Gregory Maguire is the bestselling author of *Mirror Mirror, Lost, Confessions of an Ugly Stepsister, Wicked: The Life and Times of the Wicked Witch of the West, Son of a Witch* and *A Lion Among Men*, which have earned him rave reviews and a dedicated following. He received his doctorate in English Literature from Tufts University, and has taught at Simmons College and other Boston area colleges. He has also served as an artist-in-residence at the Blue Mountain Center, the Isabella Stewart Gardner Museum and the Hambidge Center. Gregory has lived in Dublin and London, but now makes his home near Boston, Massachusetts, with his partner, their two sons and daughter.

Praise for Gregory Maguire:

'As moving and tragic as it is refreshing and scurrilous . . . [an] outstanding novel' *Independent*

'A vision that fantasy writers will find hard to resist' *Publishers Weekly*

'Highly absorbing . . . Maguire's precise, slightly archaic language . . . sweeps the readers through this mysterious and fascinating story' *Booklist*

'An outstanding work of imagination' *USA Today*

'A magical telling of the land of Oz before and up to the arrival of Dorothy and company . . . A captivating, funny, and perceptive look at destiny, personal responsibility, and the not-always-clashing beliefs of faith and magic. Save a place on the shelf between *Alice* and *The Hobbit* – that spot is well deserved' *Kirkus Reviews*

'A staggering feat of wordcraft . . . [Maguire] has created . . . one of the great heroines in fantasy literature' *Los Angeles Times*

'Captivating and beautifully written . . . a rich canvas of colorful characters and fantastic events rendered by an artist attentive to every surface a

HERTFORDSHIRE LIBRARY SERVICE
WITHDRAWN STOCK FOR SALE
PRICE

D0243485

By Gregory Maguire

Novels in the Wicked Years
Wicked: The Life and Times of the Wicked Witch of the West
Son of a Witch
A Lion Among Men

Confessions of an Ugly Stepsister
Lost
Mirror Mirror

A
LION
AMONG
MEN

Gregory Maguire

headline

Copyright © 2008 Gregory Maguire

The right of Gregory Maguire to be identified as the Author of
the Work has been asserted by him in accordance with the
Copyright, Designs and Patents Act 1988.

Published by arrangement with William Morrow,
an imprint of HarperCollins Publishers

First published in Great Britain in 2008 by
HEADLINE REVIEW
An imprint of HEADLINE PUBLISHING GROUP

First published in paperback in 2009 by
HEADLINE REVIEW

11

Apart from any use permitted under UK copyright law, this publication
may only be reproduced, stored, or transmitted, in any form, or by
any means, with prior permission in writing of the publishers or, in the case of
reprographic production, in accordance with the terms of licences issued by the
Copyright Licensing Agency.

All characters in this publication are fictitious and any resemblance
to real persons, living or dead, is purely coincidental.

Cataloguing in Publication Data is available from the British Library

ISBN 978 0 7553 4822 0

Typeset in Columbus by Avon DataSet Ltd,
Bidford-on-Avon, Warwickshire

Printed and bound by CPI Group (UK) Ltd, Croydon, CR0 4YY

Headline's policy is to use papers that are natural, renewable and recyclable
products and made from wood grown in sustainable forests. The logging and
manufacturing processes are expected to conform to the environmental
regulations of the country of origin.

HEADLINE PUBLISHING GROUP
An Hachette UK Company
338 Euston Road
London NW1 3BH

www.headline.co.uk
www.hachette.co.uk

For Maurice Sendak

King of all wild things

The moment one definitely commits oneself, then Providence moves as well. All sorts of things occur to help one that would never otherwise have occurred. A stream of events issues from the decision, raising in one's favor all manner of unforeseen accidents, meetings and material assistance that no one could have dreamed would come their way. Whatever you can do or dream you can do, begin it. Boldness has genius, power and magic in it. Begin it now.

– Goethe, by attribution

A statement about luck is a statement about the mind, not about the world . . . We find what seems to have been the lucky break or the big mistake, and so we thank our lucky stars that we took the road less traveled or curse the fates that sent that little wavelet that flipped us on our backs. With hindsight, we seem to see that everything preceding the pivotal point was leading up to it, tending toward it, and that everything following it grew from it.
To any observer outside the lucky one himself, however, luck is simply chance. Chance is neutral.

– Eric Kraft, 'I Consider My Luck,'
from *Brothers and Beasts: An Anthology of
Men on Fairy Tales*

Contents

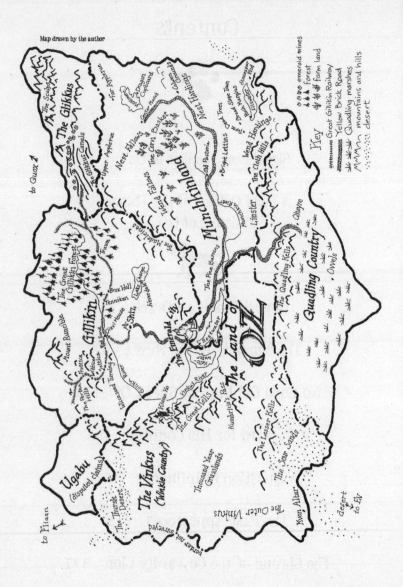

Map drawn by the author

Significant
Families of Oz

= marriage   (~) wedlock

The House of Ozma

——— *The Emerald City* ———

Ozma Initiata
|
(many Ozmas and several Ozma Regents)**
|
Ozma the Bilious = Pastorius (the Ozma Regent)
|
Ozma Tippetarius

The Thropps of Munchkinland

———— Colwen Grounds in Munchkinland ————

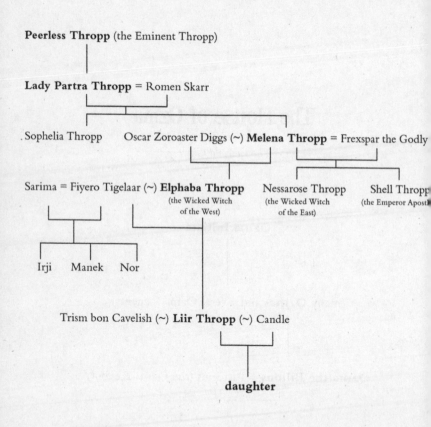

Peerless Thropp (the Eminent Thropp)

Lady Partra Thropp = Romen Skarr

Sophelia Thropp   Oscar Zoroaster Diggs (~) **Melena Thropp** = Frexspar the Godly

Sarima = Fiyero Tigelaar (~) **Elphaba Thropp**
(the Wicked Witch
of the West)

Nessarose Thropp
(the Wicked Witch
of the East)

Shell Thropp
(the Emperor Apostl

Irji   Manek   Nor

Trism bon Cavelish (~) **Liir Thropp** (~) Candle

daughter

The Uplands of Gillikin

Frottica in northwest Gillikin

Larena Upland = Highmuster Arduenna

Galinda Upland (aka Glinda) = Lord Chuffrey of Mockbeggar Hall
(Throne Minister)

The Tigelaars,
Arjiki chieftains of the Vinkus

*Kiamo Ko on the slopes of Knobblehead
Pike, the Great Kells of the Vinkus*

Marillot Tigelaar = Baxiana of Upper Fanarra

Sarima, oldest of six sisters = **Fiyero Tigelaar** (~) Elphaba Thropp

Irji   Manek   Nor   Trism bon Cavelish (~) **Liir** (~) Candle

daughter

A Brief Outline of
The Throne Ministers of Oz

Augmented with notes about selected incidents of interest to students of modern history

The Ozma Years

- The matrilineal House of Ozma established.

  The Ozma line descends from a Gillikinese clan. It originally claimed legitimacy through a purported divine relationship with Lurlina, fabled creatrix of Oz. Depending on the claim, history records between forty to fifty Ozmas and their regents.

- The last Ozma, Ozma Tippetarius, is born of Ozma the Bilious.

  Ozma the Bilious expires through an accident involving rat poisoning in the risotto. Her consort, Pastorius, becomes

Ozma Regent during the minority of Ozma Tippetarius.

- Pastorius rules over central Oz.

  He renames the hamlet known as Nubbly Meadows, near the ancient burial ground of Open Tombs, as the Emerald City (EC). Declares the EC as the capital of united Oz.

- The Great Drought begins.

- By air balloon, Oscar Zoroaster Diggs arrives in the Emerald City.

  Diggs successfully mounts a palace coup d'état. Pastorius is murdered, and the infant Ozma Tippetarius disappears. She is presumed slain, perhaps in Southstairs Prison (built over the Open Tombs), though an evergreen rumor claims she lies enchanted in a cave, to return only in Oz's darkest hour. Diggs becomes known as the Wizard of Oz.

The Wizardic Years

- The Emerald City renovation is completed.

- The Wizard of Oz orders expansion of the Yellow Brick Road.

  This serves as a highway for the armies of the EC and aids in the collection of local taxes from previously independent populations, especially in Quadling Country and on the eastern flanks of the Great Kells of the Vinkus.

- Animal Courtesy legislation enacted (known also as the Animal Adverse laws).

- Munchkinland secedes from Loyal Oz.

  Under the rule of Nessarose Thropp, Eminence of Munchkinland, the secession is conducted with a minimum of bloodshed. The 'breadbasket of Oz' maintains an uneasy commercial relationship with Loyal Oz.

- Nessarose Thropp dies.

  The arrival in Oz of a visitor, a Dorothy Gale of Canzizz (sometimes translated as 'Canzuss' or 'Kanziz'), results in the death of the Eminence. Speculation suggests her sister, Elphaba Thropp, will return to Munchkinland to mount a more aggressive campaign against the EC than Nessarose ever did.

- Elphaba Thropp is vanquished.

The so-called Wicked Witch of the West, onetime agitator, now recluse, is subdued by the powerful Dorothy Gale.

- The Wizard of Oz abdicates the throne.

  The Wizard had held power for almost forty years. The reasons for his departure remain a matter of speculation.

The Twin Interregnums

- Lady Glinda Chuffrey, née Upland, is briefly installed as Throne Minister.

  The Animal Adverse laws are revoked, to little effect; Animals remain skeptical of their chances of being reintegrated into human society in Oz.

- The Scarecrow replaces Glinda as Throne Minister.

  The Scarecrow, a figure of uncertain provenance, is often assumed to have been installed as Throne Minister by palace apparatchiks sympathetic to Shell Thropp, an ambitious upstart engaged in mercenary espionage. The Scarecrow proves to be a weak figurehead – a straw man, figuratively as well as literally – but his tenure allows Shell Thropp to avoid having had to challenge the popular Lady Glinda for the leadership. The Scarecrow's whereabouts following the end of his abbreviated realm are never revealed.

Some historians hold that the Scarecrow serving as Throne Minister was not the same Scarecrow who befriended Dorothy, though this assertion is unverifiable.

The Emperor Apostle

- Shell Thropp installs himself as Emperor of Oz.

  The youngest of the three Thropp siblings, Shell claims rights of ascendancy through an adroit manipulation of Palace power brokers.

from Wicked

In came a boy from Three Queens rolling a table like a tea tray. On it, crouched as if to make itself as small as possible, was a lion cub. Even from the balcony they could sense the terror of the beast. Its tail, a little whip the color of mashed peanuts, lashed back and forth, and its shoulders hunched. It had no mane to speak of yet, it was too tiny. But the tawny head twisted this way and that, as if counting the threats. It opened its mouth in a little terrified yawp, the infant form of an adult roar. All over the room hearts melted and people said, 'Awwwwww.'

'Hardly more than a kitten,' said Doctor Nikidik. 'I had thought to call it Prrr, but it shivers more often than it purrs, so I called it Brrr instead.'

The creature looked at Doctor Nikidik, and removed itself to the far edge of the trolley.

'Now the question of the morning is this,' said Doctor Nikidik. 'Picking up from the somewhat skewed interests of Doctor Dillamond ... who can tell me if this is an Animal or an animal?'

Elphaba didn't wait to be called on. She stood up in the balcony and launched her answer out in a clear, strong voice. 'Doctor Nikidik ... It seems to me the answer is that its mother can. Where is its mother? . . . Why is it taken from its mother at such an early age? How can it even feed?'

'Those are impertinent questions to the academic issue at hand,' said the Doctor. 'Still, the youthful heart bleeds easily. The mother, shall we say, died in a sadly timed explosion . . .'

Deposition of an Oracle

1

The time came for her to die, and she would not die; so perhaps she might waste away, they thought, and she did waste, but not away; and the time came for her to receive final absolution, so they set candles upon her clavicle, but this she would not allow. She blasphemed with gusto and she knocked the scented oils across the shroud they'd readied on a trestle nearby.

'God love her,' they said, in bitter, unconvincing voices – or perhaps they meant *May the Unnamed God love her, our unrepentant sister Yackle, for we certainly can't.*

'Sink me in the crypt,' she said, speaking directly to them for the first time in years. 'You're too young to know; that's how they used to do it. When the time came for an elder to go and she wouldn't, they settled her down in the ossuary so she could chummy up to the bones. Supplied her with a couple of candles and a bottle of wine. Let her get used to the notion. They came back a year later to sweep up the leavings.'

'Mercy,' said whoever was nearby to hear.

'I insist,' she replied. 'Check with Sister Scholastica and she'll bear me out.'

'She's raving mad,' said someone else, chocolately. Yackle approved of chocolate, and indeed, everything edible. Since Yackle's eyesight had gone out for good a decade earlier, she identified individuals by the degree and idiosyncrasy of their halitosis.

'She's always been raving mad,' said a third observer, Vinegarish Almonds. 'Isn't that rather sweet?'

Yackle reached for something to throw, and all she could find was her other hand, which wouldn't detach.

'She's doing sign language.' 'The poor, deluded dovelette.' 'Clinging to life so – whatever for?' 'Perhaps it isn't her time.'

'It is,' said Yackle, 'it is, I keep telling you. Won't you fiends let me die? I want to go to hell in a hand-basket. Put me out of my misery and into the Afterlife where I can do some real damage, damn it.'

'She's not herself,' said someone.

'She was never reliably herself, to hear tell,' said another.

The bedsheets caught fire spontaneously. Yackle found she was rather enjoying this, but it helped neither her reputation nor her rescue that the only liquid nearby with which to douse the flames was cognac.

Still, Yackle was not to be dissuaded. 'Isn't there a Superior in the House?' she asked. 'Someone who can lay down the law?'

'The Superior Maunt died a decade ago,' they replied. 'We work by consensus now. We've noted your request to be interred alive. We'll put it on the agenda and take it up next week at Council.'

'She'll burn the House down, and us with it,' muttered a novice, sometime later. Yackle could tell that the innocent speaker was talking to herself, to stoke her courage.

'Come here, my duckie,' said Yackle, grasping. 'I smell a little peppermint girl nearby, and no garlicky matron hovering. Are you the sentry? On our own, are we? Come, sit nearer. Surely there is still a Sister Apothecaire in residence? With her cabinets of nostrums and beckums, tonics and tablets? She must possess a sealed jar, it would be dark blue glass, about yea-high, pasted over with a label picturing three sets of crossed tibias. Couldn't you find this and pour me out a fatal little decoction?'

'Not a spoonful of it, I en't the grace to do it,' said Peppermint Girl. 'Let go a me, you harpy. Let go or – or I'll bite you!'

Out of charity to the young, Yackle let go. It would do the poor girl no good to take a bite of old Yackle. *The antidote en't been invented yet*, and so on.

Hours and days pass at elastic rhythms for the blind. Whether the pattern of her naps and wakings followed the ordinary interruptions of daylight by nighttime, Yackle couldn't tell. But someone she recognized as Broccoli Breath eventually informed her that the sorority had decided to bow to Yackle's final wish. They would install her in the crypt among the remains of women long dead. She could approach bodily corruption at whatever speed appealed to her. Three candles, and as to nourishment, red or white?

'A beaker of gasoline and a match as a chaser,' said Yackle, but she was indulging in a joke; she was that pleased. She nominated a saucy persimmon *flaucande* and a beeswax candle scented with limeberries – for the aroma, not for the light. She was beyond light now.

'Good voyage, Eldest Soul,' they sang to her as they carried her down the stairs. Though she weighed no more than sugarbrittle she was awkward to move; she couldn't govern her own arms or legs. As if motivated by a spite independent of her own, her limbs would keep ratcheting out to jab into doorjambs. The procession lacked a fitting dignity.

'Don't come down for at least a year,' she sang out, giddy as a lambkin. 'Make that two. I might be old as sin itself, but once I start rotting it won't be pretty. If I hammer at the cellar door don't open it; I'm probably just collecting for some public charity in hell.'

'Can we serenade you with an epithalamium, as you go to marry Death?' asked one of the bearers, tucking in the shroud to make it cozy.

'Save your doggy breath. Go, go, on to the rest of your lives, you lot. It's been a swell, mysterious mess of a life. Don't mind me. I'll blow the candles out before I lower my own lights.'

A year later when a sister ventured into the crypt to prepare for another burial, she came across the hem of Yackle's shroud. She wept at the notion of death until Yackle sat up and said, 'What, morning already? And I having those naughty dreams!' The maunt's tears turned to screams, and she fled upstairs to start immediately upon a long and lively career as an alcoholic.

2

The other maunts gave no credit to the drunken gibberish of their cowardly novice. They assumed she had succumbed to panic at the threat of war. Immediate war, local war. You could smell it in the air, like laundry soap, or an ailment in the sewers.

From the occasional evacuee who stopped to water his horses, Sister Hospitality gleaned what news she could. She broke her vows of circumspection to share with her fellow maunts what she learned.

By late spring, the four divisions of Emerald City foot soldiers massed on the north bank of the Gillikin River had been joined by a fifth and a sixth. Conscription having thinned the countryside of its farmhands, General Cherrystone released teams of men to assist in harvesting first-growth olives and early kindle-oat. The army then requisitioned most of what it had gathered as its fee for helping out.

'Indeed,' whispered Sister Hospitality, 'tavern owners are said to be bricking up the better ale behind false walls. Their wives eavesdrop on tipsy officers and gossip over conflicting rumors. No one is sure of anything. Is the army constructing an underground canal into Munchkinland, to leach the great lake of its water? Is a new weapon being perfected upriver that will make an invading army invincible? Or are these maneuvers merely war games to intimidate the Munchkinlanders into making concessions?'

Her confidantes shook their heads, dizzy with the intrigue of it, which seemed oddly like life in a mauntery except more so.

'The mood of the season,' hissed Sister Hospitality. 'Pray for peace but hide your wallets and your wives, and send your children away if you can.'

The maunts were infected with this impulse even though they had no wallets, wives, or offspring to bother about.

Sister Hospitality, peering with relish through the peekhole in the porter's lodge, allowed her mind to roam beyond what she could actually see, elaborating on the square of visible landscape with fond remembered notions of the wider world.

Despite armed conflict, fields of wheat will grow

taller, she thought, the color of bleached linen. They will pull this way and that in the breezes. Sparrows will wheel at the sound of gunfire, horses rear and dig at the air, pigs dive under their troughs.

In households? Pots go without blacking, sheets without blueing, and water drops on goblets dry into the housemaid's nightmare: poxy glass. Aprons go unironed. Upstairs grannies go unvisited. Shiny knives and spoons cloud with a mat of tarnish, as if hoping to hide in the coming gloom.

The unvisited grannies, in stone houses by the wheat field, can't remember their husbands or children. They worry their hands, though, hands that could do with a rinsing. The grannies think:

We start out in identical perfection: bright, reflective, full of sun. The accident of our lives bruises us into dirty individuality. We meet with grief. Our character dulls and tarnishes. We meet with guilt. We know, we know: the price of living is corruption. There isn't as much light as there once was. In the grave we lapse back into undifferentiated sameness.

Sister Hospitality paused in her reveries, not knowing if she was thinking her own thoughts or imagining some unknown crone's. She slammed shut the small panel and returned to her chores.

In the garden, no one approached with a rake to pull away last year's matted leaves. The tulips came up crippled. The bas-relief pagan goddess, sculpted into the western wall before unionism had commandeered this ancient temple site for a cloister, had grown a beard of winter moss: no one pulled it away. A useful disguise in time of war, maybe. Who could fuss over that?

Maybe the Unnamed God would grace them yet. Maybe the coming war would prove to be rumor, fear, nothing more.

The apple blossoms trembled and fell. No one gathered them.

The cats lost their chance to practice hunting, as even the mice had fled.

In the herb garden, a spiderweb grew on the sundial. No one swept it away. On bright days, laddered shadows crept across the oxidizing numerals, giving the numbered hours new accents, one by one, until the sun went down or the clouds came in. Any variety of darkness can silence a sundial.

Maybe there would be no armed conflict, the maunts commented encouragingly. But each maunt in her own way felt the curse of war's inevitability.

Sister Laundry would no longer dry the sheets in the sun, for they looked like white flags of surrender and no one wanted soldiers garrisoned in the mauntery. Sister Hospitality began refusing shelter to wanderers through these isolated reaches, lest they turn out to be secret agents. Behind closed doors, Sister Apothecaire availed herself of a calming beverage usually reserved for those in medical distress. Sister Petty Cash had bad dreams. 'The cost of war,' she murmured, her voice trailing off.

'We've no reason to fear either army,' insisted Sister Doctor, when the subject came due for an update at Council. 'Three weeks ago, when the Munchkinland marauders swept by, making their inept preemptive strike into Loyal Oz, they didn't stop to rape and plunder us as they passed. They hoped to wreak havoc on the Emperor's forces massing to the west, but it appears the upstarts have managed only to wreak a spot of bother. Sisters, be sensible. Now the Munchkinlanders are in – what's it called? – hot retreat. Fleeing for their lives. They'll be too distracted to drop in for a refreshment while they're being pushed back to their own borders. Lighten up.'

The maunts, pledged to obedience, tried to lighten up, though Sister Doctor's customary brusqueness of diagnosis seemed, perhaps, inadequate to riddles of military strategy.

Still, the House of Saint Glinda in the Shale Shallows, meant to be remote from worldly concerns, stood this month like a Gillikinese sycamore trying to camouflage itself in a Quadling rice paddy. An exceedingly prominent target. There was no other establishment in the district so capacious, so securable, so fitted with supplies. Most of the maunts felt it was only a matter of time. And when the time came, which army would knock at the doors? The home team or the rebel rabble? The well-trained Emerald City army forces or the Munchkinlander militia, that ad hoc volunteer swarm? Though the mauntery stood in Loyal Oz, the maunts, by dint of their spiritual allegiances, considered displays of patriotism inappropriate, if not gauche. Though they did wonder: Would either adversary show mercy to the self-quarantined isolates of a religious order?

'Of course they will,' argued Sister Doctor from the lectern. 'We are the exemplars of mercy. We set the standard, and an army has no choice but to respect our standards.'

The maunts nodded, respectful but unconvinced. Men were beasts. Everyone knew that. It's why most of the women had entered the mauntery in the first place.

Dinner conversation revolved around nothing but military operations. These days the women had to raise their voices to be heard above the sound of military skirmishes. Practice charges, they hoped. Trees were being felled for the construction of catapults: Who could think properly with all that racket? Who could pray – or, put another way, who could stop praying?

To add injury to insult, a projectile of flaming pitch and straw went astray and landed on the leads of the chapel, so the Council was burdened with the added annoyance of home repair. It was impossible to persuade skilled trade to venture behind the battle lines. Sister Hammer did what she could, but even so.

Nightly, from the bluestone bartizans, Sister Doctor reviewed the campfires of opposing forces as they shifted back and forth, west and east. A sally, a retreat: one could read the campaign from this height. Mutton for supper; one could smell the menu.

Blinking with encouragement, she reported that the Emerald City brigades looked set to push the Munchkinlander upstarts back to their borders and perhaps beyond, farther east, right into Munchkinland proper. Sister Apothecaire, a displaced Munchkin of the shorter sort, wasn't able to suppress a bark of affront at this naked sympathy for the Throne. So Sister Doctor shut up about the rumor that the Emperor was going to use the Munchkinlanders' misadventure as an excuse to invade and to capture the lake of Restwater, finally to sever dissident Munchkinland, the breadbasket of Oz, from its own water supply. Political pundits had long predicted this action: The Munchkinlander militias had cooked their own goose, but good. Done Loyal Oz a great service, they had, by ceding the moral high ground, handing their enemy a legitimate reason to retaliate. Very smart of them. The little morons.

'Remember to breathe,' advised Sister Doctor to her companions. 'It is, after all, the secret of life.'

Obediently, the maunts breathed, if not much easier, and they sang songs of gratitude for having been spared – for those who *had* been spared, they took pains to remember.

They paid for their neutrality in baskets of apples, in buckets of water pulled from their well. They fed the professional Emerald City Messiars as fully as, three weeks earlier, they had fed the stumpy little Munchkinlander farmer-soldiers. They never stinted at feeding the hungry, as long as the portions could be lowered over the wall in a basket, as long as the hungry didn't need spoon-feeding. There was a limit to everything: eggs, bandages, breath, even mercy. If the maunts beggared themselves, who would be left to offer even half a mercy?

When Sister Doctor and her lowly and disgruntled colleague, Sister Apothecaire, went forth to tend to the wounded, they left by a back door, and under cover of darkness.

3

Some miles south — away from the nickering of cavalry horses, the cloudy antiphons of the maunts — the night-time sounds of Oz took on a more arbitrary rhythm. A breeze in the higher branches of trees. The percussive *thunk* of a frog objecting to his neighbors.

Silky passage of water snake, *chirr* of midnight mosquito. Woodland Oz going about its nocturnal business. Adequate peace.

Safely buried in deep forest, the infallible Clock counted out the seconds of its life in waltzing ticks like hazelnuts dropping into a wooden bucket. *Tik tik tok, tik tik tok.*

The dwarf and his company of superstitious boys snored on. The Clock's only female attendant, a woman of uncertain age, kept the night watch against reconnaissance scouts or beasts or light-fingered mendicants. She was still new to this troupe – and she owed them her life – so she did what she was told, picking up what information she could as it fell her way.

She'd learned that now and then, sometimes for years at a stretch, the Clock of the Time Dragon dropped out of sight. The acolytes of the Clock would shutter up the preposterous thing. They trusted in its own infernal charms to protect it. And maybe the boys were sensible enough to do so. Whenever the sergeant-at-hand called back the company – a few starry-eyed converts compensating for any no-shows – they apparently always found their treasure in working trim. Sometimes it would be overgrown with forest ivy or moss. Dead leaves, tendrils of cobweb. Perhaps a kind of natural camouflage the Clock called to itself. It didn't matter. The handmade masterpiece snapped right back to business. The play of its gears remained deft, the tension in its belts and chains keen. Its mechanical advantage was said to have been augmented by a stubbornly adhesive magic.

The night watchwoman, a novice in service of the Clock, had asked the sergeant-at-hand their destination.

'We meander as whimsy dictates unless the Clock gives explicit advice,' he'd answered. 'Whimsy is fate, too: just less knowable.'

'Did whimsy bring you to rescue me, Mr Boss,' she asked, 'or were you bound by advice?'

'That's what they all want to know.' The sergeant-at-hand, a dwarf with regrettably sloppy habits of dental hygiene, leered his mustardy smile. 'But it's confidential, my darling, my dimple. Trade secrets indeedy.'

For five weeks the self-appointed acolytes had been pushing and dragging the towering Clock, which was mounted on a wheeled flatbed. They kept away from farmhouses, going overland through pastures and paddocks. If they had to pass through a small village, they waited till midnight.

The equipage rocked and lurched like a small ornate ship on stony seas. Above, the clockwork dragon supervised. How much of Oz those dull eyes had taken in. Oz rehearsing itself, rearranging itself decade after decade. Whimsy and fate, destiny and accident. The fall of the house of Ozma, the dirty years of the Wizard, the rise of impeccable Shell, holy Emperor of Oz. Fortunes, in any case: changeable fortunes converted into the changeless facts of biography by every passing tick of its mechanisms.

After the Clock had rescued her, its sergeant-at-hand had briefed the newest convert. 'We pick our way with superior caution,' the dwarf told her. 'Everything's tinder-hot now and ready to conflagrate. We have our task. The Clock tells us so. Quietly, quickly, like mice stealing between the toes of battling manticores and basilisks, we inch forward as we're told.'

'Imagine what it's seen since we last brung it along to an audience,' one beardless boy said. 'Imagine the stupefied Squirrel or idiot Monkey coming across this in the greenwood! Sitting all 'lone and full of itself, like a pagan temple! Without us to service it, you think our smoky friend here would rouse itself and deliver a pronouncement?'

'For a chattering Monkey? Get real. That ever happen, I'd like to see so! Fun for the Monkey who goes shrieking mad and he drop right out of his tree!'

The dwarf knew, but did not say, that in those quiescent periods in the forsaken outlands, creatures did creep up to sniff, to examine, even to climb over the peculiar heap of marvels. A dense woods is not off-limits to its own residents. And woodland creatures take notice of everything invading their territory, including fate.

Monkeys, venerable and caustic, lost no opportunity to chitter. Parrots, much given to expressing their opinions, gossiped in serrated squawks. Younger, more timid habitants approached in their own time. A garter snake and his sister. A raccoon with a tendency to morbid depression. The odd lion cub among them.

The newest vigil keeper didn't worry so much about animals. Let them come up and sniff. It was men she avoided as best she could. So she liked this task of midnight watch. In company but still alone. The lads in a loose jumble of limbs, their wizened old sergeant-at-hand shifting in his creaking hammock. She could move around as she liked. It wasn't that, if awake, this lot would plague her much. They knew better. But she enjoyed the privacy. To the veteran of prison, solitude can offer few unsavory surprises.

She removed her shawl and hung it on a branch, and with steps that whispered in the pine needles, she approached the water. A small cove of Restwater, Oz's inland sea, made an intimate bathing chamber. Once out of sight of her sleeping companions – out of sight should they awaken, that is – she unfastened the clasps of her tunic and lifted it over her shoulders. Beneath, she wore a binding sheath, which she loosened and began to remove, folding it back upon itself as she exposed her stomach and then her breasts.

She wasn't thinking of her breasts, still full and high, though the hormone-whipped lads often did. She was thinking of white paper and dark ink, and the difficulty and danger of scoring a page with lines of ink, to make it sing, if it could. If she could make it.

But if it sang, perhaps it would say something other than she intended. Perhaps it couldn't help but say who she was, where she was, though she kept all things hidden that she could manage.

Books could seem to unleash all the hallelujahs of hell – she had known one that could, in her past; it was a volume of enchantments known as the Grimmerie – but even books that did not detonate into history, as the Grimmerie had, could still whisper their private secrets. And her appetite to write was countermanded by a dread of being read and recognized.

Her breasts, loosened from their cotton corset, itched; they rolled outward, toward her biceps. Absentmindedly she caressed first one and then the other with the back of her hand. Then she untucked the sash that secured her skirts. She hung the skirts on nearby branches, further curtaining herself from mortal eyes, should any be open.

Before she stepped into the still water, she ran the fingers of her right hand along the scar between her legs. This was not for pleasure – there was no pleasure left – but as a test of assurance that the seal had not been broken.

Solitude, continence, silence: custody of her own history; custody of any future that might have descended from her, squawking and looking to suck.

Satisfied. More than satisfied, relieved, she arched a foot to enter the water. But before she did, she saw in the flat green of the pond's surface a reflection of a moon. At first she thought: Now there's a surface safer to write upon than paper. The circular page of the moon in the water – words written in water are sure to wash away, and the moon itself no wiser.

Lowering herself to her haunches, preparing to bathe, she realized she was not entirely unobserved. She could see upon the water a curlicued sort of growth like a backward question mark. She knew it for the reflection of the head of the dragon to whose service she and the others were committed.

The dragon's eye was red, red in the green water. Red, unblinking, unblinkered.

You, you can look all you want, she thought, but even so she slipped into the water hastily.

What words she had thought to write on the face of the moon were washed away from her as she submerged, trying to disturb no one, nothing. Trying not so much as to interrupt a current, even trying not to shatter into soft-edged platelets the green moon in the reflection. Trying to sidestep having any influence at all, now and till the end of her life.

4

At dawn Sister Hospitality was summoned to the back door of the mauntery when the medical team returned, accompanied by a tall, stooped figure.

'We are not housing soldiers,' hissed Sister Hospitality. 'You know I made that perfectly clear at Council, Sister Doctor.'

'Whatever this fellow is,' said Sister Doctor, 'he is not a soldier.'

The chap was wearing a traveling cloak with a hood finished with bristles of greasy fur – or that is how Sister Hospitality saw it at first. When the visitor dropped the hood, she realized the fringe of fur was an unkempt mane, and the man in need of sanctuary was in fact a Lion.

Sister Hospitality snapped, 'Who is this, then? What class and category of aberration? A deserter? A conscientious objector? A visitor from the press?'

'An emissary on a neutral mission,' replied Sister Doctor, removing galoshes caked with gore better left unidentified. 'He is taking advantage of the safe passage here allowed by the forward front of the EC Messiars. And we welcome him, Sister *Hospitality*.' She spat out the name.

The Lion studied the floor as if expecting to be turfed out. An unlit cigar dangled in his mouth, a pad of paper projected from his vest pocket, and a pair of spectacles fitted with green-glass bifocal lenses hung on a chain from his velvet lapel. Sister Hospitality noticed some greying mane hairs stuck to the front of his cloak. His posture . . . well, it made Sister Hospitality square her own shoulders in a superior way.

'Brrr,' said the visitor.

'Let me fetch you a warming cocoa,' said Sister Hospitality, without much enthusiasm.

'No,' he replied, 'cocoa disagrees with me. Brrr, I was introducing myself. Brrr, the name.' He handed over a card on which was scribbled an illegible note to himself. 'Sorry, other side.' There it was: BRRR, three rs. COURT REPORTER TO THE EMERALD CITY MAGISTRATES.

Sister Doctor and Sister Apothecaire hung up their own robes – Sister Apothecaire using a lower hook. Sister Doctor stumped off in her stocking feet without further comment. Her diminutive associate blushed by way of apology. 'Sister Doctor and I must enter our activities in the Log of the House,' said Sister Apothecaire to their guest. 'Please excuse me, too. Sister Hospitality will see to your needs.' She left the Lion standing among the cleaning buckets, the barrels of cornmeal, the bins of dried beans.

Sister Hospitality went to hang the Lion's traveling

cloak in a clothes press. When a pocket twitched, Sister Hospitality recoiled with a shudder and she tried unsuccessfully to disguise her curse as a cough.

'Oh, my guard cat has scared you good,' said the Lion – almost approvingly, thought Sister Hospitality. 'Nearly forgot about my little kitty-thingy. It's been following me since Shiz. I must be the first Lion it ever saw, and it's become smitten. Look at it, the little dollop.'

The cat may have been white once, but it was old enough for its fur to have thinned. 'I never saw such a thing,' said Sister Hospitality. 'It's distinctly offensive. Creepy. Almost transparent. Male or female?'

'That much isn't transparent, I'm afraid. Everything else is.'

'What ailment does it suffer from?'

'Cats don't usually last as long as this one clearly has,' said Brrr. 'That's my guess. A cat gets old, its fur goes white, it dies. This one's got some years on it, looks like, and if cat fur is white to start out with, how much paler can it go? Look.' He rubbed the cat's arthritic spine, and a net of hairs came off on the pad of his paw. He held them out. Each hair looked like nothing so much as a thread of glass.

'Revolting,' said Sister Hospitality, charitably enough.

'Look, it hardly has a shadow,' said Brrr, and this was almost true; the morning light of the vestibule slanted through where the cat stood, stretching arthritically on the flagstones.

'What name does it answer to?'

'Have you ever known a cat to answer to anything?' said the Lion. 'But I call it Shadowpuppet, for old as it is, it still enjoys the game of stalking prey.'

'If it's as fragile as glass, it will be pleased to learn that our own mousers have recently fled,' said Sister Hospitality. 'Cats can be so territorial. Present company excepted,' she continued, leading him up the stairs toward a receiving parlor.

'Oh, I'm territorial enough,' said the Lion. 'Still, Shadowpuppet never leaves me, and I think I can scare off your convent cats if they come back.' He lifted Shadowpuppet, because the stairs were too steep, and Sister Hospitality would not pause even for a cat of advancing years.

'May I ask, what *is* a court reporter, Mr Brrr?' Sister Hospitality pushed the drapes back to let in sunlight the color of old bandages.

'Sir Brrr, when I'm at home,' he corrected apologetically. 'Title awarded by Lady Glinda herself, at the conclusion of that little Matter of Dorothy.'

'Beg pardon,' said Sister Hospitality, no tone of regret to stain her inflection.

'Not that I use it,' he hurried on. 'The house has fallen on hard times. I do pickup secretarial work to make ends meet. Now, to business. I am dispatched by the Lord High Magistrate of the Emerald City to make enquiries of a member of your – tribe? Flock? Whatever it is a body of maunts calls itself. You know, like a swarm of bees, a murder of crows, a parliament of owls.'

'I've heard that lions consort together in a pride,' said Sister Hospitality.

'Those that let others join,' interjected Brrr. 'Let's not go there.'

'Call us a deference of maunts, if you must. And deferential, then, within reason, we'll try to help. Do you know the name of the maunt you have come to ask about? Though we take new names as our obligations require, most of us remember what our original names were.'

The Lion steadied the spectacles on his nose. Dander flecked the lenses; no wonder he peered and blinked at the small notebook in his paw. 'I can't read my own writing. Jackal?'

'We have no Sister Jackal.'

'Sister Quackle? No, perhaps a C. Cackle?'

Sister Hospitality said carefully, 'Oh, dear. I wonder if you could mean Yackle. She was laid to rest over a year ago.'

'Was she an oracle?'

'Sir Brrr. We are a convent of holy women. We don't trade in prophecies. What would a seer be doing in a mauntery?'

'You haven't answered my question. Was she an oracle?'

'I can't possibly answer that question. I was not her confessor.'

'Who was?'

Sister Hospitality thought. 'Actually, she didn't have one. She wasn't professed, I think.'

'Would someone here know if Yackle was an oracle?'

'The old Superior Maunt might have, but she's gone too.'

'Holiday?'

'The Final Holiday.'

'Sheesh. Occupational hazard in this place?'

'Growing old? Yes.'

Brrr explained. A knotty little concern in the courts had prompted a senior magistrate to call for a finding. Brrr had been dispatched by order of the Stamp of the Emperor to pursue the matter in any direction. From a side pocket he produced a notarized writ of entry flecked with bits of bread crust. He flattened it with a paw. The legal penmanship crosshatched the vellum into illegibility. 'This authorizes any enquiry I want to make, as it happens.'

'Are you bullying me, sir?'

'I don't need to bully the likes of you,' he replied, tapping the paper. 'This is the bully.'

'I haven't the mind for this, nor the time,' said

Sister Hospitality. 'Nor am I the authority in the House; we are governed by a Council. But I can and must report to them what you say. Why don't you tell me *precisely* what brings you here?'

'Highly secret and hush-hush.'

'I respect that. I'm Sister Hospitality, after all, not Sister Rumormonger. If hospitality requires confidentiality, I'm qualified.' She made a shushing gesture, tapping her forefinger against her pursed lips, then whispered, '*I'm all ears.*'

The Lion muttered to himself a little, weighing his options. Finally he allowed this much: He had recently spent a week in the Gillikinese city of Shiz, going through the deposit library of Shiz University. He had required to see the papers of a onetime governor of Crage Hall, long since departed into the Afterlife, rest her soul. A Madame Morrible. The frumpy little scholaresses at the desk had put up an argument, but he'd prevailed.

'And what did you find, pray tell?'

The Lion appeared to be governing a small temper, as if he thought Sister Hospitality's curiosity unseemly. When he spoke, though, his tone was even enough. 'Since you ask so nicely: Cryptic notes in what looked like the deceased headmistress's hand identified a questionable personage known only as Yackle. An entity of some sort, but what sort? An agent of whom? If an oracle, was she a charlatan or a savant? And the way these investigations go, don't you know, one thing has led to another. The Motherhouse of the order of Saint Glinda, in Saint Glinda's Square in the Emerald City, had known a Mother Yackle but had sent her away for retirement. To a mission chapel, a benighted outpost in the Shale Shallows. And so, as they say in the pantomimes, ta-da!'

The white cat settled in a patch of sunlight and began to clean itself. It all but disappeared.

'I do so wish you'd come sooner,' said the maunt. 'There's a little thing called armed conflict going on locally.'

'Don't I know it.'

'You ought not to have bothered. There's nothing I can do for you now. Whoever Yackle was – an ancient madwoman older than sin itself – she's passed away, and to the best of my knowledge she was never an oracle anyway.'

'Think again!' said a voice at the door.

They turned.

'I knew you'd be here sooner or later,' said Yackle, 'but it took me the better part of the season to get up the stairs. Glad I'm in time.'

The Lion, not knowing precisely what he was seeing, merely gaped. Sister Hospitality sloped to the floor with the clop of a collapsing ironing board. 'You seem to have killed her,' said the Lion to the newcomer, affably enough.

'All those months that I couldn't manage to kill myself, and I slay the righteous with my first remark?' said Yackle. 'There's gratitude for you.'

The Lion cocked out a sleeved elbow. She gripped it. He guided her to a chair. Her voluminous winding sheets were unstained by ordure or blood; they were merely dusty from having been trailed through the basements. He could detect no stink of corruption. 'The odor of sanctity,' said Yackle peremptorily.

'You are an oracle,' said Brrr. 'You're the one I hoped to find.'

Shadowpuppet sniffed around the edges of Sister Hospitality, who came around and sat up. 'You're blind, not to mention dead, Mother Yackle,' sputtered the maunt. 'How could you make your way upstairs?'

'My inner eyesight seems to have been improved with my little reprieve from the distractions of dailiness,' Yackle admitted. 'I could remember every step taken to cart me downstairs, and how high the door handle was, and so on.'

'No time like the present,' said the Lion, extracting from another pocket a pen and a small pot of ink with a cork stopper. 'The tides of war go backward as well as forward, and some army might wash up here by teatime. I'd never be able to concentrate if there were men ballyhooing about. Distractible that way, but there you are.'

'You have no business leaving your bier and barging in here as if this is some sort of a – a *saloon*,' insisted Sister Hospitality in a honking voice, but they banished her and set to the task.

5

He didn't like the look of Mother Yackle. Who could? She was a walking cadaver. Her eyes rolled, ungovernable but to the spectacle of her inner sight. Her lips were thin as string. Her nails had kept growing while she was interred, and they made a clacking sound like a set of bamboo blinds being lowered against the noonday sun. When she went to scratch a place on her scalp, she misjudged the angle of approach and nearly punctured her own eardrum.

It's been a long time since I have seen Death this close up, he thought. This is Death refusing to die. She's a centerfold for a mortuary quarterly.

'I was quite a looker in my time,' she said. Was she reading his mind, or only being smart, to know that she must be hideous?

'Oh, had they invented time as long ago as that?'

'A comedian,' she observed. 'I come back from the very gates of death to be interviewed by a vaudeville wannabe.'

'Let's get started.' He flipped open his notebook. At the top of the page he wrote a note to himself: *Interview One. Don't vomit.*

She paused so long that Brrr thought perhaps she'd expired. My timing, he thought. Just my luck, if I believed in luck. I only believe in the opposite of luck, whatever that is.

But then she exhaled again. 'What do you want from me, kind sir?' Her vowels were lengthy, as if she intended to wring out of her words every drop of nuance they might supply.

'I'm conducting an investigation,' he said. 'Official business. Consider the codes quoted and the documents flashed at you. You're blind, you can't read them anyway, so take it on faith. We don't have a lot of time. I'm chatting up anyone who had anything to do with a Madame Morrible. Your name has come up.'

'That's no answer,' she said. 'My name comes up everywhere if you dig deep enough. I want to know why Madame Morrible's archives are being combed. Why are you bothering?'

'The Courts are building some kind of case, and I'm preparing a background paper.'

'A court case with Madame Morrible as a lead witness? I knew she was talented, but if she can give sworn testimony from beyond the grave, she has better connections than I thought.'

He snorted at this, and while his guard was let down, she jabbed at him, 'Or are you sniffing around here for the young fellow named Liir? Last I heard, he'd disappeared into the lawless lands.'

The Lion started but hoped she hadn't picked up on it. Once in his regrettable past he personally had known someone named Liir, a ragamuffin boy who had lived out west with the famous Witch. But Brrr would keep his own counsel. He sang softly in a lullabye voice, '*I* need to take *your* deposition, good granny. Don't you worry your tired noggin over poor little me.'

'I needn't answer you merely because you ask,' she said. '"In this country everyone must pay for everything he gets." Isn't that what the old bastard, our dearly departed Wizard, used to say?'

He hadn't figured on her sass. 'Perhaps you've been comatose through the current troubles. Oz has an Emperor now. One with an iron will, as it happens.'

'Threats don't work on the chronically dead,' she replied, 'which is close enough to what I am to make no difference. So try again, mister. You tell me something about yourself first. I want to know who I'm talking to before I decide. And what you're really after. And for whom you're working. And what immunity from prosecution I might be afforded. My testimonial privileges. Then we'll see if I feel like rewarding you by answering your questions.'

He took a breath in. 'And don't lie to me,' she continued. 'I can be vexed when I find I have been lied to.'

Where to start? Always the question. 'Well, for one thing, I am a gentleman sporting a very fabulous weskit,' he said, partly mocking, and to see just how blind she was. But he regretted the gambit at once. If she leaned forward to feel his vest, she'd rip it to shreds with her nails, and it wasn't in such good shape to begin with, actually. Second-hand, if not fourth-hand.

'Not a spot of mange?' she asked. Did she know he was a Lion, not a man?

'I'm not talking about my own hide. I mean I'm decked out in a gentleman's item. A bespoke article. It swims on me a bit, since I'm leaner than I once was, but it's a Rampini original. Teck-fur detailing, with a kind of red highlight. Can you see color?'

'No, but I can smell it,' she said. 'Yellow, yellow, yellow.'

The cozy old invalid was sneering at him. He unsheathed his claws, just for a moment. Let her droopy ears catch the release of each horny talon from its velvet socket.

'A shame to start off on the wrong foot, don't you agree?' he said. Plaintively, almost a miaow, to the castanet shuffle of his claws sliding against one another.

She heard his feline assertion. 'You *are* a Lion,' she said, and whispered theatrically: 'the king of the forest, no less!'

She used just the perfect phrase designed to poke the embers of his childhood into flamed memory despite his resistance. *The King of the Forest.* He shuddered involuntarily, hoping she couldn't hear his jowls jiggle.

She pressed her advantage. 'I'm neither a judge nor a jury. I'm a witness. Tell me who *you* are, Sir Brrr, and how you got here. And tell me the truth. Then maybe I'll comply. You weren't already weaselly when you were young, were you? Even weasels aren't very weaselly at first.'

With elegant steps, looking sore of paw, Shadow-puppet paced to the legs of Brrr's chair and purred to be picked up. Brrr obliged. The cat calmed him down.

Taking this deposition would be one campaign he wouldn't screw up. For the love of Ozma, wasn't he the equal of this crazy old coot draped in a tablecloth? And he had his writ in hand, permission to take her into custody if need be. He would get the goods if they were to be gotten.

If it was to be cat and mouse here, he had the genetic qualifications to play the cat. He had the motivation. He had the might of the bloody Court to back him up, too, if need be. He would redeem his reputation among the great and the good of Oz, and he'd wipe the smirks off their goddamn faces with his own beribboned tail.

'You're an oracle, I'm told,' he said. 'You ought to be able to see my youth, if you want to.'

'I like to hear it told,' she replied. 'I have an appetite for childhoods. Insatiable, as it happens.'

The Nursery in the Forest

1

The particularity of other folks' youthful memories always mocked Brrr. *The first visit to Grandmama's! When the coconut fell on the teacher's head! The time that baby Albern almost choked!* How we laughed, how we cried. How we remember. Together.

His first and oldest past was undifferentiated. Unending forest. Unremarkable seasons. Loneliness without hope of relief. How could Brrr *imagine* relief from loneliness when he hadn't found companionship yet? What goes unnamed remains hard to correct.

Brrr didn't know if his mother had died in childbirth, or been stricken with amnesia. Or maybe she just lit out because she was an unnatural mother. A loner or a schizo. Or maybe she was drummed out of the pride for low behavior. He used to care which it was.

Though of course he didn't take it in at the time, he also grew up without the benefit of a tribe of his own. No aunties to fill in the blanks about what his mother had been like, and where she had gone, and why. No growly father hiding a whiskered grin of affection even as he set to cuff his darling cub, raising him up right in the ways of the family.

His earliest memories — gluey hazes — involved skulking about the Great Gillikin Forest north of Shiz like — like a skunk, like a grite, like one of those creatures who can become repellent even to their own kind. Like a human.

In later years as an arriviste in the Emerald City — having sat through a number of poetry readings — he found a way to characterize the Great Gillikin Forest. After a second sherry he could wax most convincingly about shrouds of spiderwebs. The dank naves suggested by rows of diseased potterpine, slatted with bars of cold yellow light. The forest floor carpeted with thornberry prickle. The stupid fecundity of the spring, the swift and unrewarding summer, the gloomy autumn, and — oh hell — the bone-taxing winter. What damned Lioness would bother to deliver a cub just to abandon him there, of all benighted places?

People nodded politely as they inched away.

The trees creaked as if the whole world were constantly flexing its muscles, about to pounce. A fern could unfurl with a snap that knocked you six steps toward a sanitorium. Owls, bats, forest harpies, badgers. A wild turkey in the undergrowth, startled into flight, making a noise of small explosives. To say nothing of fog. He hated fog. And poison ivy. And don't even mention snakes.

Or elves. Or any beast larger than a runtling pig.

The first humans he could remember coming upon

were the mad Lurlinists. Brrr spied on them from behind screens of bracken. They dabbled in heathen rituals. Smoke and incense, singing in minor thirds. That sort of thing. He'd deduced language from them, language of a sort: an orotund pitch derived from religious prosody. Somewhat off-putting, as it turned out. It hadn't helped him to act the part of an alley cat later on, when he'd wanted to flee into the demimonde.

But he had loved the contrapuntality of discussion even before he quite understood that words possessed dedicated meanings. Eavesdropping on two travelers arguing over which way to go: savory plum nectar to him, blanket and kisses and mother's milk to him. The lilt of human voices in conversation, the nasal sonority, the fermata silences – he learned to hold himself very still in dappled shadows for the reward of it. Rhythm and tempo came first, vocabulary followed – but he never practiced, except to himself in secret bowers. As a young Cat he was still larger than a human, and if he spoke stupidly he might identify himself as nothing but a big lummox.

How had he survived his early years? He'd eaten nothing but forest turnips, shallots, the pinker of the edible fungus. He'd stalked human travelers and eavesdropped on their campfire chats to try to pick up anything that approximated street smarts, though he didn't even know what streets were yet. Watching occasional romantic exercises in the firelight, he'd learned more. Not that he'd been able to put theory into practice very often. More's the pity.

'Your childhood,' said Yackle coaxingly, as if she could smell his thoughts. As if she could sniff out those passages he hadn't chosen to retail at drinks parties.

Her words lulled him. The past, even a bitter past, is usually more pungent than the present, or at least better organized in the mind.

2

He didn't exchange a word with a mortal soul until he was nearly full grown, which for a Lion takes about three years. Therefore, he was slow to pick up on the concept of hunting, even though he'd heard it mentioned.

The memory stung still. He crossed his legs, as if the old witness sitting there in her death-linens could hear the vascular effort of his veins trying to retract his testicles. He smoothed the Rampini coat over the little loaf of his stomach.

Hunting . . . well, it was what he was doing now, too, wasn't it? No handgun in his vest pocket, true.

Just the privileges of the law, notarized by EC heavies.

He remembered the first time he'd heard the noise of rifle-shot. From far enough away, it had sounded like a distinct filament of thunder, a single flayed nerve of it. Brrr knew tree rodents to be smart; if they were careering away from the retort, there was good cause.

He lay low, in a kind of declivity – not a Lion's usual response to aggression, but how was he to know? Before long a quartet of uniformed men came near. They pitched their tent, and lit their campfire, within a few yards of where he had dropped like a felled potterpine. It took the Lion a few moments to realize they were responsible for the portable thunder. The rifles leaned against one another, reeking still of burnt gunpowder.

He was afraid his body odor would give him away, or the rumbling of his stomach. The hunters were noisy from drink, though, and he had nothing much to fear from them except what he learned about hunting. They traded tales of knocking off deer, skinning and mounting ocelot, tanning the hide of elk, beheading lions and having their skulls stuffed with sawdust and their teeth waxed. And spheres of polished onyx inserted in the emptied eye sockets.

Brrr's blood went slow, as if turning to gelatin. Even when the last hunter had nodded off, and the campfire collapsed into bright char and hiss, his whiskers never twitched. Were the hunters to sniff him

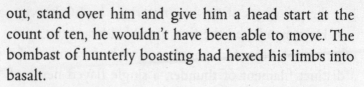

out, stand over him and give him a head start at the count of ten, he wouldn't have been able to move. The bombast of hunterly boasting had hexed his limbs into basalt.

The hunters woke before dawn. One of them all but pissed on Brrr, but the guy was sufficiently hungover not to notice. They kicked sand over their campfire and hoisted their rifles and packs, and crashed like rhinos away from Brrr's sanctuary.

He resigned himself to living in hiding for the rest of his life: to remain a rogue, unattached and unnoticed. And safe. Though what kind of a life would that be? He remembered with the instant nostalgia of youth the Lurlinists singing their anthems, the rare hikers chatting over landmarks, the lovers twisting by firelight against each other, as if trying to relieve a fatal itch. The choice of renunciation he was making was gloriously disappointing and refreshingly sad.

It was his first adult decision and therefore almost immediately revoked. A few days later he stumbled – literally – across the inaugural test of his mettle.

Evening. Brrr had been on the lookout for a growth of sweet forest pumpkin, which he especially favored. He hadn't seen the fellow on the ground, and he'd stepped right on him. The pressure of his paw had awakened the hunter out of a torpor of pain. 'Help,' said the man. Brrr leaped back, as terrified as he was surprised.

It was the youngest of the four hunters, the least

offensive, though no saint either, by the stench. The fellow's leg had been all but snapped off in a trap of some kind. Flies were making a banquet of the pus.

'Open the trap,' begged the poor sod. 'Let me free, or else eat me at once. I've been here days beyond telling.'

Surely it can't be more than three days, thought Brrr, but he didn't contradict.

'I can't bear another night,' claimed the fellow.

'The very dark,' said the Lion. This didn't seem enough, so he added, 'Isn't it very very *fright*-ful?' It was his first remark to anyone other than himself, so it was the first time he heard himself sound like a pantywaist. What was that all about?

'I beg you. Mercy, for the love of the Unnamed God.'

The Lion backed up, his rump high in the air, his whiskers a-twitter.

'Release me or do me in – one or the other,' said the man, and fell to moaning. 'Kill me and you can chew this wretched leg off my torso at last.'

'Actually, I'm very vegetarian,' said the Lion, proud of the *actually*. Is this how conversation was supposed to go? Your turn.

The young man reached again, for what must have been the ten thousandth time, to try to open the trap by force, but the thing was built to hold. He hadn't the strength by himself, and the trap wouldn't yield.

'You pull that side and I'll pull the other,' said the

fellow. 'Together we can open it. Then, maybe you could cart me to a settlement, or at least to a stream. I've been rotting here with nothing to drink but the dew I could lick off the vegetation.'

But the Lion found the teeth of the trap alarming. 'That's a very iron mouth,' he observed. 'Far too very dangerous. Look what it's done to you.'

'It's sprung, it can't spring again. Hunter's traps don't work like that.'

Brrr shook his head.

'You imbecile. You flathead. I'm begging you—'

'I can't risk it. There are those who rely on me for support,' said the Lion, thinking: *Myself, for one, and one is enough*. 'Besides, I haven't those curving shrimplike fingers you have. I can't just purr the thing off you, you know.' He was trying for a jocular tone, but it seemed to lack smack, and the hunter's distress was, well, distressing. Brrr pawed about, keeping a fair enough berth, sniffing and tossing his mane. 'So this is a hunter's trap, and you're a hunter. And I've just put the two concepts together. Aren't you a little bit very ashamed of yourself?'

'I'll give you anything. Every nickel florin I own. My father's cottage — it's freehold, no mortgage, running water, two fireplaces, stunning views.'

'A cottage among very human cottages?'

'Nicely done up. You wouldn't even have to redecorate.'

'Cottages filled with the fathers of hunters? I don't think so.'

The man fell back, stunned into silence, and then began to weep. Quietly, noxiously. The Lion was appalled and faintly offended. This wasn't quite as much fun as he'd imagined. The human raised himself on an elbow and managed quaveringly to say, 'You have a pride nearby – someone old enough to know how to show mercy to a stranger in your kingdom . . .'

'I'd go for help,' said the Lion, 'but I'm afraid no one is very near.'

'Help is near enough. If not from your clan, then from mine. I just got separated from my pals. Not long ago, really. They probably only made it back to the base camp by now. And look, in case the base camp has pulled up stakes, there's a small cadre of the Wizard's forces stationed at Tenniken. I'm one of their number – hunting with my mates on behalf of the regiment. They're loyal to the Wizard of Oz! They will come for me if you tell them where I am. Soldiers don't abandon their own.'

'A soldier-hunter.' A new concept. 'A lesson for us all,' said the Lion cautiously. 'Wish I'd had a soldier for a mother, then. Loyalty to the pack: what a thought.' But that was rumination, not conversation. He tried again. 'Have you enjoyed visiting this very neck of the woods?'

'Are you tormenting me?' The lad – he was hardly

more than that – sat up as far as he could. 'Am I hallucinating all this? Kill me or save me, as you wish, but for the love of the Unnamed God, do it soon. I'm all alone.'

It was this last remark that moved the Lion to pity, or pity of a sort. He knew about being alone. The weather was always cold there.

He padded forward and put his big head down on the man's chest. The man swooned in fear or disbelief, whereupon the scattershot snare in his chest slowed to a more stately thud.

The Lion considered creeping off. The whole thing was so embarrassing. Yet he remembered conversations usually concluding with 'Good night' or 'So long' or at least 'Piss off.' He didn't want to be rude and leave without the correct valediction.

He wrinkled his nostrils and sorted out the ribbons of odor. The pheromones of panic and anxiety (the young soldier's and the young Lion's, both). The salty sting of male sweat, and the cinnamony reek of human feces. Dried urine (faintly aphrodisiacal), dried blood (an astringent to the curled outer segments of Brrr's olfactory fissures). And mold, but not common leaf mold. This was mold on parchment that had been sized with bleaching.

Brrr had few words for those apprehensions, which were nonetheless tantalizingly distinct. He followed his nose and discovered a satchel of four books. They were dropped a few yards beyond the trap. He picked them up in his mouth and brought them forward to the soldier. He smelled the ferrous note of the belt buckle and then its complement, the tooth-sting of processed tin. The soldier wore a medal on his chest. Even in forest gloom the shine on it was enthralling.

The Lion fell in love. He sat down with front paws laid out together, like a sphinx, until the felled hero began to stir.

'I brought you your books,' said Brrr.

'Oh. I hoped you were a dream,' murmured the soldier, which Brrr first took to be a compliment.

'I thought you'd want them.' He walked the parcel over to the soldier and he didn't mean to drop it on his head. 'Whoops. Sorry.'

'They're not mine, you monster,' complained the young man. 'They're for you.'

'I have no learning,' said the Lion, 'or I'd be happy to read aloud to you to pass the time.'

'You mock me for someone else's crimes. Lion, I throw myself on your mercy.'

'What can I do for you?'

'What do you think? I don't want you to *return these books to the library*!' yelled the soldier. 'I want help! Go for help, you cretinous beast!' He was quite pretty, weeping.

'Wait here. I'll bring you some water to drink.'

'I'm not going anywhere, 'cept to the breast of Lurlina if you don't hurry.' The soldier ran his fingers over his shaven scalp. 'I wish the bugs would wait until I was fully dead.'

The Lion returned. It was hard to balance water in a scooped-out gourd, and most of it had spilled, but a few drops moistened the soldier's parched lips.

'Since you can't wrench this iron mouth off my leg, please go get my comrades,' said the soldier. 'If they've given up on finding me, they'll reconnoiter at the barracks in Tenniken. Tell them that Jemmsy sent you. They won't forget their Jemmsy. I'm their favorite. I'm like their little brother.'

'Jemmsy, is it? Jemmsy, I can't have anything to do with soldiers! Soldiers and their campaigns, Jemmsy. Really.'

'Don't kid yourself,' said Jemmsy. 'Everyone sleeps with the soldiers, in the long run.'

'If I'm not mistaken, Jemmsy, you were among that troop a few nights ago, Jemmsy, boasting about bagging pussy and all that? Weren't you, Jemmsy?'

'You totally don't get it. But this is my punishment? To be lectured to death by a talking Lion?'

It was at this remark that Brrr first surmised that not all Lions could speak.

'You're raving, perhaps from starvation,' said Brrr. 'Jemmsy, let me find you some food at least.' He lit out in the direction of Tenniken, in the direction that the fallen man suggested, and when he came across a slope of ripe strawberries he picked several quarts with his mouth and brought them back, delivering them one by one with a roll of his tongue.

The water had revived the soldier enough to be more aware of his pain. 'Don't stop to feed me,' he groaned, cramming the fruit in his mouth. 'Don't come back with a salad course. Just get my mates. Get me some fucking help. Don't I merit that much mercy?'

'I can't actually tell. What's your medal for, Jemmsy?'

'Courage in the line of fire.' Jemmsy began to bite his nails.

'And why do you wear it, Jemmsy?'

'To give myself courage.'

The circularity of this was beyond Brrr.

'You want it? The medal? Take it. I don't deserve it anymore, anyway. Going to pieces like this.' He unpinned it from his jacket. 'You can fix it to the belt lashing those books together, and wear it around your mighty thigh.'

Brrr had to keep from stealing a look to see if his thigh was all that mighty. 'I haven't earned it,' he said. 'Jemmsy.'

'It will be your passport in Tenniken. No one will harm you if you come in aid of a soldier of the Wizard's army. If you deliver the news of my incapacity to my brothers-at-arms, they won't forsake me. Soldiers take care of their own. Low ranking though I am.'

Brrr came forward and accepted the token by opening his mouth and gumming Jemmsy's hand almost up to the elbow. It tasted lettucy, watery, unwashed. The hand was limp on Brrr's tongue, and for a moment neither of them moved.

Then, extruding the hand through closed lips, and ejecting the badge onto the pile of books, Brrr said softly, 'Pin it there on the belt, as you suggested. When I go, I'll take the books with me, too.'

'Bless you,' replied Jemmsy. 'If I were not to survive, would you tell my fellows to remind my father I loved him until the end? And forgive me my crimes against you and your kind.'

'I have no kind,' said Lion. 'But okay, sure. If it'll make you happy. What crimes might those be, Jemmsy?'

But Jemmsy had rolled over on his side, and he put the saliva-wet hand into his groin and drew his knees up, as far as the trap would allow. He didn't speak again.

Gratitude, thought the Lion. He gripped the satchel belt in his mouth and left. He found, though, that the farther away he got, the less he could be confident of the small association that had sprouted between him and Jemmsy. Did a conversation constitute a friendship? If so, this was his first friendship, and he wasn't sure how fragile it might prove to be. How could he abandon the fellow, just like that? What if Jemmsy fell asleep and had a bad dream, and cried out, as the Lion had so often done?

He circled back, then, but by old habit he settled out of sight in a shadowy clot of fallen and rotting tree limbs. He watched his friend sleep, and struggle against the trap, and grow still. Brrr reviewed the matter as best he could, inventing rhetorical forensics from the ground up.

On the one hand, Jemmsy and his companions had *set* that very trap. Or things like it. They were hunting him, or his kind. His *kind*. Right? Right? So now the soldier had him. Jemmsy had caught himself a Lion, just perhaps not in the way he had intended.

On the other hand, maybe experience – of any sort – was only valid if it caused you to redefine your terms. *Courage*, for instance. The courage to go versus the courage to stay? Which was more very couragey?

Any decision he made, Brrr realized, would affect his friend's future one way or the other.

His heart burned with affection when, in a fever, the man called out, 'Lion. Friend Lion! Have you forsaken me?'

It's good that I am in your heart to give you hope, thought the Lion, hope unto death. He lay as close to the soldier as he dared, to keep the man warm at night until there was nothing left of him to warm. Even when

Jemmsy died, and the smell grew worse, the Lion hated to leave the body.

'Now I'll go for help,' he said to the carcass. 'You've been very patient.'

Jemmsy didn't reply.

'What's the matter, cat got your tongue?' said Brrr, but his tone sounded off and he closed his mouth.

My first conversation, he thought, and his bound had a new spring to it. He was nearly giddy. Of course, the finish had been awkward – death is a real stifler of repartee – but on the whole he thought it had gone rather well.

A conversation and a friend. Jemmsy had called out 'Friend Lion!' So the friendship had been short-lived but real; now that it was dead, it couldn't be revoked. It was preserved inviolable in his heart. And the medal shone like a portable compliment. The medal advertised Brrr's own courage as he headed to Tenniken to keep his promise. He would deliver the news of the fallen Jemmsy to those grieving companions-at-arms. And through them the news could go on to Jemmsy's father, that puzzle of a creature, for being capable of abandoning his son to the care of the army.

'The heart of a Lion,' murmured Yackle, almost purring herself. Brrr resisted the temptation to imagine she was being snide, but he couldn't resist the domino-patter of memories, one after another, that had concluded his childhood. The momentum of the mind can be vexingly, involuntarily capricious.

3

So the next memory toppled forward, a tremor following upon a tremor. Jemmsy. His body seeping into the ground like a pudding at room temperature. How long had it been since Brrr had thought of Jemmsy? The scab torn off, after all this time; a smell of earth leaching from that opened wound. The smell of those childhood woods from as far back as his mind could pick its way.

When was his unspoken pledge to Jemmsy hijacked by ambition? How soon was his hope to deliver the news of Jemmsy's death superseded by his hunger for the reward of gratitude? Or had it not happened as baldly as all that?

He couldn't now remember. Only the terror and giddy release at having a destination at all. Tenniken. Tenniken, a garrison town, and nearby, a soldier's grieving father. A brick hearthside where Brrr might curl up like a house cat, like a surrogate son, purring, domesticated, basking in the warmth of approval.

He felt perverse and new, flayed by raw luck. For the first time, he felt naked. He felt he could outrun his timidity just by doing the job right.

Getting to Tenniken. Returning Jemmsy's medal of honor. Exchanging the tin ikon for the real thing: a sensation of righteous bravery he could own for himself.

It was going to take a while, though. He had to venture beyond the paced edges of his territory. Like all creatures who mark their boundaries, he could tell when he passed into the treacherous unknown. The musk of the undergrowth seemed foreboding.

The pictures in his mind grew more lovely, perhaps to distract him from the fear of being afraid. The cozy garrison settlement, and a place to eat. With any luck it would be a beer garden. Flowers, stripped of their nettles and thorns, madly fomented in pots set on window ledges and stoops. Candy-colored birds in silver cages, birds who didn't threaten like forest vultures with those nerve-jangling cries, but who actually sang. On pitch. And trilling maidens at the town well, picking up the melody and embellishing it. That sort of thing.

It would have been hard to say just how this picture came into his head. It must have been cobbled together from bits and pieces of things he had heard in the woods, long before he could understand them. Though what a pretty picture! The maidens with their scuttles and pails, and every cobblestone glistening, and every windowsill laden with fresh fruit pies cooling, and every housewife generous with her pies, and every schoolchild blithe and gay. And every father appreciative, especially Jemmsy's father. Brrr could hardly wait to get there.

He rehearsed these visions to put himself to sleep at night, troubled upon a bed of foreign moss.

He'd gone six days or more, practicing conversational gambits aloud – 'Hello, I'm very new in town' – 'Hello, are you very in need of a new friend, one with prior experience?' – when he crossed through a thicket to the edge of a blueberry patch. The fruit hung heavy, cobalt and black and pink, and a small creature, perhaps the size of a human cub, was driving its snout through the offerings.

Brrr couldn't help himself. 'You must be very brave out here all alone in the woods,' he began. The cub froze and turned an eye like a blueberry upon the Lion. Brrr straightened his shoulders and tossed his head to aerate his mane into magnificence, whereupon the cub fell to the ground on its back, its small stained paws cupped below its furry chin.

'Sweet Lurlina,' said Brrr, 'I'm slaying them right and left with my conversational wit.' He went up to look closely. The cub wasn't dead, but shamming: Brrr

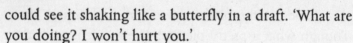

could see it shaking like a butterfly in a draft. 'What are you doing? I won't hurt you.'

'Just my luck,' said the Bear cub, for that's what he had turned out to be. 'I break the rules and go off on my own, and the King of the Forest arrives to devour me.'

Brrr almost turned around to see the King approaching. 'You don't mean me? How very droll. Get up, I won't hurt you. Rise. Why are you lying there as if you've had a very cardiac episode? It's unsettling.'

The Bear cub sat up. 'If you insist. You promise you won't hurt me?'

'I'm very promising. Why did you collapse like that? Do I look like a hunter to you?' Brrr was more curious than offended.

'It's what you do if you're facing long odds,' said the Bear. 'You play meek and helpless in front of a sterner foe, and that kick-starts a sense of noble mercy in them. That's the theory anyway. I never had need to practice it before, but it seems to have worked. My name is Cubbins.'

His placid delivery sounded mature, though his voice strayed trebleward. Brrr replied hopefully, 'Lost and alone and very abandoned by your clan?'

'Just taking a break from the endless hilarity of it all. They're downslope a ways at the stream's edge. You're not here to scatter us to kingdom come?'

'Hardly. I need some directions.'

'The King of Beasts needs directions?'

'Will you stop with that?' said Brrr. 'I'm not even a very local celebrity. Just passing through and minding my own very business.'

'Well, with that medal and all,' said Cubbins. 'You look official. Is that why you say *very* so very often?'

Young as he was, he was ribbing the Lion. 'Take me to your leader,' said Brrr, exerting *very* control. 'Please.'

'Such as she is,' said Cubbins obligingly. 'Actually, I'm the boy sheriff of our group, but since you stumbled upon me and showed me mercy, I'll oblige. Follow me.' The Bear cub led Brrr along a ridge and down a trail to the edge of a broad, shallow stream. 'Look who found me when I was lost in the woods,' called out Cubbins.

'Liar, liar, pants on fire,' said the others. There were five or six of them, full grown: some burly companions at play and an aging old thing resting in kind of a shabby bath chair, half in, half out of a pool.

'Don't mind them. They've spent the afternoon with a comb of fermented honey,' said Cubbins.

Brrr picked his passage on stones across the stream, taking care not to let the pads of his paws get damp.

'Oooh, a toady right from the git-go,' said one of the older Bears. 'I oughta known it, a sissy missy, the way she goes mincing across those stones like she's afraid of ruining her mother's silk stockings.'

'Enough, Bruner O'Bruin,' said Cubbins. 'This creature was kind to me.'

'What's your name, Lord Lion?' asked Bruner O'Bruin.

'Brrr,' replied the Lion, shaking his mane, trying to make a theatrical shimmer out of word and name alike. 'Who are you lot?'

'The last, best hope for Oz. Movers and shakers,' said Bruner O'Bruin mockingly. He got up and shimmied, his rump poking out. The others guffawed. Cubbins rolled his eyes and offered the Lion a sip of water from a battered iron ladle.

'We're what remains of the court of Ursaless, the Queen of the North,' said Cubbins. 'Fallen on hard times, but good at heart, I hope. That's Ursaless over there.' He indicated the oldest one, who was getting up from her chair to stretch. She was immensely tall. Even at her apparent age, white whiskers and all, she towered over her companions. 'Ursaless, say hello to our guest.'

The Queen had a ratty sort of coat, and no clothes to speak of but a tiara three sizes too small. A sash that read QUALITY LIQUORS AT INSANELY LOW PRICES rode from one shoulder to the opposite hip. She grimaced. Perhaps she was troubled by arthritis.

'Queen of the North?' asked Brrr.

'Queen of the Northern Bears,' Cubbins amended. 'Not that there are many of us left in the wild. Our kin and cousins are easily seduced by the lure of human

comforts — beds, running hot water, whist champion-
ships, you name it. Still, some of us hold on to the old
folkways, and Ursaless is our leader.'

The Queen lumbered over on all fours. 'The Lion
comes to pay his respects,' she observed, looking him
over through mild eyes. 'It's been some years since I've
seen Lions in these parts.'

'You've seen a Lion around here before?' Brrr
found a new reason for conversation: the examination
of history. 'How very marvelous! I've never met another
Lion. Who was it? Where did they go? Did they
happen to misplace a Lion cub, do you know? Did they
look like me?'

'Don't be tedious; I have no head for details,' said
Ursaless. She examined her nails and frowned.

'Oh, but if you could remember a scrap!' he
insisted. 'A very scrap!'

She turned her head so only one eye rested on
him. It looked cold. 'Your Highness,' he added.

This relaxed her. 'Sometimes I recall oddments
without even trying. We'll see what happens.
Meanwhile, what brings you to our encampment?'

'I'm headed for Tenniken,' he replied. 'The human
settlement, where I understand soldiers are stationed.
Soldiers loyal to the Wizard of Oz.'

'Tenniken,' she repeated, hummingly. 'Do we
know Tenniken?'

'Tenniken's not to be worth knowing,' said Bruner

O'Bruin, 'if we're not there making it worth the while to know.' His voice was confident but he turned his head away as he spoke, as if not wanting to meet the Queen's glance.

The Queen continued. 'Caraway Coyle? Bungler MiGrory? Shaveen Brioyne? Anyone remember Tenniken?'

'There's so much past,' said the one called Shaveen, a female who sat picking nits from her armpits. 'I don't think Tenniken was worth remembering, if we ever knew of it. Otherwise we'd remember it.'

'She's right as usual, our Shaveen,' said the males. The concert of their agreement seemed to satisfy the Queen.

Ursaless turned back to the Lion. 'We can't help you in this, either, I'm afraid. Tenniken means nothing to us.'

'Didn't we go on a scavengey romp there?' asked Cubbins. 'I was only a mite of a thing last spring, but isn't Tenniken where the train engine scared us, racing by?'

'Don't listen to yourself,' said Ursaless fondly. 'You're too young to have learned to forget what isn't needed. If we can't corroborate your assertions, there can be no useful truth to them.' She cocked an eyebrow at Brrr. 'Would you care for some honey?'

The Lion shook his head. Their lopsided version of conversation was unnerving, and he was losing the confidence he'd been struggling to maintain. 'I'll just help myself to another sip of water and be on my way, then.'

'What way is that?' asked Ursaless.

'I'm going to Tenniken.'

'Never heard of the place,' she stated firmly. 'Any of you bruisers heard of Tenniken?'

'Not I,' said Caraway Coyle. Bungler MiGrory put his head in his paws and began to snore. Shaveen Brioyne said, 'I think we talked about this once before, but maybe I'm thinking of someplace else. Or that we talked about something else.' She absentmindedly ate a nit. 'I like to talk,' she said, almost to herself.

Ursaless turned back to the Lion and asked, 'What's your name?'

'I thought I'd mentioned it,' said the Lion. 'It is Brrr.'

'That's a nice name,' said Ursaless. 'Brrr sounds like a Bear. Do you have Bears in your background?'

'I very much doubt it,' said Brrr. 'I may be mocked by some for the way that I walk, but I believe I am very much Lion.'

'Why did your parents give you a name so like a Bear, then?'

'I had no parents,' he replied. 'Unless you've remembered seeing any around here? A pride of Lions on a march of some sort?'

'Someone gave you a name, or did you name yourself?'

This question hadn't occurred to him before. He hadn't named himself — so where *had* his name come from? 'I don't remember that I had parents,' he replied.

'All *Bears* have parents,' said Ursaless. 'Caraway, you have a father and a mother, don't you?'

'You're my mother. No?' Caraway sounded dubious. It was Ursaless's turn to cough and change the subject; she couldn't answer authoritatively.

'Were I you, I would find my parents and ask them why they named me something like a Bear.' Ursaless hurried on. 'Then you can come back and tell us.'

'Though chances are we won't recognize you,' said Shaveen.

'Except Cubbins,' said Ursaless fondly. 'You will, won't you, fondness?'

Cubbins turned his head so she couldn't see him rolling his eyes at her.

'I can't find my parents, I don't even know who they are,' said Brrr. 'For all I know, they're dead. Besides, I am on my way to Tenniken. A human town to the south.'

'Oh. Humans. Hmmm. I've never been convinced they exist, humans.'

'Of course they do,' inserted Bruner O'Bruin. 'That's where all our cousins go when they can't stand their cousins anymore.'

'They go to be humans?'

'No. They go to human places.'

'Like Tenniken,' said the Lion, pushing it now, but unable to resist. 'You know, Tenniken. The human settlement, where I understand soldiers are stationed. Soldiers loyal to the Wizard of Oz.'

'Oh,' offered Ursaless, attentive, 'the great WOO.'

Cubbins intercepted that one for Brrr. 'WOO. That's what we call the Wizard of Oz. The Great and Wonderful WOO.'

'And if there is such a creature,' said Ursuless, 'may he stay where he is and we stay where we are. Anyway, we're not subjects of any Wizard. He doesn't rule the Great Gillikin Forest.'

'Far from it,' said Caraway Coyle, belching.

'He's never even been here,' said Shaveen.

'We'd tear him limb from limb, if he existed,' said Caraway Coyle. 'Watch me do a three-quarter snarl. It's so cool.' He obliged, looking suddenly like a hydro-encephalitic dog with a mosquito in its nose.

'I thought he was the Wizard of *all* Oz,' said Brrr, trying to bring them back to it.

'Anyone can name himself whatever he wants,' said Cubbins. 'Wizard of Oz or WOO or the King of Beasts.'

'I know this much,' said Brrr. 'He sends human soldiers into our forest.'

'A good reason to stay out of his way,' replied Cubbins. 'Deep down, we wild Bears are unrepentant followers of Ozma, though she has been long disappeared from the public eye and is presumed dead. Still, we carry a torch for her. In her time, she was less hostile to beasts in the wild than the current administration is. May she come again. They say she will return to rescue Oz in its time of tribulation.'

'Who says?' asked Brrr.

'General prophecy. Common sense. I don't know.'

'People who say it, say it,' barked Ursaless.

Cubbins continued. 'Well, all I want to know is, what's keeping her? It's tribulating enough these days. Threat and panic everywhere you turn. We have to wait until it gets worse?'

'Listen to smartypants there. We never believed in Ozma,' said Ursaless. 'I never did, so you never did either. I'm the Queen.'

'I don't believe in *you*, so there,' said Shaveen, though when the Queen glared at her she pointed at Brrr.

'You have your hands full, governing this crew,' murmured Brrr.

'Well,' said Ursaless, 'some say the brighter among us left for the human world. More possibilities for advancement, et cetera. Maybe they had more get-up-and-go. Personally, I think it takes *character* to stay here and hold down a court. Maintain a presence in the ancestral wild. The forest bucolic.' She made it sound like a paradise, the pestering flies, the drunken circularities repeated by an inbred family. 'Anyway, when we bother to believe in her, we wait for the return of Ozma. No good comes of commerce with humans. Mark my words, you Lion.'

'But do they come back? Your cousins in the human world?'

'Cubbins, can you help our guest? I'm growing weary of giving an audience.' She let loose a flagrantly stagy yawn, and returned to the dollop of honey dripping off a wedge of comb the size of a small boulder.

Cubbins nodded to the others and jerked his head to the Lion: this way, friend. The Lion followed him, trying hard not to waggle his rump. As he passed, though, the Bears made remarks under their breath.

'Captivating family you have here,' said Brrr, when they were far enough away to avoid being overheard.

'Go easy on them,' said Cubbins. 'They can't really help it. It's what happens to us Bears.'

'You go loopy on honey?'

'I don't think the honey has much to do with it,' said Cubbins, 'though I can't really be sure. I don't care for fortified honey yet, so I don't partake. Still, I've observed that a taste for the stuff develops as Bears mature. In any case, I suspect it's just that we don't have much of a race memory, that's all. Bears are creatures in the present. Any Bear who finds that the present just isn't *enough*, well, that Bear strikes out for the human world – the Tenniken of which you speak, or other parts. Maybe they want to see if they can acclimate themselves to a weight of memory under which humans live and are pinned. I have no idea if they manage, for they never come back. Maybe the WOO gets them. Who knows?'

Perhaps that was what happened to Brrr's parents. Maybe they entered the world of humans. But he didn't want to talk about it to Cubbins: all this curiosity was a new thing. Likely born of hearing how lovingly his friend Jemmsy had remembered his own father as he lay dying. For the first time Brrr tried the gambit of changing the subject. 'How did you come to be sheriff?'

'I'm just the youngest. The youngest is always everything important, except the Queen, of course. I'm the sheriff, and the bursar, and the accounts receivable department, and the chaplain and the social affairs committee and the historian. As soon as someone accidentally has another cub, I will yield my place to him or her. The youngest is in charge around here. We forget as we grow. Or did I already say that? It worries me when I repeat myself accidentally.'

'You're fine,' said Brrr.

'You haven't said why you're leaving the wild for a human settlement.'

Brrr didn't want to speak yet about Jemmsy. It was his secret. His mistake, maybe, or maybe the key to his own rare and beautiful future. In any case, he wasn't sure if he wanted Cubbins coming along. Cubbins was a lot more adorable than Brrr. Cubbins might move into the cottage of Jemmsy's father while Brrr was kept on a leash in the yard.

'I have some books to return to a library. For a friend,' he said, becking his head at the leather-bound stack of them.

'Books!' said Cubbins. 'What are you doing with *books* in the Great Gillikin Forest, for crying out loud?'

'Returning them. As I said.'

'But where'd you get them?' Cubbins was riven with book-lust. 'Let me see, may I? *Three Treatises on the Liberty of Speaking Beasts.* What's that one with the faded gilt – *Ozma Incognita.* Oh, my. A trove. And chosen to appeal to the likes of us.'

'Well, don't get your grubby paws all over them. They're not mine to loan.'

'What's this silvery emblem?'

'A medal,' said Brrr. In a softer voice, with a tone of hesitation, as if nearly too modest to continue: 'A commendation for bravery, as it happens.'

'I'd never have guessed it,' said Cubbins, piercingly earnest, though his eyes were still on the books.

'If you don't mind, I have a schedule to keep,' said the Lion. 'It's a busy life, mine. As I'm learning. Now, can you set me on any sort of a path that would be useful, do you think?'

'The Tenniken that we Bears have never visited and don't believe in lies south by southwest,' Cubbins said without sarcasm. 'The only way I can tell you for sure brings you uncomfortably close to Cloud Swamp. Though maybe you wouldn't mind that the way we Bears do.'

'I never heard of the place.'

'Cloud Swamp? Oh, it's a soupy section of the woods. A wetlands, I suppose you'd call it. Not all that far from here, most of the time, though it has a weird tendency to be migratory. Imagine not knowing about Cloud Swamp.'

'I had no parents to tell me about it,' said Brrr dryly.

'Well, it's the haunt of the Ozmists.'

'Ozmists. Who are they? Secret defenders of the deposed line of Ozma that I'm learning about?'

'Good guess. But no. Ozmists are – well, for lack of a better term, I guess you'd call them ghosts. Or particles of ghosts.'

'Migratory ghosts.' Brrr tried to keep his voice level. 'Ghosts ancient or modern?'

'I don't know. We Bears avoid Cloud Swamp most of the time. Perhaps we give up our pasts, as you have seen, whether we like it or not. But ghosts – wow. Ghosts are nothing *but* pasts. Look, if your parents are dead, you might find one or both of their Ozmists in Cloud Swamp, and at least learn why they called you Brrr. And maybe why they went and died on you, and so forth.'

'I never said my parents were dead.'

'No, you didn't, but where are they, then? Living the high life among other talking Animals and humans in the wonderful welter of Oz?'

'If they are ghosts – well – can *ghosts* hurt?'

'You mean, can they hurt you? I doubt it,' replied Cubbins. 'They're just notions, aren't they? Dissolving shrouds of an individual? Still, to be fair, don't take my word on it: For all I know, it's ghosts who have spooked us Bears into being so forgetful. We can never remember if we ever accidentally ventured into Cloud Swamp. I only know we haven't been there since I've been in charge. That's all I'm sure of.'

Brrr wasn't sure he relished the idea of meeting the nub of an idea without its mortal husk, though he couldn't think how to say this.

Cubbins shrugged. 'Just a thought. Maybe you don't want to know if your parents are dead or not. If it doesn't appeal to you, head on past. You'll find your Tenniken. To the south, more or less. But I don't know where it is exactly. Someone else will have to tell you.'

'Too bad,' said the Lion. 'If you'd had better information, I might have paid you with one of these books.'

Cubbins looked disappointed, but he spoke with characteristic brio. 'It's okay. Anything I might read I would only forget sooner or later.'

'It must be hard to be the only Bear with a brain,' said Brrr.

'I'd love to come with you. But someone has to keep this passel of friends on the straight and narrow. If I didn't remind them, they'd forget the answer to the tired rhetorical gibe, Does a Bear shit in the woods?'

Brrr didn't want to share with Cubbins any final glory he might achieve in Tenniken, but on the other hand, if Brrr were accidentally to meet up with the Ozmists he intended to avoid, company in the form of a little Bear sheriff would be welcome. 'If you walked away from here, your family would forget you in a minute,' said the Lion. 'What kind of a loss is that? Don't sacrifice yourself to them. They won't even notice.'

'I get something out of this,' said Cubbins. 'It doesn't hurt to have a family, you know, even a troubled one. At least I know where I am. What are you looking for in Tenniken, anyway? You think your parents went there?'

Brrr snapped his mane. 'It's my own business,' he said.

'You really should start at Cloud Swamp and find out what you can, you know. It might help you narrow your search. Why spend time hunting for forebears if they're dead?'

'Thanks,' said Brrr, 'but no thanks.' Then he gave up his airy attitude. 'Truth to tell, without a companion, I don't dare venture into anyplace called Cloud Swamp.'

'Cloud Swamp? What's that?' asked Cubbins, but when the Lion shot him a look, the cub's eyes were twinkling in mischief. 'You better get along now. My family party here is agreeable, but they can be disagreeable, too, and the mood can shift in an instant. Better make your way before they get suspicious that you're going to kidnap me or something. One thing they do know is that they'd be lost without their baby cub to give their lives what little meaning and history it still has.'

'And you went out hunting for blueberries on your own.'

'One misdemeanor a day is enough, I suppose.'

'It's been a mighty pleasure,' said the Lion, and he meant it. He was sorry to leave Cubbins. 'Good luck to you. If I ever make it into the human world, I will hope to run into you there someday, too. You deserve better than this.'

'Life is unpredictable,' said Cubbins. 'I don't imagine we'll meet again, but who knows. I'll look for a Lion with a sway in his swagger. Just kidding.'

'If I wanted to avoid Cloud Swamp, now,' said the Lion, 'which way would I go?'

'From this point on the streambed, you may choose left or right. If you can just keep to the uplands, you'll skirt it entirely,' said Cubbins. 'Good luck to you, very Brrr.'

4

Ursaless, the Queen of the Bears, had said it straight: *Sometimes I recall oddments without even trying*. Who knows when memory, unbidden, will burst out and take hostages? Clearly the question of Yackle's had snapped some ancient chains Brrr had used against all this.

And this wash of recollections had become a slick along which Brrr careered, like it or not. Brrr's recall of what had happened *before* seemed limited to apparent causes of what had happened *next*. The future reshapes the memory of the past in the way it recalibrates significance: some episodes are advanced, others lose purchase.

But his intention, starting out, had been to avoid Cloud Swamp. Hadn't it? His curiosity about possibly meeting his spirit-ancestors was more than mitigated by the fear of coming across the ghost of Jemmsy. Wasn't ready for that. Not until he had delivered the medal to Jemmsy's father. Not until Brrr deserved his own personal medal for courage that a grateful pride of grieving soldiers might press upon him. Not till he could show his missing clan that he had survived on his own. Survived and triumphed. Cloud Swamp could wait until then.

Though wherever Tenniken might turn out to be, Brrr couldn't seem to get there without tending downslope. Every path that he found leading upland reversed its grade, perversely, around the next stand of houndstooth hedge or outcropping of granite. Leaving the path also proved futile: he'd met an interlocked network of chalky cliffs, too sheer to climb. The chasms that he came across proved too wide to leap. And again with the houndstooth hedge.

Eventually, despite his hopes to avoid any lowlands, hunger drove him downhill, as in the moist gloom he could see knuckles of cobbleberry vine displaying their sweet green fruit like so much vulgar jewelry. Brrr fell on the treat avidly. The aftertaste of the cobbleberries was tart, reminding him that the berries were in second growth. The spring was moving on.

He became possessed by the notion that time might harbor a hunger of its own, a hunger it fed by gobbling up long strings of minutes, courses of hours, harvests of seasons one after the other. This notion, too, was probably born of watching those Bears in their eternal present, unaware of time passing, unaware of cobbleberry vines forcing out a last, tangy collation of the season.

A few moments later, Brrr wondered if perhaps the berries he'd gobbled down had begun to ferment. His usual gingerish footing became a bit heavier, even clumsy. His head grew dense, and a miasma of unde-cipherable impressions closed in on him like marsh gas. Not long thereafter he fell to his chin and rolled over onto his back, dozing with open eyes. The stars lifted their myriad eyes to watch him wince over the clenching of his intestines.

If the stars showed, it must be nighttime. No cloud of ancestors on the horizon to obliterate the constellations.

Very few forest creatures were out and about tonight at their nocturnal chores and hobbies. In fact, he could detect no motion but the papery rustling of wind in sedge-grass. No frog dove into the stagnant ditchwater. No mockingbird traced her alibis into the gloaming.

There weren't even any mosquitoes, which was not only pleasant but impossible, especially in a swamp.

A swamp it certainly was; perhaps a rising one. The small hillock on which Brrr had settled seemed ringed by a steely salver of water – so calm that the constellations were reflected in it perfectly. You couldn't make out the seam where the water ended and the sky began. It was more like being aloft among the heavenly bodies than adrift below them. The air was uncolored, characterless, neither sweet nor cold, neither clear nor moving.

Poison cobbleberries? Maybe, he thought, I have died, and so all life around me has died, too, for what proof have I that life should go on when I do not? After all, what kind of a life is it that is not pestered by insects? A perfect one, and since life is not perfect, this cannot be life.

With a sense of calm, or was it a paralysis, he realized the stars were moving toward him, very slowly, growing infinitesimally larger but no more distinct. At first he thought: Maybe these are the ghosts of trees that have rotted in Cloud Swamp, for that's where I must be, like it or not.

Then it seemed like a host of shimmering midges in a *corps de guerre*. (Was this where all the insects had gone? Magnetically drawn to the hollow-in-life that a ghost colony might be, filling in the vacuum with the smallest fleck of indivisible yet visible living matter?)

Now they were airily shaping themselves into bouquets, like giant heads on tapering necks, like volutes of blossom on slowly spiraling stems. Nearing and nearing, possessed of both presence and distance.

'I don't believe in ghosts,' said Brrr, to himself or to them, or both. Hoping they might be offended and leave.

They began to circle about him. The nearer they drew, the more of a family feeling they took on. Was it because, once a creature became a ghost, it shirked off the differentiations of biological diversity and, uniqueness annihilated, became just shades of life? Footfalls of the past?

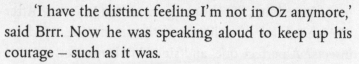

'I have the distinct feeling I'm not in Oz anymore,' said Brrr. Now he was speaking aloud to keep up his courage – such as it was.

The specters wreathed themselves around him. As they tightened the circle, their separate margins began to merge. Before he was swallowed up in a blancmange of foggy apparition, he gave out a thunderclap of a roar. It appeared to make no impression on the creatures, but he was glad he could still roar. It meant he wasn't dead. Presumably.

'Excuse my volume; I have no self-control,' he said. Well, why not talk to the phantoms? He had meant to avoid Cloud Swamp at all costs, but opportunity was presenting itself. And conversation was his only skill.

'Begging pardon for the intrusion. Frightfully thoughtless of me,' he went on. 'Is there a spokesperson among you who can answer a question or two? If you've time to spare?'

There was a sort of drumming in the air, as if a billion miniature throats were clearing themselves. Languidly the sound resolved, its pitch rising and consolidating toward a common note. But it died out, bearing no word for Brrr upon its pressured breath.

'Allow me to introduce myself,' he said more forcefully. 'I am, in actual fact, the King of the Forest.'

No reply. The apparent lack of interest on the part of a congress of ghosts shamed Brrr. It also frightened him. Of course they would realize he was no kind of king at all. He organized his thoughts with more honesty.

'I didn't come here to disturb your rest,' he stated. 'Indeed, I hoped to pass without pestering you. Shall we just nod courteously and say 'Good-bye' or 'Piss off' or whatever's appropriate and then breeze on our separate ways?'

The assemblage of ghosts seemed to hover, listening, or drumming its fingers against its forearms, so to speak. Tacit. As yet uninvolved.

'Wait,' said a voice, not Brrr's, but a normal worldly voice. *Jemmsy?* The Lion swiveled his head, not certain from which direction the sound approached.

Cubbins blundered down the side of an invisible bluff, snapping the branches of an invisible birch tree to break his descent. He splashed through the vision of ghosts and arrived at Brrr's side with slicked thighs. Under one arm dripped a wedge of honeycomb.

'I forgot to tell you that you need to offer a tribute if you want to speak with the ghosts,' said Cubbins.

Another little secret about conversation. How did folks learn to get on in this tricky verbal negotiation called chat? How much had it cost him to grow up without the banter of family life?

Still, Brrr was glad to see the boy sheriff. (Out on his own again, the little dickens!) Almost as glad as if Jemmsy himself had coalesced out of a matrix of midges, free of an iron snare, smiling a soft-cheeked

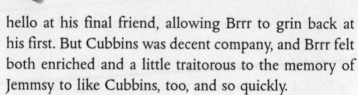

hello at his final friend, allowing Brrr to grin back at his first. But Cubbins was decent company, and Brrr felt both enriched and a little traitorous to the memory of Jemmsy to like Cubbins, too, and so quickly.

He said, hiding his gratitude, 'How do you know you need to offer the ghosts a gift if no one in your tribe believes in ghosts?'

'I asked Ursaless. She claims never to have seen the Ozmists, but she insists this is the way it's done by long-standing custom.'

The Lion raised an eyebrow. 'Don't ask,' said Cubbins, sighing. 'I don't expect to follow her line of reasoning. I just listen and obey.'

'But you're not allowed to go running off alone,' said Brrr. 'Isn't one disobedience a day enough?'

'You are brave enough to strike out on your own,' replied the cub. 'And ten minutes after you left, no one could remember you had been there. So I realized you were right. What is there for me in the court of Ursaless?'

'They're your family!'

'They're not the whole world. I can always come back if I want.'

Brrr spoke cautiously. 'What if you can't find them? What if they have moved on?'

Cubbins laughed. 'Move? That's the whole point of the Northern Bears. They never move on. So I'm taking a cue from you . . .'

He put the comb of honey on a rock in the

clearing. The midges swarmed nearer it. In the act of crowding together their apparition took on a more coherent aspect. Not a human face, perhaps not even a face at all, but something with an enriched identity.

'Are ghosts *bugs*?' whispered Brrr.

'Who knows? Next time you squash a roach, you might be doing in old Auntie Groyleen again. Or maybe bugs are the largest part of life without individual character, so they're useful vessels for ghosts. I have a theory—'

All at once, words were spoken in the clearing. It was like the echo of a sound divorced from its original imprint. The Ozmists spoke in one voice.

Barter, said the chorus ominously.

'"Barter"?' whispered Brrr. 'What's that supposed to mean?'

'Another word for *chat*, I think,' Cubbins replied. 'I'm guessing they will tell you what you want if you tell them what they want.'

'Is this more advice from Ursaless?'

'Common sense. Which as you know doesn't come from Ursaless. Shhh, let's find out what they want.'

Brrr cleared his throat. 'All right, then,' he started. 'As long as you have granted me an audience, I would like to ask about the possible ghost of a Lion or Lioness who might have joined your, um, ranks. Or even a whole pride of Lions. Not just any spare Lions, but mine. My kin.'

When a certain velocity had been reached, the Ozmists trained their vibrations nearer to a common key, if not a single note. They managed to communicate a message in some fashion that was neither words nor music, quite. Still, the Lion and the Bear cub listened closely.

We note your query, they managed to communicate. *By way of payment: You tell us first — Is the dreadful Wizard still on the throne of Oz?*

'You should know more than I do,' said Brrr, playing for time. How embarrassing to be asked a question he couldn't answer. 'You're ghosts, after all: you're spirit and transcendence. I'm just plodding along with my nose to the ground here, wet behind the ears and a long way to go.'

We have no more experience of the future than the living do, they said, but their voices went out of keen registration, and it sounded like hundreds of voices intoning the same thought at once. *W-w-w-e-e-e ha-v-v-ve n-n-n-o-o-o mor-r-r-r experiesnshchshe . . .*

'And you hunger for future history,' said Brrr.

This day you live in today is the impossible future to us, said the Ozmists. *Is the Wizard still squatting upon the throne? We crave to know the future.*

'All well and good,' said Brrr, 'and what I know, I will share gladly. I recently met some soldiers in the forest — one special soldier particularly — serving in the forces of the great and powerful Wizard of Oz. So I can answer that much, if not more: The Wizard of Oz is on the throne of Oz. Do I get an answer in reply? Are fragments of my ancestors figured among your midst?'

The Ozmists glowed, small cyclings in place. *We stir, we steep, we sift, we shift among ourselves for clues to your question*, they said.

Brrr waited. They said no more.

'Are they taking inventory?' whispered Cubbins.

'I don't know.'

'Well, tell me this, then,' went on Cubbins excitedly. 'While you're figuring out whether his parents are among you Ozmists, perhaps you can tell us about who is *not* there. Is the missing queen of Oz, Ozma, among your kind? Was she murdered in her infant cradle, as some have said? Or is her spirit still abroad in its human form?'

The Ozmists reared – twenty, thirty feet in the steamy air.

'Scratch that last question,' Brrr called in a loud voice. 'Never mind. We'll soldier on as we are. You are dismissed.' Hoping that he and Cubbins could be dismissed, too.

But the Ozmists replied, *There is little time left – the act of our compressing into community unsettles the vapors. You ask the impertinent question all Bears ask, and you will pay the price. Ozma is not dead. But you bring us no news of our lost Oz – you break the contract. You will pay.*

Cubbins's small jaw dropped. 'News!' he

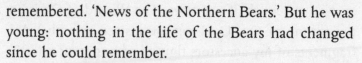
remembered. 'News of the Northern Bears.' But he was young: nothing in the life of the Bears had changed since he could remember.

Brrr wanted to say, *Lie to them, tell them anything!* But he didn't dare. The Ozmists were everywhere and could apprehend the faintest whisper.

'News,' said the Lion, trying by his tone to communicate an instruction to fabricate – another first – 'Cubbins, give them, you know, the *news*. The newest news!'

Cubbins looked wildly about as if trying to see modern history in the making among the jeweled rash of phantoms. His eye fell on the stack of books that Brrr carried, and he grabbed the top one. 'I have – to hand – the latest news – here!' He read the title: '*Ozma Initiata: The Birth of the Throne Line.*'

But even Brrr could tell this was history, not current events.

'Or . . . or . . .' Cubbins tore through a second book. '*Animal Magic, or, The Secret Spell of Language.*' He whipped pages filled with charts. 'A grammar textbook. You know, language is always changing, they say: ever new. Refreshing itself—'

As if a compression of thunderclap had been unpacked, a low sound began from the center of the wheel. The Ozmists swayed their rotating mass laterally across the marshy ground, passing over and (it seemed) through the Lion and Cubbins until the Animals were in the center of the swarm and the noise became deafening.

Bear, if you don't believe in keeping your bargain, we thrust you out before we make you one of us!

'I don't believe in ghosts,' said the Lion, trying to stand before the small cub – but the Ozmists were everywhere, and there was not enough Lion to encircle Cubbins. The sound of the Ozmists raked through them both, but Cubbins held his paws over his ears. Then the Ozmists disappeared into the rising vapors from a visible marshland. In their place rose curtains of brainless flies and midges, deterred for a moment by the honey but ready, Brrr guessed, to turn and attack them.

Cubbins was already scrabbling up the slope, which now seemed to permit it. With flummoxing of limb and tail, the Lion followed. Soon he'd overtaken the young Bear.

This is what it feels like to be a piece of shit, thought Brrr; being pummeled on all sides by the world, forced forward, outward, into naked stink and light. But he and Cubbins danced as they ran, a sense of relief and escape energizing them. They avoided the steam of salt geysers that were sprouting up through invisible fissures, but they couldn't avoid the hot rain that pelted down.

His eyes closed against the sting, Brrr smacked into boulders and tree trunks and clawed his way through brambly growth. By the time they emerged from Cloud Swamp, day was dawning in the teeth of an ordinary rainstorm.

'What did we get from that exercise?' he asked Cubbins, once he felt able to speak without his voice breaking.

'Wet,' said Cubbins.

'Well, yes. But from the Ozmists?'

Cubbins looked at Brrr. 'I don't believe in Ozmists,' he said. 'Bears don't, you know.'

The Lion snarled, as if to say: No time for your funning, Cubbins! The Bear's eyes looked back at him, flat, less glossy than before. Perhaps it was the overcast sky.

'They said Ozma is still alive somewhere,' ventured the Lion.

'People can say all sorts of things,' said Cubbins. 'Where did you get those books?'

'From . . .' But he couldn't finish. Didn't Cubbins remember?

Cubbins was pawing them and looking at the spines. '*Ozma Incognita.* That sounds interesting. What are you doing with these books?'

'I don't know,' said the Lion after a while. 'I don't have much use for them.'

'I'll take them off you. I like the idea of books,' said Cubbins. 'Here's another one with color plates – look! *Lurline and Preenella: A Fairy Tale of the Poor.* How stupendous! We don't see books around the Great Gillikin Forest often, you know.'

'You don't say.' He tried to keep a wobble out of his voice.

'If books show up anywhere in the woods, they're usually not far from a trap of some sort. Bait, you know. Humans plant books in the woods, hoping to attract the urban talking Animals who have gone to ground here, escaping the Wizard's laws against them. I suppose you're aware of this?'

'I suppose.' He sighed.

'And hunters, perhaps with guns, waiting nearby.' Cubbins was turning the pages. 'If you picked these up from the woods, you're lucky you didn't get snared in some beastly iron-jaw thing with rusty teeth.'

'Guess luck is my middle name.' But it was too dreadful. 'Will you know how to get back to your clan?'

'My clan?' said Cubbins.

'Don't forget *that* part! Ursaless and the others. Bruner O'Bruin, Caraway Coyle. You know.'

At the sound of the Queen's name, Cubbins grinned. 'Oh yes! Of course! My mind had wandered for a moment. Well, I'll take these books off you if you like, and be getting back to my kind. We admire books, you know, we Bears. We read them over and over.'

'Good.'

'We never get tired of them,' said Cubbins in a

voice gone soft, as if the fact of his dimness was trying to dawn on him. 'Because we forget them as soon as we finish them. We can start reading them over right away.'

'If you don't mind,' said Brrr gently, 'I will take the medal, though. I need to bring it to someone.'

'Suit yourself,' said Cubbins. 'In fact, I'll loop it around your neck on this leather belt. I can carry the books in my arm. There, how's that?' His small brown arms reached up. In the effort to put the strap over Brrr's head, he gave the Lion a bear hug around the cranium. The coarse Bear fur was slicked into tapering points and it rubbed agreeably against the Lion's mane. 'What is the medal for, anyway?'

The Lion couldn't answer, *Courage*. He couldn't speak for a while; he just turned and walked away. He glanced back only once. Cubbins was staring at a page of the book, and shaking his head, and wiping his eye with the back of his paw. Growing up, growing dead.

As he padded south, Brrr considered the all-but-fatal interview with the Ozmists. Maybe Bears who had genuine news they could barter were released unharmed. Maybe these were the Bears competent enough to take their chances in human society. If so, Cubbins had sacrificed his own ambitions in order to help Brrr summon the phantoms.

Still – on further reflection – had any of it actually happened? And why should Brrr presume that Ozmists, being ghosts, were telling the truth about anything? If they could be legalistic and harsh to a Bear cub as guileless as Cubbins, perhaps they could also lie — about whether or not Ozma was still alive, even about whether or not Brrr's pride was among their particulated number.

The alluring stars in an apparently endless sky had, after all, been a disguise for the cloud of spirits. Ghosts perhaps could lie in death as well as creatures could lie in life.

Under a green bay tree he stretched out, thinking: If even the ghost of the past can harbor a motivation to dissemble, where can any ignorant Lion sensibly place his trust?

Perhaps nowhere. Perhaps lying down and playing dead, as Cubbins should have done with the Ozmists, was the only legitimate response to the villainy of life, the aggrandizement of very matter.

In any event, the Ozmists hadn't spoken in the voice of Jemmsy, a new arrival in their midst. Neither to hector Brrr for his mistakes nor to hurry him toward his goals. So the Lion would continue to Tenniken to deliver to Jemmsy's father this precious medal, and to deserve his own. On his own, unpartnered, but by the ghost of a chance, maybe, wiser than a day ago.

5

Some weeks later, when the Lion emerged for the first time from the Great Gillikin Forest into the world of human affairs, he paused to wash his mouth out with well water and straighten his mane as best he could. It wasn't vanity so much as nerves. He'd never seen an entire hive of humans before.

The first people he saw gave him a bit of a berth, to be sure, but at least they didn't run shrieking behind slammed doors. They kept their little toy noses in the air. Their little toy ankles, tucked in those little booties, kicked ahead in the best, most dismissive manner. He couldn't fault the town citizens for self-possession.

He finally managed to startle an old woman who was nearsighted enough not to see him coming. He'd been practicing his inaugural remark for weeks and was pleased with his delivery.

'Beg pardon, madame. I'm enquiring after the garrison of soldiers I'm told is stationed at Tenniken,' he said.

The woman's crabapple chin bobbed up and she fished for a pince-nez in her reticule. 'Goodness, a Lion,' she observed, when she could. 'Why ever would you imagine you could find soldiers stationed at Tenniken *here*, of all unlikely places?'

By which he learned he had emerged too far to the east. Not in Tenniken at all, but on the high street of the Gillikinese settlement called Traum.

'You charming idiot, get out of my way,' she concluded. 'I've a daughter-in-law to annoy, and I must be to it. If you can't tell the difference between a military garrison and a market town, you've got a screw loose, I fear.'

How was he to know? He blushed, though he was not sure if a blush would show in a Lion of his naturally high coloring.

Still, a handsome place, this Traum. The town was prosperous, old enough to boast some architectural character and even charm. Half-timbered almshouses and taverns. Stone guild halls clawed over with ivy and roofed with mossy slates laid in patterns of chevron. Escutcheons of painted wood advertising the trades.

'Do you know the way to Tenniken?' said the old woman. 'Someone will tell you, but not I. I must get going. It doesn't do to be stopped in the street today, not with those ruffians and ragamunchkins about.' She snapped her spectacles into their case and pushed away.

Brrr continued on, curious, feeling braver every moment. Traum must have seen Lions before, to judge by the way its denizens affected a worldly disregard to the visitor in their midst. At least this was how he read it at first. In truth, like the first old woman he interviewed, the citizens of Traum had other matters on their minds.

The Lion paced the merchant arcade, stopping to sniff at a rope of garlic hanging from a peg, or to watch through an archway as a glassblower plied her gassy art. He would ask for directions to Tenniken in a moment, as soon as he could catch someone's eye again. But Traumanians were deeply skilled at averting their gazes.

In any case, the need to ask for directions seemed less urgent the more he saw of Traum. This was an old establishment, and he was a very young Lion, after all. So much to command his attention! A steam engine on a rail track. Gutters that ran with clear water. A unionist minister in dark leggings and an accusatory beard, pointing its hairy finger at every passing sinner.

'Are there any soldiers in town?' he asked a schoolchild, the only human who didn't intimidate him. The girl pouted and began to suck her thumb in reply.

'No soldiers when you need them,' remarked the child's chaperone, a teenage sitter. 'The town is crawling with angry trolls, so are we supplied with a military presence this week? No. Of course not. Naturally.' She dragged her charge off into a side street. 'Come, Gritzolga. The nasty trolls will eat you if you don't behave. They like bad children like you.'

The Lion asked a question or two of some jittery

shopkeepers who were folding up their shutters early. They didn't stop to reply. At one emporium, however, where a shipment of porcelain was being unloaded from a wagon, the doors remained open so the workers could haul in the wares. A few of the more chattery of the townspeople were converging there. The Lion stooped to enter.

'Traum: the crossroads to nowhere,' said a young clerk with a voice that broke in midvowel. 'Or everywhere: it's the same thing, en't it?'

'I don't know Traum from Tenniken, or a troll from a trolley car,' said Brrr, admiring his own cleverness.

The clerk rolled his eyes. 'Looking to buy a good map?' He pulled out a colored chart of the district.

Brrr had never seen a map before. He struggled to make sense of the scraped lines and shaded patches. A wispy gentleman, in looking for some snuff, leaned over the counter to see. 'I taught geographics and natural civics to unteachable boys for thirty years,' he said. 'Allow me to explain.'

The Lion learned that Traum had sprung up in a gentle valley between folds of forested hills. The valley allowed for a train line originating in distant Shiz, to the southwest, and running to Traum and beyond. To the northeast, the line was built on steep and inhospitable ground. Trellised and buttressed in precipitous style, the tracks climbed upslope until they reached the quays of the famous Glikkus Canals.

'Famous to some but not to all,' said Brrr.

The old fellow took a pinch of snuff. He was warming to his subject.

'The Glikkus channels are carved by some natural event of such mind-numbing antiquity that their origin can be explained only by myth. They serve as a merchant's route to the emerald mines in the western Scalps of the Glikkus. The mountain natives – called Glikkuns, though none can deny they are anything but trolls, really – take advantage of those natural waterways and our industrial rail line to bring their emeralds to market.'

'Yes, but which way is Tenniken from here?'

'Traum is the trading post for the whole emerald industry. Why do you want Tennikin?' asked the clerk. 'We have quite a line of emerald souvenirs, including a kind of fudge peppered with emerald dust.' The lone box of fudge wore a mantle of ordinary dust upon it, suggesting that the delicacy was more a novelty than a necessity.

'Is Tenniken *on* the rail line?' asked Brrr.

'Look, there's some stumpyfolk now,' said a burgher's wife, clutching her shawl about her, as if to preserve her respectability, even at this distance. 'Stars and stitches, but they give me the goosey shivers!'

Brrr regarded the Glikkuns through the open door of the establishment. They were stout and stubby. Like many creatures who spend a good part of their lives underground, they were bleached out.

'If we Gillikinese are pale, at least compared to the darker tribes of the Vinkus and the ruddy bloody Quadlings, Glikkuns are downright albinoid,' murmured the doddery gentleman, who apparently couldn't resist a spontaneous lecture. 'Am I right? Am I right about this?'

'They look like walking farmcheeses to me,' agreed the good-wife.

A Glikkun family group loitered outside, deciding whether or not to venture into the shop. A blond moss capped the scalps of them all, from the papoosed newborn to the elders. The eyes of trolls, what Brrr could make out through their perpetual squint, glinted like steel, the pale white irises appearing to rise in blue albumen. Both males and females sported hunches pronounced enough to need wrapping in dedicated hunch-coats, each secured by buttons and straps and elasticized hems.

They carried short, stout dirks in skarkskin sheaths.

'That's their chief,' whispered the schoolmaster. 'A woman named Sakkali Oafish.'

A troll woman in leather leggings and a grey scarf rubbed the belly of her pregnant companion and scowled around her.

'She's just got wind of the scam — I mean the scheme,' said the clerk. 'Oooh, dark night, alley, that carving knife: not for me.'

'When their babies want to suck, the Glikkuns offer the knife instead of the tit,' said the goodwife. 'Puts 'em off milk at once and stunts their growth, making 'em more Glikkuny than ever.'

'The Wizard of Oz wants emeralds, he gets emeralds,' said the schoolteacher. 'The Wizard of Oz makes the laws. In this case, the law of supply and demand. He demands it, they supply it. End of discussion.'

'The Wizard of Oz,' said the Lion, remembering the question of the Ozmists. He wished he had the nerve to say 'The WOO' in a superior, derogatory tone, but he didn't trust himself to be able to carry it off.

'The Wizard of Oz, yes. You just crawl out from under some rock? – the chief potentate, if self-proclaimed, of the whole beloved country, thank you very much. He has recently kicked off a schedule of public works in the Emerald City that requires a goblin-hoard of emeralds. A fourfold increase from the usual amount requisitioned. The Glikkuns have stepped up production in their mines and arranged for transport of the emeralds to Traum. Here they collect their fees in cash and grain and medicine.'

'And vermouth,' intoned the clerk, knowingly.

'You serve trolls in here, don't you,' said the goodwife.

'Their coin weighs the same as yours,' said the clerk. '*Madame.*'

'The economy of Traum relies on the trolls,' said the schoolmaster. 'And I don't know why they should be complaining. Business has never been so brisk for them. Ever. But, my dear boy,' he continued to the clerk, 'I do think you could make a legitimate argument for barring the door against an angry mob.'

If the seven-person family group outside constituted a mob, it wasn't entirely angry. The Glikkun baby chortled as it sucked on a sugar stick.

'What's their gripe?' asked Brrr, going toward the back of the shop, pretending to inspect the wares displayed there – a line of women's foundation garments. Camisoles, bustiers, smocks, and pantaloons.

'Close the door up, mercy on us,' hissed the goodwife to the clerk.

The schoolmaster rooted through his purse to pay for his snuff. 'Sakkali Oafish has just gotten wind of an . . . an irregularity, shall we say, in the arrangements. The Traum merchants are paying the Glikkuns the going rate for emeralds, fair and square and in conformance with trade agreements – but our merchants are transporting the crop of jewels by rail down to Shiz, and they have begun to mark up the wares fourfold. For the simple job of loading emeralds onto the trains and unloading them several hundred miles south, the merchants are getting fat on the labor and product of the Glikkun miners.'

'The Glikkuns get their due,' said the clerk, 'as I

hear it told. The guild of traders has never stiffed the trolls a penny farthing.'

'Contracts hold, but contracts can be unfair, too,' asserted the gentleman.

'We're in the wrong place at the wrong time,' said the goodwife. 'I'd have been a smarter woman to have gone visiting my sister in Tenniken like she asked me to instead of finding myself here on this day of all days.'

'Tenniken! The home of the soldiers,' said Brrr. 'Can you get there by train, do you know?'

'*I* can. Not certain trains are serving the likes of you.'

'I don't understand why we're seeing trouble today,' said the young clerk, whose pink-ham face was going pale and his voice cracking in higher registers than before.

'Aren't you paying attention?' snapped the schoolteacher. 'Sakkali Oafish has just learned about the trade inequities. The merchants taking twenty florins for every five the trolls get. She's spitting nails. She's declared she'll call a strike unless the agents of the Shiz merchants pay double the negotiated rate for the emeralds they take, starting with the current shipment. Today. Before the Glikkuns leave. But the agents for the Shiz merchants are balking, saying that they aren't authorized to enter into a new agreement, nor do they have the funds on hand to pay an unanticipated surcharge. Of course the Glikkuns are mad as hornets. And like all trolls, stubborn to boot. The whole town is waiting to see if they start to riot.'

'Our husbands are getting their guns,' said the goodwife. 'They'll take care of the matter. The Traum civic militia drills once a week.'

'Drills for ten minutes, drinks beer the rest of the evening,' replied the schoolteacher.

'My Aimil is in the service and he can shoot to kill at fifty yards even when he's dead drunk.' She sniffed in pride. 'Good lad.'

'I hope your Aimil is stopping for an ale then, because there will be shooting here before the moon is up.'

'Mark my words. They'll show those Glikkuns the business end of a blunderbuss. Do some good, to boss the clammy little pasty-blobs about,' said the goodwife.

'Severity rarely helps in instances like this,' replied the gentleman.

'You setting yourself up as a court of justice all by yourself?' The goodwife raised her chins and rounded her lips as if tasting something unsavory. 'Why en't you going to live underground with the mole folk, if you endorse them so pitifully?'

'I'm not a court of justice – merely a commentator for our ignorant visitor,' said the schoolmaster mildly. In the spark of their little exchange, the Lion had retreated farther into the shadows.

'That petticoat will never fit you. It's a petite,' said the clerk, either nastily or trying to make a joke and diffuse the situation. 'A *lady* is petite.'

'I'm shopping for a friend,' replied Brrr, as frostily as he could, dropping the garment. He had thought it was some sort of headdress, with its lacy eyelets and scalloped hem.

'I suppose you're friends with *them*?' asked the burgher's wife. 'You arrived with them, and all?'

'I never did.' Brrr tried harder for a tone of offense. 'I have nothing to do with them.'

'If you're not their weird bodyguard, then why en't you chasing them away for us? They'd run from you soon enough.'

'I have nothing against trolls,' said Brrr.

'That's a medal you got on your chest, en't it?' She glowered at him. 'A medal for what? Valor in the line of shopping?'

'I was hoping to find the soldiers' garrison at Tenniken. This is all a mistake.'

'What the soldiers wouldn't do with the likes of you!' She pursed her raspy lips at him and lowered her chin to look out under her brow, like a lizard from under a rock.

He stopped trying to explain. He only wished he could fade into the shadows in the shop the way, so conveniently, he'd been able to camouflage himself in the shadows of woodlands.

Before the Glikkuns outside could move on, the lane was filled with the stutter of drumming. The Traum Defense Brigade, no doubt. The goodwife looked hopeful at the thought of an encounter.

Not yet ready for a face-off — not with the baby troll drooling into its bibbing — Sakkali Oafish turned her group toward the doors of the shop.

'My virtue,' said the goodwife to the clerk. 'Shut the door, can't you?'

The clerk strode forward and said, streetward, 'We're closed to all but residents with town accounts.'

Sakkali put her foot in the door jamb. Her glance betrayed little fear. When she spoke, her voice was low and full of rasp. 'Is that so? Then the Lion lives in Traum?' One hand settled on the infant's scalp, the other one on the hilt of her dirk.

A silence ensued. 'She has a point,' said the clerk to Brrr. 'You'll have to leave.'

'This is unseemly,' said the schoolmaster. 'There's no need—'

'I insist, or I'll summon the merchant defense,' said the clerk. 'I can't tell the boss that his shipment of deluxe Dixxi House dinner services got shattered in a brawl.'

'I don't have the stomach for shopping today,' said Brrr at last.

The door closed behind Brrr. He could hear the angry click of the bolt against the strike. Apparently that honorable schoolmaster had elected solidarity with his fellow citizens.

'You choose to stand with the aggrieved,' said Sakkali Oafish admiringly.

'I choose no such thing,' snapped Brrr. He looked up the way, and down. He wanted to get out of Traum before things became more unpleasant. 'I don't suppose you know the way to Tennikin? Where the soldiers are?'

'The Wizard's soldiers?' Sakkali Oafish spat at their name.

'I knew a soldier who was—' But Brrr couldn't think of how to describe Jemmsy.

She was quick, that Sakkali. 'You knew a soldier who betrayed his orders by befriending you?'

The local militia turned into the high street. A motley mob of overweight merchants, nervous teenagers, that same miserable minister with his beard. Some pitchforks, a rolling pin, several guns looking all too dangerous.

'I have a job to do,' said Brrr. 'I'm sorry for your trouble with soldiers, but I can't stick around and sort it out. I have an errand of mercy for the father of a dead friend.'

'You're not going to leave us to face this human mob unarmed,' said Sakkali. 'What kind of Lion are you, anyway?'

At which question the Lion discovered the rhetoric of silence.

In any case, the trolls were hardly unarmed, he thought to say (but didn't); fellow Glikkuns were showing up from an alley here, a chapel gate there, supplied with pickaxes.

The local militia raised their muskets. The Glikkuns stooped to loosen cobbles from the roadbed. From the stove of some upper-story kitchen, out of sight, a teakettle hissed like a small storm of rain beyond the hills.

Once again, thought Brrr, my chief talent: wrong place, wrong time, wrong key. 'Not my fight,' he tried to explain. 'I have a promise to keep . . .'

Backing up, twitching his tail in consternation, he heard a holy sound of bells splashing from the steeple. Like the Lurlinists' music, only pretty. Brrr had not heard such melodic resonance before, and it sounded notionally of resolution, somehow.

Yet all around the town square of Traum, the hands of worried citizens were clanging gates closed, making an iron music. Wooden garden shutters slapped into place and were barred from the inside: You could hear the oaken music of the slats dropping. The free passage of the high street and the market square, within moments, became a pen. A closed run for an enemy trapped within.

This is how a market town defends itself when it lacks an army garrison, thought Brrr, and only then did he realize he had been paddocked, too.

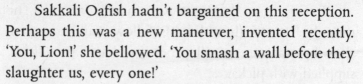

Sakkali Oafish hadn't bargained on this reception. Perhaps this was a new maneuver, invented recently. 'You, Lion!' she bellowed. 'You smash a wall before they slaughter us, every one!'

'But – but – I have business in Tenniken—' He wasn't refusing, he wasn't – so what was he doing?

A barred iron gate right before him in his face, and all the pitching against it, to no avail – for it was strong, and he only a cub—

Before he could shake the thought free, return to language, a shot rang out, or two. Brrr was lately familiar with gunshots in the woods, but here in the open, in a town built of stone and slate, the echo was terrible. Stupefied, he recoiled sideways, involuntarily, and he pitched into the stone arch of a covered well. Dizzied, dazed, he stood long enough to see Sakkali take a stone at her skull. She was brought solidly to the ground, like a sack of rice tilting over onto its side. He staggered and fell, and was sick on the cobbles.

'Here, here,' cried the other Glikkuns, a small citizenry of them in their gravelly tones. Sakkali – dead or alive? – no one could tell. Two small fierce trolls lifted her body with hoarse grunts like chortles. 'Lion, to gate, to wall, for one, for all.' Two or three of them leaped upon him. They hauled Sakkali's barrel-like form with them.

'No,' he murmured, hoping only they could hear, 'play dead, play dead! It's your only chance.'

He shook them off and rolled onto his back, showing them how, letting his forepaws fall limp upon his chest like the unbuckled ends of a belt.

The trolls battered down beside him, as if he were a rampart, but only for an instant. Rifles were being aimed from all directions, and a supine Lion was a useless Lion to the Glikkuns. They abandoned him, making a rush for the lowest and weakest-looking of the gates, where a single sharpshooter was able to pick out one, two, three of them, and then the others took Brrr's advice too late, and played dead, and were taken into captivity.

Initially – that day, the next – the Traumanians went through a show of celebrating Brrr. His refusal to evacuate the Glikkun trolls was called brave; his collapse in the high street was deemed an act of public sacrifice. A masterstroke of mob-control strategy. Pacifism in the course of strike busting. Brilliant.

For a while Brrr believed the public relations campaign, until it dawned on him that the constant advertisement of his refusal to defend the Glikkuns diverted attention from those who had actually carried out the assault. Then he began to suspect that within any cry of applause may lie coiled a hidden sneer. Perhaps a well-deserved sneer.

He made plans to leave Traum as soon as it felt safe to do so, which was some weeks. He traveled by train toward Tenniken, afraid all the while that vengeful Glikkuns might dynamite the tracks. Run the carriages off the rails. Reclaim any cargo of emeralds in transport. Then hunt through the passenger cars to locate the Lion's cowardly carcass and do to it what he had allowed to be done to the members of their tribe.

He found that his reputation preceded him. 'Just my luck. The Champion Lion himself,' said a portly journalist in the dining car, scribbling notes on a stenographer's pad. He looked fondly over the tops of his reading spectacles and lifted a glass of sherry to the Lion, who had been assigned the second dinner sitting and directed to the journalist's table. 'Have I heard that the grateful citizens of Traum pressed upon you a small purse, in gratitude for services rendered?'

'Yes,' said Brrr, with some reservation.

'Whatever funds they came up with would have been less than what they'd have had to pay the Glikkuns.'

'Indeed,' said Brrr. Some of which he had spent in the dry goods store, buying a vest in which to keep his cash. And a cane, to give him gravitas. 'It was just a token honorarium.'

'As befits a token hero. And look at that simply glorious medal for courage, to celebrate your achievement.'

The twinkle in his eye was deadly. Brrr feigned an attack of indigestion and excused himself. Alone in a stinking loo, he found that his alibi of intestinal ailment had come true.

When he emerged, he didn't return to the dining car but wandered in the opposite direction. Upon reaching the last car on the train, he opened the rear door and stood on the juddering platform. Out of sight of anyone else, he allowed himself an unseemly spasm of shame. Then, when the train rattled onto a trestle bridge, crossing some dark unpleasant lake, Brrr let the medal on its leather belt fly out to hit the water with a final gleam.

Now it is over before it has really begun, he thought, my quest for approval. Only for Brrr it was never over, not really. An accidental half hour in the wrong village. His curse.

The train stopped at Tenniken later that evening, but Brrr didn't alight.

An onward pitch to his life now, a few arts and skills – rolling over, playing dead, making mistakes, making conversation – but no destination.

Trusting in the amnesia of Bears, in the incapacity of Ozmists to identify their constituent citizens, Brrr hoped that his mortification at Traum would be as quickly forgotten. He was not so lucky. He hadn't yet had enough experience with humans to know that the thing they hold dearest to their hearts, the last thing they relinquish when all else is fading, is the consoling belief in the inferiority of others.

6

The air in the mauntery parlor seemed to have settled, as if nothing were alive but the past. 'Not too much to say about the first years,' he concluded. The room had a funny buzz to it, though. Old granny *vigor mortis* was listening so cannily that the Lion began to wonder if he had shared more about his origins than the sentence or two he remembered speaking aloud. She's a tricky one, he thought.

'Talented, rather than tricky,' she cut in. 'But how did you come upon the name Brrr?'

'If you can read my mind,' he said, ' – which frankly I find an abuse of my fucking privacy – then you know already.'

'I don't read minds, and you haven't got enough of a mind to browse through anyway.'

'What's being an oracle, then, if you can't read minds?'

She replied, 'I can only guess at what you are thinking, and truth to tell, I'm not quite up to room temperature yet. Playing dead myself has caused me to lose a little of my usual concentration.'

'I don't know who named me Brrr,' he told her, 'and it doesn't matter. Now you tell me of *your* own origins. For the record. For when I file my findings.'

'None of us knows our own origins. We only know what we're told by our parents and the mythography of our national anthems.'

'Don't hold out on me. Look, I gave you what you wanted. I offend you by being honest? Get used to it. Story of my life, which you can stay the hell out of.'

'I'm the last one to be offended at human behavior,' she replied calmly, 'so a Lion's petty moral conundrums mean even less to me. Besides, I'm no blushing spiritual nosegay myself.'

'Well, then, get on with it, will you? Why are you implicated in Madame Morrible's journal? I haven't got all day. I can't read your mind, I can't even read your expression, since your eyes are so screwed up. The Court doesn't want minor philosophies. It wants the facts.'

'Why should I tell you anything?'

He mused. 'A barter system. Like the Ozmists proposed, once upon a time. You want something of me, too. Don't you? You must, since you've taken pains not to die till I got here. Well, you scratch my back, I'll scratch yours.' He grunted. 'You look like you got a mighty arthritic hunch on your back.'

'Don't flatter yourself. Whatever could you do for me?'

'You tell me.'

She sat silent. He'd got her thinking. He was sure

she was bargaining, too, though he didn't yet know over what. He'd promise her the world to get this job over with. She wouldn't live long enough to collect.

He slapped his notebook against his forehead as if to attract the attention of a simpleton. 'I'm *ready when you are.*' He flipped the book open again. 'It's your relationship with the Thropp family that the Court is tracking down,' he said. If she called him on his dissembling – his peddling not a lie so much as a disguised truth – he'd have proof that she was the real deal, not a charlatan.

He was gratified at her response. In her chair she reared back a little, her dry, flaking nostrils flaring like those of a panicky horse.

'For what use does the Court want my deposition?' she demanded to know.

'When did you come to be involved with the Thropps of Colwen Grounds, Munchkinland?'

'Has she come back?' said Yackle. 'Is she here?'

'Who?' said Brrr. He stifled a wince of triumph. It had worked. Even a seer could be startled, it seemed. 'Which one do you mean?'

'Elphaba, of course,' said Yackle.

And, dullard that he was, Brrr could sense it: The mention of Elphaba, of her sorry history, had hurried a flush into Yackle's old veins. Whoever she was herself, old Mother Yackle, death-defying crone, she was still human enough to be corrupted by feeling. After all these years, an ounce of regret or something else very urgent still tainted the bucketful of blood that seeped beneath her bunched, crepelike skin.

He saw this. He had her. He wasn't as stupid as he thought.

'Has Candle been found?' she said. 'And Liir?'

She had mentioned Liir before. Well, some folks just knew the wrong things to say. Liir was another thorn in the Lion's own sore past, and he didn't want to think about how casually he'd sauntered away from the homeless boy without a second thought.

Brrr flipped open his notebook again. 'It's your turn to talk, Yackle. And I got evidence from other sources to check your statement against, so don't try slinging some phony hash at me, fair enough?'

She chewed on the nail of her little finger. It looked as if she were dining on the fin of a lake narwhal. Beyond the room, a gust of autumn wind rattled the drying ivy clinging to the shutters. 'I hear a noise of marching,' she said at last.

'The Emerald City divisions are tramping their muddy boots into Munchkinland,' he said. 'Didn't you know that? On the grounds of retaliation. Self-defense by way of colonization, probably.'

'I never attended to human politics.'

'That's sound practice. Stay far away. Very far away. Listen, you want the background? So far as I can pick up, our glorious Emperor asserts that *he* is the de facto Eminent Thropp, the satrap of Munchkinland. Because his great-grandfather was the Eminent Thropp those three, four generations back. Shell, the Apostle Emperor, claims a right to the manor house of Colwen Grounds, to the demesne, and even more so, to the governorship of the province. So he's about to re-annex the Free State of Munchkinland.'

'But the Eminent Thropp had daughters, and the rights of inheritance pass down through the female line. Even I remember that much.'

'Ah, but Shell is the last of the line, and both his sisters, Elphaba and Nessarose, died without issue.'

'But did they?' cried Yackle.

'What do you know about it,' he asked, 'and furthermore, to the point, why do you care?'

His voice was brutal, even in his own ear. He must be anxious, more than he wants to show, she thought. But she had no room for him right now, when her own tinderbox of memories was flaring to the strike. Her eyes, which had not yielded up moisture for a decade, went gummy, and her heart went hard and soft by turns.

'Tell me when you first became aware of them all,' he said. 'Why not? It might help. You may be an oracle, but no oracle can know everything.'

At that remark of his, her sloppy tears did fall. When they dropped on her immaculate winding sheet, small tear-shaped holes burned through, showing shadowy flesh, rucked like flaky pastry.

'I will hold you to your promise,' she said, when she could speak, 'or I will kill you.' Standing, she gripped the back of the chair as if she were at a Testimonial Pulpit. What was left of her irises rolled up into her head, slowly. It turned his stomach so far around he felt he could taste his own shit.

She didn't begin to speak until there was nothing left but the whites of her eyes, like bloodshot stones embedded in her skull.

When did I first become aware of them? Of the witches of Oz?

No Good Old Days to Speak Of

1

'You can start with your own origins.' He kept his voice soft, almost a purr. 'Name, place, and date of birth. The usual jolly rigamarole.'

'Well, I don't know my origins.' Her voice sounded faraway. Maybe she was speaking slowly because she was manufacturing lies, or maybe it took her a while to reclaim a notion of the past. 'Lost in the mists of time, I'm afraid.'

'You mock me, you mock the Court.'

'I mock nothing and no one. First thing I can remember, I woke from a stupor and I sat up. Like a newborn I was naked, stupid, and without control of my bowels and bladder. But I was resplendently wrinkled and I wasn't blind the way babies are. My breasts pointed at my toes. I wriggled my toes and I tried to wriggle my breasts. I smelled of ginger and pearlfruit jelly and I was devilishly hungry, so I got up and began to explore. I found a mirror on a wall and noticed that I had eyes, and I saw the flaccid skin barely managing to hold these eyes in their sockets. I had moles on my earlobes, and my hair was lank and grey, and my back hurt. I could talk, so I knew how to curse. I was already well on my way to bodily corruption, you see.'

'But where were you – in a room, on a bed? What district?'

'Some room, some bed. Some hostel for indigents, I suppose. I didn't linger to find out. I stole a robe and some slippers from a cubby in the washroom and I tottered out the door. I found myself in the city of Shiz in northern Oz. I appeared older than most of the sentient life that waddled or cycled or ambled by.'

'Did you remember your name?'

'Those who don't have a name can't remember it, can they? Sir *Brrr*? If I'd had a name before, I didn't know it anymore. So I had to name myself. In a market-place stall I found a portfolio of rotogravure prints and I examined the pages. The collection advertised itself as artistic interpretations of characters of folklore. I saw gnarled old Kumbricia, I saw the fairy queen, Lurline, and her sidekick, Preenella. I saw the dragon who dreams the world and the tiny pixie-mites who afflict the undeserving with plague. Then I came across a page showing an elderly dame with a walking stick and a jackal on a leash. She carried the moon in a basket on her back. It was pretty. The script said "Yackle Snarling," and though I didn't know the story she features in, nor any story, I liked her name. Yackle. I didn't know if "Snarling" was her second name or her occupation, so I left it off.'

'Didn't you see a doctor? Anyone propose it might

have been a stroke?' He wasn't being tender, just comprehensive. 'Probably your mental gears just slipped. It happens to the feeble.'

'Those who don't know the concept of medicine don't think to consult physicians.'

He tried a more soothing voice. It came out snide. 'A little therapy, or a stiff drink, and maybe the memory of your past life would return.'

'Maybe,' she replied. 'But I don't believe in past lives.'

'Any twinges about your lost childhood? Snatches of déjà vu, that sort of thing? Did you ever pick up something silly and common like, oh, bootlaces or, or . . . butter rolls . . . and stare at them in case they jogged your mind about your past?'

'I didn't imagine the past, yet, so I didn't miss it. It was as if I was freshly minted as a senior. Some are born blind, some cranky, some superior. Some' – and she waggled a finger at him – 'are born green. I was born old. Old I came into the world, and older still will I leave it, if I can ever figure out how.'

He wrote in his notebook: *Claims to have amnesia about her youth. Dotty? Honest? Clever? Canny strategy to avoid her legal liabilities?*

'We're here to do some discovery about your relationship with the Thropps,' he said. 'Can we continue?'

'I thought you said it was Madame Morrible's connections you were tracking down.'

'Madame Morrible. The Thropp sisters. There is some overlap, as you bloody well know. Now just start where you can, and I'll cut you off if you ramble.'

'I don't think I like you,' she said, 'but since this is nearly a posthumous tea party to which I've been invited, maybe it doesn't matter if I like you or not.'

'You came from your coffin to talk to me,' he reminded her. 'You must have had *something* to tell me now, right? Got some beef you're eager to turn into hash. I'm your willing audience. I'm all ears, I am.'

She cocked her head sharply. She wasn't befuddled in the slightest. She just didn't like him. It showed loud and clear. Not that he cared. He was only doing his job. 'Get on with it, before those army boots start tramping back this way,' he said.

Was she ready to talk? She thought it over. Would she inadvertently give something away before she had finished vetting the Lion for a possible ally? So far he didn't look promising. Sitting before her, waxing his mane with spittle, twirling it into points. She could hear the motion, her ears were that keen. He was behaving like a pantomime villain training his mustachios.

Maybe he was only a ruse, a warm-up. Maybe she'd emerged from her clammy bier for the one who would follow this oily character.

Oracle though she was, she couldn't see in front of her own nose.

2

Brrr tapped his pencil. Patience wasn't his strong suit. Still, he was trying to listen to her with the severity of attention she had paid to him.

With a plain demeanor, I could sidle by unnoticed. I had no charm to speak of. The older woman talking to herself in some gutter isn't an uncommon sight, and passersby rarely bother to interrupt her.

I found it useful staying a bit unwashed. No one wants to look too closely at someone wrapped in strong body odors. That made it easier to sidle along in the background, to watch slit-eyed and sideways at the goings-on of a crowd. To size up a mark. To pick up what I could about this mystery of my existence.

So I stumped about Shiz. I kept my eyes down and my ears open and, for the time being, my big mouth shut.

These were the days before the Wizard arrived – yes, get your pen, I'm going to be as specific as I can, though the patterns of politics always eluded me. But now I know enough to realize that I emerged from my first sleep into the halcyon last days of the line of

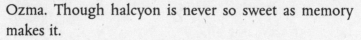

Ozma. Though halcyon is never so sweet as memory makes it.

Vain Pastorius was squatting upon the throne as the Ozma Regent. He ruled in the Emerald City in the stead of his infant daughter, the Ozma Tippetarius. He was a piece of work. Dim, bullnose-chinned Pastorius. What is this in human time? Fifty, fifty-five years ago? Being born without any childhood to speak of — my 'olden days' have a different meaning than yours! — I never could master time. It seems a long while ago, anyway. Pastorius, that old fool. Both sybaritic and syphilitic. Cocooned in silk, drunk on compliments warbled by his ass-licking courtiers. Those were days of expensive balls in the court proper, and of bawdy carnivals of patriotic sentiment outside the palace walls. To distract the urban poor from the deprivations of the Great Drought, about which no one could do a thing.

'Those days,' she asserted. 'You wouldn't remember. You weren't whelped yet.'

'Tell me. I'm all ears.' He listened like a doe just noticing a leopard on a limb.

'You want the three historic segments of my earthly life? I've lived through a good deal of these modern times, if you can call it living. I'd arrived, preaged and preshrunk, a crone at birth, just at the end of the Ozma regency, before Pastorius was deposed by the Wizard and the infant Ozma was secreted away, probably murdered.

'Then came the Wizardic reign. Nearly four decades of the Great Head, as power consolidated in the Emerald City. Animals were disenfranchised of their rights; and the green shrike of a witch, Elphaba Thropp, flew the skies in agitation. Her sister, Nessarose, presided over the breakaway state of Munchkinland.

'Following the Wizard's abdication of the Throne, the brief and blameless twin interregnums – first of Lady Glinda, that bottle blonde, and then of the so-called Scarecrow, who came to power and left it again faster than a pile of autumn kindling responds to a winter torch.

'The torch of piety, that is, as wielded by Shell, the Apostle Emperor. Younger brother of Elphaba and Nessarose. He swore he was divinely positioned by the Unnamed God. For all I know he is his, he is his—' She nearly gagged at the thought, and rotated her hand in the air, a forward roll. 'He is history.'

Brrr didn't want to lead her on, to give her anything to work with, if she was indeed an oracle. Let her show facility with those unholy talents. Yet he was curious, too; he couldn't help saying, 'The Emperor Shell is still on the Throne in the Emerald City. No opposition to his royal prerogatives allowed.'

'But of course. Who can gainsay a prince personally chosen by the Unnamed God?'

He nodded: go on.

I heard about current events, naturally. Shiz is a university town from way back, and undergraduates reading history do blather so.

I minded my own business on the pavement – well, begging a little, picking pockets, too, for I saw that was how common folk fed themselves. I figured out that inventing little prophecies – doling out appealing lies – brought in some cash.

I bought my bread and beer from the small change I could earn by pretending to be a seer. I was persuasive enough, a competent liar, and I looked the part, so I developed a clientele. I wore a shawl, like Yackle Snarling. I had fun worrying my hair into a nest of scowls. When I had put a small purse aside I took a room above a tonsorial parlor and I invested in a line of herbal comforts. Limited-liability curses, bogus love charms and the like. I traded only in minor hexes, for I wanted no trouble with the constabulary.

It was fun for a while. I examined tea leaves at the bottom of a cup. I studied the crow's feet on either side of a spinster's face and I made up some nonsense about strangers and romance. I never could figure out why romance is so desirable, having felt nothing of the sort myself. Maybe because I was desiccated in that department. With no eggs to hatch, I had no reason to kiss and canoodle, and no appetite for it, either. But those with an experience of canoodling seem reluctant to leave the possibility behind, even when their romantic prospects are limited due to the insults of aging. Onset of severe personal ugliness.

Then I got in a spot of trouble. A local brouhaha, nothing you need worry yourself about. I made a bad investment prediction and a couple of Shiz financiers who were trembling on the edge of ruin fell into it. When their goons came after me with a vengeance, I developed a sudden yen to see the other sights of Oz. So I considered lighting out for the Emerald City, which, while still being built, was already the biggest conurbation in Oz. Finding me there would take some doing, and I hoped they wouldn't manage it. Still, you have found me. A goon on whose payroll?

Brrr thought: Is she just making this up because of my own admission of being morally obtuse as a cub? Trying to soften me up by saying, see, we're equally untethered to conventions of right and wrong?

A court reporter's first job, though, is to report what is said. Let someone else authenticate it. Someone with more to lose. Hah – as if there were such a creature.

'Very interesting,' he said, and made some notes. Then he regarded them dubiously. He had invented a shorthand all his own to compensate for his inability to hold a pen in the human style — wrong muscle groups for that. But sometimes he couldn't read his own scrawl. He hoped he wouldn't come a cropper when it was time to dictate to his transcriber back in the Emerald City court stenographers' bullpen. She'd slap his face, and her colleagues would snort and titter. The flatheads.

'You haven't answered my question,' he said. 'I had asked about when and how you first came in touch with the Thropp family. When you became aware of them. And I'm trying to find out why your name was scribbled in the notes left in the archives of a clandestine Wizardic operative named Madame Morrible.'

'One has to start somewhere,' she replied. 'Because I developed a reputation for clairvoyance in the demimonde of Oz, I attracted the attention of a family retainer of the Thropp contingent. It all goes back to that.'

'Still, can we get to the point? I haven't been tracking the progress of the military units around here, but if the skirmishes around us heat up, the Emerald City Messiars or the Munchkinlanders may need to fall back to regroup. I wouldn't be surprised if this House is commandeered for a garrison by nightfall. I plan to be finished up and on my way before that happens. I have no interest in hobnobbing with soldiers. Not my type.'

'Don't bully me,' she snapped.

He straightened up. This was one of the nicest things that had been said to him since his release from custody. 'The Thropp family,' he insisted.

'You next,' she said. 'This is a bargain, remember? What happened when you debuted in property society? Civilization and its malcontents?'

The Lion's voice was testy. 'You are under order of the Emerald City Court of Magistrates to comply with my request for information. I don't have to answer your nosy questions. I'm done auditioning for you. I've said all I have to say.'

'You didn't tell me if you ever found the soldier's father. As you promised. Do you keep your promises? I'm merely asking.'

'You think you can shame me? You'll have to work harder than that.'

'Shame you? Hardly. I have no capacity for that,' she said. 'No capacity and no interest. I'm not involved in shame. Morals are learned in childhood, and I didn't have any such holiday called childhood. I'm merely curious.'

3

They sat in silence, both of them unwilling to yield, and after a while a maunt came in. She carried a plate piled with rye brisks smeared with a paste made of ground tadmuck and onions. Neither Yackle nor Brrr thanked her – neither was willing to be the first to show the weakness inherent in courtesy.

While the maunt fussed about with napkins and condiments, Brrr listened to the world.

The Mauntery of Saint Glinda in the Shale Shallows sat only a little distance from a forest of oakhair trees. Brrr knew that the higher branches of the mature oakhair tree developed long tendrils. In early autumn, the tendrils produced dense little acorns that swung until, finally, they were heavy enough to snap off and drop to the ground for seeding. Before they fell, though, the weight they exerted pulled their long threadlike stems tighter and tighter. When the wind arose from the south, if it ran close enough to the earth, it could produce a sound as of thrummed harp strings. A kind of foresty moan. Lurlina, or whatever damn goddess was responsible for the development of flora in Oz, hadn't bothered to tune the oakhair's reproductive system. The sound was less like an orchestra agreeing on a common pitch and more like a bevy of banshees considering what creature to feast upon for their supper.

The sostenuto lingered. The transparent cat began to vibrate slightly, as if in sympathy, like the ringing of a wineglass struck with the blade of a knife. The noise an ornamental paperweight might make if it could purr.

The maunt left, closing the door soundlessly behind her, no doubt vexed that she'd been able to overhear nothing of the interview. The wind pulled longer, half-strangled moans out of the forest, until, to drown out the noise if nothing else, Brrr caved at last, and spoke first.

'I hate that sound.'

'What sound is that?' asked Yackle, pawing on the floor for a biscuit she had dropped.

'The oakhair chorus. Can't you hear it? I thought the blind developed keener hearing as compensation.'

'I can't hear it. I have other compensations,' she said. 'Like a sense of taste. I don't suppose that helpmeet supplied us with any gin? I found this little snack offensive.'

'Only water, I'm afraid. I could do with some ale.'

'You say,' said Yackle, 'that your emergence into Traum was your first experience outside of the Forest. Are you sure of that?'

'No,' he replied. 'It's even been suggested to me that I could have wandered out when I was too young to perceive it. So what? That's as good as if it hadn't happened, right?'

'Perhaps,' she answered. 'Or not.'

'You might well have had a childhood yourself,' he said. 'Suppose you lived eighty years of some life choked with drama and feeling, and then you had a stroke or some other illness. When you came around, in that basement in Shiz, you were like a child again. The slate wiped clean. It's been known to happen to the elderly, Animals as well as people.'

'No, no,' she replied. 'Even those whose memories are corrupted by illness still have their pasts pocketed somewhere. But I have nothing to remember – no childhood to flee from. Don't you understand? I think that's why I can see the future – to the extent that I can. I suppose it's your principle of compensation. I can't remember the past, so I can remember the future.'

'All right, then. Prove it to me. Remember for me what is going to happen to me when I get back to the Emerald City with the information they want. Which you're about to give me.'

He was playing with fire, but what was there left to lose? Not dignity – he couldn't lose face with this harridan, who couldn't see his face to begin with – or could see it all too clearly. One or the other.

'You don't really want to know.'

'Or are you the scam artist that most oracles are?

Look, I gave you my shame, which you asked for. Tell me about the Thropps, then. The Thropps.' He tapped his pencil on the notepad. 'Or are you losing memory capacity so fast? The bucket leaking while we sit here? Your past draining away?'

'If I only had a past. I have no past.'

He grinned at her, wondering if she could intuit an expression. 'And if I don't get what I'm looking for, I have no future. So begging your pardon, can we hurry it up?'

4

He watched as she descended into what memories she had. The poor old macaroon. What possible good could come of her in the end? Of any of us, he amended.

Did her memories sting and surprise, as that sudden recollection of a cage had done, coming over him in Traum at the height of the troll massacre? And returning to him now. Always a cage, no?

I remember more than you think.

I can't always tell what it means, though. Every oracle is a scam artist, even those with talent.

My departure from Shiz. Under cover of night I packed up what little I owned and I spent my last coin on a midnight carriage to the Emerald City.

The journey – it means nothing to your investigation. But I do remember sucking on the edge of my lace shawl, to savor a taste of potato stew I had trailed the garment through. I was at wit's end. I was spooked by the challenge of the Emerald City, but I desired it, too. I hoped I could glean something from some other old crone at a bingo parlor or a chapel testimonial. Maybe I could hear that someone else had been born old. Then I might learn why I was so blighted.

I can feel you sneering in sympathy. You think effeminate beasts are the only ones who don't know their places?

So I came to the Emerald City to find my fortune, a toddler in the body of an octogenarian. I was astounded at the capital city's noise and breadth and stink and lights and attitude.

The Emerald City, so called, wasn't hugely emerald yet. It was more like a work in progress. Its name was a developer's advertisement looking for investors. The green jewels being dug up in the Glikkus mines adorned only the Palace. The urban squalor around the Throne house looked like a heap of pigsties.

Nonetheless, the Emerald City was beginning to practice the art of self-squawk.

Eventually, I saved up enough of my little pilferings and filchments to launch a new practice. I'd learned my lesson, though. No more financial advice. And I wouldn't take on a client unless she — it is nearly always a she who cares about the future, isn't it? — unless she promised not to call in the authorities if my reading provoked some catastrophe or other. In such an event, I declared, I'd consider myself released from our contract and I'd have to lower a chastening spell upon her.

I hadn't any such talent at spells, mind you — I was never a witch of any stripe — but my talent for lying proved useful. Clients always acceded to my conditions. They were so greedy to know things.

And as I peered at them, and as I struggled to see the ways that they could lie to me as well as to themselves, I found out new things about them. And about myself.

Without a childhood, you see, I had to lightfinger an education from someone.

Don't glare so. I can hear you glaring. Yes, the Thropps. I'm getting there.

In my third year at work in the EC — old Pastorius was still in power, parading his baby Ozma up and down the Ozma Embankment — I had a visit one cold autumn afternoon from a middle-aged domestic. Her name, she said, was Cattery Spunge, but she was known around the estate as Nanny. Well-upholstered in the rump and cushiony of bosom — professional attributes as a governess, I guess.

She liked saying *estate*, she adored saying *she was known*. She wore her affectations of gentility like so many foxfur castoffs of her lady employer.

It came out soon enough that this Cattery Spunge had served as overseer to several generations of a prominent family. The clan was headed by the Eminence of Munchkinland known at home as Peerless Thropp or, when in government circles, the Eminent Thropp.

Yes, we've reached the Thropp family at last.

Cattery Spunge brought with her a small pot of common ferns. She pushed it across the table toward me as I was clearing away lunch. Scraps of congealed tar-root and mash, I'm afraid. Proof of my humble station. 'I don't barter,' I said at the sight of the fern. 'I take cash only.'

'It's not a present,' said Cattery Spunge. 'Nor a bribe. Nanny wouldn't stoop to bribery.'

I left it where it was. Green things tended to wither in my company. Milk sours, children cry, cats develop hairballs. I'd have made one hell of a mother, believe me.

'Go on,' I said to her, refusing to touch the plant. She fussed at the clasp of a garish carpetbag, making sure I saw the handsome obsidian rings on her chafed hands.

Not too old for romance, I guessed, though beyond child-bearing years. Not twitchy enough to be in legal trouble. Too stout to be vexed by a wasting illness. 'An eminence named Peerless Thropp,' I said, to get a hold of anything. 'I'm not quite sure about eminences. I have never been to Munchkinland.'

'An eminence is the senior member of the local governing family. Munchkinland has maybe a dozen or so established families, don't you know, and the Thropps are the most prominent. The Eminent Thropp is superior in station to all other Munchkinlander gentry. I believe the term *Eminence* is specific to Munchkinland, though I can't be certain. I have never traveled much. Happy at home, you see.' She grimaced. 'Quite happy indeed.'

So we were getting somewhere. 'Peerless Thropp is still alive—?'

'Yes. A widower. So he's the Eminent Thropp. More or less the governor of Munchkinland. One daughter, Lady Partra, who married and bore two daughters of her own, Sophelia Thropp and Melena Thropp. I helped raise them both. The former went mad, in the most respectable way, and is housed offstage. The latter, Melena, I did with what I could. High spirits, that one.'

A decayed gentlewoman of loose morals, I inferred. 'Go on.'

'Melena could have had anyone, but she suffered chronically from spite. To vex her family was her chiefest aim. She refused an alliance with another eminence's son, as Lady Partra had proposed. Instead, Melena eloped with a minister of the unionist faith. The husband is far beneath her. Frexspar, his name. As if it matters. As if he matters. Stationed in the hardscrabble outback of Wend Hardings.'

Yes, I remember this all. As if it were yesterday. But you must consider that my mind wasn't stuffed with eighty years of my own memories. There was little to displace.

The Nanny enjoyed reciting genealogies. 'Melena is the Thropp Second Descending, you see – she will become Eminence when her grandfather and her mother are both dead. The honor passes through the female line, just as with the Ozmas. This is assuming, of course, that her mad Aunt Sophelia doesn't rap out a claim to the title and the family seat, et cetera. Few think she's capable,' observed Nanny, 'but in any instance she has no issue, so sooner or later the title will revert to Melena Thropp.'

All this palaver. 'Why have you come, Miss Spunge?'

'Call me Nanny.'

I resisted the invitation. She continued. 'My sweet Melena, the Thropp Second Descending, is still young and fertile. I want some salve, some charm, some hedge to ensure that any second child would be born — without blemish.'

'The first child?' I said.

'Elphaba,' said Nanny.

A chill ran through me. I who hadn't known chills before. I didn't ordinarily deal in medical charms. 'A serious blemish, I'm guessing, or you wouldn't be here.'

She nodded. A tear fell, and I knew it to be genuine.

I continued. 'They put the unhappy infant out of its misery, I assume.'

'Hardly. As if they could. That child has a will stronger than springtime.'

'Her infirmity, then? You must be blunt if I am to be of help.'

Nanny pushed the potted fern closer. 'Green. Skin as rich as that. I brought this so you could see. The child is a year old now, poor dreadful thing. I don't ask you for a corrective for her condition — only for a prophylactic to save Melena Thropp, her mother, against a repeat disaster. To benefit a second child, not Elphaba. Elphaba is condemned to sorrow.'

'Elphaba is condemned to nothing,' I found myself saying. 'Nothing is written for her, which means everything is possible.'

I looked at the fern, which did not wither back at me.

'That's a fancy opinion,' said the family retainer,

but I could see she was a bit shaken. 'Nanny expected something more in the line of an herbal remedy. Not a prophecy.'

'This is not a restaurant. You take what's on offer,' I said, but I was surprised at my vehemence, too.

'As long as you're feeling prophetic, why not push it a little bit further?' she asked. 'I mean, a Nanny's job is to prepare for all eventualities, so it would be useful to know what to look out for. Plagues, boyfriends, the rotten tread in the tower stairs, that sort of thing.'

I was torn at the audacious request. Who was I? A scioness of nothing – without an evident mother, I wasn't even a bastard. Having anything to do with a prominent family seemed risky from the start. Still, I was intrigued. I wasn't given to vaulty sorts of sentiments, but the report of a green girl had captured my attention. I felt a little bit of a one-off myself – perhaps there was a kinship effect.

'I will need to have something to hold,' I said, playing for time while my mind raced.

Nanny put her hands in her satchel. At first I thought she meant merely to remove them from the tabletop so I wouldn't get any ideas. Then I saw she was fussing about. 'I suspected as much,' she said. 'I came prepared. This isn't my first visit to an oracle, you know.'

'Why didn't you go back to the oracle you'd seen before?'

'She died, alas, when a marble bust of Pastorius fell off its pillar and brained her.' The Nanny got to the punch line first. 'Yes, yes, if she didn't see it coming, one questions her professional skills. So she probably deserved to die.'

I snorted to be polite, yet not so loudly as to impugn my colleague, may she rest in peace. Whatever that might be like.

'Still,' said the Nanny, continuing to rummage about, 'who of us really can see our own deaths coming?'

I didn't know back then that this would be a problem of mine decades hence: that I couldn't find my own death. 'Have you got anything in there?' I asked.

The Nanny withdrew some prettily carved beads, ivory or the like, and a golden garter worked with repoussé trim. 'The beads were made by Melena's husband, the minister,' she said. 'They're inscribed with symbols of the Unnamed God, I'm told. To me they look like denomination emblems from foreign monetary systems, but what do I know. Like I said, I haven't traveled much.'

I took the beads. They felt cool and aloof in my hands, and spoke nothing to me. If I'd hoped for a jolt of spiritual connection, I was disappointed. 'Let's see the garter,' I said. 'And this belongs to your Ladyship?'

'Did. Does. That is . . .' And here the Nanny began to blush, remembering I was supposed to be a truth-teller. 'I came away with it in my belongings, somehow, last time I visited,' she admitted. Meaning she stole it. I nodded without disapproval; I wasn't above theft myself, though it was the edible thing rather than the beautiful that I usually lifted.

I felt it, to little benefit. The woman who wore such a decorated legging expected her legs to be explored by admirers. That was all, and I'd already figured out as much. I handed it back. 'Is there nothing else?'

'Oh, you *are* good,' said the client. 'Here you go.' Next she fished out a small bottle made of green glass with a cork stopper in it. It stood so-high, about, and a paper label was affixed to the front. Yes, I remember what it said; give me a moment. It read MIRACLE ELIXIR.

'You have miracle elixirs, so what are you coming to me for?' I asked.

'I need all the help I can get,' she replied.

I picked at the label with my finger and some of it came off. A scrap of paper at the end of the word, showing part of the ornately inscribed X and IR – XIR, it looked like, or – LIR. I examined the dried glue on the back, as if it might be a pale word in a secret language. It was a glob of dried glue, no more, no less.

Still, the client wanted theatrics, and I think I was more alert than I'd ever been. I found a porcelain mortar and I burned the scrap of paper, and looked to see if I could read words forming in the arabesques of smoke. I couldn't. I mashed up herbs and crystals and added some oil of gomba, and heated the whole mess in an alembic. I counted backward by seventeens. All the usual party tricks.

Then I popped off the cork and took a swig of the miracle potion.

I'm not a poet, and despite my profession I'm not particularly good at description. The taste burned and stank, and I felt the liquor in my eyes stew. Waves rose and fell in half formation, like apathetic ghosts, like anemic fogs. I could almost see – I reached, mentally – I could almost read what it meant. But it was shapeless as most dreams really are; we put onto our dreams the shapes we think with during the day, depriving our dreams of the message they are trying to deliver. Such it was with me. There was so much life, it was so vivid: but I could only think of it with the experience of life I had already had. And despite my evident age, that wasn't much experience at all. It was like a five-year-old, upon learning the alphabet, being presented with a copy of the annotated *Great Morphologies* of the ancient tutorix Gorpha vin Tesserine. A child might be able to count the numbers marking off the footnotes, but not much more than that.

Nonetheless, I put my hands flat on the table and felt the surface of the wood grain, and tried to release my mind. The wood meant 'usefulness in death' to me; the wood meant 'you may be dead and you may still serve.' I had never tried to read the lifelines of a piece of timber before.

'Are you quite all right?' asked the Nanny, beginning to gather up her things, including the bottle. Apparently I looked as if I were about to expire, or explode.

'You have to leave the way you came,' I said to her.

'I only saw the one staircase,' she asserted.

'That's not what I meant,' I said, though I wasn't quite sure what I did mean, or if it had anything to do with her at all. 'History waits to be written, and this family has a part to play in it.'

5

'Hah,' said the Lion. 'You have to leave the way you come in? So what did you mean by that? You have to go out of the world the way you came into it? Imbecilic and diapered?'

Yackle didn't speak. He pressed his point. 'Did you decipher your own gibberish? You've been trying to die as a human, but if you never were born as a human, you're barking up the wrong tree. Ha-ha.'

She was silent for a long time. Her hands moved as

if she were picking up the green glass bottle in her mind, all over again. When she spoke, her voice had an opacity to it.

'So you did have something to give me after all,' she said. 'You come in all rough edges and smarmy clothes, and it seems you have something to say.'

He shrugged. He didn't know what she meant.

'That's why I've been down in the crypt for a year without having the pleasure of a visit from a gentleman caller named Master Death. My first prophecy, and I read it wrong. "You have to leave the way you came." That was for me. Not for that Cattery Spunge.'

'Don't look at me,' he said. His paws went up and flat like the palms of a human hand, protesting. Like a Bear cub playing dead. 'I'm not certified.'

She was shaken. She left the chairback and meandered to the window. She stood there for a long time. Then, as if trying to change the subject, she said, 'Someone's got a cook fire down there. One of the houses to our west.'

'You can see now? Or are you "seeing" it?'

'I'm smelling it, you blasted bog-wart. The wind is pressing up from the west, and I remember a few stone cottages out that way. If we're in as much of a skirmish moment as you say, I'd have thought the residents of the small farms that supply the mauntery would be huddling in our great hall for protection. That's the origin of this establishment in the first place, after all – a keep.'

'Apparently whoever lives out yonder isn't scared, though.'

'Not scared of war? Hmmm.'

'Or maybe more scared of starvation. It's harvest season, and the troops have been tromping their bloody jackboots all across country. Flattening whatever modest crop of autumn wheat the locals can manage to eke out of this unforgiving soil.' He walked to the window and stood next to her. 'I'm right. Their house stands amid three small fields of grain ready for harvest. If they leave that harvest too long, the armies will trample the fields for a camp, or bloody it with an encounter.'

'Still, if the farmers become the next casualties of war, they're not going to be able to enjoy their wheat rolls. So why stay and guard their useless harvest? They should get out of the way while they can.'

'Maybe they've had enough of life. Maybe they've had their share.'

'Who has had enough of life?' she said.

'You did,' he answered. 'You laid yourself down to die.'

'I laid myself down to go,' she corrected him, but then she began to cry. He assumed she didn't really know what she meant. It must be no fun being an oracle for everyone else and being clueless about yourself.

Before they could return to their chairs to continue, a bell rang in the mauntery. The glass cat slept on. 'It is time for prayers before dinner,' said Yackle. 'Shall we take a break now?'

'You're going to pray?' he asked.

'I remember the old ways of this place. I'm going to find a cleaver and trim these pesky nails, for one thing. Then I'm going to sit in a chapel among people who pray,' she replied. 'You may have a writ from the Emerald City, but I suspect it doesn't require me to reveal the metes and bounds of my religious doubt.'

He shrugged again. 'Will you join me?' she said, aggressively.

'We have hardly started,' he said. 'You've told me about meeting the Nanny, and how you came to learn about the Thropps. That's just scratching the surface. Tell me something more about that Elphaba – the Wicked Witch – before you go. For all I know you'll be assumed bodily into the Afterlife at the end of prayers tonight.'

'Wouldn't that be nice,' she replied and headed for the door.

Then she turned. 'The Nanny had come for advice about her employer, about that Melena Thropp – the mother of Elphaba and, eventually, the mother of Nessarose and our current benighted Emperor of Oz, Shell, too. I supplied her with something, some pinlobble leaves cut with milkflower or something. I don't even remember. Useful, though hardly magical. I never met Melena or her husband the minister. I never met Nessarose or Shell. And that Elphaba – that green girl! – well, we know what happened to her. I was on hand for bits and pieces of that, too.'

'Go on,' he said.

'I'm out of here,' she said, scraping her hand in the air, hunting for the doorknob. 'But don't you see what I'm saying? I had had my first genuine vision, even if it was induced. Something about possibility. All that misty apprehension, those swirls of image trying to form into something intelligible . . . in all that, I perceived force and hope alike. And I saw that I would be a real oracle, whatever kind of oracle I could manage to be. My calling wasn't just a joke.'

'Elphaba's tools of the trade,' he urged her. 'The broom. The crystal ball. And wasn't there a book, some book of magic?'

She wasn't taking the bait. 'The elixir had awakened in me the potential to read for meaning. I would read for meaning. It's as simple as that. You see, I had been waiting for something to focus my attention. I needed to find something in order to sense a meaning to my life, in this earthly prison of Oz. Maybe I was like the orphan duckling who has to find a friendly dog or a hen or something that might serve as a surrogate mother.'

'Take it from me,' said Brrr, 'not everyone who is

devoid of a mother seeks out a surrogate.'

'Tell it to the judge,' she replied and left the room.

Like many a blind person, her spatial memory seemed keen. She creaked and tottered away toward the chapel. He listened to the hem of her winding sheet whispering along the floorboards.

It would be fun to hear the scream of some young novice who hadn't yet heard the news that Yackle had risen from the nearly dead. All he could hear, though, was the arpeggios of melody in the oakhair trees.

Not many miles to the south, on the banks of the Vinkus River, a stand of young deciduous trees grew fairly close together. A forest fire some eight or ten years earlier had leveled the foliage, so what had sprung up in the ashes was of first growth, and all roughly the same height. Had Brrr possessed a spyglass, and had he thought to train his eyes in that direction, he might have caught a glimpse of a strange and troubled head swimming above the tips of the adolescent trees. It had ears like a dragon, and eyes like a dragon, but its tread was continuous, more like a serpent dragging its huge tail than like a quadruped galumphing along. But Brrr had no such spyglass.

6

The Clock was moving rather slowly; the lads who pushed and pulled it were struggling across the terrain. It felt as if they were hauling the wagon over a series of railway ties without the benefit of steel runner rails, since the ground was fretted with half-submerged roots of oakhair trees.

The dwarf and his new recruit walked ahead, picking out the best route. They would need to stop before long, as the sky was paling.

'We shall want to take special care, Lady Lucky,' said Mr Boss. 'Usually we like to sidestep troublesome neighborhoods, but our advice this time is to thread our way among contentious populations of nasty, armed men. Reach a safe haven just between them – a tall stone house where custom requires we be granted sanctuary.'

'Sanctuary comes at a cost, however hidden,' she replied.

'Oh, our private Missy Prissy condescends to comment!' The dwarf skipped in place. His mockery was affectionate, but it knew no restraints. 'Do tell, darling.'

'I mean nothing by it. Just – just that no rescue comes free.'

'You're sulky, you're surly, because we impressed you into service after we saved you from that dolorous tower. That's the thanks we get. My feelings are hurt.'

She shrugged. Perhaps she did mean that. Some weeks ago, in her life before now, her aging employer had locked her in the top floor of a stone turret. She'd been retained as a nurse, but he wanted more than medical care, and she had refused to yield to his advances. (Well, she couldn't even if she'd wanted.)

He had gloated at her from below, by turns cajoling and threatening, until one morning, when a grape had become lodged in his windpipe. She couldn't throw herself out the high window to revive him; the drop was too steep. She couldn't beat the door down (she had tried that). She watched him stagger to his knees and clutch his throat, and look up at her. He couldn't speak. She had all she could do not to sing down to him, 'Did you take your tablets before your meal?' When he fell, his body made a shadow and then a stain on the terrace.

She feared starvation, but scarcely a day later the dwarf and his crew came along with their awesome Clock. The Dragon had stretched its armored swanlike neck nearly as high as her windowsill, and she had been able to escape, exchanging one affectionate fiend for another. But at least the dwarf and his toothsome boys had sworn against sex with a woman, so they were a better company to keep for the time being.

Mr Boss deduced that his reticent recruit was in a perplexed mood. He asked, 'What were you doing in the service of that Grandpa Ogre, anyway?'

She looked hither and yon. Though the boys were far enough ahead not to hear, she didn't want to talk about most of it. She said, 'My invalid master professed that in exchange for chores I could perform, I could barter for my freedom. I had three years to go when he became cross with me and locked me in that tower. It was too high to escape from, unless one wanted to jump to one's death. Once in my childhood I had thought I could fly – but I had no wings of my own. It took your dragon with its own wings to reach its neck up so I could crawl on top of it, and scramble to safety. Did the dragon tell you I would be there, or was it just my luck?'

'Please! I don't dabble in contingency theory. Too rich for my numbish skull.'

'How long am I beholden to you for your kindness?'

'Ah, that I *can't* say. The Clock spells out its designs of fate only as far as it wants me to know them.'

They were silent. More companionable than usual. The dwarf in his way was as indentured as she was in hers. She had seen him set up the Clock only once, to put on an exhibition for a petty brigand who'd come across them on a stretch of paved road and threatened them with a pistol. She'd watched the sergeant-at-hand ratchet the gears until the whole tall instrument was quivering with tension. They all stood back as the Clock invented a little entertainment. She didn't yet know if the Clock was merely distracting, a tiktok cleverness, or enchanted.

A puppet arrived under the arch of a little proscenium up top. He looked uncannily like the brigand, right down to the gusseted Lincoln-green tunic and the pistol. The puppet looked this way and that, as if to make sure he was alone. Then he sat down and clasped the pistol, barrel upright, between his legs and began to stroke the shaft of it.

No children's puppet play, this. She'd closed her eyes.

'That's filthy,' murmured the bandit, somewhat approvingly.

She heard the puppet rocking back and forth. Though there was no sound, she could tell by the quickening of the rhythm that the big pop was near. 'Stop,' she'd tried to say, but her voice had fled: She knew no one was listening to her.

'Whoa,' said the bandit, 'you've got some nerve—'

She had peered between lashes, she admitted it: The mouth of the pistol had fountained a surge of foamy blood all over the trousers of the puppet, who fell back, sated and, it seemed, dead.

Worried that the Clock was not just illustrative of

morals but perhaps a hand of fate, she'd whirled to see the brigand. He was slack jawed at the performance (though that was the only part of him slack), and he hadn't yet noticed that the boys had liberated him of his considerable wallet and his pistol both.

They kept the cash and the bullets and returned the pistol before releasing him. They had nothing to fear: He tore off crashing through the underbrush like a fox from hounds.

The blood was good, no? asked the dwarf. Juice of blood oranges and pomegranates thickened with cream of tartar. The Clock is talented but needs some fuel from time to time.

She hadn't asked how it came to be that the Clock was supplied with a puppet resembling a chance highway robber. Such a turn put paid to the notion of chance at all. Still, in some ways that was consoling: She could stay where she was, clandestine and still, and freely believe that this must be her fate. The need to decide further was removed from her, which made something of a rest.

'I won't keep you longer than I'm directed to,' said the dwarf now, as they headed toward the sanctuary he had divined might take them in.

'You did me a service by rescuing me. I'm not looking to leave you. I have no plans but to keep out of sight. I merely worry at the thought of armies massing around us.'

'Armies are only hunters in formation. Upright teams of precision hunters.'

'Once I hunted for information, but one of my informants was killed. I have retired from hunting, Mr Boss. I am no fan of the spoils of the game.'

He reached out to pat her wrist but she tucked her hands in her shawl. Such reticence she showed! Hoping to further this unexpected moment of confidences, the dwarf asked her, 'How would you feel about a Lion hunt?'

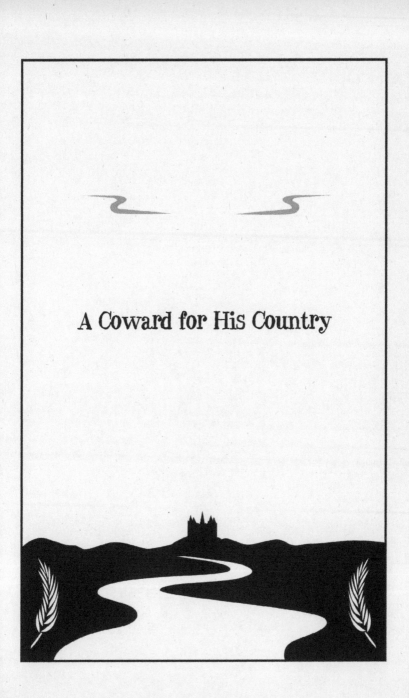

A Coward for His Country

1

A Lion at rest.

How old was he now? Thirty-eight? Forty? How long had he been waiting to see some shade of the world other than grim yellow?

That oracle, who was blind with age, could see more than he could. Damn her.

Was she holding out on him? Running for the chapel just when they were closing in on the questions he most needed to ask? Where is the Grimmerie? Where was Elphaba's rumored son, Liir – where had he disappeared to? If anyone in Oz might know, it had to be Yackle. Yackle wasn't the only person who had cared about Elphaba – there was Lady Glinda, among others – but Yackle was the one who had been able to see into the darkness of Elphaba's life.

A vision like that – what he wouldn't give to have some . . . some sense of scope. Some perspicacity. But he could never see forward. Even the act of looking back – at how he had gotten himself hip-deep in muck, again and again – even that was hard for him to fathom.

Well, he wasn't giving up this time. He'd proved useless at his earliest tasks, like finding Jemmsy's father. A total loser and no mistake. He'd always run off at the first sign of trouble. But now there was nowhere left to run. It was this or prison.

So he let her see of him what she would, with her oracle's inner eye; she didn't need to hear him voice his reservations about himself out loud. There were things he would never say to any female, whether she was a Lioness or a human, a judge or an oracle, a petty whore or a pettier maunt.

A male usually had made up his mind before you began to talk to him – so why bother? – but a female, because her mind was more supple, was always prepared to become more disappointed in you than she had yet suspected possible. Yackle would prove no exception, he was sure.

How different his life might have been if he had emerged from the Great Gillikin Forest right at the outskirts of the town of Tenniken instead of at Traum. Sure, now he knew: A talking Lion would have had a rough go of it anywhere under the Wizard's jurisdiction. Yet if Brrr had been able to deliver the medal of honor back to Jemmsy's father, he'd have had an early experience of reaching a goal. Of not being diverted.

But remembering what had happened in Traum – even thinking about it today – had been a mistake. Living with amnesia, the way those cretinous Bears in the Great Gillikin Forest did, was the only sensible strategy.

The word *lionized* had more than one meaning.

His youth, his stupidity, had been no more than that. Stupidity was forgivable in the young. But when he'd lain down and played dead in Traum – it had been no more and no less than a collapse of his enfeebled sense of himself – he'd made himself into an emblem of complicity. 'Remember the cowardly Lion,' the humans had said in Traum. 'He laid down his life for us.'

Sunk in a fug of self-loathing, he'd bypassed Tenniken entirely. Paid the conductor extra to stay on to Shiz. (No other Animals rode the train that day, though, sealed into his own mortification, he hadn't noticed. Later, he wondered if some good burgher of Traum had bribed the conductor to allow Brrr to board at all, just to get him out of the vicinity.)

Still, the sight of the outskirts of the ancient university town caught Brrr's attention, drawing him out of his funk. He peered through the grimy train windows. First, the great manufacturing plants. Brick factories with glass transoms, spewing noxious plumes out of zigzaggy smokestacks. Closer to the city-centre, terraced housing for millworkers. Their laundry yards swarmed with small human cubs, at play with their skipping ropes and stones.

And then into the close, gnarled, ancient university center of Shiz. Its separate colleges in promiscuous adjacency. Each boasted an ivy clawed gatehouse through which passersby could glimpse serene quadrangles ... brilliant chapels, lecture halls ... science labs chasing the latest developments in two dozen separate branches of enquiry.

The Lion had taken stock of the smart little city, the jewel of the province of Gillikin. He'd explored its nests of colleges and its clubs and its manicured parks and canals, and then he'd set himself up in a better class of residence. Not far from Ticknor Circus, with its array of bistros and bathhouses. A sunny, top-floor den in a purpose-built brick mansion block called Ampleton Quarters. Suite 1904. Fully furnished and featuring the most up-to-the-tiktok in water closets.

Was he aware that he might be trading on a reputation as the very Lion who had inadvertently advanced the Wizard's plans in the emerald trade, helping to squelch the spontaneous labor revolt? Innocent as he was, it would have been hard for him to discern the ways in which he was receiving undue advantage. His first time in a city – or the first time that he could remember. No other Lions seemed to live in Ampleton Quarters; but then, he tended to hurry to his flat, and avoided the biweekly tenants' meetings because he didn't want to be bullied into serving on any committees.

He kept his mouth closed as much as possible. And comparatively speaking, a Lion cuts a fine figure; the world admires a glossy mane, a sultry-surly growl. One can make an impression without saying much, and Brrr learned that he was not bad-looking, as Lions go.

But being good-looking has its own penalties. The public will not let a comely face walk by anonymously; it must find out who owns it. By the end of his first social season in Shiz, Brrr had made the grade. He enjoyed the occasional off-night, back-alley shenanigans but he built a more formal life on the strength of his reputation as a hero.

He didn't consider marriage. He didn't have the stomach for it. Instead, he invested his little nest egg in a portfolio of diversified stocks managed by a Shiz bank called the Gold Standard. In the first few years it swelled agreeably. While the rest of Oz was still suffering the effects of the long drought, and farmsteads in Munchkinland were being repossessed for back taxes, the industrial base of Gillikin allowed waistlines to amplify and chins to double. Brrr grew prosperous, and lived like it. He kept to himself. Cultivating the reputation of a mystery presence about town, he avoided close contact of a genuinely intimate nature, and therefore – he hoped – he might be excused for failing to see the social coercion, the repression on which the Shiz haut monde was built.

He took in shows. He meandered through galleries. Without much attention to the topic at hand, he attended the occasional public lecture at Three Queens College or Briscoe Hall; it seemed to be something the well-heeled *did* in a university town like

Shiz. He never took notes, although sometimes he tried mentally to assess his compounded interest for the quarter while the lecturer was nattering on.

Brrr especially enjoyed those presentations on the subject of art history, not least because the lights would go down when the gloriously colored illuminatums were to be cast upon a white plaster wall. In the darkened hall, no one could notice if Brrr was paying attention or not. Thus, freed of anxiety, he found he did appreciate the lectures. And he stayed awake, unlike some.

His earliest love was for manuscript pages. 'A singularly fine example of the monk known to us now only as the Ur-Scribe. This from Shiz's most antique bound codex,' droned the master. 'Notice the three-ply wreathing adorning the left margin. Green foil made from the crushed talons of dragons, very rare; and observe the flecks of gold as well: a hint that the artist still possessed Lurlinist tendencies, though the early unionist text posits the Unnamed God's superior station.'

'And the blue on the third strand?' asked a woman of a certain age, decked out in blue furs herself, fluffing a storm cloud around her chin.

'Perhaps a kind of alibi color, to throw those sniffing for heresy off the scent,' replied the master. 'We can only speculate.'

'Perhaps he liked blue,' said the aging dilettante.

Her eye was bright and, yes, blue. 'I certainly do. I find it . . . stimulating.'

'If we might proceed,' said the master wearily.

Brrr talked to the woman at the reception hour. 'He's so distinguished, our guest scholar,' she gushed, 'but he thinks me crass. He *won't* find time in his research schedule to visit my newly decorated salon – oh, it's divine, eighteen panels of bleached pearlwood – and help me decide on what to hang. And where. I'm so cross with him.'

'Have you a fine collection?' asked Brrr.

'I've no eye to decide if it's fine or not,' she replied. 'Why don't you come have a look, tell me what you think?'

When he said he would, she introduced herself as Miss Piarsody Scallop. She was rather long in the tooth to be a Miss, and he wondered if he might have been invited to her home for reasons other than art appreciation. Nonetheless, he took a risk, and discovered Miss Scallop to be genuinely rich, and genuinely interested in – if paralyzed by – the ambiguities and obscurities of art.

Thus he finally found out that he did possess a native skill, that mysterious commodity known as a good eye. Cousin, perhaps, to perfect pitch, or a sixth sense. He became adroit at buying and selling small prints and sketches and advising ladies of leisure about the works gracing the walls of their salons. He could turn a tidy profit in the bargain, and he did. He lived off his interest and never touched his capital.

One evening, in the magnificent diamond-paned lectorium nestled next to the Deckens College chapel, he heard a titter in the room and sensed faces turning his way. He blushed without knowing why and waved a little, as if to show he had been paying quite close attention, thank you very much. He *did* try to concentrate for the next few minutes, to deduce what had happened. The lecturer, a Madame Morrible from Crage Hall, was treating the audience to the benefit of her impressions of – what was it? – the Animal Adverse laws (or the Animal Courtesy acts if you used the jargon of punditry) – as they pertained to higher education at Shiz.

'Exceptions are always possible,' insisted this Madame Morrible, fluttering one hand to simulate the sparkle-dust of mercy while waving the other hand in the Lion's general direction. 'The Animal who serves our beloved Wizard is accorded all the privileges he so richly deserves. The creature called cowardly by some has had the courage to accept the epithet. Another name for cowardice is the courage of no convictions. A true hero can tolerate being called a coward for one's country. No?'

He wasn't quite able to follow the gist of this. He wasn't ashamed. He'd had no education, after all; it was a miracle he could walk into a place like this and hold his head up! He applauded with the rest of them, but he couldn't think of a single remark to make during the Q-and-A period.

He got up to stretch, collect his greatcoat and huge bespoke dove-grey evening gloves. He turned to mumble appreciatively to the lady on his left and he saw that she was moving away quickly as if to avoid having to chat. He turned again, and the gentleman on his right was doing the same.

He looked the room over, in that way one does, pretending to expect to find one's best beloved, or at least a crony, and readying to sigh loudly, a public display of regret, dash-it-all! – and at last it dawned on him that he was the only Animal in the room.

On reflection, walking home, he concluded that this had been the case, in the circles in which he traveled, for some time. He had never noticed.

Still, he didn't yet have the wherewithal to know if he had become a laughingstock. He began to pay attention. Was including Brrr on a guest list a sleight-of-mockery to amuse the disdainful? An Animal in Society – in these days, in these hard times, with the Animal Courtesy acts! – had he become a joke? A beloved old joke? Was treating him like a hero a part of the joke? It might be just so. His allowing it to happen – showing up at dinner parties as the outré guest, dandified and powdered and beribboned – that was his part of the joke, people assumed. He had no shame.

Good for him. He was a token of the Wizard's clemency and understanding.

Perhaps they weren't as cruel as they seemed. He pondered it. The Cowardly Lion? Sure, it sounded like a slur of sorts, but he'd looked on it as almost a kind of stage name, a title. He'd assumed they meant it affectionately. He had been very young when he'd made his name, after all.

Then, at last, and who knows how, the word began to get out that he'd been paid for playing dead all those years ago.

The Traum massacre. The journalist in the train's dining car, all those years back, had coined a phrase, the Cowardly Lion. The tag was an insult in remission, ready to metastasize in the public consciousness now that Brrr had established himself as a public figure.

The Lion who wouldn't fight. The pesky Glikkuns who were mowed down. The big old peaceable pussycat. The dead trolls. The wussums with his wittle Wion's tears.

Ah, but Brrr would have survived the shame of it a little better had he not taken the purse.

He'd been too wet, too inexperienced, too damn hungry to think twice about accepting it. In the end, as the stink of a questionable past began to bloom around him, it wasn't as much the cowardice people commented upon, but that Brrr had been paid handsomely.

We all make mistakes. But we're not supposed to profit from them.

What could he do next? The rumors kept doubling the amount of the sum he'd been awarded. If he'd had anything like such an initial investment, he'd be the wealthiest Animal in Oz by now. In gossip, presumed wealth is always overestimated by garish exponentials. That in itself was a burden to him.

He couldn't give the money back to the hard-up burghers of Traum; that would be to acknowledge some sort of wrongdoing, and he'd done nothing wrong except to be young and ignorant.

Besides, he could never afford to give back the amount of money folks now said he'd earned on his first day in human society.

In any case, giving publicly to charity was thought unseemly. He'd only be able to contribute anonymously. And while this might help his soul, it wouldn't salvage his reputation.

He tore his mane out at nights, sleepless and distraught. But he kept accepting invitations, for suddenly to drop out of society might also signal a sense of failure, of guilt. The soirées became ugly but he kept showing up, in part to prove he wasn't scared to show up.

Then one evening, as he stood under the stone portico of the Sir Chuffrey Opera Palace, waiting in a queue of the great and the good for the next available landau, Brrr was approached by a young blueblood. 'The Cowardly Lion! You're the Lion from the labs at Shiz University,' he said. 'Aren't you? The little orphaned cubling! Doctor Nikidik tried to sever your language stem. I was there. I remember.'

'I was never in Shiz as an infant,' he replied, affronted, though as he spoke he realized he couldn't be sure of this. Who remembers their own infancy?

It was a Margreave's son, deep in his cups, slurring his words and making a scene. 'Brrr. Is that right? I remember – the doctor named you Brrr because you shivered like a kitten with the flu.' Only it came out 'shivered like a shitten.'

'Nonsense,' said Brrr. 'This is my first episode in Shiz. I should remember an earlier visit.'

'The cage,' prompted the inebriate, 'a cunning little cage! I remember because your name was pronounced like the first syllable of *berserk*.'

Avaric Tenmeadows, the Margreave's son, it turned out, had attended some classes with Elphaba. The dreaded Wicked Witch of the West, as she'd come to be known. On the day in question, she'd witnessed the dustup, swore the Margreave's son. She had!

Heads turned. The Witch was big news just then, because her sister, Nessarose, recently had orchestrated the secession of Munchkinland from Oz. The Thropp family was in dudgeon, both sisters alike. No one yet had taken any measure of their baby brother.

Overnight – as the rickshaws and buckboards and broughams pulled sloppily into the rain – the Lion's reputation was tarnished in another way. Suspicious through association. Complicit. A familiar . . .

The Witch had rescued the poor little cub from the experiment, said a letter to the editor, signed *Anonymous* (*a pensioner*).

No, it was a pair of fey boysies called Crope and Tibbett, said someone in a gossip column. The Witch actually wanted the cub killed so she could drink its baby Animal blood.

No, the Witch had hexed him, that poor little Brrr.

Are you kidding? He'd been hexed at Brrrth. Ha-ha.

I wish I'd been hexed with a trust fund like his.

Within a few weeks, vaudeville comics on the variety stages of Ticknor Circus were mocking Brrr's precision in speech. When he made an attempt to talk street-thuggy, they mocked that even more.

What astonished him – when he had achieved the distance from the events to interpret them without rages – was the extent to which a comic accusation could, by dint of repetition, begin to be taken as received wisdom. The Witch, after all, was on her way to becoming feared and despised, but she was still only a distant threat. Whereas if the Lion was her familiar – hah! It made the threat of the Witch seem more like a joke.

When the joke faded, the sentiment remained. The bemused tolerance that had attended his myopic insistence on being a civilized Animal in Shiz began to evaporate. His silvered tray was empty of calling cards; the morning post brought fewer and fewer requests to call, to dine, to take a promenade through the Scholars' Arbor, to attend a charity function at considerable cost. He was stuck with a stock of expensive old mettanite engravings he couldn't shift, and he owed a bundle on them.

Miss Scallop began to be not at home to him, when, on her receiving afternoons, Brrr came to call.

In the week that no such invitations arrived, and the columnists grew snarkier in their insinuations, Brrr finally saw what others had seen many months, even years, before. Things were not going well for talking Animals in general, and for a talking Animal with a tainted reputation, for having been defended by the Witch, a known enemy of the state – well, if he didn't get out soon, it would be his own fault.

One morning over coffee, a political cartoon showed a dandified Lion mincing along with bank-notes stuffed in his beribboned mane. The caption read:

> *Quivery Brrrr.*
> *What's up with her?*
> *What's she prefer?*
> *What makes her purr?*

No loyal Cat
Should act like that.
The heart of a cur
In expensive fur.

The offending newspapers slapped to the floor, the Lion made his plans quietly – there were no friends to share them, after all – and then he disappeared from Shiz, leaving three months' rent owed on Suite 1904.

He needed to avoid the Emerald City to the south, so he couldn't go there. If anything the Animal Adverse laws were stricter in the capital. Yet, though some free Animals were said to be migrating westward into the Great Kells, the Lion could summon no enthusiasm for the wilderness outback of the Vinkus. He'd become too accustomed to his creature comforts. And he had no interest ever in revisiting the Ozmists or the Bears, or any other denizens of the Great Gillikin Forest. Shame? Been there, done that, as the wags said.

Instead, therefore, he made his way cross-country to the southeast. He wandered about, doing odd jobs and stealing from barns when hunger required it. In the best of times, a Lion can't cause trouble in rural neighborhoods and get away with it for long. And these were not the best of times by a long stretch. So he lived in an unsettled way. He roamed the lower slopes of the Madeleines, hunger in his guts, burrs from hack-thistle in his pelt.

These were years of loping along, fits and starts. He would take a job on a farm — he wasn't above hauling a wagon if it meant dinner — but the farmer was inevitably brutal, or stupid beyond tolerance, or offensive, or a sorry joke of a human being. Brrr didn't think of himself as *losing* his jobs, but leaving them when the moment was ripe. (That moment so often came the moment he was fired.)

Once he discovered a pride of Lions trying to make a small conclave for themselves in some caves on the eastern slopes of the Madeleines. They had never been to Shiz, nor to anyplace more thrilling than the nearest market town. Nor had they any memory of abandoning a cub in the Great Gillikin Forest as Brrr had been abandoned. They were not his family, they attested. Far from it. None of their number could commit such a heinous act. Furthermore, they didn't keep up with Lion tribes in other free-range zones.

At least, that was what they said at first. One evening on watch, a distinguished old auntie Lioness allowed that communiqués among the outlying prides had once been common. 'There were human campaigns to separate prides of Talking Beasts from the rest,' she insisted. 'The great WOO has never trusted Animals. I heard from a relative in the Great Gillikin Forest that the usual single poachers were being joined by a more systematic cohort of army hunters. They were intent on eliminating the larger Animals who might get wind of the Animal Adverse laws and mount an attack in defense of their citified kin. The Forest is not all that far from Shiz, as you must know.'

'As far as I understood, Animals in the wild have little to do with their domesticated cousins.'

'Every pride is different, dear,' she answered softly, 'as every Animal is.'

'Have you ever known a pride that abandons its young?'

'Not willingly. I did hear once of an attempt to cull Lion cubs from their mothers,' she continued, more blithely than he could have thought possible. 'For use in laboratory experiments, whatever *those* are. One queries if said mothers relinquished their cubs in exchange for their own liberty. *I* never would of course.'

By now Brrr was cynical enough to look at her sharply. Was she revealing a hidden secret of this pride? Might they all have been lying to him? Could she herself . . . ?

But this pride, to the last one of them, was marked by a dark tuft of fur at every chin, and he had no such marking.

So all she was revealing was the capacity of a Lion even to entertain the thought of such a betrayal, even if by someone else.

He didn't bid the auntie good night, for he didn't think it would be one; and it wasn't.

Still, he learned from this pride of tuft-chinned Lions a certain coherence of attitude. A Lion pride could be a kindly casual crowd. They didn't indulge in aimless ancestor worship, but unlike the court of Queen Ursaless, they didn't forget each day as it happened, either. They were wary of others and tended to avoid large groups of nomadic Animals, even those they might easily disperse by a show of claw. Not precisely pacifists, but not the fierce Lion of human legend, either.

For quite a while they admired Brrr and treated him like a respected cousin visiting from the glamorous, dangerous city. He amused them with tales of goings-on, quite a few of them true. He settled with them, a raconteur-at-large, a personality that brought their humble forest lives some distinction. He made an effort to court a few young Lionesses (one at a time, of course), but his overtures were rebuffed. He was too foreign, too silver of tongue, for them to take seriously. He thought he could wear them down – wear them all down – by his amused tolerance, his capacity for sticking around. He could make himself indispensable.

But eventually the Lions began to mock his drawing-room parlance, and not in an affectionate manner. He was too gilded a lily for their rustic clan. If he could not mate because none would mate with him, he would be bound sooner or later to fight for tribal dominance, and – oh, the idea of it – they could never allow a dandy such as Brrr to lead their pack. He should think of moving on. Soon.

So once again he would have to get up and leave, before things got ugly.

By the time this thought occurred to him he had been with the pride of Lions some few years, and the departure was more painful to contemplate than he'd imagined.

Evacuating a sordid situation was beginning to become a habit.

During a night plagued by insomnia, he steeled himself to go. The sad dawn came, a soft-yolk sun blearing through vermilion clouds. Like an effect of the later period of the great la Chivarra. And there was a watery softness to the weather. Maybe it would be all right.

How old was he now? He pondered as he stretched the sleep-kinks out. Haven't I earned the right to a decent life? Or could that ever be a right?

He had nothing to pack, no satchel, no clothes. He'd abandoned all his fine rags in Ampleton Quarters, Suite 1904. Naked as a brave Animal, he looked left and right across the clearing one final time. No one was awake but for a shy cub who was nuzzling a makeshift dolly in her mouth.

'I'm off, then,' he said to the little thing. She turned her head and closed her eyes as if she hadn't heard.

'Don't be such a little coward,' she purred to her fake baby.

2

What a piece of work he'd become! He acknowledged that. A ludicrous figure padding his way overland, with no particular destination, nor much of a yen to settle on one.

Indeed, the farther he got from the pale of the Lions, the more desolate the landscape became, and he in it. The rises known in Gillikin as the Madeleines — for their gentle ridged shapes, like the spongy cake so beloved of schoolboys — were less appealing on the Munchkinland side of the border. Their name changed, too. The Wend Fallows. Wind-reddened, turnipy hills that, lower down, broke up into a network of arroyos, most running south by southeast. Beautiful to no one but the stray hermit or mendicant. What streams there were flushed into the mighty Munchkin River, which fed Oz's largest lake, Restwater.

But — martyrs roasting on an open fire! — Wend Fallows was ugly as sin. A furzy sort of brown nap coated the hillsides, like a mold that has died but refuses to stop clinging. On south-facing slopes, caterpillars had ravaged the spindly trees. Their leaves looked less lacy than skeletal. The water was brackish; the salt lick, licked out.

An arid good-for-nothing sort of landscape in which Brrr might as well make himself at home.

It was neither the place nor the time of his life in which he thought to find romance. Indeed, any expectation of intimacy initially sparked by his early friendships with Jemmsy or Cubbins seemed to have petered out, leaving nothing. He therefore hove into the sight of a tribe of – what were they – Ocelots? – without paying much attention. Almost devoid of the instinct for self-preservation now, he loped upon them and moved to pass through, looking neither left nor right at them as they lay, sprawled and unafraid, in the thin junk-woods that pestered the terraces and leveling slopes of the Wend Fallows.

He wasn't so much displaying a proud profile as daring the Cats to be affronted, and to fall upon him with claws.

They did neither. A leader of some variety stood up and blocked his way. 'It is poor manners in these parts to traipse through a party without stopping for a meal,' said the creature, a male.

'Didn't presume to be invited,' said Brrr.

'You're in such a hurry?' The tone was guarded, perhaps hostile.

'No hurry,' said Brrr, and then — a little hostile himself — 'and no appetite to speak of, either.' He neither raised his brow to be superior nor lowered it.

'Stay a spell, then. Join your neighbor Cats in fellowship.' He flicked his eyes left and right, circling the pack in. 'We are a family tribe called Ghullim, and I am the chief, known as Uyodor H'aekeem. We have not met you before, I think.'

Brrr decided to withhold his name for the time being. 'I'm not from these parts.'

'Advance guard for your pack?' Uyodor sniffed the wind for further company.

'Traveling alone,' said Brrr. 'By choice,' he added, which was mostly true.

'A rare creature, to brave the landscape on your own.'

'Not much of a landscape.' He couldn't keep from adding, 'And so not much bravery required.'

'Still, you've met a peaceable sort, we Ghullim. We don't like strangers to pass through without getting to know them, for strangers can become enemies, but friends? — friends can never return to being strangers again. Don't you agree?' He whipped his tail, aerating his punctuation. The wind hissed in Brrr's eyes.

'Oh, quite,' said Brrr, 'though a conscripted friendship is a conceit I've never encountered before.'

'No conscription,' said Uyodor H'aekeem, 'no coercion: only conversion, and by affable means!

Piyanta, Zibria, come escort our new friend to table.' He enunciated the word *friend* with a crispness and decorum that suggested something like a legislated honor.

Piyanta and Zibria rolled up on delicately articulated paws. They were maidens of a piquant variety, and in a human affectation their eyes were smeared with kohl.

'Follow us,' they purred, and led Brrr away – he was not protesting – to a shaded clearing up a small rise, where a pair of tree elves was busy stirring a pot over a fire. The smell of a savory stew enhanced the sense of welcome.

'You will be our guest,' said Uyodor from a distance. 'Ghullim custom insists on it. Treat him well, young ladies.'

'Guest, schmest,' muttered one of the tree elves. 'I call it indentured service, myself.'

'Me, I live to cook,' replied the other elf staunchly while looking around himself this way and that. Sotto voce: 'Shut *up*, Twigg.'

'Shut up yourself, Stemm.'

Brrr paid them no attention. He had never seen tree elves before, but having heard of them, he considered them beneath regard. 'Are you allowed to talk with me?' he asked his female consorts.

'To talk, to befriend, to enrapture,' said Zibria. Piyanta giggled and looked in one of Zibria's ears, as if studying to see if she had any brains at all.

'Then I ask a question, if I might.'

'You might.'

'I don't recognize your species. Your profile confuses me. You resemble Tigers in your musculature, but you are smaller. And your coats – like dried mint leaves, the markings, rather than stripes . . .'

'We're a rare kind, we are,' said Zibria. 'Perhaps a one-of-a-kind species. We have Spice Leopard in our Tiger makeup.'

Brrr raised his eyebrow. He hadn't known interspecies generation ever to work. True, in the wide scope of society, it was inevitable that shady romances between members of separate species would occur from time to time, but they were frowned upon at best and rarely produced offspring in any event. Now, he thought, an aberration that had yielded a most sumptuous type of cat – look at Piyanta lying there, amusing herself by batting at a butterfly – a dollop of femininity curled upon itself, in a coat of golden-brown scallops. An exquisite she, a remarkable she.

'Does the Ghullim clan have a name?' he found himself asking. 'As a species, I mean? I can't quite place you.'

'We don't need to name ourselves. Let others try,' replied Zibria.

'Merchants of Oppression?' offered Twigg. 'Slaves to Your Glorious Past?'

'Soup's nearly on!' sang out the one who'd been

addressed as Stemm. 'And yummers, is it a winner today, folks!' He brandished a ladle like a mace. 'Who wants firsties?'

'The guest,' said Zibria. 'Of course.'

'Not hungry,' said Brrr, thinking *poison* or the like.

'Still, it's only polite to accept our humble fare,' said Zibria.

'Not as humble as all that,' said Stemm. 'We been working on this batch since sunup. No rest for the weary, that's what I say.'

'No rest for the idiotic,' said Twigg. 'Dish up a portion, brother-at-arms, before I bash your brains in. Not that you have many.'

The tree elves conspired between them to carry a shallow bowl of the viscous liquid over to Brrr and set it down on the ground without spilling too much of it. Potatoes like soft stones gleamed in the broth.

'Garnished with elf spit!' cried Stemm, and made as if to prove it.

'That's an elf joke,' said Twigg, cuffing him. 'Go on, eat up. It's good.'

'Please,' said Zibria.

'I couldn't,' said Brrr.

'You should, please,' inserted Piyanta, 'for Ghullim custom requires us to hold off our own meal until the guest has partaken, and I am particularly hungry this morning.' She loosed a sour-pink tongue between pearly dirks of tooth. Brrr nearly swooned. Whatever they called themselves, or resisted calling themselves, they were a perfect beauty of a tribe.

He obliged, in the name of courtesy. If he were poisoned and died today, what difference might it make? He'd have perished in golden company, and little complaint at that, among all else to fret over.

And the soup wasn't bad, actually.

He finished his portion, and the elves then served Zibria and Piyanta – from the same pot, Brrr was pleased to note. He rolled over on his side and stretched his aching legs. He didn't think Lions had been meant for hillside meandering, not the way his limbs felt today. But to lie here in a wash of faintly pulsing pain and watch those pretty tongues lap and lap . . . well, he could bear it just now.

Before the elegant pair of damsel Cats could return to conversation, though, a third creature walked through. At first Brrr thought it was Uyodor H'aekeem again, for the stance was regal and the attitude curt and guarded. Then he saw that the newcomer was a female.

He was on his feet at once.

'Scatter,' said the newcomer, and Zibria and Piyanta left, drops of soup raining to either side.

The ladycat sat herself down. The tree elves didn't offer her a meal (perhaps there was none left). They clung to each other and hid behind the pot.

'First things first. I see you've been fed,' she said. 'I

am Muhlama H'aekeem. The daughter and only child of Uyodor.'

He waited to be urged to sit again, but she didn't mention it, and after a while he didn't dare.

As if continuing a postprandial colloquy, she commented, 'You are a brave Lion, to waltz in among the inestimable Ghullim without introduction or apology.'

'I don't know your Ghullim ways,' he replied. 'I don't fathom the ways of communities in general, come to think of it. I have lived a while among Lions, but I am not essentially one of them. You must forgive me the brutality of my manners. Ignorance, I promise you, not superiority.'

'Well, of course, not *superiority*,' replied Muhlama. Her eyes were anthracite – hard, fixed, aqueous – but her tone had the faintest uplift of irony. 'Where are you headed?'

Brrr had no destination. In a sense, his life of motion and restlessness, in successive waves of unsuccessful campaigns, had washed him up, cast him ashore on the lip of this very morning, with no further horizon to crave or even imagine. 'Where am I headed? I suppose I was headed here, although I didn't know it.'

Muhlama turned her head. It dawned on Brrr that they were perched on a blunted promontory above the encampment. While he was more or less on display, an ornament on a ledge, so were the splendid cats arrayed below. It was a larger tribe than others he'd encountered in the wild. He could examine their social organization as if it were drawn out in a textbook diagram.

'Has the Ghullim clan a name?' he asked. 'A species name, I mean?'

'We are the Ghullim family. We need no other designation among ourselves. But I have known others to call us Ivory Tigers, which seems to be a nod to the apparent Tiger among our ancestors as well as to the Spice Leopard markings, which to some look like angle-cut slices of vanilla pod laid in imbrications.'

Muhlama H'aekeem, an Ivory Tigress. And below, her father *en couchant*, his forearms set decidedly as andirons. Marmoreal, he rested upon an ornate carpet knotted in golds and green silks. Back and forth among the cool stand of ferns behind him, his Ivory Tiger tail moved, like the head of a Water Cobra.

Around Uyodor H'aekeem's carpet churned the workings of a government more regularized than any that Brrr had witnessed in the Animal provinces. Several elder Ivory Tigers, ambassadors or senators of some sort, conferred among themselves in tones soft and serious. Other male Tigers, disarmingly casual, patrolled the perimeter of the camp. The Tigers weren't dissolute like Bears or paralyzed by endless arbitration like humans, but regimented and alert. Brrr realized he must have been given clearance to stroll into this group.

Nearer, he could see Piyanta and Zibria and their cousins in a kind of open cloister, reclining behind a netting of pale golden gauze suspended from the branches of larch trees. The young females tended to one another's needs with a simple affection that seemed both kittenish and provocative.

A few rapscallion youngsters were being taught the algebraics of pouncing by a seriously trim grandmother warrior. She was not afraid to draw blood with the cuff of her paw, though Brrr could hear no mew of complaint from the erring student.

'Is there a queen?' he found himself asking, thinking of Ursaless, that dowdy collapsing pillar of Bear.

'Are you referring to Ozma?' Muhlama nearly spit the word.

'I was not. I meant was your father blessed with a consort.'

'Uyodor H'aekeem does not take a mate for life,' said Muhlama. 'Like so many tribes in Oz, we are a matriarchy. But if a Chieftess bears no female offspring, her oldest male cub becomes leader until he dies or is challenged successfully by an upstart. Uyodor, the son of our last Chieftess, has held sway since before my birth.'

'And you are in line, then, to lead the Ghullim when he dies.'

'I stand in no line,' she snapped, but that was a revelation she regretted at once. (She had a temper, he saw.) The rate of her breathing had changed; she was holding her breath – holding herself together, holding herself back. 'You are correct. If tradition is followed, I am the next to rule.'

He decided to change the subject. 'Since you mentioned her, I wonder if your clan believes that Ozma will return to rule Oz again?'

She snorted. 'Ozma? Can you credit anything about the heap of gossip surrounding her? The washerwoman myths of a holy saint Ozma, our savior and our guide – hah! Those baby bones are halfway to dust now. The Wizard in the Emerald City is far too smart an operator to have sequestered that child somewhere off-site, where she could grow and thrive and command an army to return and reclaim her throne. We wait for no deliverers here, and we need none. We are in readiness when our terrain is threatened, and no Wizard of Oz nor any other agitator will co-opt our independence or receive our tribute.'

The vigor of her testimony seemed disproportionate, since his remark had been casual. This was a tribe that reveled in its iconoclastic identity with lethal earnestness.

'I only wondered,' he said. 'It does seem to be an enduring story, that the baby Ozma was hidden somewhere when the Wizard accomplished his coup d'état.'

'Inane. What reason could that mad potentate possibly have for allowing a potential rival to survive?'

'I don't know.' The Lion felt out of his depth when talking political strategy, especially if the discussion became heated. 'I heard someone posit that if the Wizard were ever brought on charges for her murder, he'd be able to pull her out of hiding and prove his innocence. Other than that, I have no earthly idea.'

'I can see that.' She rolled over on her side and looked at him without blinking. He felt he had never been scrutinized up close so intimately, and it took every scrap of willpower not to flinch at her velvety appraisal. 'You are a naïf who has traveled widely. I can tell by how you speak. It takes a certain kind of independent spirit to remain aloof when one has gotten around.'

'Independent spirit is a polite way to put it. I prefer to think of it as a character flaw.'

She laughed a little and her tail lashed against the stone beneath her.

He asked her, 'Why did the Ghullim allow me to approach, when you clearly approve of your own independence?'

'You showed no sign of being a threat to our security.'

He had to acknowledge they had read him correctly, but still that seemed an incomplete answer. 'Are you looking for something from me? News about the Emerald City, say? It is some years since I was in Shiz, where EC goings-on were always the hot topic.' He did not add, *And I left in disgrace*, but he imagined Muhlama H'aekeem was smart enough to guess his shortcomings.

'We have a network of informers, should we need a key piece of classified information. Anyway, it was I who gave the signal to let you in.' She rolled onto her back so he could see the bits of torn autumn leaf, red maple and lavender pearlfruit, caught in the hot white-gold of her under-trunk fur, spangling it like jewels, from her neck to her loins.

'But why?' He found he had to lower his volume or he was afraid his voice might break.

'Diversion,' she said. 'Do you mind?'

'How could I mind?' he replied. 'I was going nowhere special, so I could hardly be diverted.'

'I mean diversion for us. For me. A distraction from the daily efforts of our military readiness. A distraction from the threat of becoming the Chieftess, which is an obligation I have no wish to accept.'

'Can't you simply refuse?'

'Refuse your duty to your father? To the tribe he governs?' She let her tongue hang out of the side of her mouth, playing corpse. 'Only in death. Have you no concept of fathers?'

'No,' he admitted. 'Mine never remembered to come round.'

'Lucky beast.'

'Him or me?'

She turned her head toward him; her chest was still exposed in the sunlight. It was all he could do to keep his eyes trained on her eyes. 'If you have never enjoyed the paternal correction as administered by your own father and master, how will you qualify to be a father when it's your turn?'

'I didn't know I would need to supply qualifications to become a father.'

Again, she laughed. 'I suppose there is really only one application procedure,' she admitted. 'Touché. But in actual fact – what is your name? – I signaled you should be brought into the circle so that the subject might be changed. I was arguing with Uyodor H'aekeem about matters of state. Our words were sharp, and I didn't want to lose my temper. In general it isn't considered seemly among the Ghullim, and for a chieftain's daughter to discredit her father's position by second-guessing him – well, it isn't done.'

'You could just walk away, couldn't you?'

'I can be rude to you, but not to Uyodor H'aekeem.' Her tone remaining precisely neutral, she neither mocked her father's name nor celebrated it. 'Or did you mean I might strike out on my own?'

'Some do. I did, of necessity.'

'I knew I liked the look of you, at least a little. You have a silly swagger about you that is entirely unconvincing. Anyone brave enough to sashay through our territory like that is either a one-off nutter or an ally worth cultivating.'

'I may be neither,' he said, and wanted to add, *or I may be something else again*. He tried to focus on her without blinking, though his tear ducts tended to empty at inopportune moments.

She leaped to her feet as if she had caught wind of salacious thoughts. 'I'm too full of energy, I can't sit still for long,' she said to him. 'I don't want you to leave yet, for I have a lot to accomplish while you're here, but I have to run, run my limbs to exhaustion, or I will claw myself to death.'

'Highly strung, are we.'

She bared her teeth at him. He went on more neutrally, 'Are you permitting me to stay or prohibiting me from leaving?'

She didn't answer but went leaping down off the ledge, a wave of golden coins pulsing through the scatter of falling leaves.

He did not feel he wanted to push his luck.

The tree elves came out from behind their pot. He had forgotten about them.

'*She's* in a lather,' said Twigg.

'Never seen her quite like that,' said Stemm.

'Have we heard something we ought not hear?' said Twigg.

'She's too smart for that; she will have known we

were quivering back here like mice,' replied Stemm. 'But nobody trusts what we say anyway, so who cares?'

'Is it like that?' asked Brrr. 'Is Uyodor H'aekeem so driven? So unyielding? Would he care that much if his oldest daughter renounced her obligations?'

'And do what?' asked Twigg. 'Run a nursery school for malformed forest creatures? It's inconceivable. Ivory Tigers live to thrive, and they thrive through keen military readiness. She can have no other notion for herself. It's not allowed.'

'She's touched in the head,' said Stemm. 'Of course, don't listen to me, I'm a dolt-bolt, what do I know?'

'Well, I know what they think,' said Twigg. 'It's all *honor* and *tradition* and *how things are done.* And how they've been done for the past twenty chieftainships. Their elegant history of independence weighs on them, their own style of yoke. Slaves to themselves. *Do as well as we have always done! Don't be the weak link in the chain of our ongoing history.* What a lump of cold congealed pottage it all is, at least to me.'

'Shall I leave or shall I stay?' It seemed demeaning to ask advice of tree elves, but Brrr was caught in indecision.

'Makes no difference to us. Stay, enjoy our cooking. Leave without permission, and we have Lion stew on the menu for the evening. Your choice. It's a free woods.'

So Brrr allowed himself to stay and be courted by Piyanta and Zibria again, though they seemed less appealing now that he'd met Muhlama. In time he asked to take a nap, and he sent them off giggling and blushing back to their enclave.

3

Was he a guest of the Ghullim or a prisoner? He couldn't answer the question for himself assuredly. If a guest, eventually he'd have to leave. If a prisoner, he supposed he ought to protest his incarceration. Still, what kind of incarceration was this? Exercise, the morning run, and rock-scramble with Muhlama and her companions. Hardly a punishment.

Brrr relaxed; what else could he do? He enjoyed the meals, sometimes cooked by the tree elves, sometimes caught and served bloody raw by the Ivory Tiger hunters. (He'd abandoned vegetarianism when he'd arrived in Shiz, though he preferred the human custom of cooking the meat.) He took part in games of hide-and-seek at which he was always *it*, because he, alone among the Cats, couldn't scale the bark of a tree nor hide in the foliage of its canopy. Even emaciated with hunger, he weighed twice what an adult male Ivory Tiger weighed.

Afternoons – a Lion's laziest time – he dozed a short distance away from where Uyodor H'aekeem held court. Muhlama disappeared. He wondered whether she was conducting her ablutions, or napping in a private boudoir, or – he tried not to visualize this – pursuing a dalliance with some other creature. It was none of his business. And he would never know: in her regal demeanor, she shone, and deflected close scrutiny, too, like a shellac.

Still, the idea burned him and teased him a little.

He had never expected to appeal to anyone. He didn't much appeal to himself. He conceded the obvious: Perhaps he was being kept around as a spot of comic interest, like the dotty maiden aunt trotted out into the family parlor to amuse the neighbors and ensure that the conversation remained innocent and droll. But so what? He was growing used to Muhlama's manner. Her high style and her higher disdain, which sometimes flowered into impatience.

Brrr and Muhlama disagreed from time to time, and she even lashed out at him, but he took no offense. Disapproval was better than invisibility.

He'd been with the Ghullim a month, or even two, when the equilibrium was shattered. One night, after a feast of braised loin of warthog served with mushrooms, Uyodor H'aekeem awoke with a start. He claimed he had been snared in a bad dream. (It seemed that Ivory Tigers rarely dreamed, but when they did, it was a bad sign.) The truth was, though, that the raw terrain was being washed with high winds and cracking branches. The chief had probably been startled by the fall of a tree nearby.

Dreams were always warnings. But what did it mean? Unfamiliar with the conventions of dream, Uyodor called Brrr to his side.

'The dream had human men in it,' said the Ivory Tiger, pacing back and forth in the teeth of the dry gale. 'You've lived in the world of men, you say. Tell me how I should interpret the dream. Tell me why I have had it now.'

'The storm unsettled you,' said Brrr. 'With your sharp ear, you heard a cry of alarm from some pitiless creature hurled through the high winds. Give it no mind.'

'It was a dream,' Uyodor insisted. 'Where did it come from?'

'Perhaps the mushrooms were off?' But this was too glib. Uyodor glared and repeated what he could of his murky midnight vision. It was less clear than ever; it had dangerous men in it. Cats, Brrr thought, could have no more revealing dreams than socks or mustard could.

But he didn't care to make things up. 'Have you considered perhaps dismissing your chefs?'

'Are you proposing poison?'

'Heavens! No.' Brrr wanted no more blood on his paws, not even the thin silly blood of tree elves. 'Perhaps your palate needs a change – your indigestion a result of a kind of curiosity for something new . . .'

The wind snatched at one of the golden veils and flew it away.

'Perhaps you need to move camp,' said Brrr. 'Maybe the dream was calling a warning to pack up and leave here before a disaster stronger than a storm should strike.'

This was more like it. The chief retired to spend the rest of the night sleepless, and Brrr crawled back into the nook he'd been designated, a cleft under a protruding slab of pinkish granite. A moon was up and the skies were clear, and Brrr could see that the tree elves had climbed into their iron pots to keep from being blown away.

At dawn Uyodor H'aekeem convened a council of elders. He gave out his orders on the legitimacy of the Lion's advice. They would retreat to a new campsite at once, cull food from fresher sources, avoid some disaster that must be coming their way at the place they were about to abandon.

His tribe reacted with the usual politesse and immediacy. Everyone except Muhlama, who without comment disappeared into the forest.

Brrr went to the cooking station to find out what to think about all this.

'Uyodor H'aekeem, the brave Chief of the Ghullim! This is a rare instance of superstition, for him,' Twigg observed. 'He prides himself on being above that kind of thing.'

'This lot stays put until there's a reason to move,' agreed Stemm. 'But, Twigg, it's not your job to judge how Uyodor H'aekeem makes his decisions. Some leaders do it with entrails, some with tea leaves, some with the knucklebones of pigs. He does it with dreams of storms, or storms of dreams. Same difference.'

'Do the Ghullim move often?' asked Brrr.

'We lose track,' said the tree elves simultaneously. 'One forest glade is the same as any other to us,' continued Stemm. 'We're doomed to servitude our lives long, so we take no interest in our surroundings.'

'Why don't you just leave?' asked Brrr. 'You aren't shackled in any way that I can see, and half the time no one is paying any attention to you.'

They seemed offended at that. 'Really!' said Twigg. 'You don't know much, do you, Brrr? They'd be lost without us, lost. None of them have opposable thumbs. How could they possibly do a roasted leg of forest goat with a side of ivory ferns and a saltberry pudding? I mean, really!'

'Besides,' said Stemm, 'where would we go? It's not as if there are dozens of tree-elf colonies sprouting up all over the place like, like ... some sort of problem in forest population control.'

'We go where we're told,' concluded Twigg, 'and really I imagine, Brrr, so will you. Haven't you learned anything about the sacred performance of your duties? You'll come along with us. Unless our employers decide that your presence drew the storm from the sky and the dream upon the Chief. In that case you will need to be sacrificed, bled, roasted, sliced, and served on a leaf of buttercup lettuce.'

'With marinated shallots,' said Stemm, rubbing his hands.

'No, that's so high summer. Let's go autumnal. Grocer's gourd stuffed with minced hazelnut in a chanterelle reduction and a wild rice pasticcio.'

'Will you stop?' said Brrr. 'I'm not going anywhere. I mean into any cooking pans, thank you very much. And you're lucky I was around to save you from the same fate.'

'We should have let ourselves be blown to kingdom come when we still had a chance.'

While the Ghullim began to break camp, Muhlama seemed stalled in a state of high dudgeon, huffing and hissing at anyone who came near. Brrr kept his distance, too. He saw that the tree elves were the ones who scampered aloft and untied the gauzy curtains from their boughs, and stacked the cooking utensils in wooden crates, and rolled up Uyodor's patterned carpet, and collected scraps and bits and souvenirs. What the Ivory Tigers provided the elves, he guessed, was some sort of security, but the elves did all the work.

Most of it, that is. A ramshackle old cart came out of storage from somewhere, and Brrr was asked to push. Twigg and Stemm would sit up top and steer.

So Brrr set his shoulder against the sloping rear panel of a human cart. This required his head to cock at an angle, and he hoped to find Muhlama looking at him with a measure of gratitude. He was earning his way, see, just like the tree elves. She didn't favor him with the pleasure of a glance, though. He worked without reward or even much assistance.

Muhlama's tone was saturated with rancor. 'Where are we going? The moon? Uyodor, do you intend to march us all the way up the slopes of the Scalps? Just how big was that dream anyway? I'm not going another step!' She seemed to have forgotten her requirement of obeisance toward her father. 'Or was this so-called dream just a ruse? Had you been planning on relocating us to the highlands anyway, and forgot to tell us? Are you mincelings just going to tramp along without saying a word?'

She had to spit in disgust, which was an elegant thing and, Brrr thought, had a certain sort of sweet sexiness to it. Though his neck and shoulders were aching.

Perhaps she wore her father down, for he selected

a new campground before dusk. Brrr found it impossible to estimate how far they had gone, but it couldn't have been five or six miles, not with the cart bumping and scraping over every inch. The downed limbs, the mess of storm. In one place an entire pool had been emptied of its water; turtles were emerging from the mud and blinking at the novelty of air.

'That's a pretty talented storm system,' observed Brrr, as conversationally as he could. Trying to lighten the mood. Muhlama paid him no mind and addressed her father, who remained confirmed about his premonitions because they had been illustrated with wind damage.

'Is this our final lodging?' she said. 'Or is this just nighty-night? You get spooked by another hurricane, and tomorrow will we continue on toward the Glikkus or the over-harrowed Corn Basket? Make our home in domesticated fields like so many cowering field mice?'

His eyes flashed, but she was his daughter and he wouldn't upbraid her in public. She would rule the Ghullim sooner or later. He couldn't be seen to erode her authority even as she questioned his.

Brrr watched. The strange flexing arrangement that fathers exert over their children. It awed him.

He also saw that the tree elves were being directed to unpack the cart, so perhaps this really was the chosen camp for the next indefinite period. If they were marching again tomorrow, the elves wouldn't be

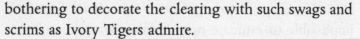

bothering to decorate the clearing with such swags and scrims as Ivory Tigers admire.

While the hunters skulked off to hunt down a supper, which Brrr supposed drearily would be served without anything by way of sauces or savories, he managed to straighten out the kinks in his shoulders enough to hobble up to Muhlama and look her up and down.

'What are you giving me the once-over for?' she snarled.

'You've spent an awful lot of time being furious today.'

'So what.'

'So' – (here it came) – 'I can't help noticing fury becomes you.'

She backed up several steps; her tail snapped. 'You – you *pack Lion*! You menial . . . beast! How dare you! You have some nerve!'

'I have little nerve,' he replied. 'But after my work on behalf of your tribe, I'm too tired to lie. Why shouldn't I tell you that you are more provocative than ever when you're so vexed?'

'You – you and your deciphering some dream of the chief's – making us move camp by your auguries.'

'Oh, stow it,' he said, flumping down in some leaves. 'I'm the only one who talks to you. I might as well talk to you honestly.'

He knew there was a sting of truth in his words. She became frozen with reserve, though her tail couldn't stop itself from switching back and forth.

He pressed his advantage. 'Why didn't you want to leave? Are you just angry at your father for his unilateral dictates? If what everyone says is true, those powers will be yours one day.'

'I don't want to rule. Haven't you sussed that out yet?'

'Why not? Everyone will look up to you, take you seriously.'

'Are you an aberration to your species?' she cried. 'Cats don't look for *approval*!'

He didn't reply. Her words were cutting, but she hadn't convinced him of anything yet, except that he could be cut by words. And he already knew that.

'I have no use for this guarded life, this wreath of security around us all the time, this . . . myopic *servitude* to ourselves,' she said more slowly. 'I have other ambitions than to be the indentured princess of an autocratic father.'

'Then why don't you just leave?' he asked. 'You are sleek enough. You could outrun any number of hunters.'

'And I'd end up like you, wandering aimlessly through the woods?'

'Things could be worse. As it seems you know. Why *don't* you leave?'

'Because it would break his heart,' she replied, voice lower still. 'It's all he lives for. Not me, not them, but for the inebriation of being ruler, and passing it on. Fathers want one single thing: that their power will outlive them. It's his only gift to me, after all.'

He wasn't sure if he believed her rationale. Nonetheless, he believed her distress. She wasn't just playing at being fussed.

'What is it *you* want?' he said again, more privately, hoping that she would surprise him with intimacy. 'Are the tree elves right? Did you have some lover-Cat in the near vicinity, and is that why you balked so at leaving?'

'Did they say that?' Her head whipped around so fast he could only see the circumference of the circle described by the tips of her erect ears. He was afraid she would lunge off and slaughter the elves.

'No,' he quickly replied, rising. 'I was fooling. It was my own thought, actually. Though I hope I was wrong.'

'You are so wrong at everything that if you ever started being right . . .' But she couldn't finish her thought. She glared at him with perhaps the coldest look ever, but he imagined he saw a fringe of possibility flaring.

'You hope you are wrong,' she repeated. She took a step back, still looking at him. It was as if she were seeing him for the first time. He wished he'd had time to comb his mane. But in all his disarray, he preened for her anyway, tossed his head with a jerk at the neck. That usually got the human crowd, but good. She didn't flinch. She moved an inch closer.

'Brrr,' she said. 'Oh, Brrr. I've been rather a selfish thing today. You doing all this work, and just to get my attention. Now I see it. Now I see.'

'I like to work,' he lied.

'And they took advantage of you. That's like them, you know. My *kin*. They make servants of guests. You realize of course that three Ivory Tigers could have pulled that cart easily enough from the front, if the elves had harnessed them into the leathers. But no, they all took advantage of your brute strength.'

He liked the way she said *brute strength*, even though his muscles were so tired that his back haunches were trembling. He hoped he was standing at such an angle that she couldn't see. From some perspectives he actually didn't look all that ineffectual, he guessed. He hoped.

'It was an honor to help,' he said again.

'Are you all right?' she said. 'You look ill.'

'I'm fine,' he said. 'It would be good to lie down and rest a bit. It has been a long day.'

'We'll go for a walk,' she said. She turned and snarled at the nearby sentries, 'We are *going* for a *walk*. Got it?'

He couldn't tell why they stood back and let her pass unrestrained. Perhaps they realized she was still spitting mad. Perhaps they saw that Brrr was calming her.

Muhlama led the way. She had a seriously keen sense of smell and followed a track through sweeping clusters of vine until, after a few minutes, she had reached the edge of a pool. Here she laid herself down, reclining her hindquarters fully, her chest torquing into an elegant curve, so her head reared back upon her neck. Nacreous shadow behind her, blue and lavender and mauve. Her eyes lowered. Her ears lowered. 'There is no one trailing us,' she said. 'I would hear them if they were.'

He sat down close. Not too close. Close enough that he could feel the heat from her pelt. Musk of a rare sort; he'd never apprehended such a naked barb of invitation. A scorched-pecan, apricoty, humid sort of appeal.

'You are so royal, you can bring on estrus at will?' A bold thing to say and would have been crude said to anyone but a princess; and indeed he meant it as a compliment.

'I *am* talented,' she replied, lifting her tail another parabolic sweep higher, 'but you give me too much credit.'

They didn't speak for a while, as the evening birds exchanged their bulletins, as the bullfrogs dove into the water out of a surfeit of modesty. A hummingbird, a whipping blossom, came along and perched on

Muhlama's ear, until it realized its mistake and fled.

'You can't be so kind to me,' said Brrr after a while. 'It isn't possible. No one ever has. I don't fit in.'

'It's I who don't fit,' she said, 'I with my strong-minded ways, my temper, my appetite to leave the very home that I am tethered to. I look a princess, I know; but I am slave here, no less than the tree elves, no less than you are. I don't belong.'

She angled her rump, and the movement of her tail changed. It became the pendulum on a metronome, counting the slow moments until she pushed her pelvis higher and threw her head back, nipping at Brrr's throat as he covered her beautiful coat with his own.

When he could think in words – was it then, was it later, he didn't know – it was simply this: Now I fit in.

His reverie was delicious. Eyes closed. He was partly conscious of the floating strings of the world, its selvages restitching themselves into a prettier apprehension. Some might call it afterglow. For Brrr it was as if a new appetite was just beginning to stir out of his dreamy slumber. But it was interrupted by hissing alarums. He hardly knew what was closing in on him until it was over and done with.

The discovery in flagrante by Ivory Tiger scouts. The forced return to the camp. The accusation of Uyodor, his recitation of Brrr's offenses against the noble line of the Ghullim camp. Was this an attempt to thwart Uyodor's regime? Was Brrr a stooge of the Wizard of Oz, working his way in here, seducing the daughter of the chieftain of the Ghullim?

'There was no seduction, sir!' Brrr was aghast. He glared at Muhlama, looking for testimony. Muhlama neither concurred with her father nor protested his accusations. She couldn't speak. For anger, for regret? Then he saw what they had seen already. She had begun to bleed. The iron stench of it, a wound too large to hide. A rivulet of orangish blood that wouldn't stop.

It seemed he hadn't quite fit in, but she'd let him try anyway.

With a cold resolve, she hectored him, too. 'Go. Don't you see? Don't you get it? Go, before they have your head on a trophy backboard. You've done quite enough.'

Perhaps because she was still Uyodor's daughter, they let him go. Though Uyodor declared, as Brrr backed away, 'You are no creature of the wilderness, Lion; you do not belong here. Should we come across you again, or should our allies, you are fair game for the predator. A marked beast. You have ten minutes before we enact our promise to seek vengeance.'

So he pelted away, but ever after he wondered why. Was it just to preserve his own life? His life had a tinny cast to it, an artificial quality, hardly worth preserving. Or had he left not so much to save his own skin as to avoid having to see Muhlama's life bleed out of hers?

In any case, he was gone. Not for the first time, nor the last: an ignoble retreat from a fray that had grown too hot for him.

Back into the wild, back into woods, back into exile. And this time he would endure a loneliness made more cutting by the recent experience of consanguinity. Or call it love, if you must.

Exiled, even unto himself, until and unless something came along to redeem him.

What came along some time later – days, or was it weeks? – near where the Wend Fallows petered out into the Corn Basket, was that toothsome morsel known as Dorothy. Another rare and delicate human, a girl this time, improbably making her way along the stretch of Yellow Brick Road that originated in central Munchkinland.

4

It was an accident of the light, nothing more, that caused the little girl and her pair of noodnik companions to leap in terror at the sight of him. Or had it been too long since his most recent wash-and-set? In any case, he steeled himself for the inevitable interview, and wondered how much of his sorry history he could gloss over. Maybe they had some provisions to share.

Dorothy, though, was not riven with wild curiosity. She seemed to take his bowdlerized biography at face value. She asked no probing questions. She just smoothed the edges of her apron and consoled her quivering little pup. 'Oh, Toto, have you ever *imagined* a Cat so big in your wildest nightmares? I hope you don't lose your lunch.' She nuzzled her face against her dog's in a way that might cause some citizens of Oz to question her sanity.

Still, he found to his surprise that he felt some small measure of sympathy for Dorothy. He was no longer inclined to consider human beings warmly, but maybe he was able to make an exception because she was so clearly a foreigner. Brrr imagined she was an orphan like himself, as humans didn't usually leave their young to wander the high road alone. And no half-decent parent of any species would hire a Scarecrow and a Tin Woodman as chaperones and *aides-de-guerre*.

'Come with us,' said the girl. 'We're headed for the Emerald City.'

Propitious words.

One doesn't know, necessarily, when one meets the trip-action person in one's life. A good teacher, a flirt behind the dry-goods counter, a petty thief wielding a knife. Any one of a thousand chance encounters might be the chance of a lifetime. Or a deathtime. A lost girl in a blue gingham skirt and a white pinafore hardly seemed a likely ambassador to a rosier future: still, stranger things had happened.

He considered joining them. What else did he have scheduled? He couldn't risk running into the Ghullim again. Neither the nabobs of Shiz, nor the Bears nor the Ozmists, nor the Glikkuns with their dirks, nor any affectionate soldier boys astray in the Great Gillikin Forest.

It seemed there was nothing in the wild for him; it was civilization itself that must be tamed. Perhaps this was his lucky break. It sure was about time.

And who better to serve as his escort back into society but this Dorothy? She possessed a writ of safe passage from Lady Glinda, who had met the foreign girl when investigating the sudden death of Nessarose, the most recent Eminent Thropp and governor of Munchkinland. It took Brrr several weeks to pry the whole story out of Dorothy, about the tornado, the plummeting house, the glittering shoes. By then he deduced that Glinda was moving the girl out of harm's way, because Munchkinland was up for grabs now that its governor was dead. Would Nessarose's sister, Elphaba, come back to Colwen Grounds and rule the seceded nation?

Every step away from Munchkinland would be a

step away from the Wicked Witch of the West, Brrr figured. Accurately or not, his name had been linked to her before; he wanted no reunion, thank you very much.

And once in the Emerald City – well, there was the famously reclusive Wizard of Oz to meet! The WOO! If Lady Glinda's offices were as well connected as she had attested to Dorothy.

'Oh, do join us. Lady Glinda is so good,' said Dorothy. 'I'm sure the Wizard will honor her request and see us. After I've come all this way – and through that dreadful storm, no less. A thousand miles from any outhouse. I won't tell you what I had to do while aloft; it was revolting.'

Laboriously Brrr figured the dates backward and concluded that the great twister carrying Dorothy to Oz was the same storm that had given Uyodor H'aekeem nightmares and begun the sequence of events leading to Brrr's expulsion from the Ghullim. He spent a few moments over a dark fantasy of revenge against Dorothy. But she hadn't orchestrated that storm into being; she was a victim of fate as much as he was. So he let it go.

'I'll come with you,' he told Dorothy and the others.

At this point – the moment when Brrr stepped into the limelight of history – he was perhaps twenty, though of course as a Lion that meant he was middle-aged. Twenty, and he'd conducted his sordid affairs and peccadilloes only in Gillikin and Munchkinland. But he'd spent his life within earshot of Oz's great capital city, which pulsed with so much power it was almost a nation unto itself – a state on its own. Perhaps what was scandalous elsewhere, in hidebound provincial centers like Shiz, would seem penny-candy stuff in a capital city. Perhaps the EC was large enough, urbane enough, to consider Brrr's trials and shames not only incidental but unremarkable.

He had little to lose now. If Dorothy's stamp of approval from Lady Glinda proved genuine, he might be traveling with diplomatic immunity. After all, Dorothy had shown him a writ on a scroll, though he couldn't read it well enough to parse its curlicued grandiosity.

The Kiss of Lady Glinda, it was called: a passport requiring its bearer safe passage to the Emerald City under penalty of prosecution to the fullest extent of the law, et cetera, et cetera.

It was signed with a flourish and a little scribble of a heart with a smile inside it, which looked to Brrr like a picture of an extracted tooth delighted to be liberated from some foul mouth.

A good deal of what happened next – the Matter of Dorothy – was a story he didn't choose to dwell upon. How déclassé, to arrive with a crippled human decked out with tin prophylactics and with a

Scarecrow, sweet enough but clueless as to his own origins – though who wasn't? Brrr liked Dorothy, though. One evening he found himself imagining her as Jemmsy in a dress and pigtails, which seemed too weird, if fun, so he steered his attentions elsewhere.

The Emerald City lifted itself onto the horizon, more pomp and glory than Brrr had imagined possible. Emerald overdrive. Even the loo paper was green, which Brrr considered a sort of design error. But *The Kiss of Glinda* worked its magic, as it were. The magnificent and dreadful Wizard of Oz agreed to meet them, though in separate interviews. Brrr's was last, and he was expecting a great Head, like the one that had shown itself to Dorothy, but perhaps the wine had been more toxic than he'd realized, for all he could see was light shining from the throne.

Steeling himself, Brrr remembered the Ozmists, and thought: *Barter!* He would negotiate for some government sinecure in exchange for having escorted this foreign dignitary to the palace. 'I have a request of you,' he began, 'O great-and-powerful-and-all-knowing Oz.'

'Courage,' said the Wizard.

'No, not courage,' said the Lion. 'I mean, well, courage *would* be nice. But I was thinking of something more in the line of a job.'

'I will give you what you most need,' said the

Wizard, 'if you bring down the Wicked Witch of the West.'

'Bring her down? I had hoped she wouldn't even come up,' murmured Brrr. The Wizard was better at bartering than he was.

Later, Brrr said to his new companions, 'I'm all for engaging in a little cut-and-run action here. Why should we do the Wizard's dirty work? He has his own military presence. The EC is crawling with soldiers.'

Some of those middle-aged military personnel might once have known Jemmsy. But Brrr let that thought pass.

'Yes,' said Nick Chopper, the Tin Woodman. 'And any one of those soldiers could take you into custody for refusing the request of the Wizard.'

'He didn't *order* us out to the West,' said Brrr. 'We're volunteering. Aren't we? Aren't we?'

They looked at him.

'We're not drafted against our will, surely.'

'De facto, we are,' said the Scarecrow. 'It's only our having a commission from the Throne of Oz that keeps those soldiers from picking you up, anyway. The Animal Adverse laws haven't been lifted, Pussycat. You don't see many Animals in the streets of this fair city, do you?'

'Besides,' said Dorothy, 'I want to go home. I'm sick of this place. Not of you, dear friends, never of you. But all this rigamarole, all this kowtowing. It's exhausting. Let's just consider this little military action something we have to go through. In any event, *I'm* going, on my own if I have to.'

'You'd kill a witch, just like that, at someone's suggestion?' asked the Tin Woodman. 'How unfeeling. You're a monster.'

'I didn't say I was going to kill her,' said Dorothy. 'Perhaps we can make a private arrangement with her. Broker a peace deal, a compromise of some sort. Who knows. In any event, my house did sort of smush her sister, and I haven't had a chance to deal with the trauma of that, what with all the festivities and so on. I mean, I need some closure here.'

The Wizard of Oz, it seemed, had them all by the short hairs. So against his better judgment, Brrr signed on to the mission. Maybe Dorothy's preternatural innocence would call good luck upon them, and he could be a partial beneficiary. And the Wizard *had* promised Brrr a suitable reward should the mission succeed.

Now, was it forward to victory? Or was it out of the frying pan into the fire? The stakes were never higher. Whatever happened, it would be impossible to retire anonymously after all this. Perhaps Brrr should have roared that tiny little Toto into an early grave and gotten out while he could.

The trip to the West was taxing in every sense. Eventually the Witch's Winged Monkeys showed up to give them a lift up the steepest of the slopes of Knobblehead Pike to the Witch's castle, known as Kiamo Ko. The Tin Man and the Scarecrow were left below, but the Lion and Dorothy and Toto were deposited in the courtyard to meet the Witch and her little entourage: the other monkeys, that lad named Liir, and the old Nanny whom Yackle, it seemed, had met all those years earlier.

Liir was the least of creatures on the scene, a scrambling *aide-de-sorcière* as the Lion remembered. Fumbling, earnest: a knockabout kid who looked as if he could fall out a tower window without much surprise. The Lion had paid little attention to him: Who knew that Liir's whereabouts would come to intrigue the high and mighty in the Emerald City one day?

And of the so-called Witch, what could Brrr now recall? His whole life had seemed to lead up to this fatal event: the instruction to murder the Wicked Witch of the West. So you would think he'd have a better grasp of that Elphaba Thropp.

Yet he had only seen her the once, really, and there she remained, stamped in his mind's eye in a kind of bas-relief, like a figure on a commemorative medal. If she really was a Witch, beneath all that witchy drag, she was an erratic one. Her body made a zigzaggy shape at the top of those castle steps, like a *W* fallen on its side. She was all angles, contorted like a cripple, twisted with rage and fear, but not with paralysis. She was anything but paralyzed.

'You!' she'd cried at him. Had she recognized him as the Lion cub in the laboratory back at Shiz? He didn't know. He hadn't the temerity to ask for clarification. 'You!' she'd cried again, and this time he quailed more deeply, thinking she meant *You traitor! How can you, a Lion, come against me, when I have fought for your weal since before you were born!*

He wanted to reply, *Show me some respect. Some of your detractors have tarred me as your familiar.* And he would have said that, and more. If he only had the nerve.

But her gaze had turned to Dorothy, and Elphaba had whipped down those steps like an oversize, bewitched eggbeater whirling on its own. What happened next, the famous dissolution of the Witch, had happened offstage, as the flying monkeys had crowded Brrr and the Witch's help-boy, Liir, into a larder and locked the door. By the time Brrr had broken the door off its hinges, the damage was done. The Witch was gone. And Brrr's reputation would be tarnished forever by dint of his presence at the castle.

Guilt by association – or a hero by popular clamor, depending on which political hack was retailing the events.

One way or the other, the Witch was gone.

After a couple of skirmishes with barbaric tribes of

the Vinkus, the Lion and Dorothy – together with young Liir, and soon reunited with Nick Chopper and the Scarecrow – made their way overland back to the Emerald City. Their hopes were high but soon daunted. By an accident of the sort one might see on the stage, Dorothy's little yapper, Toto, took a grip on a closet curtain and gave a tug. Only useful thing the fool animal ever did. The Wizard was revealed as a mere mortal, and a bit of a charlatan at that. As clever with his hands – all those tiktok inventions, those terrifying images he projected – as he was with his diktats and fiats and fatwahs. Oh my.

In the confusion that followed, the Emerald City Irregulars were showered with junk. Tchotchkes you could pick up at a five-and-farthing store.

As the Wizard rummaged through a drawer, he spoke over his shoulder. 'My research associates are thorough when they need to prepare the case for honorifics. You, my friend, are known as the Cowardly Lion – oh, don't be bashful! Your history precedes you! I shall give you just what you deserve: a token of esteem suitable for wearing at Court.' He came up with a tin medal on a sash of green and gold. It wasn't suitable for wearing to the church rummage sale, unless you intended to dump it in the hand-me-down box. The sash was stained with creepy beige spots (don't want to know what *that* was) and the medal said COURAGE! It had been so clumsily produced that the first three letters were afflicted with bloat. The only legible part read RAGE!

'Thank you, your Ozness,' said Brrr, hoping it was a joke, hoping if he played along he'd end up happy. The WOO placed the medal around his neck. Had Jemmsy's medal for courage been as cheaply manufactured, as odious? Brrr lifted the medal to sniff it, to bring back Jemmsy. A pin mounted on the back cut the softer part of the pad of his paw.

'I can't accept this—' he began to say, but the Wizard had moved on to address Dorothy, and the little girl was beaming in such high hopes of an exit visa from Oz that the Lion didn't have the nerve to interrupt.

Still, as they were dismissed and ushered away, Brrr continued to imagine that he might somehow parry the dubious honor into a rehabilitation, perhaps even a position in the Wizard's court. He was mistaken, though. His timing couldn't have been worse. The Wizard's long reign had come to an end at last. Oscar Zoroaster Diggs, the great and powerful WOO, abdicated the throne and departed the Emerald City by a hot-air balloon, said to be the way he had arrived four decades earlier. Why, why leave now, when his adversary, the Wicked Witch, was finally done for? No one was certain. Perhaps the crafty old geezer could hear that palace knives were being sharpened for a use more sinister than the carving of rump roast.

'Cowardly Lion,' said Dorothy to him, snapping

her fingers in his face to get his attention. 'With any luck my visit is drawing to a close, and I need to talk to you before I go.'

He roused himself from the lethargy of resentment. Dorothy shut the door to the chamber of the shabby guesthouse in which he was lodged. There was no direct light, given that to the north a government bureau loomed six stories above them. 'Sadly in need of redecoration,' said Dorothy, smoothing her skirt over her behind and sitting down on the chenille bedspread, 'but nothing compared to what Auntie Em and Uncle Henry are faced with, given that I set out from home bringing the whole house with me.'

'Are you making the rounds, dispensing last little bromides? You can save your breath.'

'Don't be like that. When the time comes for me to leave, I know you won't want to make a public fuss over me. So I've come to say something in private.'

Brrr hadn't actually planned to attend Dorothy's valedictory session. He just nodded at her: Go on.

'I love your pals, you know; the Scarecrow and the Woodman. But I love them for their quaintness, while I love you for the animal in you.'

In most Animal circles referring to one's animal instinct would be considered a ferocious insult. But Brrr thought it best not to challenge Dorothy to a duel at this stage. He'd probably lose.

'You see, I grew up on a farm. I had a little pet hen

once. She followed me around, in and out of the kitchen, into the farmyard. She couldn't speak, of course. We're talking Kansas, where free speech in general is not highly prized.'

'Is there a moral to this story?'

'One day she crossed the road. Do you know why the chicken crossed the road?'

'Is this a joke?'

Nothing was a joke to Dorothy. 'Because I was on the other side,' she finished. 'I was standing on one foot and singing a little song about, oh, I don't know what. And that brave little hen crossed the dangerous road to be with me.'

'What happened to her?'

'One Saturday night Uncle Henry wrung her neck and Auntie Em made chicken stew. I cried and cried but actually she tasted pretty good.'

Brrr shook his head. 'I'm not getting the point of this, Dorothy. I think you've been away from your own kind too long.'

'*That* is exactly my point!' she exclaimed. 'You see, I lost my parents, too. Auntie Em and Uncle Henry aren't even relatives. They wrote away to an orphanage in Independence, Missouri, requesting someone because Auntie Em needed some help around the house, what with her sciatica. I'm who they got.' She chewed the end of one pigtail. 'Perhaps they regret it now, or maybe not. Hard to say.'

'Dorothy,' said Brrr, 'I was about to take a nap.'

'Sorry. The point is: You and I are more alike than you think. And ornery as Auntie Em could be, and pigheaded as Uncle Henry is, they are my own family now, and I miss them and love them. I would cross the road for them, like my pet hen did for me. You must feel no different about your own family.'

'With all due respect, I have no family, Dorothy.'

She put her arms around him, which was an odd comfort.

'Take care of Liir,' she whispered. 'Okay? He has no family either. And he's a little . . . well, dim.'

'I don't have any obligations to that boy.' Brrr was all too aware how he had failed Jemmsy and Cubbins. Better that Liir should get on in his life without being shackled with a big burly Lion for a sidekick.

'For me?' she said. 'If the Witch was his mother, my word: it's my fault he's an orphan now, too. Like me and you both. I can't bring him home with me, and I daren't leave him alone. He needs someone, Brrr, and so do you.'

He pulled away from her, uncomfortable with this consultation. She sat with her hands folded in her lap, gravely. She was waiting for a promise. There was something eerie about her gentle manner and her steely patience. Winds would wear a cliff down to a stony strand before she would change her mind about the goodness of the world.

He had to love her for it. He kissed her furrily. He knew she was taking this as a promise to regard Liir as his own family, but he was just getting rid of her. He wasn't in a position to take care of a minor, not when he was so minor himself.

'Good-bye, Dorothy,' he said. 'I hope they learn to love you at home as much as we love you here.'

'Well,' said Dorothy, standing up, 'I'll tell them they just better.'

5

Within a few weeks of Dorothy's departure, Glinda formally took the Throne. Brrr was able to get an audience with her, and, after a little fawning and purring, he wheedled a title. Sir Brrr, Lord Low Plenipotentiary to the market environs of Traum. It was, as he thought and others joked, a cruel blow: about as undistinguished a peerage as it was possible to acquire. One could pick up higher honors going through the garbage. Lord Low Plenipotentiary was a title without an estate, a job without a salary, an honorific without a voting voice in the Council of Agreement, which Lady

Glinda had promised to reconvene after a lengthy hiatus.

And Traum? *Traum*, of all places? Lady Glinda was depositing him at the site of his public humiliation. Had she meant to rub his nose in it? Or in her giddy innocence did she hope to give him a chance to return as a conquering hero? He didn't know and he didn't bother to visit his district and find out. Let them get on without him.

He drank too much during the day, and he lost track of that agitated kid, Liir. When the Lion learned that the Scarecrow had been nominated to succeed Lady Glinda to the Throne – the Scarecrow elevated to be the Head of Oz, while the Lion groveled, a Lord Low Plenipotentiary! – well, he lost more acreage of guts to stomach acids.

Anhedonia, a doctor said. Fear of pleasure.

He almost bit the doctor, for the pleasure of it.

He might have survived the indignity if he'd had a circle of companions. Anything like a confessor, a crony.

But Dorothy was gone, disappeared perhaps the way Ozma Tippetarius had disappeared, too. The Scarecrow was busy with regal affairs and rarely met his public. (Some said he wasn't even the same Scarecrow, but an imposter. Brrr never got close enough again to venture an opinion on the matter.) And Nick Chopper was filled with the romance of labor rebellion, getting in bed with dubious sorts to hatch out schemes to organize the tiktok workers, the mechanized servants of Oz. Change was in the air, everyone said – change of every sort except spare change: not that kind. Times weren't better, they were just – different. Times were hard in a new way. You could be grateful for the novelty of it, but only up until teatime, when dried rye brisks and plowfoot jelly made their baleful appearance on the table. Unless you were Palace, of course.

He might have survived it if he had never learned to read. But what else was there to do but hang out in cafés frequented by the demimonde, sip stale tea or watered-down plonk in the Burntpork district, and scrutinize the cast-off newsfolds?

THE WORTHY SCARECROW HOLDS A PALACE RECEPTION.
Dateline: Emerald City

Peers of the realm, from the level of Minor Establisher and up, gathered in the glittering Ozma Arcade last night in one of the season's most exclusive soirées – See and Be Seen! Tizzy Splendthrift, society spy, reports on a very naughty party held last night in an undisclosed private residence in the tony district of Goldhaven, to which Oz's glitteramuses, the great and the good from as far up the

social pyramid as can be mounted, got up to
no good – and we do mean *up* . . .

Whipping the pages so hard they tore. The financial
columns and the editorial pages arguing about whether
Nick Chopper was well connected enough to bring the
Throne's attention to a proposed scheme of merit-
credits for the tiktok workforce . . . Whether it would
be any good for Oz . . . The social obligations, if any, of
rewarding clockwork for ticking on time . . . The
suffering of laborers and their families if a general
strike was called . . . NICK CHOPPER: BLEEDING HEART OR
BLOODY HEARTLESS?

Brrr didn't care. It was the parties he wasn't invited
to, the salons, the committee meetings dedicated to
raising funds to repaper the libraries in imperial Ozma
style, now that it was no longer forbidden to speak her
name . . . The drunken lunches of the newsmongers
who laughed at the excesses of the high and mighty!
He'd have been glad enough to rag on his former
friends, had he been invited to do so.

Then some journalist, writing under a *nom
d'espionnage*, published a column questioning the
correctness of the Palace's having awarded even so
much as a Low Plenipotentiaryship to a Lion who had
been, after all, a collaborationist. He'd worked at the
Wizard's bidding, hadn't he – when more respectable
Animals were imprisoned, or had fled into the outback?

A collaborationist. Working for the Wizard, who had done so much to oppress the Animals of Oz. When once Brrr had been tarred as the Witch's familiar, now he was a lackey of her enemy. He was a turncoat for all seasons. You couldn't win.

Perhaps, the argument went, if the Cowardly Lion were stripped of his honors, hardworking Animals would feel justified, at last, in returning to the cities and towns of Oz and entering the workforce again. Hadn't Brrr been known as a Cowardly Lion? If he were all that brave, he'd surrender his honors himself, voluntarily, for the symbolism of it. His apology to the nation.

Let him be rehabilitated as a common citizen and join the Animal workforce that Loyal Oz hoped would soon be returning from exile – those who hadn't been exterminated, that is. Bring back the Animals as a backup labor resource. Show the agitated millworkers they could be let go if they made trouble.

So off then, outa there, but good. Brrr tried not to think of the injustice of it, but of course the injustice greeted him daily. Was there any reason he should be so embattled other than the maliciousness of fate?

He didn't avoid the thought of Dorothy; he didn't need to. She evaporated out of Oz as successfully as the Witch herself had. One would have thought Dorothy had been brought from abroad for no other reason than to have her wet way with the Witch. But that was paranoia, wasn't it? Fuck Dorothy. In a manner of speaking.

And as for his promise to keep an eye on Liir – well, Liir had his own history to follow. He had disappeared into the crowds of the Emerald City. Just another urchin on the make, a feckless little whippet cast aside by the powerful. Let him dodge his own fate as best he might; he was not the Lion's cub, after all. Brrr had his own hide to protect.

Back to the wilds, once again, where the knowledge of his demotion by way of low promotion could prove less bitter, less public. He'd have to avoid the Ghullim, of course. If Muhlama H'aekeem had lived, she might be the Chieftainess now. And if the networking of the Ghullim was as keen as they boasted, they'd have heard that their runaway Lion had been marginalized by the indignity of petty honors. And tarred with the worst taunt of all. *Collaborationist.*

No, he'd avoid the Ghullim. Avoid them all. Avoid the whole damned mess of his whole damned life up to now.

6

After Dorothy.

Brrr entertained the notion that he might go back and take up again with that pride of tuft-chinned Lions in the western Madeleines. As far as he knew, he was the first Lion with a title. Maybe the pride lived far enough from the EC to have missed the curse of 'Collaborationist!' Maybe it would decide to be impressed. Reconsidering their early dismissal of him, they might conclude that they had been too provincial to recognize his merits first time around. Why not?

But these years on, the Lions had scattered. The outback of Gillikin hadn't proved hospitable to Animals, even to those who had never forsaken their natural habitats in the wild. From smaller Animals who still lingered, reluctant to give up the old neighborhood, Brrr learned that the tuft-chinned Lions had migrated east into Munchkinland. 'Though I'm told,' continued an opinionated Squirrel with a cleft palate, which made his words hard to grasp, 'that times have been no easier for the Animals in the Free State of Munchkinland than they are in Loyal Oz. The Great Drought is blind to national borders. Larger Animals have had to withdraw into less salubrious quarters.'

'Like?'

'The more hardscrabble reaches south of the Yellow Brick Road. Nest Hardings, Wend Hardings, and the ghost hamlets on the banks of Illswater.'

'Ghost hamlets.' Not Ozmists, for sure; they maintained their haunts in the Great Gillikin Forest. Or had the Cloud Swamp been affected by the drought, and had the ghosts migrated, too?

'I mean the old farming villages in southeast Munchkinland – the last sorry bit before Munchkinland peters out into the uncrossable desert. Those desolate places that even humans have no more use for. Or that humans abandoned once the Animals began to move in.'

'I'll head that way.'

'I'll come with,' said the Squirrel succulently.

'Not if you value your nuts. Forget about it.' Brrr was done with finding mates on the road.

He headed east, learning to nurse his grievances like so many fond memories. To take them out in his drowsy hours, in his dreams. To fasten upon them in the doldrums of insomnia. He remembered how the frowzy Miss Piarsody Scallop had tended to her mysterious ailments with all the devotion of a postulant. He dedicated the same zeal to his rash of insults, kept them raw by constant attention.

The death of Jemmsy. The taunts of the Bears. The dismissal by the Ozmists. The Traum Massacre. The lovely but brutal sex with Muhlama, and his subsequent exile from the Ghullim.

And then the taunts. *Coward. Witch's familiar.* 'Little Miss Sissy' in one popular musical parody that was all the rage the season he fled from Ampleton Quarters. *Lord Low Plenipotentiary*, for the love of Lurlina. Collaborationist.

A Lion, even a lily-livered one, can roam about an unfriendly landscape more easily than, say, a Badger or a slow-moving Cow. The Lion was shunned but not otherwise abused. He kept to himself. He could get little work in Munchkinland; farmers husbanded their farm chores zealously.

One night he fell asleep on the edge of a cornfield, and dreamed of a happier past. When he woke up to take a leak, he heard his own voice muttering in his ears. He had been talking to the rangy scarecrow set up to frighten predators. It was an odd thing, nothing like his erstwhile pal. Neither male nor female, Animal nor human, the creature had a woman's apron, a farmer's soft felt hat-for-chapel, an Ox's collar, and a cunningly arranged strap of sleigh bells. Its head was a gourd of some sort, softening in the back, and the seeds falling out of an abrasion in the vegetable skull were being nibbled by field mice. 'Get away from my man Jack!' roared the Lion, but when the mice scattered in terror, he had to weep. He'd come to this: lording it over dumb mice in drought-slackened fields. And talking to a dummy, the best he could claim as a friend.

He crossed the border from Gillikin into Munchkinland near the southern edge of the Madeleines. He wanted to steer wide of the Ghullim, so he headed southwest toward the spot where the Yellow Brick Road breached the Munchkin River across a span of nine murthstone arches. On the far side, the terrain lay down and refused to move, not even a wrinkle in the dustland. Suitable for little but subsistence farming. None of the great Munchkinland bounty you'd find in the Corn Basket farther north. Just scrappy farms worn grey with wind and regret.

One job he could take, and he did without mortification, was the carting of manure from farm stables. In this wasteland, farmers couldn't manage a decent yield of crops without manure. So the stables were shit factories. Whether the Animals were glad enough for their oats to shit on demand, Brrr didn't know, and he took pains not to ask. Coming face-to-face with a Stallion in tethers, Brrr behaved as if he were a mute Lion, or perhaps ignorant of basic Ozish. He had no doubt the Stallion could see right through the ruse, but it still seemed correct to feign being dumb.

He got the job done, was paid in innards and offal.

He slept apart, alone, and stayed until his insomnia flared up again, at which point he moved on to the next farm. A constantly changing horizon seemed the only prophylactic against his obsessive review of his grievances.

The next horizon, sometimes just the next farm, was always more promising, until it proved not to be so, after all.

This way, Brrr made his slow progress southeast through Munchkinland until he'd reached the hardscrabble district known as the Hardings.

The Squirrel had been accurate in his description. In the towns of Three Dead Trees, Rush Margins, and the inappropriately named Center Bounty (Center Spite was more like it) the hounded creatures had hunkered down and made the best of a bad situation.

By now he was finally beginning to understand what had happened to the Animals in Oz. The professionals – the chattering classes, also the twittering, clucking, nickering, and braying classes – had gone underground. Some of them literally (Moles, Rabbits, Badgers), some symbolically. As a rule, many of them were so long removed from any kind of manual labor that they hadn't fared at all well when trying to take up again the practices of their ancestors.

They made their living, such as it was, in the townships of southeastern Munchkinland – the stony dales and blackened, brackish rills, the treeless hills supporting only gorse and broom and the occasional weary flock of sheep, for their weary wool, or peppermilk colts, for equally wearying cheese. The

Animals crowded, cheek by bristly jowl, or wither by wen, in stone crofts and stone hovels and stone lean-tos and stone corncribs built in a more hopeful time.

Brrr continued his career in down-market picaresquerie. A month in Three Dead Trees, two weeks in Broad Slope Town, then a longish stint, almost a year, in Rush Margins, the surface of Illswater glinting with a hard beauty in the occasional shock of sunlight. More often the skies were streaked with grey. It never grew very warm here, even in spring, what with the winds constant as tidal wash. They endlessly speckled the windowpanes with sand carried in from the eastern deserts.

But eventually even Rush Margins grew unbearable, too, and Brrr forged his way against the wind, ever farther south. He wondered if he harbored a secret compulsion to leave Oz entirely, to enter the trackless desert from which, it was said, there was no return. To dig himself a grave in the largest sweep of cat litter nature could provide, bury himself like a turd there. Outside the legal reach of Oz itself, outside its memory if he could only arrange that, too.

One evening on the south slope of Illswater, not far from Stonespar End, Brrr came upon a neglected parsonage. It had been dedicated to the use of a unionist minister – Brrr recognized the symbols carved over the lintel. He nearly passed it by, having no more use for the blandishments of piety than he did for political capital. A voice called from an open window, though, offering a firkin of water, and one didn't turn down a drink even if it came at the cost of a spiritual seduction.

It was an ancient Ape in a quilted velvet smoking jacket so old and frayed that it betrayed no clue as to its original color. He beckoned with palsied knuckles. He called himself Mister Mikko. He shared digs with a Boar named Professor Lenx who, due to deteriorating hips, was confined to a wheeled cart that the Ape could only barely manage to maneuver in and out the garden door.

Both of them were too elderly to do much but remember the good old days when they were tenured lecturers at Shiz.

'Tenured,' insisted Mister Mikko, 'until we were untenured.'

'Sacked,' said Professor Lenx. 'Pass the saffron cream, will you, old darling?'

A joke of sorts. Saffron cream was a thing of the past for these two.

They housed the Lion equably enough, making certain he understood it was only temporary. Brrr tried to resist the urge to scoff at their fusty mannerisms. The way they insisted on offering him two-thirds of whatever they had in the larder was unctuous and superior. He ate it anyway.

'You're looking for a home, but we have only the two sleeping chambers here,' observed Mister Mikko.

'We're gentlefolk of a certain generation, don't you know, so we wouldn't bed down in shared quarters like cattle.'

'Certainly not,' said Professor Lenx. 'Never think of it. The very idea.'

'Too cozy. Not our style.'

'You assume I care.' Brrr managed to sound offended, obscurely.

'Well, a Lion on his own . . .' The way their voices trailed off. *Suspicious*, they meant. 'At loose ends.'

'My end is anything but loose.'

They didn't like that style of badinage. 'And food is in short supply, of course. Had we gardens like the ones in College now, it might be another matter. The vegetables! Do you remember the vegetables, Mister Mikko? The sweet summer scallions, the tomatoes, the blue runner beans! And when the corn was ripe! Hallelujah season.'

'Indeed I do remember it well, my dear Professor. Though also I was partial to the formal walking gardens, the parterres, the flowering cherries, the borders of myccasandra and iris . . .'

'Shiz could do gardens well. Here, alas, if we get eight potatoes a season, we're lucky.'

'The gardens of Crage Hall! I *do* remember. The year that the transplanted termite ivy from the Lesser Kells went wild! It took the staff five years to root it all up. They even needed to demolish an ancient Lurlinist shrine because the migrating root ball had lodged itself there.'

'Would that we had a problem with invasives now.'

'We do. We're being invaded by dirt.'

They laughed. It was as if Brrr were no longer there. Their memories were stronger than the present moment. Brrr felt as if he were the new invasive.

'I have been to Shiz myself,' he ventured.

'Oh well, dear boy, many go to Shiz,' said Mister Mikko.

'And many leave it,' said Professor Lenx.

They looked at each other as if they were discussing the deepest philosophical principles. Then they laughed at the same instant. 'Good riddance to bad rubbish!' Their simultaneity was cloying but kind of sweet.

Over dinner – a noxious potato porridge and sandwiches on stale bread – the subject returned to Shiz. Naturally. Brrr learned a good deal more about the Animal Adverse laws enacted during the Wizardic reign. Early on, when professional Animals could still quit their positions and freely cross the borders, Professor Lenx had fled too quickly to liquidate a sizable portfolio held by a Shiz fiduciary house. He assumed the funds had since been co-opted by the Wizard's financial ministers, but he had no way of knowing.

'I daren't write to enquire. I don't care to give

my location away, you see. Old-fashioned reticence about money matters, and cautious that way,' said the Boar.

'No one would call you cowardly, old darling,' said Mister Mikko, which sounded like a riposte in a disagreement between them that stretched back years. 'A little mustard on your cheese butty? I think so. Let me spread it for you.'

Perhaps it was a thrill of sympathy for Professor Lenx having to endure that particular slur – *cowardly!* – or maybe Brrr was simply relieved not to be the target of the criticism himself. He found himself saying, 'I actually had a profile in Shiz once – of a sort – and of course I am now formally a Namory, by order of Lady Glinda.'

'A Namory! And you didn't mention it till now. You are too humble, *Sir* Brrr,' said Professor Lenx. 'May I humble you further with another spoonful of pottage?'

'There's a shortage of certain kinds of labor in the Emerald City these days,' said Brrr. 'Domestic work isn't yet open to Animals again, it seems, but there are other opportunities. The WOO is history, gentlemen. Your old stomping ground, Shiz, has become ringed with factories. I understand Dixxi House to the north of Shiz is begging for a workforce. The Animal Adverse laws are greatly relaxed, and the EC is making all sorts of overtures to exiled Animals.'

'Well, we're far too old to enter the workforce,' said Mister Mikko.

'And I'm crippled,' said Professor Lenx. 'Not to mention that my field was mathematics. I specialized in diluted equations.'

'Did you say deluded equations?' Mister Mikko posed this piously.

'Ha-ha, exceedingly ha. What a robust sense of humor you have. Too bad it isn't equaled by your sense of history. Or perhaps you taught histrionics, I quite forget, as of course one would tend to.'

As much to smooth over the comedy of professional sniping as for any other reason, Brrr said, 'If the EC's ministers of labor are really interested in wooing back the Animal workforce, they would be smart to free up any funds appropriated from Animals who had to leave under the Wizard's "courtesies."'

'We didn't *have* to leave,' said Mister Mikko. 'I did teach history, young Sir Brrr, and I know that much. We could quite as freely have chosen to go to prison, you know. *That* option was never denied us. So we are considered to have departed of our own volition.'

'You know what I mean,' said the Lion. 'The banks could institute an amnesty of sorts. If Animals were permitted again to invest and profit, they might be more likely to lend their shoulders to the wheel of industrial progress. The powers that be should consider this.'

'Well, I wouldn't trust the current administration

any more than I trusted the Wizard of Oz, may he rot in hell and all babies sleep well, thank you very much.' Professor Lenx worked at a bit of rind with his tongue and then spat the mess out of the side of his bristly mouth.

'Tut-tut. And I just swept that dung heap,' said Mister Mikko, and spat in concert.

'Oh, the Scarecrow's not smart enough to be devious,' said the Lion.

'Stupidity is as dangerous as cleverness,' retorted the Ape.

'More so,' said the Boar.

Brrr looked at the two of them, noting their infirmities, their indignities, their brave courtesies to him. He didn't like the old codgers, nothing so drastic as that. But if he had been of a certain class of urban Animal, he might have gone to Shiz University himself, once upon a time. He felt a tenderness at the idea. They might have been his very professors. For a moment he pretended they were, and he was a devoted student who had made good in the world, and was looking after their interests, the old dears, now that they couldn't manage much for themselves.

'I attended a few lectures now and then,' he told them, playing at the fantasy. Well, attending lectures open to the public, that was true enough. 'I once had a private practice trading in small original etchings under glass, the occasional watercolor. I grew to know quite a bit about old paper, and the fugitive qualities of certain pigments . . .'

'Oh, you don't say! But how bizarre,' said Mister Mikko. 'I don't suppose you ever came across a Miss Quasimoda? She was a White Ape who taught drawing from life. Quite scandalous.'

'With you involved, I shouldn't wonder,' intoned Professor Lenx.

'I mean the drawing from life,' huffed Mister Mikko. 'The very idea!'

'No, no, I never did,' said Brrr hurriedly. 'I don't remember anyone's name from that time, except for a headmistress of one of the women's halls. Someone named . . . Madame . . . Madame Morrible.'

The silence could have been scraped with a putty knife.

'She was in cahoots with the Wizard,' said Professor Lenx shortly. 'That's what was said in the SCR, anyway.'

'Of course she was, she and that little tiktok agent of hers. Gramitic.'

'Grommetik.'

'All due respect. I am certain it was Gramatic. *Gramitic.*'

'Your certainty has more bare spots than your scalp does.'

Mister Mikko bared his old teeth at his colleague and turned back to Brrr. 'Don't mind Professor Lenx;

his mind is going. I don't suppose you ever came across a Doctor Dillamond? A Goat with expertise in several fields, history and science among them.'

'The history of science,' murmured Professor Lenx. 'The science of history.'

'I never did. And I'm sorry for mentioning Madame Morrible. I didn't meet her personally. She presided over teas for the visitors – community relations, that sort of thing, a town-and-gown tension-mitigation scheme. She lectured once or twice. I don't remember the topic.'

He did, though. The Animal Adverse laws, and the Wizard's mercy.

'Doctor Dillamond,' said Professor Lenx. 'A fine scholar.'

'And an early admirer of Elphaba Thropp's, as I recall,' added Mister Mikko.

Brrr took the chance that was presenting itself. 'I don't suppose you remember an occasion in which an infant Lion cub was brought into a laboratory in Shiz? For some kind of treatment?'

Professor Lenx and Mister Mikko exchanged glances.

'Much was done that is best not to remember,' said Mister Mikko softly.

'I think I might have been that Lion cub.'

A grave silence as, in the next room, a few coals fell from their little heap.

'We might all have been that Lion cub,' said the Boar.

The Ape got up to clear. The cups trembled in his hands. When he left the room, the Boar leaned forward. 'We did not approve,' he whispered. 'Please don't speak of this again. He gets very upset, the old fool.'

'It was *my life*,' said Brrr.

'And this is ours, what's left of it. Spare us, and save yourself. You're young enough. Look: You have survived. Bless you, dear sir. Bless you, and shut up.'

As Mister Mikko cleared away, Brrr pushed Professor Lenx's cart into the front parlor, where it took up half the room. The Lion stirred up the fire while the Boar sunk into a reverie about Madame Morrible and the last golden years of an integrated university life. When Brrr settled in a ratty old upholstered chair (just covered with silvery Ape hairs), he didn't speak but thought about Animals in exile and the need for a modern workforce in the factories.

There was an opportunity here. Staring him in the face. Rehabilitation of a sort, if he worked it right. If he had the mettle to do it.

During afters, Brrr made his proposal over a bitterroot sherry. He offered his services as a go-between. He would return to Shiz and present himself to the appropriate authorities as Professor Lenx's agent. He would ask 15 percent of any funds he was able to locate and arrange to have released. Everything notarized and formalized.

'I know you're young,' said Mister Mikko. 'Well, youngish. But have you really the nerve to return to Loyal Oz?'

'I am a Namory,' he reminded them. 'I once got a medal from the Wizard of Oz himself. And for a time I counted the Scarecrow, who sits upon the Throne, a personal friend.'

'We move in lofty circles, yet we wear such a nobly frayed jacket,' said the Boar, as gentle as he was wry.

Brrr pressed his case. 'I ought at least to be able to get an audience with him, if the banks give me a hard time.'

Professor Lenx couldn't control his trembling as Mister Mikko, with a more capable hand, labored over a contract engaging Brrr as a financial agent.

'Assuming on the Loyal Oz side of the border that the Shiz bank honors its terms, will the Eminent Thropp here in Munchkinland allow the funds transfer?' asked Brrr. 'I don't know much about monetary policy. And who is the current Eminent Thropp now, anyway?'

'With the deaths of both Elphaba and Nessarose, the title of Eminent Thropp ought to have reverted to Shell,' said Mister Mikko. 'I mean, given the absence of the issue of the women of the line. For, like the descent of Ozmas, the Eminenceships descend with a matrilineal bias. But Shell is said to be a playboy in Emerald City gambling parlors. Also a regular visitor to girlie arcades. He's shown no inclination to give up the high life and waltz back here to govern a rogue state. One suspects his political sympathies, if he's ever developed any, would have conformed with the Wizard's, anyway.'

'Who else has emerged?' said Brrr. 'I mean, to pick up the county where Nessarose left it when she died?'

'Bit of a local scrabble,' said Mister Mikko, 'but if we had the money you might bring us, we'd put it on the Eminent Pastor in Old Pastoria. Her name is Mumbly.'

'Her name is Mammly.'

'Her name is immaterial. Mumbly, Mommy, *will* you let me finish, old darling? She keeps to herself. She's distantly related to Pastorius, who was the last Ozma Regent before the Wizard's takeover. She probably has the most legitimacy to stand up to the Emerald City in case of an attempt at reannexation, though I don't know if she would. I don't think she has the conviction of exceptionalism that Nessarose possessed.'

'We use the same currency, in any event,' added the Boar, 'so how could there be a prohibition against our reclaiming our retirement funds?'

Brrr left them to their nattering and sunk into a haze of anticipation. Could this work? A legitimate job serving two populations at once? If he helped to resolve the labor crisis, surely that would confer upon him a legitimacy that had hitherto eluded him in human society?

It had been several years since he'd left the Emerald City. He could return in triumph, circling north to Shiz first, of course, to begin the negotiations.

He fell asleep in front of the fire and dreamed of gratitude.

In the morning, Brrr managed to cadge from the two old bachelors an advance on future earnings – a sack of fifteen mettanite florins. With mounting hopes he made his way back overland to Shiz. Back from the farthest habitable corner of Munchkinland, back to life. Scheming all the while. He'd spend a third of the money on a new wardrobe, first; then secure a pied-à-terre in a respectable neighborhood. Someplace better than Ampleton Quarters: that was important. People would notice.

For a week, no more, he would bring himself out to cafés and concerts. He'd condescend to recognize none of his former associates. It would be enough to be seen. *Brrr's back. Brrr's back in town.* Delicious. He'd returned: a Lion unafraid of human society. Let it be said of him that he was the first of the Animals to emerge from hiding. *He's the first, you know. Who'd have thought it of him?*

Let it be said that he held his head high.

His mane is a ruff of bronze. Adversity has strengthened him! Let that be said, too.

His knees were shaking, though, behind the panels of his red velvet greatcoat – cut intentionally long to hide just such a syndrome – when he got up the nerve, at last, to present himself to the governor general of the banking house identified by Professor Lenx.

He gave his name as Sir Brrr, Namory of the Palace of the Throne of Oz. He didn't specify his rank nor identify his district, which proved a smart move. The governor general apparently thought it impolite to enquire. (An Animal Namory was an aberration in and of itself, so far, and perhaps, Brrr speculated, the GG of the bank didn't care to be seen ignorant of the conventions, however newly established.)

Somewhat shocked by Sir Brrr's request, the banking officials couldn't quickly enough find out a reason to reject his petition. In the end it was a matter of deciding what fee to apply against the withdrawal sum for the backbreaking work of having kept Professor Lenx's deposit secure all these long years, while said absentminded Professor had gone lollygagging about without so much as a postcard over the holidays.

When they announced the amount that they would take – 30 percent – Brrr was shocked. He understood at once that he had undersold himself as to the percentage of his own fee. But how easy to exaggerate by 5 percent what the bank had charged, and pocket the difference. He was worth it. Without his skill at negotiation and his nerve, the Animals back in Stonespar End would be getting nothing.

Carrying a letter of assurance, Brrr traveled back to Munchkinland. He avoided the high road, fearful of bandits – he was carrying cold cash – so it took a while to arrive. In the time he'd been gone, Mister Mikko had suffered a viral infection of some sort and lost all his teeth, and he refused to come out of his room.

For his part, Professor Lenx was irate to learn that his investment, far from growing, had lost 50 percent of its original value. But to have some cash was better than having none. He thanked Brrr profusely with tears and scratchy embraces, and introduced him to a neighbor from Three Dead Trees, a crippled old Tsebra, whose family also had a sizeable trust fund in a Shiz cash emporium . . .

Thus did Brrr's career as a professional adjustor of personal finance – his own – root and thrive. He took new digs in Shiz at the top of a converted palace. He had a private lift and he hired a personal valet – a human, what a delicious touch – and from his salon at night he could see the glittering lights of the banks reflected in the black waters of the Suicide Canal. The pelt of a tiger was draped across the piano.

7

A Lion could move in circles that others could not. Once he established himself as a professional arbiter, Sir Brrr began to demand – and get – the more useful sort of testimonials. Letters from the proper officials that permitted his passage across the Oz-Munchkinland border at the checkpoint called Munchkin Mousehole. A good thing, too. Much safer than the off-road scurry that black-market enterprise favored. Still, the fear of highway robbery remained strong, since the wheels of the rented phaeton had bronze rims that rang out an alarm – the progress of money over here! – as they struck the yellow brick paving.

Brrr's valet doubled as a chauffeur. He carried a cosh and a pistol and looked like a bandit himself, which was perhaps useful. His nose ran constantly and he seemed to enjoy his toddy at all hours of the day and evening, which Brrr overlooked since everything else seemed in order. He was called Flyswatter.

The need for Brrr to approach his old chum the Scarecrow in the Emerald City had never arisen. A good thing, too, as the Scarecrow had stepped down or been stepped over. Indeed, Flyswatter – speaking for the demimonde – insisted that the Scarecrow had disappeared. The power in the EC now devolved upon the improbable person of Shell Thropp, who had boasted publicly of his estrangement from his famous and powerful sisters, Nessarose and Elphaba. And then he had ordained himself Emperor.

On what authority? He'd had a conversion. The Unnamed God had chosen him to lead Oz. The Unnamed God had selected in Shell a servant and a steward of this great people, this deserving nation, this heap of goodness, this blessed verdant pasture ringed by stinging deserts . . . well, the rhetoric was almost as bountiful as the moral surcease with which Oz credited itself.

Brrr took little notice, except to be glad he hadn't needed to approach the Palace of the Emperor of Oz. Instead, he involved himself in more traditional credits of the double-entry bookkeeping sort.

The banks didn't like seeing their deposits dwindle, but those in the know were always muttering about the cost of an impending military strike. Who could say when deposits might be impounded by the Throne for the purpose of funding the army? If the banks could charge 30 percent for every withdrawal by an Animal and then use magical accounting to disappear their earnings as thoroughly as Ozma herself had been disappeared, they were in some ways ahead.

Any in-house scruples were easily suppressed. A certain Loyalist strain had never accepted that Shiz banks should be holding Animal funds in the first place. Tainted!

So the banks prospered in the short term, and hid their gains; the Animals received some capital after a long period of penury; and Brrr thrived. His own account accumulated like – well, like magic. He paid off old debts involving Ampleton Quarters, and he invested shrewdly in the less gaudy of Hiiri Furkenstael's gilded engravings. Not for trade, but for his own pleasure.

The Lion ran into Piarsody Scallop one afternoon at the Fine Engraving Exchange this side of Ticknor Circus. She had not aged well, growing purple in the face and kitted out in an unsuitably girlish gown, all white ruches and pink furbelows. Her boot was undone because she suffered from elephant ankle. The malady forced one shoulder lower to the floor than the other, but Miss Scallop bolted upright with surprise to see him. She came stumping across the sawdusty floor with both hands flung in the air as if she were about to hurl a watermelon. He cut her.

He lived it up, he put on weight, becoming almost portly as befitted a gentleman in middle age. He ate well. It showed.

He called it gravitas, but it was mostly gravy. He was swimming in gravy.

Until the gravy boat spilled him.

It happened so slowly this time, so genteelly, that

he didn't even see it coming. He paid little attention to conversations in the club about the need of an Animal workforce to shore up the Gillikinese manufacturing sector. No significant improvement noted in that area yet, worried the captains of industry. But Sir Brrr – he used the title now – didn't feel implicated. For one thing, he wasn't a laborer himself, as was patently clear. For the second, though he had initially proposed to the Shiz banks that a loosening of monetary policy would result in a rise of Animal workers hunting for jobs, the bankers seemed to be exercising due patience. The banks were still culling huge fees from the withdrawals. 'What do they have to complain about?' he muttered to his valet, expecting no answer. Flyswatter gave him none.

Whatever else was barked and bellowed, Loyal Oz saw no return to the Animal Adverse laws. In fact, those hoary old containment strategies were retired in ceremonies dripping with public symbolism. COME HOME TO OZ read the full-page government advertisements.

'Ha,' said Brrr to Flyswatter. 'Come home to Oz. That'll be the day.'

'What day would that be, sir?'

Brrr explained. The Animals who had emigrated to Munchkinland or to the outback of the Vinkus remained cautious about emerging from their obscurity. Hardly better integrated into the Free State of

Munchkinland, where the Wizard's Animal Adverse laws had landed a weaker blow, many Animals nonetheless lived in relative tranquility. 'Exiled for a generation now, some of them, they go largely unmolested about the rural reaches of the Hardings and the Fallows. They keep to themselves. They've found their safe haven and they'll stick to it. Smart of them, too, don't you think?'

'I wouldn't know, sir.'

Brrr thought it over. Few Animals tried to reinvent themselves in Shiz or the Emerald City as he had done. Abroad – in Fliaan, in Ix – it was another matter, but the sands that surrounded Oz made it likely that anyone who managed to survive an oversand trek to a foreign country stayed there.

Oz – Loyal and not – remained, in all its own breadth and vitality and distance, isolated from anything like a comity of nations. The vessel had yet to be built that could sail the desert sands on sledge runners, though inventors and madmen had imagined such a thing for generations.

'Troops amassing on the Munchkinland border, they say,' he murmured to Flyswatter once. The valet was giving him a whisker trim. 'That long-anticipated strike against Munchkinland's life support?'

'What life support would that be, sir?'

'The lake called Restwater. Huge thing. Don't you read the papers?'

'I keep to myself, sir.'

Brrr turned to the financials. It looked as if Shell, the human Emperor of Oz, had run his treasury bankrupt by building up the military for the possible invasion.

'That's enough for now, Flyswatter.' Brrr decided to get to the bank. He'd seen that the Emperor's chancellor had ordered an audit of the banks, hoping to find pennies of taxable profit.

The bank manager was too busy to see him. He came home and watched the matter unfold in the papers, listened to the gossip in the clubs.

Hold on, cried the auditors. What's this? Shiz deposits draining into the breakaway state of Munchkinland?

Possibly funding the military of that upstart nation?

And in a time of social unrest, what with the labor shortage, the drought still upon them, the tax base eroding as incomes fell?

Fie, cried the chancellor, and the bankers shrugged, and the *fie!* rolled off their shoulders. It lay like a judgment upon the shoulders of Brrrr.

Or perhaps Flyswatter turned him in. In any event, the constabulary showed up one morning and the valet had bolted, so Brrr answered the door himself. He was wearing a regrettably adorable robe, beige satin woven with stripes of darker beige, and pink piping, very cuddly, very oh-what-a-night – and his mane went every which way. Bumblebee advocates of the new journalism – on-the-spot flash-lit photogravures – were waiting behind the shoulder of the constable to ambush the Lion.

'Aiding and abetting the enemy,' said the constable, as if pronouncing a sartorial crime. 'Is that a Rampini knockoff?'

'It's an original,' said Brrr, letting it drop to the floor. The nakedness of Animals always made humans profoundly uncomfortable. It was the best he could do as a protest, given such short notice. 'Am I allowed to dress myself?'

'We're gentlemen here. Make it snappy, though.'

CLAP HIM IN CHAINS said the caption that evening, and IF SIR BRRR LIKES STRIPES SO MUCH, WE CAN SHOW HER SOME STRIPES IN A PRISON GARMENT.

Clap some more as he is led to prison, was the point, and we go free for the virtue of our fingering him.

'I am only a delivery service,' Brrr declared to the court registrar. 'You want the bankers, not me.'

The registrar raised her eyebrow. Brrr knew she was saying: Bankers are always pure. Bankers are purer than priests. Something about money insulates them in virtue.

'I charge you with fraud, to start with,' said the first magistrate he saw in Shiz, known as the doorbell magistrate for his job of cobbling together the initial court definition of an indictment. 'You're a villain.'

'I charge you with exaggeration,' shot back the Lion. 'I'm a fall guy.'

The accusation of fraud was entered into the register – fraud perpetrated not against the victims, for some reason (who regards victims?), but against the banks themselves. Fraud in the service of treason. (Had he been turned in by one of his pool-hall cronies?) The complaints were written in such convoluted language that Brrr couldn't follow them. Nonetheless, his gizzard seemed cooked, but good.

His offer to pay back to the banks any funds deemed to have been illegally skimmed off the released Animal accounts was met with 'no comment.' The court wasn't in a mood for bargaining. Brrr spent a few weeks in a holding pen, no worse a lodging than that old ministerial croft in which Professor Lenx and Mister Mikko were entering their dotage. One night the Lion was bundled into a special convicts' train that traveled at midnight from Shiz to the capital. Within a mile or two of the Emperor's Palace, Brrr knew, hunched Southstairs, the underground prison carved on the site of a megalithic tomb. He imagined the place as a massive mouth of Oz. It ground its stony gullet, waiting for Brrr's carcass.

But there were a few steps to endure first, the joke of applying for an appeal in the Emerald City, the punishment of having to wait for a hearing until the meanest magistrate was free of social obligations. The usual foul skirmishes.

By dint of the judgment against him his assets were frozen pending appropriation. (Someone had to pay for his incarceration in Southstairs, and better the accused than the state.) He wasn't a lamb thrown to the lions – he knew that – he was a Lion thrown to the lethal but dominant Lambs of the Unnamed God.

Then, if you could call it that, a stroke of luck at last. Someone serving as a Friend of the Court had recognized him in chambers; it was the Margreave of Tenmeadows, a Gillikinese noble named Avaric. For his own amusement if nothing else, Avaric worked in Secret Affairs, an arm of the Palace defense team. Before Brrr's final appeal review could be canceled due to insufficient cause, and before he could be led off to prison, Avaric arranged a meeting between the criminal and the sentencing judge, a professional scold named Miss Eldersdotter. At the Court's discretion the Margreave was allowed to attend.

'You are a Namory, as I understand it,' said Miss Eldersdotter. Her shiny jaw bristled with so many ugly hairs she could have knitted herself a chin wipe out of them.

'Sir Brrr, Low Plenipotentiary of Traum,' he replied.

'The first Animal so honored,' interjected Lord Avaric.

'All the more reason to set an example,' snapped Miss Eldersdotter. 'You should be ashamed of yourself, Brrr.' Her refusal to use the honorific was nothing less than a taunt. He governed his temper.

'I am mightily ashamed of what has happened,' he said coolly.

'And well you might be.' Her eye was trained on documents. He expected if he kept replying she would keep answering his assertions so as to have the last word. *I remain deeply ashamed, Your Honor. As it should be, Brrr. And as it is, Your Honor. I would expect it to be so, Brrr.* And on. And on.

Then she looked up and said, 'Not the Cowardly Lion of the incident out West? That little contretemps with the dainty Dorothy? You do get around.'

'The same, Your Honor, though I don't include the sobriquet on my letterhead.'

Lord Avaric snorted. Even Miss Eldersdotter had to twitch a smile into submission.

'So you had doings with the Wicked Witch of the West and her witch-boy.'

'Doings would be putting a mighty fine gloss upon it. I accompanied Dorothy to the West and spent the evening in question mostly locked in a kitchen storeroom.'

'You know the lad called Liir. Her son, some say.'

'He won't be a lad anymore if he is still alive. I knew him for a few weeks, and that was the end of it.'

'Have you an opinion as to whether he really was her son? Did he ever show signs of any particular talent at spells?'

'He showed little initiative in the time I knew him, and no promise of any sort.'

'Still,' she said noncommittally. 'Still. And even so.'

'We may have an opportunity here,' said the Margreave.

'I begin to see what you are on about, Lord Avaric. Would you like to present your proposal to the Court? Since we are about to be off-record, Miss Saucerly, you may break for an early tea.'

Miss Saucerly fled. Miss Eldersdotter took off her magistrate's wig to reveal a flattened little steel-blond hairdo, spare and dispirited. She fluffed her hair with Miss Saucerly's pencil as Lord Avaric spoke.

Brrr looked out the window, his future in the hands of others. He listened, but not too closely at first, afraid to become hopeful about whatever Lord Avaric was proposing. Miss Eldersdotter asked a few questions and made a few notes. At one point she dispatched a pigeon to the Palace, requesting information from someone, and the pigeon returned twenty minutes later, the reply scribbled on the back of the same scroll.

Thus was the plot hatched to transpose Brrr's punishment from incarceration in the highest security prison in Oz to a civic alternative: government service. By virtue of his experience with the Wicked Witch of the West and her putative son, Liir, Brrr would be engaged to do some research for the Courts and for Secret Affairs.

He would find out what happened to Liir after he was last seen some eight years ago, suspected of having holed up for sanctuary in this very mauntery of Saint Glinda in the Shale Shallows. He would poke around for this and that among the Witch's effects. Interview a few witnesses.

To what end? Brrr insisted on following the point. Not because he would take it into account — just — because. Curiosity may have killed the cat, but he was a big Cat and had a higher tolerance for curiosity than some.

'Lord Avaric will explain. Case retired.' Miss Eldersdotter closed the file and rubbed her temples. 'Before you take up your new assignment, Brrr, I wonder if you could illuminate me about that aspect of your career involving the assessment of antique prints. I inherited a set of moldy old things from my widowed aunt in Tenniken, and I suspect they are worth a pretty bundle.'

All kinds of possibilities emerged. He held his tongue until his thoughts settled in his mind. Then he said evenly, 'I am afraid the market has changed so much since I was professionally involved, Your Honor, that I would no longer be qualified to offer a judgment.'

'Well,' she said, 'so few of us are.' And she all but leaned back in her chair and kicked up her heels, laughing at her own little self-coronation.

Suppose Miss Eldersdotter's widowed aunt had been the mother of Jemmsy the foot soldier. That would make the magistrate and Jemmsy first cousins. But if she were so related, Brrr didn't want to know. Poetic justice could be just that ironic, but why allow it to trounce upon his frailest feelings?

Once the plea bargain had been struck and approved and signed in triplicate, and the copies filed and their receipts stamped in triplicate and themselves filed, he was free to leave his cell. In a brougham, Lord Avaric arrived to collect Brrr at the door of Saint Satalin's Nook for Petty Criminals. The Margreave proposed luncheon at a respectable establishment, but Brrr said he had no appetite. This was only partly a lie, as he certainly had no appetite to be seen dining in public.

So Avaric took Brrr on a walk along the Ozma Embankment, where they couldn't be overheard by pedestrians. Avaric had a little device called an air pistol that, when fired, made a sudden bang, and the nearby avian population involuntarily launched themselves into a frenzy. The swans on the canal hammered the water with their powerful wings, thwacking the lilies, splashing themselves airborne. No small winged spies remained near enough to overhear Avaric's revelations.

'You're right to ask about your obligations to the Court,' he confided to Brrr. 'Secrecy is all very good, but an agent can best do his job if he knows the parameters.'

Brrr pulled the collar up around his ruff. He was furious, but he was free. The Ozma Embankment was in spring bloom. Butterflies, untroubled by the salute of the gun, pasted themselves on the limbs of miniature ornamental quoxwoods. Bees reprised their hymns to the goddess nectar. A street sweeper in leg irons sang, too, some pagan paean to Lurlina. The roses were a week from cresting. His eyes watered at the notion of how swiftly this could have been swept away. The beauty. The bastards.

'I don't know why you took my part,' he said to Lord Avaric.

'Don't be craven,' said the Margreave. 'It wasn't high sentiment, believe me. As I hear it told, you were once labeled a Witch's familiar, back when she was public enemy number one. And — how talented you are, really — you've also been tarred as a collaborationist, taking the part of the Wizard against your own nativist Animal population. Both the left and the right have called you seditious. You're despised by all. That's a good profile in our line of work. If you've had some actual practice in betrayal, you're better able to carry off the scheme again.'

Brrr did not reply. He had never considered

himself either a defender of the Witch or a collaborationist with the Wizard; that had been an interpretation of the press and general public feeling. As if guessing his thoughts, Avaric continued, 'Don't mind me. A traitor can skew his moral compunctions around any new endeavor and make it seem the correct and even laudable course of action. That's also part of the makeup of a spy: the ability to convince himself of the rightness of his aims.'

Brrr found the courage to say, 'Sir, I am no spy.'

'Well, that's just fine,' said Avaric, unflappable. 'You're just a Namory who has narrowly escaped imprisonment for treason. How lucky that you have such patriotic impulses. All ready to help the nation in a little fact-finding mission! And since you're no traitor either, as I see you are about to claim, you'll have no qualms in working on behalf of Secret Affairs.'

They had reached the place on the Ozma Embankment where one could turn around and look back along the Grand Canal to see the Throne Palace. It stood shining on its little blunted peninsula above the reflecting basin. The emeralds in its facade winked like reflections on a lake: at this hour, from this point, the palace looked as if it were built of the purest water.

This prospect was the subject of dozens of mettanite etchings and coldstone engravings. He knew it as he knew the back of his own paw. But seeing the view for real, in stone and jewel and waterway rather than in watercolor washed over ink on paper – well, it thrilled one to the bone, even as the power the Palace represented gave one a cramp.

'From what I hear tell,' Avaric was saying, 'Old Elphaba, that crankina on a broom, once gave the Wizard of Oz a page from a book she called the Grimmerie. She was tempting him with it, using the book as a bargaining chip to arrange for the release of a political prisoner named Nor. The good Wizard refused to negotiate with a terrorist like her, but, frankly, he *was* tempted. He'd had knowledge of that magic book for some time, and he wanted it. The single page he managed to get from Elphaba that day was responsible for the knowledge of how to train dragons for use in military maneuvers.'

'Some book,' said Brrr cautiously.

'How much more the Wizard might have achieved had he gotten the whole book! But the Wizard abdicated – some say he was deposed, as he deposed the Ozma Regent before him – and notions of those magic gospels were forgotten for a while during the short, giddy reigns of Glinda the Good and the Scarecrow after her.'

'Yes,' said Brrr, unable to resist boasting about his connections. 'I was once quite au fait with the Scarecrow, as it happens.'

'Indeed you were. Of course you were. Then you will remember how Shell, Elphaba's brother, ascended to the throne in that smooth, unresisted way. The Scarecrow as good as a butler, the way he melted away without a murmur.'

'I was traveling at the time, but I learned of it later.'

'It was Shell's ministers, combing the Treasury for negotiable commodities to fund his army, who came across the page on dragons.'

Avaric explained further. Since the writing on the reverse side of the page had seemed to be the second half of a spell, not otherwise identified, no one had paid it much mind at first. But then the Emperor had engaged a scholar of magic at Shiz – a Miss Greyling, spelled *g-r-e-y*, or maybe it is spelled *g-r-a-y* – something like that – to decipher what she could of the spell's conclusion and to infer, if possible, the spell's name and intention.

'That would take some talent,' Brrr ventured.

'She spent several years over it,' continued Avaric. 'Eventually she made her report to the Emperor. As near as she could tell, the verso of the manuscript page was the second part of a spell to reveal hidden inscriptions. Codes, watermarks, the like. A universal spell for the deciphering of runes. Perhaps even the location of individuals in hiding; could it be? Either that or, perhaps, a recipe for oatmeal fritters. It was hard to be sure.

' "What we need," our Emperor Shell replied, "is the rest of this text so we could use it to reveal the location of the Grimmerie to us. A circular ambition, but once we had the Grimmerie, what else we might be able to do!" '

'What does the Grimmerie look like?' asked Brrr. 'Not that I was ever one for books or that sort of thing. My expertise was limited to flat pieces done on private presses.'

'Few could ever have seen it,' said Avaric. 'So there's no reliable description. By the size of the page that Shell has in his treasury, it is a big codex, a tome — a foot square, perhaps.' He looked narrowly at Brrr. 'You were one of the few to go to the Witch's castle while she was thought to have it in her possession. I mean, the others — dead or disappeared. The entire Tigelaar family, who held the castle called Kiamo Ko before the Witch took up residence, was captured and imprisoned. One of them, that child named Nor, escaped from Southstairs a few years ago — she might know the whereabouts of the Grimmerie.'

'Well, ask her.'

'You find her and ask her. Also, the boy named Liir, who some say is Elphaba's son, had gone to Southstairs hunting for her. Perhaps he had seen the book, too, and was looking for his half sister to work with. But he also has gone into hiding. Oz is just riddled with hidey-holes, to judge by the number of useful folk that we can't seem to locate. Can you imagine what a boon it would be, if the government could get its paws on the rest of the spell – to say nothing of the rest of that book?'

'Surely the Witch's castle has been searched?' asked Brrr. He didn't want to go back there again; he'd almost rather sign up for a season in prison. Those flying monkeys – it made his flesh creep to remember them.

'The place was turned inside out,' said Avaric. 'Or so I understood. Nothing left there but an old family retainer and the monkeys. No, the guess is that someone took the Grimmerie from Kiamo Ko. But who – and why – is a mystery – and where it is now is an ever bigger mystery.'

'To whom does it actually belong?' asked Brrr. 'I mean, if Liir actually is the Witch's son, I suppose it is his book, really.'

'It belongs to the government,' said Avaric. 'I hope I haven't misplaced my trust in you, Brrr.'

'Not at all. I was merely making conversation. Wondering if perhaps Liir had found it after all, somehow.'

'I don't think he has,' said Avaric. 'Because the betting parlors have it nine to one that when or if the Grimmerie falls into Liir's hands, he would find a way to use it against the Emperor.'

'Is our national security policy governed by the odds in betting parlors?'

'You're funny,' said the Margreave in a voice that

betrayed little evidence of amusement. 'Liir led a sort of protest of sorts against the Emperor seven or eight years ago. He commandeered a huge armada of Birds and they flew over the Emerald City. He had the Witch's broom and her cape. If he gets his hands on her book, too, there's no telling which corner the trouble will start in. The fact that things have been so quiet this past decade suggests he is looking for it as hard as we are.'

'Maybe he isn't,' said Brrr. 'Maybe he's melted away like his so called mother. He's done his conscientious objection—'

Avaric started.

'I mean his rabble-rousing,' continued Brrr. 'And if the rabble refuses to rouse itself further, why bother? Maybe he's retired to the country to take up croquet.'

'He's certainly gone to ground,' agreed the Margreave. 'But it isn't Liir we want, specifically. It's the Grimmerie. Keep your eyes on the matter at hand. My advice is to start with Madame Morrible. She was, apparently, engaged by the Wizard to keep Elphaba under some sort of surveillance. She died two decades ago, but her effects are archived in the college of Shiz University, where she was headmistress. Crage Hall, it's called. Start there.'

When they were about to take their leave of each other, Brrr asked, 'How will you have me report?'

'I trust you,' said Avaric. He pulled his cloak about his shoulders. Despite the spring efflorescence, a cold wind had sprung up, smelling of old ice. 'You are the Cowardly Lion, dear fellow. You will fulfill your commitment to the Throne or find your pardon revoked. One can always trust a coward to behave in a certain manner; they are predictable as rust. That's why you're so useful.'

'You are too kind,' said Brrr.

Avaric laughed. 'You can't even do obsequy with any conviction. The perfect spy. Here's hoping for your sake, and for ours, you can carry it off.'

Freed to wander about again, though without his glad clothes. Brrr was reduced to seconds bought off the rack at the Poor Fair Boutique in the Burntpork district. A Lion snatching for a Rampini knockoff and fighting over it with a toothless gentleman who wanted it, he said, to make purses out of. Brrr won the tussle but lost his dignity. Well, as if he had any left to lose.

Supplied with a sheaf of writs and a small purse for expenses, Brrr headed back to Shiz. It was eerie to be middle-aged, tramping about the quadrangles as a functionary of Secret Affairs, where once as a dandy he had sprung along the graveled walks in an opera cape and a daringly rose-scented cologne. Everything now looked as seedy as he felt. He didn't know if this was the aging process – the retreat from insouciance – or if the university was falling on hard times.

He'd met the archivist, Miss Greyling, a stoic in sensible shoes, and he decided that she was nuts. She couldn't work the latch on the casement window, or remember with which hand to shake Brrr's paw – nor whether touching the felted pad of an Animal was gauche or daring or illicit or morally profound. How could she deduce what the half-a-spell was saying? It would be a half-magic not worth the coin, he guessed. Her credentials, in addition, seemed dubious. But she was devoted, and flustery, and her cheeks grew pink if he let his language get coarse, which he did now and then, to remind her that he was, after all, an Animal.

'Oh, sir,' she'd say, 'muffins at Lurlinemas, I shall scream!'

He was amused, and also chagrined. So it comes to this. I say naughty things to aging spinsters, to get a rise out of them. What a wolf I am. What a loser.

She found him the name of Yackle, though, and in time, with worryingly few other leads scrawled in his notepad, Brrr made to leave that hothouse atmosphere.

A glass cat had been sitting, grooming itself at the porter's lodge. Perhaps unused to seeing a Lion in the streets of Shiz, the cat had gone all devotional and even romantic, purring up a storm in its aging larynx. So this is what it's like to have a pet, thought Brrr, and while he didn't encourage the creature, he didn't kick it away, either. It had been too long a time since anyone, creature or human or Animal, had purred in his presence.

Why did the cat cross the Yellow Brick Road? To

reach the Lion waiting on the other side.

Brrr had accepted the companionship. It was a novelty. He named it Shadowpuppet for its bright transparency, for its tendency to skulk in the shadows as if to keep from being overheated by the sun.

Going overland again – into the part of Oz most likely to see military activity – was no picnic. Until the first sign of battle, though, he preferred imminent danger to the froufrou of cottage guest rooms for hire. The lavender sachets, the geranium-mint teas, the caged songbirds embellishing the air with the pretty sound of their distress. Spinsters can decorate their own hearthsides with handiwork and camouflage, but to the Lion it seemed another sort of prison.

However, he was striking out in a new direction, and that had some merit. He had always relished the look of a virgin horizon. He headed due south, bypassing the EC, southwest toward the place where the dead lake called Kellswater most nearly approached the great reservoir of Restwater. The provinces of the Vinkus and Gillikin met here, and the Free State of Munchkinland to the east nudged up against them both. It was, quite possibly, the hottest spot on the map just now, due to the need for fresh water.

The various biddies from their porches agreed: Just north of the oakhair forest he would find the Cloister of Saint Glinda in the Shale Shallows. He nodded and kept on. With luck the old bitch, Yackle, would still be clinging to life. If she'd survived to this unholy age, she'd be a pushover. He wasn't worried about it.

He would pursue any lead he could to learn from Liir, or from any source, the whereabouts of the fatal book of magic known as the Grimmerie. Even daring to dart about a landscape gone noisy with the movement of infantry divisions. Where, in a slightly horrifying night, he had come across Sister Doctor and Sister Apothecaire tending the wounded, and persuaded them to let him and Shadowpuppet accompany them back to the mauntery.

He sat in the darkening room. Early evening was always the hardest to negotiate. He tried to concentrate on the immediate. The wind had died down a little; the oakhair forest moaned less strenuously. A moon was rising; it would be ducking in and out of clouds tonight. The world first in shadows and secrets, then in naked prominence.

Nothing in his own life was worth remembering, really. Every turn had promised reward, and delivered something less. So in truth, searching out the twists of someone else's life – be it Madame Morrible's, or the wretched Liir's, or even old Yackle's – was a downright comfort. A welcome distraction. It was diverting to consider lives that had been as hobbled as his own troubled existence.

From a witch's familiar to a collaborationist of the

Wizard to this: a civil servant yoked to the information agencies. Abhorred by the right and the left alike, as Avaric had said. In some ways, rounded upon by everyone, Brrr had nothing left to be, to become, but himself.

How limited, even sour a prospect, though.

One may, oh, cook poorly, or be socially graceless, or invest unwisely, or fail to achieve the best of personal hygiene. But one doesn't want to live wrong – from breath to breath, from start to finish, to get it wrong, so wrong, so fully wrong, that one has never had the glimmer of an idea that it might be better. Or does one? Maybe if you're going to get it that wrong, it's better to get it all wrong. The proverbial stupid ant crawling on the hat brim of the prophet, eager only for the shade behind the prophet's left ear, and ignorant of the civilization-altering sermon it is witnessing.

8

The acolytes of the Clock of the Time Dragon banged cooking utensils into dirty kettles, tying up their sleeping rolls. Their anxiety at the sound of distant cannon was obvious through their overeager laughter. Boys in the neighborhood of war.

'We're pulling up stakes here, Missy Morosey,' called the sergeant-at-hand, but when she didn't arise to hurry to them, he just cursed under his breath and continued knotting ropes to secure the carriage. There was too much to be done to waste his breath trumpeting at her when she decided to go deaf.

Her back was turned to them, her head bent as if listening to an interior argument. She was alone in the way that the terminally ill, crowded into an institution, are alone. Had she a mirror to study her own features, she'd have noted with approval the early silvering of her hair, the spatter of liver spots on the edge of her temple. These would have helped her overlook that her skin still glowed, almost as if backlit, with the enviable sheen of youth.

But she wouldn't have a mirror. She cared to see in her own face neither shades of the hopeful child she'd been nor glimpses of the schemingly wanton maiden she'd become. In recent years, she had bridled at compliments – 'How like a sylph you are! How maidenly!' – as if the efforts to survive her calamities and do useful work had proven incapable of maturing her.

The clearing was striped with oakhair strands. They'd been vibrating earlier, but as night drew near, the winds lapsed, the music stilled. It was almost time for a candle, but she didn't want to go back to her cohorts at the wagon. Bellow though they might, they wouldn't leave without her.

She balanced a pen in her hands, musing.

She had been trying for years to write, but even when she managed a line or two, she couldn't or wouldn't use the personal pronoun. The habit of alibi prevented her. Anyway, she was no longer convinced that she possessed a character so resolved it could boast about itself: *I*, *I*, *I!* When she did write it, it was followed by a period. **I**. It might as well be her initial, as in 'I. sat alone in the way that the terminally ill, crowded into an institution, sit alone.'

Her reservations weren't rooted in aesthetics. She knew little about that branch of opinion, and cared less. Beauty and its refinements. Hah! If she had to consider her aversion to the unslakable *I* in terms of theory, she supposed she would speak about the elegance of justice: Your *I* and my *I* are of equal weight. Or about the central paradox of equality: The *I*, the singular first-person pronoun, had to be eradicated in order to sustain the argument about justice's brash lack of interest in individual history – even as justice existed to champion the rights of such histories to exist. I and I and I and I, all the land over.

The dwarf barked at her. 'Dizzy Lady Lollipalazy! We may have to break camp before our scout returns with news of those pesky troop movements! Skedaddle before we know whether we're making ourselves targets or skirting the skirmish! Put away your note-paper unless you prefer to be swallowed up in cannon smoke. Though whether it's the cannon of the EC professionals or the stumpy little guerrillas, we can't yet tell. Are you listening, Twit-Twit-of-the-Mountaintops?'

After a while she uncorked a bottle of dark red ink and wrote a few words.

The madder the battle, the saner the peace.

She didn't know if this was true. She wrote to ask herself questions. Was there any reason that peace should ever be sane? Perhaps war was too mad an endeavor for the world to survive intact; perhaps its aftermath was always corrupted. The I. who considered this was not without corruption, she knew.

She thought, but didn't write: The louder the cannon, the deafer the peacemakers.

This was nearer to what she wanted, but it was not right.

She sighed. Given how the writing impulse had first emerged, no wonder it was so hard to get the correct words.

Some years before signing on as a nurse to a dirty old coot, she had taken up a position as a gentleman's comfort in the squat industrial Gillikinese town of Red Sand. She learned her trade, mastered it, to useful effect. One evening she maneuvered herself from a shadowy nook in the Hall of Salt Fountains right onto the lap of a northern Gillikinese supplier of iron ore. He gave his name as Serbio, which she knew to be false. No matter; she used alibis in her line of work, too.

After a brief and teasing carriage ride, she ended up in his bed in a lodging house in one of Red Sand's seedier streets. The smell of hot refuse, brimstone, and tarnish entwined, issued from the drapes; the factories were working overtime.

Her client was drunk and handsome though tending to portliness, and he had a wife at home who wouldn't let him have his way with a riding crop. While I. could pretend abandon with a finesse verging on the uncanny.

Her client had left her there naked in the brownish lamplight while he answered the lodge keeper's knock at their door (the interruption seemed to stoke rather than quench his ardor). The lodge keeper complained. Would Master Serbio please see to the inconvenient visitor at the street door as the lodge keeper was retiring – again, and this time for good?

She had expected the interruption – it was why she was here – though she hadn't figured on the beating. But if she could deliver the goods, the unexpected welts on her naked skin might be seen as badges of honor.

As soon as Serbio left the room and trotted down

the hall of the rented chambers, she rose flinching from the bed to accomplish her task.

Her backup team having worked out the scheme properly, she was ready. They'd had word that while Serbio was visiting from the western edge of the Glikkus, a munitions manufacturer in Red Sand was hoping to make a secret negotiation with him. The deal would need to be sealed before Serbio headed home to the slopes of the Scalps, site of the iron-ore mines. She needed to find out: How much blue iron ore was Serbio selling to the arsenal in Red Sand? And how often? Only certain kinds of firearms were prized in infantry maneuvers – the Pollinger redoubler, especially – and the iron ore used in the casting of Pollinger gun barrels was derived primarily from Glikkun sources. So figuring out which factory was producing the bulk of Pollinger artillery, and how frequently, would give a clue as to how the Emerald City generals planned to prosecute an invasion of Munchkinland.

If the bulk of the munitions were being manufactured here in Red Sand, then the invasion would likely start in the south, as (with a carefully planned overland water carry) artillery could be shipped from Red Sand to the Shale Shallows by way of the Gillikin River. The goals of the invasion most likely would be limited to wresting the great lake and its water supply from Munchkinland.

If, on the other hand, the iron ore was being

reserved for the new munitions factory in Traum, the EC invasion strategy probably involved cutting across the Glikkus Canals – braving those trolls – and dropping into Munchkinland from the undefended north. A march through the Nest Fallows – a summer holiday for foot soldiers! – then on into Center Munch and Colwen Grounds. Capture the capital first rather than its plum asset, Restwater.

I. had planned the seduction; she had worn the red picandella with the lace reveal; she had done her hair in pearl rosettes. Into the recess scooped out of her abalone-clad toiletry kit she had fitted a slim notebook with curved pages (each cut to fit with a nail scissors) and a pencil shaved to an inch.

The birds in the cage on the landing, though, she hadn't planned on. At the sound of the knock on the street door at midnight, they had gone mad with song. (They hadn't uttered a word at the noise of the cudgel or at her bitten-off cries. Perhaps, like so many, they had tendencies of voyeurism.) Now they were shrieking alarums.

On tender and bruised soles she had hurried back to the chamber, praying that all other fly-by-night tenants, even if they'd awakened, would be cowering with their illicit bedmates, hoping to escape notice. Once past the age of twenty, few like a surprise midnight visitor. She had grabbed her skirt and returned with it, its wings wuffling, and she'd flung it over the cage. The birds fell silent at the unexpectedly immediate sunset.

She'd crouched at the top of the stairs, shivering in the cold. She'd listened and heard one, two vital words; and then a bonus, something about an increase in orders next spring. And a second bonus – another supplier was being brought on to help the Pollinger manufacturer – might Serbio consider a reduction in his bulk prices, and meet his competitor's prices? A lower figure per unit ton . . .

Her client began to haggle. She had to admire a businessman able to defend his turf while standing in a freezing hall in nothing but button-bottomed pantlettes.

It was enough. Reclaiming her skirt, she stole back to the chamber and made three notes in pencil while the birds began to clamor again.

They covered the noise of Serbio's tiptoed return. He had wanted to find her cowering with her head under the pillow, her rump exposed; she was busy writing instead.

'A letter to Mama about what a naughty girl you've been?' he said, though his arched eyebrow defined his attention as keenly suspicious.

She gasped and managed not to fling the book away from her. She said the first thing that came into her head.

'Notes for a story.' A long pause. 'I write fancies;

they only come to me when I am in distress.'

She pulled her skirt over her lap, making a game of it, but Serbio grabbed her paper, saying 'Whaddya fancy then, so I can provide it times three, heh-heh?'

Blessings on the team member who had insisted she learn code. 'This looks like dragon drool,' he said. 'Words en't involved here.'

'I was just starting,' she said.

'Tell me what your big idea is, that you got to get up from your sweet bed of pain to write it down.'

Maybe it was his mention of Mama. Just in time, she remembered a story from her childhood. She had no way of knowing whether it was a famous legend or an invention of her own mother. 'It's about a Witch,' she said, 'a Witch who has a sudden yen for a dinner made out of fox babies. But the fox mother howls down the moon, which rolls like a grave door in front of the Witch's cave. And there the wicked old Witch stays, for ever so long.'

He wasn't so drunk as not to be dubious; the unexpected business negotiation at midnight had corrected his thinking. 'All that in this little sketch, these scratchy lines?'

'I was just beginning,' she said.

'I'll sit and watch you write,' said Serbio. 'You can read it out loud as it occurs to you.' He dropped on his knees by the side of the bed and pulled the skirt away from her lap. He dug his hand. 'I don't know whether we should beat that old Witch out of her cave,' he said, twisting. 'What do you think? What do you think we ought to do?'

'Once there was a fox mother,' she said, but where she had avoided weeping earlier, the memory of the story retold in this situation gave a greater grief.

The diversion had worked. She had escaped with the information required, which she supplied to the go-between the next morning over a market stall. 'Did you get hurt?' asked the intermediary, pretending to examine potatoes as he slipped the written information into his vest.

'I'm not sure,' she replied, 'it wasn't covered in the story I told.'

For a while after that, she'd survived the worst of the injuries brought on by her espionage by escaping into stories. They served as a kind of supple armor when she was naked, a place to which her mind could retreat. Over and over again she told herself the story of the Witch and the fox babies, like singing a song in her head to give herself bravery – the same thing those filthy noisy birds had done that evening. Later, sometimes both bruised and confused, she collected herself by trying to scribble things down. Not the notes in code – that system, amazingly, had remained undiscovered. But shreds of tales.

She became involved in the work. For a short time it became her salvation. She remembered how her aunts had read the same novel over and over again, for it was the only one they had, and how in their bleak spinsterhoods they had thrilled over false adventures in an invented world.

Then she gained some distance, and lost some momentum. She began to see that her stories were an argument through incident. What had seemed arbitrary, even magical – events unfolding out of her pencil as if it were her pencil doing the thinking – she now deduced as a reductive patterning, a false simplification of the world. Narrative shapeliness was a fiction in and of itself, a lie. The pencil was lying about how much meaning the world was capable of.

Any conclusion she could ever reach was false, because the validity of any conclusion could not be proved by any creature still imprisoned in the throes of life, and therefore still ill educated about myriad cause and final effect.

So after some years, she gave up the experiment of fiction. For a while or for good, she didn't know. When she was engaged as a helpmeet and a nurse by the elderly widower – the Ogre, she called him – only to be locked in a tower to watch from above as he died, words failed her yet again.

Now sitting just outside of the company of the Clock, her saviors, she watched her pencil trail the paper and, avoiding language, make a long arcing line, a tree trunk of sorts. She added odd hooping branches bent like geometrically accurate arches. A stylized willow, a perfect fountain of green.

Sometimes, when words began to raise welts in her skin and panic in her breast, a drawing would suffice. It came from nowhere, this pure tree on the page. Perhaps it was code of another sort, and she could not yet read it.

The sergeant-at-arms said, '*Ilianora!*' At the sound of her name, she had to stir; she had no choice. 'The runners are back,' he continued, 'we've worked out our route. We're right in the crosshairs of the EC militia approaching from the west; we've got fifteen minutes to get out of their way. If you don't come now, we'll leave you here! And bye-bye, Baby Beauty!'

The dwarf turned to the others. 'North we go, boys, north to the edge of the woods but not out into the open, for we don't know precisely where the Munchkinlanders are, and in the evening light we don't want them to mistake us as their foe. We don't want to draw their fire. Haste, or we'll be collateral cost before midnight! If I haven't lost my touch, sanctuary should lie just ahead of us.'

The boys to their harness, the dwarf to the seat up front. She tucked her pencil and her notebook into her apron pocket and pulled her veil back over her brow. Then she turned to join her family.

'I'm coming,' she announced, for it was her history to do so, and she could no more avoid her future than

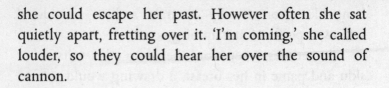

she could escape her past. However often she sat quietly apart, fretting over it. 'I'm coming,' she called louder, so they could hear her over the sound of cannon.

A Question of Influence

1

The glass cat made a sound of complaint; Brrr returned to the present.

'Oooh, Shadowpuppet, supper will be coming soon. These poor servants of the Unnamed God won't let you go hungry. Their brief doesn't allow it.'

The cat came to his lap and licked at some old crumbs caught in the pilling of Brrr's weskit. Brrr petted it, trying to provoke a purr. This was the only warmth Shadowpuppet could show, a tonal warmth: Its body was immune to changes of heat and cold, so far as Brrr could tell.

What an advantage. Maybe it came from old age. Something to anticipate, a reprieve.

Even ancient Yackle seemed somewhat inert, emotionally: She was enduring her apparent immortality with stoicism. He'd be driven mad if he thought the blandishments of death were to be denied him forever.

He tried to escape those memories that had crowded upon him this past hour: his disastrous incompatibility with clans either Animal or human, like the Ghullim, like the Shiz banking circle; his mistakes with rogues like Dorothy or Elphaba. His humiliation at the bar of Miss Eldersdotter.

Collaborator. But to collaborate implied a betrayal of one's natural tribe, and if one didn't have a natural tribe . . .

Perhaps Yackle possessed a shred of mercy; perhaps she had taken herself away not to pray, but to get out of the room while the more heinous memories surged upon him. Perhaps she'd been able to guess that, between Traum and this off-center cloister, he had endured a lifetime of collapsing hopes and misadventures.

If so – if he could credit the old bitch with that much feeling – he had a little to thank her for. Though given his record, he was probably wrong. He was another pawn in another campaign, and hadn't sussed out yet what her angle was.

In any case, Yackle would be coming back from chapel soon, unless she'd died a death holier than the life she'd led. Meanwhile, the small stars showed up one by one, picking their way slowly, reluctantly, through the gloaming. (He'd preferred overcast nights ever since the creepy atmospherics of the Cloud Swamp.) The stars made a rash in a sky that glowed the color of those mythical seas painted by Dobbius and his followers. A serpent green wash overlaid with a smudge of blue-coal Conté crayon applied with forefinger. In another ten minutes the green of the heavens would drown under the black, and night would be fully and legally arrived. For now, the day played its last hand, the sky reveling in its fullest dimensionality, flaring up into all directions: height, breadth, depth, lastingness.

The noise of cannon, distant but not comfortably distant enough, corresponded with the sound of Yackle approaching down the hall, a sloughing and sighing presence.

She came into the room, hitting backward at the helpful hand of the novice who had been guiding her. 'Enough, you crow; go pester some other poor wren. I'll break my hip if I've a mind to, and nothing you can do about it.'

'Begging pardon, Mother Yackle, but Sister Doctor asks me to show the Lion to his evening chamber, and you to yours. I bring you here just to say your good evenings, and then I'll bring you on.'

'I'll sit here in the dark. I don't need a bed.'

'I'm not wasting time at sleep,' said Brrr. 'Can't you hear that gunfire? Whatever is happening is coming closer. Let's finish up here and I'll be on my way under cover of darkness, the way I came. I have no intention of spending a night here.'

'I'll wait outside,' said the novice. 'I'll give you ten minutes. I am not at liberty to countermand Sister Doctor's orders.'

The young woman retreated, and the door closed. Yackle bumped her way to her chair; Brrr didn't offer to help her. She seemed more tired, though hardly an ounce more dead than before.

'Restored, I trust?' said Brrr bitterly.

'They haven't changed, those women,' said Yackle. 'For what seems like decades I sat among them, wondering how they did it, all that continence of emotion, all that rigor and fervor. I still wonder. I wasn't really made for this world.' By her tone he knew she meant the world at large, not just the mauntery.

'Sentimental religiosity?' he asked. 'It claws at one, doesn't it.'

'I haven't the goods to define it. Not to defend it nor belittle it. It just gets the better of me, that's all. How can they sing those hymns to an Unnamed God? What is the point?'

Not for him to answer, not that one. 'Why are you so sour? You are a maunt, after all. Or masqueraded as one all these years.'

'I make as few claims for my spirituality as you make for your courage,' she snapped. 'The truth is, I wish I were deaf as well as blind. Relieved from listening to the biddies going at one another. Sister Doctor is in charge, more or less, but her aide-in-the-surgery, Sister Apothecaire, has never forgotten that Sister Doctor was elevated while she was passed over. The rub of it hasn't mattered much for years, I imagine, but with an invasion of Munchkinland by the Emperor's forces about to happen, well, that stout little Munchkinlander Sister Bulldog-Apothecaire thinks Sister Doctor is proving too neutral a leader.'

'Very psychologic of you.'

'Don't mock me. The scorn on both sides is deafening. *Toadying appeaser*, thinks Sister Apothecaire of Sister Doctor. *Bloody hotblooded peasant*, thinks Sister Doctor of Sister Apothecaire. You suppose I can't hear all this in how they intone their prayers?'

'You do have good ears,' said Brrr. 'Quite a liability to your peace of mind, I can see that.'

'Go to your rest,' she said. 'I'm not going to talk to you tonight, so you might as well sleep. Should you have to run mighty fast in the morning, a good night's sleep will benefit you.'

'I haven't got what I need yet,' he said.

'You're not going to get it now,' she answered. 'I'm going to sit here a while, in the dark. I am thinking about whether to say any more to you at all. It's possible I might. But I would like to grumble to myself a bit, and I don't want to be overheard.'

'It's time, Sir Brrr,' said the novice timidly.

She led him to the staircase, which dropped down a wide high stairwell. Above the polished wainscoting on the walls opened a large window with clear panes set in the center, colored borders on the sides. Brrr stood on the top step, waiting for Shadowpuppet to catch up. Brrr lengthened his spine, his neck, to look over the edge of the windowsill, over the curtain wall of the mauntery, to see if he could locate any sign of army divisions or sharpshooters. The sky came down almost to the ground – a flat geography in these parts. Nothing to see but a house or two with some lights on against the dark.

A house right in the way. Poor fools.

'Sir Brrr,' said the novice, using an aggrieved tone to chivy the Lion. He picked up the glass cat, resisting an urge to heave it at the novice's skull, and followed her without speaking again.

The room to which the novice led the Lion was fitted with three clerestory windows. They were too high for him to leap through, should the place be attacked at night – the worries he carried with him! – and in any instance they were probably too small, too, since he'd put on something of a paunch despite the hard times.

Supper came, and it didn't sit well, so it went the way it came. Shadowpuppet kept a distance, wrinkling its glassine nose at the stench.

He found he couldn't sleep on the hard straw mattress, so he curled up on his coat. The stone floor was cold, and Brrr shivered enough to drive Shadowpuppet to the other side of the room, as if the small moony cat was afraid of shattering.

He tossed and twitched, avoiding the last yoke, the worst of it, but as he grew more tired his resistance thinned; and then it was upon him.

The men with their prods and harpoon guns, the net, the ignominious net. The surrender to capture, the terror in the cage, the shame. The accusations, the sentencing. The surgeon with his sedative, a needle and a plunger. Then the scissors of four or five barbers snipping around him, all at once. 'Mortification is good for the maturing beast,' said a voice, the surgeon's, someone's. 'Strip him of his honors, shave his mane, prune him down to nothing, and if he survives he will grow up stronger.'

A shorn head, the sign of a collaborationist.

He couldn't and wouldn't place the memory; he wouldn't give it credit for being true, even. He couldn't see himself either as a Lion cub or as a gentlebeast financier. The truth remained: He was a hollow in the midst of his own life. He'd never achieved a personal stature, a standard by which to guess the stature of others.

Perhaps it was a dread he had only imagined. If it really had happened, he didn't want to remember the details. Better that day should stay dead.

Relieved of that darkest recollection, Brrr slipped into sleep at last. He dreamt, and he knew he was dreaming as it happened, which was curious in and of itself, the more so because on the whole Cats rarely dream.

The long lean form of Muhlama H'aekeem extended in his dream thoughts, stretching elegantly, as if she'd just awakened from a nap by a jungle pool. He licked her spine as she arched it, each vertebra articulating in a sensuous fold one at a time. The goodly form of an Ivory Tigress—

In his dreams she was in estrus, and the smell was like a firecracker in his chest, creaking and ticking to detonate; the firecracker, as if it were something he'd swallowed, moved down, to burn his loins and swell his Lion's scepter. (King of the Gillikin Forest. In his dreams.) She lashed at him with her tail lovingly, tauntingly: Mount me, mount me now. Her head turned slightly back toward him, the smile like a snarl, the snarl like a smile, and her eyes half-closed, and the rhythm of her rocking causing the obsidian opacity of her eyes to seem splashed as with sea spume, were there such a thing as a sea.

He growled and moaned in his dream, and woke himself up before the accident of release, so he was left pitiably alone. For an instant, a kind of ghost-image of the dream lingered on the inside of his eyelids: The sight of Muhlama H'aekeem prancing away across an outcrop of limestone. She was too far for him to fall asleep and catch her again, and finish his conquest. Too far for him to tell if she was hurt and bleeding – if it was that time – or if she was still the young tempestuous Cat, the runaway from her royal family.

He rolled over on his side, unwilling to look and see if Shadowpuppet had witnessed his midnight indiscretions.

Sleep did not come back. All that unintended testimony he delivered to himself, at Yackle's canny questions, had brought Muhlama back into his catalog of defeats. He had buried so much. Like a kitten hiding his little birch–twig feces, he had dug in the sand and buried the memories of so many calamities.

Where would she be now, if she had lived?

It wasn't that I loved her, he told himself. She never let me know enough about her to know if I could love her or not.

Neither, he whimpered to himself, neither did I let her know myself.

Old, old Brrr, crouching in a cold room. Thinking about a saucy Cat from his salad days. What a sad picture of a creature he was! Poorer in every way, except broader of imagination about the treacheries we practice upon one another.

For instance – he nearly smiled at the cleverness of it – he had grown quite capable of thinking *opportunist* of others. After all, perhaps Muhlama had never loved him. Perhaps she had sized him up (quite literally) and invented a strategy designed to make her ineligible to rule after her father, old what's-his-name. Yuyodoh. Uyodor, that was it.

If her birth canal was ripped, bled out, scarred, inoperative, she could not bear young to carry on the practice of leadership of the Ghullim. She could abdicate without the tribe's objection. She could name

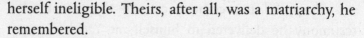

herself ineligible. Theirs, after all, was a matriarchy, he remembered.

Across the room, the ancient cat spit as if it could imagine what Brrr was stewing over. He had to suppress an urge to fist up his paw and smash it to shards.

He looked at the squares of blackened-turquoise sky punching into the chamber, and the paler turquoise stars twirling on their invisible stems. A moon was rising, bleaching out the stars: Thank Lurlina! He was sure he heard a clock tick, though he had seen no clock on any wall or table. He counted the steps into time that the ticks made, one at a time, until he fell asleep again and could count no longer.

This time he did not dream.

One of the few mercies afforded us.

2

Rooms, moods, tenses away, Yackle sat on the floor, her legs stretched out at right angles to each other and to her spine. She was spry from ankles to the bottom of her rib cage; above that, her torso was boled and contorted. Much like the beleaguered Glikkuns with their humps, she guessed. As she imagined them, anyway.

She didn't sleep, though. Sleep was no blessing to her, not until it was the final sleep. Waking up was a daily cruelty, an affront, and she avoided it by not sleeping.

She didn't sleep because she didn't need sleep. She didn't, it seemed, need to see, or really to eat. She hadn't required to move her bowels nor relieve her bladder in over a year. Everything seemed to come and go through her lungs.

So she sat and clasped her knees, stretching her backbone. She listened to the sound of ticking. She hadn't remembered the maunts being much for clocks; after all, they lived as much as they could manage in holy time, which was an anomaly, a contradiction, a tautology: the time in which time has no meaning. A paradox. What was the word?

She wasn't losing language, was she?

She couldn't be losing touch.

An oxymoron, that was it. Holy time. Hah.

Though how she longed to slip into it, even though she didn't – couldn't – believe in such a notion. This must be, she guessed, how the young felt about the nonsense stories of fantasy that their grandmothers told them – the youngest of three daughters to lose her way in the forest. The little copper fish in the mythical blue sea. The funny one about the quill pen that made wishes come true – verbatim. Children played at those stories; they dreamed about them. They took them to heart and acted as if to live inside them. We live in our tales of ourselves, she thought, and ignore as best we can the contradictions, and the lapses, and the abrasions of plot against our mortal souls . . .

And anyway, here she was doing the same: imagining herself inside a clock, the *sprock-sprock* of the mechanism inching along the circumference of an hour. The play of the gears, the lunge of the pendulum, the creep of the hands, the aperture of *now* simultaneously opening and closing at precisely the same ratio forever. But there were no clocks in the mauntery except for the sundial, which spoke its moon-hours as silently as its sun-hours. Of this, the more she thought about it, the more sure she became.

Is it the heart, my old heart, she thought – or whoever's old heart lives in my old chest? Can I now hear it ticking like a timepiece?

Or has the mauntery itself become a clock, a tall, rooted old stone clock, and the maunts, in their nervous twitchy sleep, the little mice that ran up and down its shifting weights, hickory-dickory mice?

But this was fancy; she was succumbing to fancy in a way she hadn't done before. How novel. She'd start seeing ghosts next, if she was lucky. Always a treat, always a hoot, this burden of living beyond the range of one's life expectancy!

She turned her head toward the window. From this point on the compass, her room faced a mounting bank of clouds, and what to the Lion looked like turquoise would have seemed, to someone in Yackle's room, a swollen sludge of violet. Yackle, though seeing nothing, imagined a sky with an octopus-ink tide rolling in, snuffing out young stars. Her instincts were still sharp, sharper than she knew.

Had she learned enough of Brrr to trust him?

She didn't need to know every tittle and jot of his mortification. What she had deduced was that, despite his many abrasions, his lop–cut life, he was still not beyond shame. And that excoriating lash that whips us all has some little benefit: It motors our aspirations to avoid its next hissing strike.

She had listened to his memories, as much as she could – some of them spoken aloud, though he may not have realized he was speaking; others of them rehearsed in silence – but her ears were good. She had found after a day that he seemed to have an endless capacity for mucking things up. Perhaps his history of fecklessness provided him the perfect alibi to be the treasurer of what she knew, and was hiding within her still.

Could she trust him with what she knew? And then, perhaps, die?

Or was this a temptation that she should avoid at all costs – even at the price of giving up the mortal death promised us all?

Then, a nervous spasm caught in her throat for an instant, and she found herself thinking on what the Lion had asked her. That old Brrr. His raw manner didn't fool her for an instant. He was no more a hard boiled truncheon than she was. What had he asked? If she perhaps possessed an *other* life, one too deep down in her memory to experience it, so all her protestations were only that: the crazed defense of a crazy woman.

No, she thought; no, it can't be. I have entertained that possibility eight hundred times before, and I've always turned away from it: no. Brrr had been right to suppose that something small would have given her former life away: a spoon, a string of celery caught in the teeth, the way clouds can look like octopus ink. Something would have caught in an earlier memory, if there had been one. But no random spark of dailiness had ever connected with any life predating the time that she woke up, born an old woman naked in a daybed.

Brrr was there before her in her mind. She couldn't picture him exactly, but whatever she could envision was rolling his eyes and fiddling with a pen he could scarcely govern. 'Why did you take such an interest in Elphaba?' he wondered aloud. 'Why would the story of Elphaba and Nessarose have caught at you so?'

'You tell me,' she rattled back, in her mind, giving testimony at midnight. Or was she withholding it?

'The mentally deranged have no capacity for

memory,' he said. 'You're the mad Aunt Sophelia, maybe. Lady Partra's other daughter; Melena's older sister; the aunt of Elphaba, Nessarose, and Shell, who is now Emperor of Oz. The real Thropp Descending.'

'Were I to believe that, I'd be guilty of delusions of grandeur,' she said, 'then I would truly be mad, and if anyone could find a way to put me away even further than a crypt, they'd be correct to do so at once.'

'I've never heard proof that Sophelia died,' said Brrr, 'and your age would just about conform, I guess, with how old she would be if she still lived.'

'That's nuts,' she replied. '*You're* insane.'

'Not I.' He smiled as he began to fade from her mind. 'You, after all, are having this conversation with yourself. I'm off asleep somewhere else.'

'Damn,' she said aloud, in the cold bedchamber.

She traced it out some more – just the highlights. How she had moved about Oz, in thrall to the idea of the two Thropp sisters. She'd begun to feel anointed, if that was the word – or condemned – to the task of living on the sidelines. To the extent that she had developed genuine powers of prophecy, she had tried to read what was happening, what might happen, and to place herself in Elphaba's way, where she could do some good.

She got a great deal wrong, of course. Infallible she was not. There she'd been at a grotty den of sexual escapades, collecting cash at the window, having read the signs that Elphaba would come by that night. She thought she could protect Elphaba from some dreadful experience. The Philosophy Club! She could remember that. The dwarf at the door, a rotten little bounder: That was where their paths had crossed for the first time. He had been dogging Elphaba's steps, too, it seemed, though she had not been able to determine why.

He was as wrong as she was, that night. Elphaba had proved elusive, often swifter than Yackle's powers of prediction could track. True, Elphaba's college chums had shown up: Avaric, Boq, Fiyero. A few others. But not Elphaba or Glinda. Instead, those two best friends had ducked away that night, and gotten out from under Yackle's distant and watchful eye – it worked back then, the eye, both eyes – and they had hightailed it to the Emerald City for their famous interview with the wonderful Wizard of Oz.

And Yackle had taken years to pick up the trail again. Elphaba had gone underground, a kind of freedom fighter with questionable ethics. She had been damned slippery – who would have thought a green-skinned girl could make herself so invisible? It had taken the best of Yackle's talents to track her down again. But find her she did, after several years, and this time her reading had been more accurate. She could see that Elphaba would turn to the mauntery (though not why, not that she would arrive with the blood of Fiyero on her wrists); and Yackle had presented herself at the door of the establishment earlier, to be there, to be ready when Elphaba arrived: and so she had been.

Yackle had kept her own counsel, nodding in her blankets like a gaga grandmother, but she'd watched. She'd slipped a hand to Elphaba, a set of gnarled fingers in the green palm, as if she were looking for help up some stairs: She had tried to squeeze strength and courage through that wordless communiqué. Who is to say it didn't help somewhat?

Had Yackle known what she was doing when she gave Elphaba the broom?

She could no longer remember.

Then, when the time was right, Sister Elphie had left for the West, to the mountaintop seat of the Tigelaars, the ruling Arjiki family. For all her life an upstart, the grit in the eye that makes it water, Elphaba had hoped to become a hermit. Hoped for forgiveness from Fiyero's widow, hoped for solace from the mountain loneliness.

But the dwarf had come back into the picture, and had delivered to Elphaba an old looking glass she had had in childhood. Elphaba had reheated the glass and modeled it into a globe – turning a mirror into an eye – and who knows what she had been able to see in its depths. The girl was talented.

Talented enough to sidestep everything except, in the end, her own death.

Though perhaps, like Yackle, death was what she had wanted the most.

Yackle groaned. The notion of being Aunt Sophelia, loopy Aunt Sophelia: curse that the idea had roosted in her! Now she'd have to disprove it to her own satisfaction. Still, it made some mad kind of sense: Why else had she spent these weird extended decades of old age stepping around the skirts of someone else's life? She had never known where the compulsion had come from. Perhaps something as simple as blood.

The house ticked, neither in sympathy nor in accusation.

When you can't die, she thought, everything sounds like a clock ticking.

Yackle couldn't see the dawn, but she could hear in the brush of movement, the wind against roofing tiles, and in the swell of birdsong that light was rising. She was tired without exhaustion, or exhausted without weariness – it was hard to put into words.

Still, she asked herself: If I am not mad Aunt Sophelia Thropp, and never was, then who put me here? Who had enough influence to knock me into a somewhat human figure in a world of more fully human creatures as well as Animal figures – and bystanding dwarves? And prophetic clocks?

If I were appointed to generate change in Elphaba's life, who had generated the change in mine? The legendary source of evil amongst us, that old she-demon, the Kumbric Witch? Or the grand, dim, fusty, decayed deity, goddess of creation, Lurlina Herself? Or the Unnamed God, more sober because more secretive? (And did *unnamed* mean *unnameable* or 'once named but name revoked'? All these years among unionist maunts and she had never asked a single theological question. What was *that* proof of, besides obduracy?)

Who gave Lurlina or any other deity her power?

The very children, maybe, who were now hearing the story of Elphaba only as the cautionary fable of the Wicked Witch of the West — her rise and fall — and believing it? Cutting their schoolyard morals to conform to the cheap lessons of a propagandized biography?

She couldn't know. Her head hurt to try to imagine. The closest she came to sleep these days was a kind of slipping sideways into a vision, and this is what she saw: The circularity of influence was like a trail of dominoes falling in four dimensions. Each time one slapped another and fell to the ground, from a different vantage point it appeared knocked upright, ready to be slapped and fall again.

Everything was not merely relative, it was — how to put it? — relevant. Representational. Revealing. Referential and reverential both.

No, she wasn't losing language. She was choking on it.

3

A mile or two on, no more than that, and the under-brush was pestered with the movement of small creatures. The company could read the escape routes of the beasts of the forest floor. 'The EC division that was approaching from the north beach of Kellswater is headed this way,' decided the sergeant-at-hand. 'Lads, look sharp; they've stolen a march on us. We want to cross their path before they get here to cross ours. If we're not careful we'll rub noses with them.'

'We'll blow them to kingdom come!' cried one of the boys, excitable but dull. His pals didn't bother to remind him they traveled without firearms. Their only defense was the dread that the oracle could inspire in the gullible. Though they had no idea how gullible the soldiers of an invading battalion could be, or if they would stop long enough to discover gullibility in themselves.

'Heave now, heave,' called the dwarf, but even he tried to keep his voice down.

The birds of the oakhair forest, who had settled for the night, revived their twitter. Ilianora thought again of the birds in the hall, on the night she had first scribbled a fanciful tale as a stay against discovery. Sing your hearts out, she thought: Let us know from which direction the danger is strongest.

But alone of the company, she walked without much fear. She cared for her companions, in a modest way, and hoped they would survive. Certainly she didn't want them to suffer. But she had a prerogative of calm, in that she alone had no obligation to the oracle or to the future they all muscled in favor of or against. Indeed, she often wondered if she were dead, or dying from the inside out, and that was the root of her calm, the reason she could surrender her character.

They couldn't continue without light now; the night had truly arrived. The dwarf lit torches and gave her one to carry. 'Go front, if you've the heart for it,' he mumbled to her. She knew the lads would be emboldened by her prominence, and that they couldn't risk affixing lanterns to the cart lest a stray bullet smash a glass chimney and the whole kindle box explode in flames.

Though what a sight that would be! Another kind of release, she supposed.

She did as she was bidden. She had a decent instinct for finding a way. The floor of the forest was fairly level, here between the lakes, and for that they all were grateful – though who could know for sure they weren't driving themselves directly into the line of fire of the Munchkinland resistance coming from the east?

Riding up top, the sergeant-at-hand had no need

of a whip. Four of his beauty boys, as he called them, in a kind of jerry-rigged harness, dragged the clockwork oracle along. The other three put their shoulders to the back of it, helping it through ruts and over the roots of oakhair trees. The wind had died down, which was unfortunate: As the company made its way through the strung verticals of the oakhair nuts, they set weird shimmering chords to vibrate around them. It sounded like piano strings long out of tune being scampered upon by mice.

Surely if the EC forces were to come upon their left flank, the soldiers would be playing their own entrance theme?

If the acolytes of the Clock stopped, and let all the oakhair strands fall silent, they might hear where else in the forest a cacophony was being struck. But the boys were now zealous and slightly mad with fear, and wouldn't respond to the sergeant-at-hand's proposal that they pause for a moment to listen.

The wagon met a gentle but longer slope than usual, and the boys grunted at their work. Though he weighed little, the sergeant-at-hand leaped from his perch to lighten the load. He came forward to walk beside Ilianora. He stood only half as tall as she did, when he was standing upright. She thought, not for the first time, *This little man, these seven boys: It sounds like a story I might have made up, back when I was writing down such fancies.*

'I've been through this way before,' he said. 'We'll level off for a bit, and unless the undergrowth is fuller than usual, we ought to be able to see Kellswater down to our left.'

'You've been everywhere in Oz,' she replied.

'Sure seems like it, after all this time.' He knew enough not to ask her about her own travels. She wouldn't answer. Waste of breath.

'How far to the northeast was the Munchkinlander encampme—'

'Shhh—'

They were reaching the flattening crest of the long slope, and the first missile flew by – not a rifle shot, as they'd expected, but an arrow. It buried its head in a tree trunk, and a second followed, and a third.

'We're in it,' he hissed. 'Boys, drop!' Ilianora clamped the cap on the lamp to extinguish it, to buy them a minute or two. But four more arrows, and the shouts of a force thrashing up the left flank of the rise: It would be only a moment before they were captured.

The moon cruelly opened her eye from behind the mounded cutouts of cloud, and they could see the silhouettes of soldiers against the steel-white water of the lake below.

'We'll plead neutrality, see where it gets us,' said the dwarf, dragging at Ilianora's hand to pull her to her knees. 'Boys, you imbeciles, get down!'

Being lower down, the soldiers were at a

disadvantage, but they were trained. Ilianora could see the crossbow aiming, could see the glint of bayonet. They swarmed – thirty, forty, fifty – a half mile out. The sound of crushing underbrush, the strum of advancing men. 'Hie, on the narrow,' cried one; the voice was businesslike as it carried, like a professional herder of cattle. 'Hist, second volley,' called another. 'Grade and scale,' said someone nearish; 'Bloody unlikely,' came the reply. A shot rang out.

'We fly no emblem!' cried the sergeant-at-hand, but another shot muddied the sound of his words. 'Fucking hell, we offer no resistance!' he yelled, irritated enough that his voice rattled into a falsetto shriek.

The Clock had other ideas about this. The great dragon head lifted from its mechanical sleep and rotated like a swan, and eyes with a dull carmine spark shifted in the dark. The leather nostrils dilated and the tin scales scraped upon one another as the armature of the wings stretched like two sails in the woods. It was, perhaps, just enough to cause the closest EC Messiars to halt, as they tried to work out what huge creature waited, glowering and creaking in the dark. The light shifted.

'Keep going!' cried the sergeant-at-hand to his pony-boys. 'Mischief is having her own say!'

The nostrils flared. Coils of steam-grey smoke fell out in slow hanks, unrolling as they dropped, thickening like gelatin beads in water. Within a moment, the Clock was shrouded in a fog that smelled of yeast and mud.

'Grade and lower!' cried a commander. 'Pox on my eyes,' cried an advance scout, quite close; they could hear him breathing and swearing, and he fell to the ground.

'I mean to keep on,' said the sergeant-at-hand. 'Walk the way forward, Miss Trip-Through-the-Trees, and pluck our way out of here, strand by strand if you must.'

The hilltop was smeared with fog, no less troublesome to Ilianora than to the Emerald City division, but she'd had the advantage of reaching the summit before their attackers, and she had seen a bit of how the land went. Along a ridge, and then down a scalloped recess; she could get them that far. She reached out and plucked a wry song out of the struts of the forest. A pizzicato progress. The company kept close behind her, and the dragon trawled a breathy cloak that did not quickly thin.

They were well away, perhaps as much as a mile, before the oakhair trees gave out, and a grove of taller stag–head oaks crowned the next gentle hump. There the company paused to rest and judge by the moon whether they had strayed too far east. The dwarf's destination was due north. Clearest route out of the danger was due north. The dragon's eyes had gone dim and the bellows of its nostrils now trailed only faint, acrid wisps. Its wings settled back in their customary place, folded across their mount with reticulated wrist-claws pointing straight up like spear heads.

'It's a bad night to be wandering in the woods,' said the sergeant-at-hand. 'Unlucky for some, though not for us. Hide your eyes lest the glint give us away.'

The company froze, looking through fingers where he pointed. Eighty feet to the northeast, a group of Munchkinlanders in tabards and boots were preparing some sort of a catapult. They were whispering – they must have heard something of the commotion downslope. But they seemed oblivious of the company of the Clock hunched on its separate hilltop. They were too involved in their own efforts at stirring something in a large spherical iron pot at least as tall as they were.

It was nothing short of a miracle that their attention was so riveted by their preparations. Yet through the dragon's breath, which continued to lay close to the ground, the muffled complaints of the EC men clearly identified their location: a mile or so along the ridge and below it, to the west. The twang of snapped oakhair strands; the cursing of the soldiers and the hollering insults of their officers.

The smoke didn't clear for another quarter hour, by which time the Munchkinlander guerrillas had slid their heavy artillery overland on something like a forest sledge, sleek birch runners that used the slick of pine needles to advantage. When the smoke thinned enough that the moonlight again struck the surface of Kellswater, the company of the Clock could see well enough. Not the attack of the Munchkinlanders, not the lobbing of the fiery pitch they'd prepared in their dreadful cup. Not the EC soldiers cowering or falling back – all that remained concealed by the great dark and undifferentiated folds of the hills, the screen of oakhair limbs. What the company could see was the metallic rings of bright moonlit water that grew out from the shore, circles interrupting slow circles, chevrons divided into shards, as one after another the EC Messiars were driven backward into the lake.

The Past Approaches

1

The dawn was a masked one, clouds making modest the exhibitionist sun.

Brrr, whose sleep had been erratic, sat up. In the corner, as yet unstruck by light, Shadowpuppet looked like watery milk. A small heap of shit, its tapering point like the head of a worm, lay coiled nearby. Brrr couldn't imagine how a transparent creature could produce opaque offal, but if this was a philosophical question in disguise, he wasn't up to considering it before breakfast.

He stood and tried to press the wrinkles out of his coat. Not that the humble maunts nor the blind oracle would care.

He couldn't see out the window; what an appetite a window awoke. He wanted to look down on the terrain, to observe the nearer wheat fields and the oakhair forests farther off. To plot, if he could, the movement of opposing militias. To note if the chimney of that small farmhouse in the wheat was issuing the smoke of kitchen fires, or had the crusty residents finally abandoned their homestead during the night?

Lacking the window, though, his eye veered inward for a last, involuntary lurch toward his most private possession, the memory of Muhlama.

She'd gone, bounding with energy away from him, up an escarpment of rocks the color of pearlfruit rinds. Now that his whiskers were starting to whiten, he could imagine all too well some male Ocelot lurking beyond the rocks. Or maybe even a Fell Tiger – someone who fit Muhlama better, both in character and in the congress of sexual organs, than the stout and Cowardly Lion.

One thing was certain; she hadn't been unpracticed at the art of receiving sexual advances. She worked herself to her satisfaction with a talent that Brrr had first mistaken for his own glorious technique. Later – again with the laters – he'd mused on her expertise. Lover in the underbrush some-where?

Felinity. You never knew, as he was the first to admit.

'Come on, Shadowpuppet,' said Brrr, nudging the old cat with a sheathed paw. 'Time to finish our interviews. Unriddle the riddles at hand, not the ones out of reach.'

The cat purred, and Brrr purred back. The best part of these late days was in their purring wordlessly together. The closest to companionship he got.

Then, hitting the society of crabby, tired, black-clad maunts on their way toward morning devotions, the best part of the day was behind them.

Sister Doctor and Sister Apothecaire were hotly arguing on a landing. They turned at his approach.

'Ladies,' he said, 'I thought charity ruled in a house like this one.'

'Mind your own business,' said Sister Doctor.

'That's your answer to everything,' snapped Sister Apothecaire. She held her hand to her side, as if she had a case of stitches; perhaps she'd been running. In any case, she was a stout little thing, and the staircase had not been built with Munchkinlander legs in mind.

'Anything I can help with?' His tone sounded grand this morning; maybe just remembering Muhlama once in a while had a tonic effect.

'You can finish your work and be on your way,' said Sister Apothecaire.

'You can join us in chapel to pray for those who died last night,' said Sister Doctor.

His ruff went up. 'Not Yackle?'

'No, but if she keeps refusing to die, we can put her coffin on wheels and slide her into Kellswater like – like—' Here Sister Doctor, who was one hard cookie, lost a startled little tear from the outside of each of her eyes. The drops rolled slowly down, like glue, as if astonished at their liberation.

'Don't be wet,' snapped Sister Apothecaire, and then gave a nervous snuffle. Inadvertently she'd made a joke of some sort. Sister Doctor glared with hatred at her.

Brrr had no use for either of them. 'But what? A

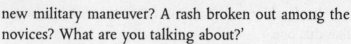

new military maneuver? A rash broken out among the novices? What are you talking about?'

'We have had news of last night's engagement,' said Sister Doctor. 'An itinerant dwarf came to our door early this morning for food, and told us what he knew. In the middle of the night, the Munchkinlander militia surrounded a contingent of Emerald City Messiars and drove them down the slope of a bluff. The dwarf saw it all, he said. The Munchkinlanders herded the hapless soldiers right off the strand of sour pebbles and into the dead reaches of Kellswater.'

'It is impossible,' said the Lion.

'They kept shooting, a volley of arrows and scattershot alike – I don't know the terms of the military trade – and the soldiers were driven deeper, waist-deep deeper; and eventually dove down to escape the onslaught.'

'But Kellswater is poison water,' said Brrr. 'That's what is said. Nothing grows there; no animal drinks at its shores.'

'That's what is said, and that's what is meant,' said Sister Doctor. 'And there is a good reason. The soldiers came up dead – their bodies began to rot once they were immersed. They bobbed like so many carcasses. Not a single soul taken hostage, no mercy shown to any man jack among them.'

'Well,' said the Lion. 'A military operation that worked, then.'

'The Munchkinlanders were unnecessarily cruel,' said Sister Doctor. 'With their penchant for thoroughness, they did in an entire regiment that might have surrendered.'

'You take a lofty point of view.' Sister Apothecaire, being a Munchkinlander herself, was denied loftiness of any sort. 'The Emerald City forces have invaded Munchkinland to annex the other lake – the big lake, the good lake. An illegitimate exercise from every angle. Why shouldn't the Munchkinlanders defend their territory any way they see fit?'

'Good water and bad,' said the Lion, wanting to avoid taking sides here. 'One lake is dead – a depthless basin of venom as far as anyone knows – and the other lake, only miles away, is the fount of life for the greatest green basket of arable land that Oz has. How can water display such variety in character?'

'You can be of help, Sir Brrr,' said Sister Apothecaire. 'If you will. The dwarf tells us that the Munchkinlanders suffered heavy casualties on the ground before they conceived of this maneuver. We have had all our cart horses and donkeys requisitioned by one militia or another over the past several weeks. We have no way of pulling a cart for the collection of suffering bodies. Would you oblige us?'

He looked at Sister Doctor, imagining she would disapprove of offering succor to wounded Munchkinlanders, since she disapproved of their tactics. But she disappointed him; her cold dispersal of mercy, such a mercy as it was, was unequivocal.

'I think we have a cart in whose harness you would fit,' she said. 'An embarrassment, I know – an indignity – but this is war, Sir Brrr.'

'I couldn't possibly,' he said. 'For one thing, there is the matter of an old injury to my spine. I try not to complain of it, but it makes some sorts of labor quite out of the question.'

'I have many liniments useful at reviving sore muscles,' said Sister Apothecaire. 'I keep a full stock of balms and lotions.'

'Then there is the deeper matter of my obligation to the Crown,' continued Brrr over her remarks. 'I need to finish up my enquiries and be on my way to file my report.'

'You will be lucky to get out,' said Sister Doctor. 'If what the dwarf tells us is true, then the Emerald City Messiars will launch an even more virulent campaign against the Munchkinlanders, and this quiet hermitage sits right in the path from one camp to another.'

'I will do what I must,' said the Lion.

'I will pray for the souls of my countrymen,' said Sister Apothecaire.

'I will hold grudges,' said Sister Doctor to them both, and she swept down the stairs. The glass cat, which had been silent throughout, hissed.

2

Brrr returned to the interrogation parlor, but Yackle wasn't there. She was in chapel, listening to liturgical music about flights of angels escorting the lucky dead to their rewards, a good rest among them.

The well of dark in which Yackle lived was something unlike what her companions assumed. Her blindness sometimes seemed to have little to do with vision. It seemed instead a kind of lack of desire, or of the desire that she imagined others felt. She experienced anticipation without the expectation of release – rather like what she assumed the libido of a eunuch might feel like. Or the spiritual ambitions of, say, a bedbug.

So in the chapel, as the maunts prayed for the drowned EC Messiars, Yackle didn't listen to the devotional longing of the spinsters around her. She who didn't seem able to die believed in death, as an article of faith – the only article of faith, and out of her reach! – though the notion of an Afterlife filled her with revulsion. Imagine the boredom of an Afterlife! All that undifferentiated yowling of praise. Yet the maunts, who had feared rape and murder or at any rate inconvenience by an occupying army, seemed ready to

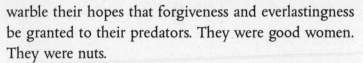
warble their hopes that forgiveness and everlastingness be granted to their predators. They were good women. They were nuts.

Rather than pray, Yackle trained her memory to recall the faded frescoes of angels that had adorned the higher reaches of the chapel walls and the vaulted ceiling. For all she knew, the images had been whitewashed over by now, angels having gone out of fashion somewhat – but beyond the hedge of her blindness Yackle could picture the paintings well. Gamine female angels in trailing robes, arching their ankles and pouting their mouths as if in perpetual erotic bliss. Wings like mattresses – imagine being an angel prettily taken against the soft resistance of her own feathery appendages. The male angels hardly less vulnerable.

How tedious to be an angel: So much holy vigor, and all directed to the Unnamed God who, without form or name or provable substance, could hardly be expected to enjoy the attentions that angels seemed eager to supply.

Probably those images had been whitewashed over. While the mission settlement of this outpost was conveniently distant from the spiritual governance of the EC, the self-appointed Holy Emperor of Oz had wielded his influence upon the varied religious and agnostic traditions of the nation. Probably the bosomy nymphs and rosy-bottomed angel boys above had been banished beyond the cloud of unknowing, a lime wash swirled with a brush. Oh, the happy memories that the soft-bristled brush must cherish!

She was working herself into a state of agitation.

She tried to concentrate for a moment on the music.

But sacred music – another anomaly. If in the Afterlife every good thing coexists eternally, then music cannot exist. Music is the stuttering of adjacent noises in sequence – stress, discord, complaint, resolve: then release – and sequence means timing. If the sound of music is simultaneous, all notes sounding at once, forever, then it is just sound. A mothy blur of noise. A sea of aural fuzz.

'*Yield up, yield up,*' sang the maunts, in a dirge written, surprisingly, in waltz time. Yackle remembered it and tapped her toes.

'*Yield up your souls*
To singe the air.
Yield up, and mount the heavenly stair.
Yield up, yield up,
You're almost there.
You've dropped your bones in the sod.
Yield up, yield up, yield up your souls
  To the darksome, nameless disappearance:
    The heart of the Unnamed God.'

When Sister Doctor approached the podium to offer a eulogy for the dead soldiers, Yackle stood up and rambled away.

3

She was almost back to the chamber where Brrr was conducting his interviews when she was interrupted by an unfamiliar smell. In the corridor's chill stony breath, a mild, milky reek of tubers. At about the level of her thighs.

'Who is it?' she said, thinking: A dog? A raccoon? A Munchkinlander she hadn't met yet? (Sister Apothecaire was the only Munchkinlander in residence, and her musk was redolent of rotting tea leaves, no matter how much lavender she doused herself with.) Then Yackle thought: I'm a bit potty – I imagine this to be old what's-'er-name, the Glikkun from the Lion's past. Sakkali Oafish. A Glikkun would smell of root vegetables; they all live underground.

But it was a male voice that replied. 'Sticky trickle, who'd have guessed this? You old thing? *Still?* What's propping you up?'

She knew the voice, from years and years back. 'Making trouble again?' she snapped at the dwarf.

'I never make trouble,' he protested, chuckling. 'I make way for trouble.'

'What are you doing here? In a cloister of religious women, of all unseemly places?'

'Not my first choice,' he admitted. 'But small and incidental as I am, no more than a straw in the floods of history, I am pushed ahead of the approaching Messiars. The Emerald City will be catching news of the attack this morning. Retaliation time. Of course it's all in the cards, don't you know? The armies are already here, prepared for the next provocation. What an obvious game, what a tedious one. But I agree: I don't like being washed up on the banks of a religious establishment any more than you do, I suspect.'

'Well, get out of here, then,' she said. 'I want nothing to do with your meddling.'

'But I don't meddle,' he repeated. 'I don't even comment. I simply perch and watch. Keep my own counsel. Lips sealed, eyes open. How have *you* managed to stay alive, you old heathen?'

'One gasp at a time. And I have no time to grant you an audience just now. Get out of my way, you imp. You hobgoblin.'

'My feelings are hurt.' His voice wheedled, almost affectionately. 'And we go so far back.'

'So far back, and no further forward,' she said. 'Get out of my way.'

'You haven't run into a Lion slouching along these corridors, have you?'

She rounded on him. 'What *is* your game, you miscreant?'

'Oh, you know me, Missus Madame Maenad. You think you're the only one with an eye to the future, but I take my marching orders from a pretty terrific instrument on wheels. I was led to believe I'd find a Lion about here. Times being what they are, I suppose I need another conscript, maybe one with claws.'

'You – you stay away from him. If you find him. He's on a mission.'

'You *defending* some craven beast? Say it ain't so. I thought you were never out for any but yourself.'

Yackle didn't answer. She just saw in her indeterminate way a kind of shadow of the Lion, slump-spined, bejowled, bewhiskered. A hat rotating in his hands, a stain on his vest. Afflicted with the twitch of always looking over his own shoulder. 'The Lion's not in play here,' she said.

She left the dwarf. As far as Yackle knew, the dwarf was as nameless as the Unnamed God – but not as blameless. Assuming that the Unnamed God was blameless in the matter of human suffering – and if you assumed that, you could have no use for such an ineffectual deity.

She ground her teeth as she moved on by. And then she thought: Maybe that sore old stump of a dwarf is my salvation, after all. Maybe the Lion is just a decoy, a distraction. Maybe it was the dwarf's impending arrival that called me from my unquiet tomb, and Brrr just happened to be in the way. Surely being in the wrong place at the wrong time seemed to be that unlucky scalawag's single occupation in life.

4

When she came into the chamber she was agitated, but Brrr hardly noticed. His own fur was ruffled at the news of the military debacle. 'We will finish our work this morning,' he said to Yackle, before she'd even had the chance to settle into her chair. 'The reprisal for last night's disaster at Kellswater is aiming right this way. I can feel it. I intend to have cleared out before it strikes. Let's get this interview wrapped up.'

'Nothing can be wrapped up,' she snapped.

'Save your irritation for the lunch menu,' he replied, as brusquely. He flipped open his notebook. The glass cat looked a little alarmed at the sharpness between them, and regarded the window ledge. But the sash was swung open this morning, letting in light and air, and perhaps the cat was just smart enough to know that it was too old to rely on being able to jump and perch without tipping out the window and plunging – to shatter into shards? – into the gravel far below.

'This is our second meeting,' said Brrr, writing it down on a new page, 'and our last one. We spent too much time dancing each other's histories yesterday. Down to business, and at once, before the army arrives.'

'And arrive it will,' she said. 'I have it on the highest authority.'

'Your deepest sixth sense?' he asked, cuttingly.

'No,' she admitted. 'Higher than that. My trust in human cruelty. But ask your question; I'm as sick of this as you are. I'd like to see your big furry behind waddling away. Or imagine it, anyway. And plant an old boot in it as you leave, for that matter.'

'You wouldn't be the first. Now listen. About the rumors circulating for a decade or so that Elphaba Thropp had a son. That boy named Liir.'

'What about him?'

'If he is her son, and if he is still alive, and if he has no sisters from Elphaba, then he is next in line to inherit the position of Eminent Thropp. He would be the de facto governor of Munchkinland. His claim would trump that of the Holy Emperor of Oz, Shell Thropp. Elphaba's brother.'

'I know who Shell is, and I know about Liir, too.'

'Can you confirm he is Elphaba's son? Or if he is alive? He was here, it seems – some years ago.'

She had no interest in giving the Lion any scrap of information that might help the EC thugs locate Liir. She spoke cautiously and shared only what she thought was redundant or immaterial. 'Yes. He has been here three times in his life. Once as a young child – perhaps even an infant – when Elphaba wasn't yet the Wicked Witch of the West. She set out from here to the castle in the west—'

'Kiamo Ko.'

'Yes, yes, whatever it's called. She repaired there for reasons of her own. She took the child with her, though where he came from originally – if he was really her issue – I don't know.'

'Don't you know through your inner vision? Can't you figure it out?'

'Even if I did know, what proof would you have? Only my word. I might as well say he was the result of a broomstick handle poking itself hot and jolly in the vortex of a tall black hat. What difference would it make? Just because I have had visions doesn't mean they're true.'

Though she had never said that to herself before.

He grunted. 'Didn't sleep well, did we.'

She glared at him as well as a blind person can manage. He continued in a more neutral tone.

'Whatever you say goes on record. Let someone else decide if it is true or not. When was the other time you saw Liir?'

'It was after he'd been attacked in the air by the Emperor's dragons, as I understand it. He was left for dead in the Disappointments a little to the south. Some do-gooder hauled his carcass here for the maunts to tend. Then a young Quadling woman named Candle, a novice, brought him back to health and life, through devices and schemes of her own.'

'You had nothing to do with it?'

She paused.

'Don't lie to me, don't *lie* to me,' he roared. 'Why bother? The whole world lies! Don't you do it, too!'

'I helped her a little,' said Yackle. How odd to feel capable of being shaken. Maybe she was dying! Her spirits lifted at once. 'Yes, I helped her, why not? I didn't know if Liir was Elphaba's son, but he might have been; I could see that. I remembered him from childhood. So I introduced a little romance into the therapeutic situation. Oh, Candle, that weird duck: She was a honey, but a mystery, too.'

'As who isn't,' he said.

'As who isn't,' she agreed. 'So I took it upon myself to stand guard upon the tower room where she was helping him cling to life, in all the ways that a young woman can and will.'

'Ways?' The Lion was all ears. His whiskers trembled.

'Don't be prurient, you old goat.'

'You said it. You mean it, too; I can tell.'

She had said it; it had slipped out. Time for damage control. 'Yes,' she continued. 'I had never enjoyed the benefit of a good leg-over. I thought she might. I thought he might. He looked rather scathingly virginal to me. Call it, what term do they use – call it transference. Call it divine sublimation. Call it a metaphor. I locked them in together and let their natures run their course.'

'And what happened?'

'I am a cupid of sorts,' she said, 'but I'm not a peeping lecher. History will decide what happened, not you or I.'

'But what did happen? I mean, whether they screwed around or not – what happened next?'

'What happened is they left the mauntery under cover of dark. As you would have been wise to do yourself last night.'

'Where did they go?'

She paused a while and then said, 'This is all old business. I suppose it can't hurt anyone to say.'

'Who are you protecting,' he rushed in, 'and why?'

Ah, but that was it, wasn't it? She admired him for catching her drift. She answered his earlier question, though. 'The maunts had once kept a little printing press off the grounds. A sideline to the religious life: producing pamphlets that opposed the war-mongering of the Emperor. Rather by accident, the press had been discovered by the Emperor's men, who more or less destroyed it. But they never traced the sedition to here. The press was housed some little distance, a day's journey or so from here. I loaded the couple up on a donkey – poor Liir was just barely alive – and I sent them on their way without confiding in my sisters. I thought that was the end of them.'

'You did.' He said it flatly, intending to be as neutral as plaster. Keep going, old lady.

'Yes, but then some short time later – weeks, I think, a few months at the most – Liir returned to the mauntery a final time. He and a soldier of the EC, a minor Menacier named Trism bon Cavalish, had torched the stables of the flying dragons and fled from the Emerald City. It was a case of political action – espionage – I don't know what you'd call it. But a force of the Emerald City under a Commander Cherrystone gave hot pursuit, and arrived at these walls just shortly after the lads did. This was before I went blind – oh, nine years ago, perhaps? And Liir therefore was perhaps twenty, his companion several years older.'

'Was Liir caught?'

'You know he wasn't.' Of this she was sure. 'Don't waste your time, Sir Brrr; there isn't that much of it left.

If he had been caught, it would be in the records. And you wouldn't be here asking about him.'

'You're right,' he admitted. 'But what happened to them?'

'Liir took the Witch's broom and he left the mauntery from the rooftops. It happened that Lady Glinda was in residence – she was a kind of patroness of the order, don't you know; years ago she changed her own name from Galinda to the more stylish Glinda. To honor the popular saint, to bury her rural origins, some other reason. Who knows. Anyway, she made an effort to get Trism out as one of her retinue, and it seemed to work at first. The team that was hunting the lads didn't dare accuse Lady Glinda of treason – not without some kind of proof. She had after all been on the Throne of Oz for a time. She still enjoyed a cherished position in the hearts of her people, though the political climate had changed so much, and for the worse.'

'Naturally. Some of us get accused of treason for no reason. Others who deserve it waft free as a bubble on the breeze. Go figure.'

'Shhh. Listen. When Glinda thought they were safely free of scrutiny, she dismissed bon Cavalish to his own campaigns. She didn't know that she was being trailed, and that the EC thugs would continue after Trism. They set upon him and beat him up. Brutalized him pretty badly, I heard, before letting him escape.

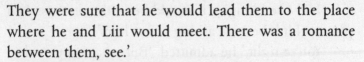

They were sure that he would lead them to the place where he and Liir would meet. There was a romance between them, see.'

'I thought you had arranged for Liir a romance with Candle.'

'Oh, la, romance will find its own outlets, don't you think?'

He wasn't about to comment. 'So they tracked Trism to the farm.'

'See,' she said, 'you know about this already.'

He purred a dangerous sound. The glass cat looked around, alarmed, as if it had discovered a thorn in its own throat.

'I never called it a farm,' she pointed out.

'I have done my research,' he admitted. 'Aren't I allowed that?'

'We choose our own bosses,' she agreed. 'Except those who work as slaves. Now in fact, Trism somehow gave those soldiers the slip for a couple of days. Not for long – they had bloodhounds on the job, can you believe it – but for a precious couple of days. Trism introduced himself to Candle, it seems, and what happened between those two – well, that I *can't* say.'

'You can't or you won't?'

'As good as the same thing, my dear.'

'But we're at the nub of it now. Was Trism jealous of Candle? Or vice versa? They shared a lover, after all. Did they go at each other like wildcats?'

'Is this germane to your investigation, or do I detect a particular interest in sexual jealousy? An uptick in your circulation? Some shallow breathing?'

'Fuck you.'

'If I'd only been so lucky.'

Shadowpuppet seemed to catch the tension. It paused in its morning ablutions and studied a spot on the wall as if embarrassed at the decline of civility.

Brrr governed himself. Don't lose it now. You're closing in on things.

'Candle and Trism. Did their mutual attraction to Liir translate somehow into an attraction to each other? With Liir off rambling on some obligation or other – out of the farm – away from prying eyes – what happened?'

Or were Candle and Trism just using each other, somehow? As he and old Yackle were doing just now?

'There are some things even oracles can't determine,' admitted Yackle. 'What I do know is that by the time Liir returned, Trism had already left. Maybe he wanted to avoid Liir. Maybe he had persuaded Candle to join him later in some safe harbor, far from the attentions of a novice magician.'

'Magician!'

'Well, if Liir were Elphaba's son, he'd be a witch of sorts, wouldn't he? Or have the potential, anyway? That's what this is all about, isn't it? Now don't *you* lie to *me*,' she snapped. 'Have I ferreted out from you what your real aim is? Are you looking for Liir? You want to get at him through any avenue possible – through either of his lovers, Candle or Trism, or . . .'

Still, she paused; she couldn't say it.

'*Or what?*' Brrr hoped that she would tell him what he wanted to know – the Grimmerie, *the Grimmerie!* – instead of what she needed to share. She kept on.

'So Commander Cherrystone circles Apple Press Farm, but Trism has already left. Cherrystone lies in wait for Liir to return. Then, just before dawn one morning, Candle leaves with a bundle under her arm. Hoping it might be the Grimmerie, Cherrystone throws all his efforts into following her. It turns out though that she has swifted away a bundle of rags, nothing more. She is deemed to have no importance – perhaps she acted the simpleton – and she is released.'

'What happened to them all?'

'Up in smoke,' she said. 'They all went up in smoke, each in a separate puff.'

They both contemplated the convenience of a private exit.

'How do you know so much?' he pressed.

'Cherrystone returned here when all his other trails went cold. He conducted an interview with the old Superior Maunt. I'm sorry to say she died a few hours later. Either from shock or due to a stronger talent at self-preservation than I have been able to manage.'

'And he interviewed you,' said Brrr.

'You know it,' she replied.

'You have told me more than you told him,' he said, 'and I didn't go the length to put out your eyes the way he did.'

'The blind see history in a different way than the sighted. Besides' – she sighed as she spoke – 'back then I had no idea I was going to prove so hopeless at dying a natural death. All that blood, all that mess—'

'Please,' he said. 'Please. I did have some breakfast.'

'It's ancient history,' she said. 'This was nine years ago. Where are they all now? How did they disappear so thoroughly? If they are still alive, Liir would be twenty-eight or -nine – Candle likewise – Trism thirty-two – and . . . And . . .'

And, she thought, the child, the child; the child whom Candle had borne? But still she could not speak.

Brrr sat very still.

She sat up straight. 'I have given you as much as I know. The truth is, once I went blind, I began to doubt my own oracular capacity. Perhaps Commander Cherrystone's terrible attack on me was exactly the thing. I can smell a person,' she said, 'I can smell a lie, but I can no longer see the truth right in front of my face.'

'You've corroborated a lot,' he agreed. 'Still, how did you know so much about the movements of Trism and Candle?'

'Candle came back, for one night,' said Yackle. 'She came back to thank me for . . . for everything. Sensibly, she wouldn't tell me where she was going; this meant I could not have it forced out of me. She was a week or so ahead of Cherrystone.'

She appeared to look out the window. 'I think of her often,' she said. 'I liked the young girl. She was braver than most.

'Braver than you,' she continued.

'That's not saying much,' said Brrr.

'I can smell a lie,' she said, 'and I believe that you still haven't told me why you're here.'

'I have,' he said. 'We're looking for Liir, don't you know? To make sure the Munchkinlanders don't rally behind him as the proper Eminence. To make sure that Shell's claim to the breadbasket of Oz isn't challenged—'

'There is no more time to lie,' she told him, rather peacefully. If she could have found his huge paw and patted it for comfort, she would have. 'You haven't really come here to find out about Liir and Trism and Candle and all. You knew most of that already. You knew about Liir and how he would suffer, thinking that Trism and Candle had fallen in love. Fine for him to love two – not so fine for him to watch two others loving in turn.'

'I take a lot of notes,' said Brrr, 'but I don't pay attention to that aspect of people's lives.'

'You don't want to,' she noted, 'because it is too close to home, I suspect.'

'None of your business,' he growled. 'If you are so ornery and right all the time, then how am I lying? What *have* I come for that you haven't yet told me? Tell it to me now and we'll have done with this interview. I can smell death frying up in the skillet alongside the lunchtime bacon. Let's finish up.'

She stood and with unerring accuracy she pointed a bony finger right along the seam of his nose. 'You want to find out the location of the Grimmerie,' she said. 'You want the great book of magic. Sure you'd be glad enough to learn where Liir is, and his little circle of oddities. But Liir isn't the firebrand that Elphaba was; he's nothing without that encyclopedia of spells. The Emperor has dispatched you here to see if I can tell you where the book is. Elphaba's magic book, and someone else's magic book before it was hers. You've been lying all along. Liir is only part of it. You want the book.'

He sat very still for a long long time. The glass cat watched with an unblinking eye.

'If you've known that all along,' he said softly, 'then you must also know where it is.'

'Ah, no, not that,' she said. 'Your comrade-at-war, then a mere commander, blinded me, and I have lost what powers I had. Tell General Cherrystone to come back and rip out my heart and fry it alongside your lunchtime bacon, and then we'll see if I can lose the rest of my powers – like breathing, and thinking, and remembering, and hating. I should be glad to let go of some of these functions.'

'Let go of the drama, why don't we. Tell me why you can't just have a vision and find out where the Grimmerie is. That's all I want. To get out of here with some hard information. We're counting in hours now, not days, before this place becomes a militarized zone. Madame Morrible's notes suggested you were Elphaba's sentry angel. No one has a better chance of knowing where the book went but you.'

'An angel!' She began to laugh. It was a hideous sight, her eyes rolling about in her skull. She clutched her ribs and bent over. 'Oh, that's rich! An atheistic angel.'

He had to wait for her wheezing to peter out. 'Please,' he said. 'What must I promise you in exchange for the location of the Grimmerie?'

'It's hopeless,' she said, her voice giddy now, as if having abandoned all hope. 'One doesn't have visions on demand. And even if I knew, dear Brrr, how could I tell you? We're at cross-purposes. The EC would use it against—'

But she went from breezy hopelessness to a sudden frenzy; her face contorted.

'Are you all right?' he said. She shook her head. It wasn't a pang of death – nothing as useful to her as that – but a grief mortal enough to carry away anyone less immortal than she continued to be.

'Stop,' he said. 'It's not that bad. It can't be.'

'What will you do if you can't locate the Grimmerie?' she asked at last. 'Who is your next witness?'

'I have none.' He slapped his notebook closed. 'Madame Morrible's papers turned up precious little, actually. She was a bit of a sorceress herself – you must have figured that out – and she was sharp enough to have known exactly what to discard. Even her references to you were cryptic – more in the line of deducing your existence by a kind of magical algebraics. And learning your name through the agency of a mechanical spy named Grommetik.'

'All that lead-up, and I've given you precious little. What will you do next?'

'Assuming I can get overland without being molested, I will have to return to the Emerald City with what I've been able to gather. The Court won't be pleased with me, but I've done my best.'

'They won't drop you into Southstairs?'

'They won't. My plea bargain has sorted that out, at least.'

'You trust the Court not to revoke its understanding?'

After this review of how his life had run so far? Only one answer. 'No. I don't trust the Court at all.'

'Then that's the first evidence of good sense I've witnessed in you.' She twisted her fingers ghoulishly. 'I will trust you, and hope that when you leave here you might come to your senses. The Emerald City will never take you in. You're too raw and obvious for them. Look, I have no other option. I'm not going to trust any dwarf with this matter; his allegiance is already pledged. You will have to do. You are a creature bedeviled with foolishness and bad luck, but if you're finally smart enough to be skeptical about the honchos in the EC, well, I suppose there is some hope.'

'Let me save you from making a mistake,' he said. 'You are too smart to trust in me.'

'I need your help,' she replied. 'There's no one else. It's come down to that. I have to trust you whether I should or not.'

Well, that was it, wasn't it? For her, for him, for anyone? Being needed? The sorry old approval game? Either it would work or it wouldn't: She had no choice.

'All right, then, tell me,' he said. 'Tell me what you have to tell me. Maybe if I become rehabilitated in the EC, I'll be in a position to help sometime.'

'You haven't given up, have you?'

'Look, if you're going to trust me, you'll have to trust me. I'll do with your information as I see fit. And you know I don't see very fit.'

'You see better than I do at this point.'

'A matter of opinion.' He closed his notebook. 'I'm putting my pencil away. Just tell me.'

'It isn't Liir,' she said. 'It's Liir and Candle together – it's – their child. I need you to stand for her, if she needs standing for. As no one ever stood for you.'

'Their child,' he said.

'Born in Apple Press Farm, while Liir was absent. Nine years ago. When Candle left with that bundle, it was to draw the watching eyes away from the newborn. She left the baby for Liir to find; she swifted away to draw the hounds off scent.'

'So that is why you locked Candle in the tower with Liir? So she would have sex with Liir and perhaps conceive a child? Why would you care? Was it because you were never nine? No, not that. It was because you would never conceive a child yourself. You were too old when you were born. You were all dried up before you even got going.'

'Very sharp of you. I suppose I deserve this. I can tell you have had many dinner parties with cognoscenti who amuse themselves at guessing the motivations of others. But my motivation doesn't matter. The thing happened, and now there is a child, a girl. And I have realized that this is why I can't die. I was present at her conception: I was her godmother, in a sense. But I haven't arranged for a guardian for her in my absence, as I tried to be one for Elphaba.'

'Why should she need a guardian?' The Lion's

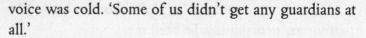

voice was cold. 'Some of us didn't get any guardians at all.'

'And you would recommend that, based on your own experience?'

'I suppose she is special,' he said venomously. 'History belongs to her, right? The next Munchkinlander Eminence in her minority? Prophecies tremble on her little shoulders? What did you say of Elphaba, that time you took a swig of the joy juice and had your first vision? Something like *This child belongs to history*, was it? Good and ill hangs in the balance, right? So she must be protected at all costs, right? She'll save us all, just like little dead Ozma? The little darling? Right?'

Yackle could not take umbrage at his tone. She understood the rage masked as sarcasm. She rubbed her shoulder blades as if they were too heavy for her own spine. When she answered, her old lips quivered.

'It's not that she is special,' said Yackle. 'It's not that she is chosen. It's that she is ours. That's all.'

He knew what the possessive pronoun meant. She is the one who is here, special or no. Whether to be glorified by history or abandoned by fate – to be accident's victim or to be prophecy's chosen child: It makes no difference. She's the innocent on board. That was all. It came down to no more than that.

'They go to war, back and forth,' said Yackle. 'The smallest indivisible part of a nation worth defending is not a field, a lake, a city, an industry, but a child.

'The child would be nine,' said Yackle in a softer voice, almost to herself. 'A nice age for a child.'

'That is,' she continued, 'I have always assumed it might be. I myself was never nine. As you know. Still, it sounds a pleasant age.'

Brrr thought that none of his ages had been particularly pleasant. Still, at this remove, he wouldn't have relinquished a moment of any of them.

'There, there,' he said. 'Don't get soppy on us. I've said I would listen, and I have listened. I've heard what you said. I didn't write it down. I've put it' – he tapped his chest – 'right here.'

The glass cat turned its head so quickly that the light winked from its ear tips. Brrr was rising from his chair and then dropping to his knees, awful creaking in his joints. He was curling up on the floor at the feet of the trembling old harridan. She was weeping into the edge of her shroud. He was purring, and rubbing his head against her ankles.

5

A knock at the door. Brrr sprang to a more dignified position at the arrival of Sister Apothecaire. 'You must forgive me,' she said in tones that brooked no dispute in the matter. 'Sister Hermit, walled up in the cenobitic tower, has broken her silence to drop down a message in a basket. An army vaster than she knows how to describe is fording the Gillikin River west of here.'

'I don't follow,' said Brrr. 'Which army, which direction?'

'West to east, so it must be the EC Messiars,' said Sister Apothecaire. As she was professed to neutrality, her tone was curt, but her sympathies lay with her own countrymen, so her eyes snapped like coal fire. 'But there's also a blaze happening to the south. Perhaps a band of the Messiars is burning the forest so as to destroy the blinds that can conceal snipers and guerrillas. They'll force a Munchkinlander retreat to the south. In any case, the Messiars are meeting no resistance so far and will be here by sunset.'

'I am on their side,' said the Lion, to no one in particular – to himself, then.

'Bully for you. You can make the tea and crumpets

for eight hundred.' Fear was turning her waspish. She continued in a rush. 'The administrative troika of the mauntery has called an emergency Council – I mean, Sister Doctor of course, and her two assistants – of which I am not one, not in the business of governance. They will propose how we shall meet the ruthless invaders.'

'Hardly invaders,' Brrr corrected her. 'This mauntery is not in Munchkinland.'

'In my book, an army intent on invading is an invading army no matter which side of the border you view it from. Sister Doctor may view things differently; that's her prerogative. I'm simply *staff*.' Her head turned to the hall, and she called out, 'Aren't you attending? *Please*. You can come in here, if you will.'

'We have company?' said Yackle.

'We have no time for company,' said Brrr.

'You have no say in the matter,' said Sister Apothecaire. 'Do you forget you're a guest here? A Council is called, and Sisters Hospitality and Cook are required to attend. So I have arranged a cold luncheon for all strangers who have sought sanctuary here. You can eat together. We will dismiss you when and if the Council decides that would be a prudent course of action.'

'I can't work under these conditions,' said Brrr.

'Courage,' said Yackle. 'Who knows what you can or cannot do?'

Sister Apothecaire made no move to help the novices, who came in with flasks of water, slit husks of pearlfruit, ham sandwiches, and a bowl of blue olives. The young women set the repast down on a sideboard and fled.

Into the room traipsed a dwarf, a woman in a plain veil, and a few muscle boys sporting tangerine tunics and leggings as well as shaved heads, which looked tangerine-ish by association.

'I'll let you make your own introductions,' said Sister Apothecaire. She elevated her chin till her nose was nearly as high as her forehead. The gesture proved she could be taller than a dwarf – which was lost on no one.

'We don't trust louts loose among the novices,' she continued briskly, 'and as I mentioned, we have an emergency Council to convene. So forgive me the indignity of this key – it is a necessity in these wartimes, and signifies no disrespect.' She departed, closing the door with a decisive slam. They all listened to hear the key turn in the lock.

'We're being held hostage by sisters in a mauntery?' asked Brrr.

'Hey, I got weak kidneys,' said one of the skinheads.

'Piss out the window,' called Sister Apothecaire through the door. 'Don't think me rude. We just can't have beefsteak lads wandering about the cloisters and hiding in the novices' wardrobes, waiting to provide them a midnight surprise. I'm sure you understand.'

'You again,' said Yackle, dilating her nostrils as a horse might.

'Me again,' agreed the dwarf. 'We seem destined to spend a holiday together.'

'Well, one of us should know about destiny,' said Yackle, 'though I confess that I didn't see this coming.'

'There's a lot more to seeing things coming than meets the eye,' said the dwarf. 'The proverbial eye, I mean, not your wonky pair. But what do I know? It always takes some—'

'I'm on a government exercise here,' interrupted Brrr. Well, he sure was, compared to a dwarf, anyway. He waved with his notebook. 'I suppose for the record I should jot down your names, and so on. Material witnesses in case this next section of my deposition is questioned by the Courts.'

'Don't have a name,' said the dwarf affably.

'Everyone's got a name,' said Brrr.

'Ask a garden moth what its name is,' said the dwarf.

'Dwarf,' said Brrr, writing. 'Ugly and hostile. Refuses to name himself.'

'Who gets to name himself?' said the dwarf. 'Come on.'

'I did,' said Yackle.

'Oh you, you're a honey, you,' said the dwarf. 'Give

me a break. Old Mama Senility gets creative.'

'I'm Ilianora,' said the woman. She dropped her veil off her forehead, revealing a sharp profile. Her white hair was lustrous and thick, no sign of yellowing. Indeed, noted Brrr, Ilianora had good skin tone, only a few wrinkles around the eyes. Her chin hadn't sunk and her color was high. Ruby plum. 'Put me down as apprentice to the dwarf. And he's not being obstinate: He has no name, or none that I've heard him admit to. When I need to address him, I call him Mr Boss.'

'Home?' asked Brrr. Her accent was curious; he couldn't place it. Might she be a Winkie?

'None,' she said. 'We're itinerants. We're the company of the Clock of the Time Dragon. You may have heard of us.'

'Yo ho,' said Brrr, recoiling. 'I've heard of that. Yes. Didn't know it was still a going concern.'

'Going nowhere fast, at the moment,' said the dwarf, amiably enough. He scratched himself at the base of his spine where, Brrr thought, a tail would have emerged had he one.

'You young stalwarts?' asked Brrr. The lads refused to name themselves. They settled down to deal a few hands of shamerika, a game that appeared to involve two sets of playing cards, a wodge of ersatz paper notes, a set of weighted dice, and a trapunto cloth map in which small brass flags could be stuck, moved, or removed. Brrr guessed that they had little to offer, and he scribbled 'seven apprentices.' He could scare their names out of them later.

'So the Emerald City Messiars are approaching by the legions,' said Brrr. 'A fine fix you've gotten yourself into, little man.'

'Truth or consequences,' said the dwarf. 'My favorite game.' He sunk his teeth into a ham sandwich and smiled around the mouthful.

'Don't eat so fast,' said Ilianora. 'You'll choke.'

'I wish,' said the dwarf.

'You sound like me,' said Yackle, surprised. 'Life gone on a bit too long for you, too?'

'Don't get me started,' said the dwarf.

'Mr Boss is none of your concern,' said Ilianora to Yackle and Brrr both. To the dwarf, she continued, 'Let's use this time to rest.'

'Fair enough,' said the dwarf. 'When we are ready to move again, we may need to move quickly.'

Ilianora sat on the floor and arranged the folds of her skirt to cover her ankles. 'Take no notice of us, friends. We'll sit silently and catch a midday nap, like your crystal cat.'

The cat opened one eye as if on cue. Never predict a cat, thought Brrr, somewhat proudly.

'Brrr, how delightful,' said Yackle. 'We have just about reached the end of what we could say to each other, and look: Look. Fate, or the Unnamed God, or brute coincidence, whatever you will call it, has

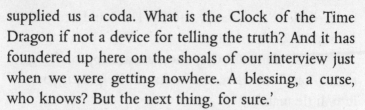

supplied us a coda. What is the Clock of the Time Dragon if not a device for telling the truth? And it has foundered up here on the shoals of our interview just when we were getting nowhere. A blessing, a curse, who knows? But the next thing, for sure.'

'I'm hardly here on official business,' hummed the dwarf through his nose, around his mouthful. 'I'm on sabbatical this year.'

'What is your business, precisely?' the Lion asked him.

'I owe *you* no answers, you nosey parker.'

'I am supplied with the writ of the Emperor,' said Brrr.

'I have a master who is an independent agent, thank you very much. I don't answer to the *Emperor of Oz*.' The dwarf was withering. 'True, I was looking for a Lion, I thought. But I have no use for a minion of the state. Don't suppose there are any other Lions on the premises?'

'Mr Boss,' said Ilianora, in an affectionate but weary tone. 'Oh, Mr Boss.' She took an ivory comb out of her pocket and began to address the knots in her hair.

'You do have your fanciful equipment with you, no?' asked Yackle. 'The fabulous theatrical clock with the Time Dragon coiled atop it?'

'He don't park it for storage this season,' intoned one of the boys, rubbing an aching shoulder.

'I'll park something in your nether nether land,' barked the dwarf. 'If something is to be said, I'll say it, or you're history. Got that?'

'Got it once too often,' murmured the lad, pretending to protect sore hindquarters, but then he fell silent.

'I don't want to talk to timepieces,' said the Lion.

'But just think!' Yackle was filled with energy. 'I've run out of capacity to see beyond the end of my own imagined nose. And who walks in but yon Mr Boss, let's call him. Accompanying a tiktok legend: a device that can sniff out the hidden. Brrr, I'll ask it about my death. I can stand to learn something new. I'm sick of being stuck here. What do you say?' She turned to where she knew the dwarf must be lolling. 'Can you do an old friend a favor?'

'In what context might you be said to be friends?' asked Brrr.

'Yeah, what context would that be?' asked the dwarf dryly.

'We've been circling around each other for years,' said Yackle. 'Why don't you take *his* deposition, Sir Brrr? He's been on the outskirts of Elphaba's life, too.'

'Pure coincidence, if it happened at all, which I'm not saying it did or it didn't,' said the dwarf. 'I had a different mission, lady. Don't involve me in your hurly-burly.'

'You *are* involved,' said Yackle. 'You wouldn't have

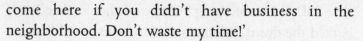

come here if you didn't have business in the neighborhood. Don't waste my time!'

'Why not? You've got plenty to waste,' he answered. 'You may not be getting any younger, but you're not getting any deader, either. No, I had reason to think I was looking for a Lion who might join us — but not this liverish lump. I must be off my game.'

'Your weird equipment knows where it wants to go, and when it wants to rest,' said Yackle. 'So it wanted to come here, eh? It can look like a tiktok extravaganza, all gears and sequins and powdery flashes of light. Traveling theater. But what it knows, and what it shows! How do you account for that? Do you send your accomplices ahead of you as advance scouts, to sniff out the local gossip, to read the local tea leaves, so when you pull into the village you know what is on everyone's mind?'

'Them? Hah,' said the dwarf. He plugged one nostril and mimed shooting a plug of mucus out of the other one. 'Haven't the brains among them to come in out of the rain.'

'Then it's a charm — I've always guessed it. Some sledgehammer of a charm, that can read the world's secrets correctly decade after decade.'

'Ninety-nine point ninety-seven percent accuracy,' said Ilianora. 'That's what the advertising panel says, anyway.'

'Hush, daughter,' said the dwarf, in a more kindly

tone than before. 'Pour me some water, will you?'

'Whose spell is as strong as that?' asked the Lion, becoming interested despite himself. 'Whose spell could teach a puppet machine to spill secrets like that?'

'One whose name I don't give out, as I don't give out my own,' said the dwarf. 'Ooh, this water is good. I've always wondered why the grand viziers of magic in the Emerald City – that is, if there are any – didn't just get to work devising a spell to purify the whole of Kellswater. Reduce Loyal Oz's dependence on foreign water. That lake is nearly as large as Restwater and if made potable could irrigate all of Loyal Oz. That would liberate the EC from its obsession with truculent Munchkinlanders, who, as I hear it told, never never shall be slaves.'

'One of the folktales I heard in my youth,' said Ilianora, 'held that the ancient old demon-witch, Kumbricia herself, lives in the depths of Kellswater, or died there, perhaps, despoiling the supply for all time.'

'You and your tales,' said the dwarf. 'One of the folktales I heard in my youth is that folktales are idiotic. Anyway, the cause is beside the point.'

'Sniff out the cause, and you conceive the solution,' said Yackle. 'But who knows. Mr Boss, Mr Boss, if you won't show Sir Brrr where in Oz the Grimmerie might be hidden – for that's really what he is here to learn – then do some good for me, your old partner and nemesis on the hems of Elphaba's life.

Show me how I might die. I've told to this Lion all that I know. Let me reap some small benefit in return.'

'The Lion works for the Emerald City,' said the dwarf. 'I should reward you for dealing him information that the EC might find useful? I've no opposition to the Emperor of Oz per se, but I've no affection either. Live and let seethe, that's my motto.'

'The Clock is off-limits, anyway; we're locked in,' remarked Ilianora, arranging a trio of white ribbons in her white hair. 'This is probably the safest site in central Oz right now.'

'A sanctuary or a trap,' said the Lion. 'I'll bark the door down if I want to. As I said. But Mister Boss-man, why are you on the "hems" of Elphaba's life, as Mother Yackle puts it?'

'You're here to interrogate the old brickbat, not me,' said the dwarf. 'En't that right? Give me that chair, you, so that I can look out the window and see if the armies are in sight.' He scrabbled up on the seat and raised himself on his toes.

The Lion could have told the dwarf what was visible: a low bolster of smoke to the southwest. The smoke must be heavy. Tendrils of it lifted up, like the heads of dark swans, then ducked down again. There was no acridity in the air, though. The wind must still be from the north or northeast.

'They're burning the oakhair forest,' said the

dwarf. 'Pushing the Munchkinlanders farther south, away from the lake, I guess.'

'Unless the wind swings around,' said Ilianora, standing beside him. 'Then it might smoke the Munchkinlanders out into the open. They'd be mowed down like wheat by a scythe.'

'We don't take sides,' the dwarf reminded her. 'Not in our brief.'

'We can take the side of mercy without being compromised,' she replied. 'Surely?'

'If it don't compromise our mission, why not?' He munched his sandwich with gusto. 'Knock yourself out with mercy, honey.'

'Mr Boss,' she said. 'The Messiars may have gotten their idea of a smoke-out from the dragon. Their fellow infantrymen were blinded by smoke from our Clock – and driven into the obsolete lake.'

'It appears Fate may have caught up with those who advertise as Fate's voice,' said Yackle, not, Brrr thought, without a touch of satisfaction. Even smugness. Professional jealousy among oracles!

'Ha,' replied the dwarf, grousing. 'Fate. Some call it fate. Some call it lunch.'

'You fault your own profession?' Yackle seemed to be enjoying this. 'Shame on you.'

'Fate brought you here,' said the Lion. 'You must admit that.'

'Listen,' said the dwarf, 'consider a pack of nursery

children on a church picnic. They are about to mount a grassy hilltop. Clouds gather while one of them stops below to tie the laces of a lisping junior. Then lightning strikes at the crown of the hill. Say it strikes the meanest child, the one who wouldn't pause to help and so has forged on ahead. Or say the cruel child has already passed to safety, so lightning kills the kindly laggard child, who is second up the slope. Or say, even, that both who act, either in churlishness or charity, cross the upland meadow safely, so it is the innocent toddler who is killed. Any of those three deaths are possible without a moral being drawn. Do you think that lightning has chosen its victim on the strength of character?'

'Then where does fate come in?' asked the Lion. 'Wouldn't this Clock of yours have been able to name what was to happen? Or any blind old oracle worth her salt?'

'Fate is only fate once it has happened. Even our own deaths are only theoretical until we croak.'

Ilianora pursed her lips as if trying to decide whether to join the conversation. She did. 'There is a fourth child at the base of the hill who can read the weather enough to know that lightning is likely. The child can rush forward to chase all the others off the mound, and she risks being killed in the process. If that brave child is slain by lightning, it is sullen fate at work. But the other children's lives have been altered. History has been vexed by the intercession of a bit player. It is what we hope for, and what we dread, too. Isn't it?'

The dwarf replied, 'I dread nothing but garlic muffins. Listen, the child who can read the portents of weather may well have hurried the others back down the slope into the jaws of a manticore, itself sensible about lightning and waiting out the storm in the down-slope shrubs.'

'Not to act is to act, too,' insisted Ilianora.

The dwarf seemed to agree with this, or perhaps he was tired of the discussion. 'Couldn't be truer, sweet-cakes, but we haven't time to keep nattering like this. I haven't been stepping sideways for half a century just to be caught, by fate or accident, in some WC in a mauntery, of all godforsaken places. Break down that door, Lion, and we can all get out, and leave these holy women to their immolation. Might be lively entertainment for a maunt, to be violated and then martyred, but I can't subject my Ilianora to the danger. Lion, the door.'

Brrr had little inclination to snap to the dwarf's commands, but he had no inclination at all to stay put. 'Always with the doors,' he said. 'When I broke through at the Witch's castle, I was in better nick.' He took off his weskit and folded it neatly as the boys surrendered their cards and collected their ivory quad-ribbed pieces. The little glass cat blinked, obedient and even docile, but it seemed ready to quit the company of oracles and acolytes.

Ilianora, with a placidity that under the circumstances suggested a mild mental incompetence, straightened the margins of her veil and stood up. 'After you,' she said to the Lion, indicating the door.

For the Lion, staying in fighting trim had never been a daily ambition. He did several deep-knee bends and sprang back and forth across the room to get his blood going. Turning to Yackle, he asked, 'Are you coming with us? Or is this what you've been waiting for? Death by an army sharpshooter? I shouldn't hang around any longer than necessary—'

Yackle appeared to have passed out.

'The sight of me taking any exercise, I know: a taxation to credulity,' said Brrr.

'She's ill,' said Ilianora. She moved without apparent urgency to the old woman's side, but her voice betrayed some fretfulness at last. The ancient oracle had sloped sideways to the floor and – oh, not a pretty thing to witness – her eyes had actually rolled back in her skull, just as oracles were said to be able to do, so the blind eyes looked inward. Only a glaucous white showed between the remaining shreds of ancient eyelashes.

Ilianora took Yackle onto her lap, like a mother to a child, but reversed.

'She's shamming,' said the Lion without conviction.

'Oooh, that's revolting,' said one of the boys. 'Those eyes.'

'She's trying to hold us here,' said the dwarf as Yackle began to shake. 'She is in cahoots with the powers that be. Pay her no mind. Lion, bust down that door before I bust your chops.' He stumped across the floor and showed the Lion a laughable little fist, so close that the pig-bristle hairs growing out of the knuckles went all blurry, and the Lion had to pull back to get them in focus.

'Can we do something to help?' asked Ilianora. Yackle had torn her robes open, and Ilianora tried to close them again. Her attempts were rebuffed by the ancient maunt's thrashing limbs. The sound unreeling from her mouth was a taper of protest; it hummed against – he could hear it now himself, Brrr could – the groan of the oakhair trees as their harp strings swung in the smoke, and shimmered atonally, and then snapped. All this he could hear, and more besides: The room had fallen so very still as everyone watched Yackle in the throes of some condition, as if in the maw of some invisible beast.

'Water for her,' murmured Ilianora, and one of the boys brought forward a tumbler of water. But Yackle's mouth wouldn't stay still enough to cup the liquid, and it drained off her face to stain her robe.

Brrr watched as old Shadowpuppet, who had kept its tail tightly wound about its furled legs, now stretched with effort and scrabbled, you'd have to say, across the floor. It put out a paw tentatively against the heavy cross-laid door, and walked its front legs stiffly up the panels till it was leaning against the door like a fragile glass buttress. The cat meowed. Brrr had heard purrs from Shadowpuppet before, but in all these weeks, nothing more expressive than a glottal hum. This complaint was vicious, like the voice of a tomcat being crossed, and reminded him, just for a second, of Muhlama's high-flown irritability.

'Let's go. We're all agreed,' said the dwarf. 'Even your shattery cat can tell that it's time.'

Brrr flipped his notebook closed. Was Yackle shamming? He wouldn't put it past her. But why would she want to hold them there? Not to do him harm – the EC Messiars wouldn't lay a finger on Brrr, not with his letter of introduction from the EC on his person. Did Yackle know something more about the dwarf than she was letting on?

But who cared? He'd gotten a good deal of what he had come for. The old bag of bones could suffer and crumple if she wanted. That was what she had wanted. And anyway, wasn't bolting from a crisis his special skill and trademark?

He turned back to stalking up and down a few more times. It moved the blood, loosened the joints, bulked up the muscles. It had been a long time since he had had to throw his weight around. Humiliating if he couldn't actually defeat a door in a mauntery, but he tried not to think about that yet. Out of the corner of his eye, he saw the dwarf rooting through the pocket of the Lion's own weskit.

'Hey, what do you think you're doing—'

Too late. The dwarf had folded the piece of official vellum into a chevron, and was aiming—

'You don't dare!'

The paper soared out the window before the Lion could snatch at it. 'Now we're all in the same boat,' said the dwarf affably. 'No one is supplied with special defenses against being aggrieved by the Messiars, or whichever army gets here first. So stop stalling, Lion. Get us out of here before the soldiers arrive.'

Brrr could have sprung on the dwarf, swiped him sideways out the window. Mashed him to an ugly organic patty, internal organs extruded like sausage meat through a grinder. Good-bye to Mr Boss's unblinking unretreating stance, his out-thrust bearded chin and agate eyes. His belligerence. His confidence. In one so small: so concentrated. Like Sakkala Oafish. Where did it come from?

Was the dwarf a Glikkun – avenging the Traum Massacre, after all this time?

No: That was his own nerves attacking him, a case of the humors. Or, as some called it, paranoia. As much to shake himself up as anything else, Brrr roared. The boys started. The dwarf did not.

The Lion tensed and sprung, rolling his spine forward and sideways, to take the brunt of the impact on his shoulder rather than his skull.

There was a gratifying thud, a shriek of splitting wood, and an echo, but the door did not split. The old oaken planks ran in two depths on the bias, they were laid tongue-and-groove and reinforced by iron braces. And the doorjamb was stone.

'Good one,' said the dwarf. 'Very nice, that. Expected no less.'

'In words of one syllable or less,' said the Lion, 'first: ow. Next: shut up. You want to take a turn, be my guest.'

Ilianora came up to Brrr to press her hands on his shoulder muscles. 'Your old auntie needs help,' she said. 'Wasn't that Munchkinlander maunt who locked us in here a healer? An apothecaire? We must find her.'

'You don't understand. If Yackle is failing at last, the last thing she wants is help,' said the Lion, shaking Ilianora off. 'But I'll try again.'

Three, four times at the door.

'Who's in a hurry?' said the dwarf. 'Not me. I can't see the army approaching through that high window. I'm too short. So I'm totally unconcerned. I think I'll sit here and teach myself to count in a foreign language. One, two, three, fuck, fuck, six, seven, eight, nine, fuck.'

'Mr Boss,' said Ilianora.

'Hey, look at the see-through pussy,' said one of the boys. 'She having the genuine hissy fit?'

'Hair ball, more likely,' said another.

'Glass hair ball? Ouch.'

Brrr thought: It's as if Shadowpuppet is as alarmed by the loss of the writ as I am. Attuned to my jitters. Some sweet, small consolation.

In protection of Shadowpuppet, if no one else, the Lion made another half-dozen lunges at the door. Eventually the wood split along the grain, and the iron doorknob and lock hung at a drunken angle. It appeared that Sister Apothecaire had left the key in the keyhole. They had some job reorienting the lock to line up, but eventually they managed, and opened the remains of the door.

'Are you coming?' said the dwarf.

'She's not in a condition to be moved,' said Ilianora. 'You go, get things in order. We'll follow as soon as we can.'

They pelted away. Their footsteps retreating down the stone stairs made an isolating sound. The mauntery echoed like a mausoleum.

Still Yackle twitched, like a blind fish unable to see the string coming out of its mouth or the fisherman overhead, but responsive to every tug. Ilianora kept one hand on Yackle's shoulder or at her wrist.

'You have a talent for comforting the sick?' said Brrr.

'None,' she replied. 'Why don't you go with them? Nothing is holding you here.'

He had no answer so he offered none. 'What's your answer to that same question?' he said.

'By long habit,' she replied, 'I don't answer questions.'

'Could we get her on my back?' said Brrr. 'Maybe I could carry her down the stairs?'

'She's too brittle, and she's still being bothered by a spell of something.'

'Maybe she'll wake up and find herself an infant this time,' said Brrr, almost to himself. 'With a cowardly Lion and a whatever-you-are for parents. What are you?'

'I'm the handmaiden of the Clock, I suppose,' said Ilianora.

'That tells me less than I want to know.'

'Are you taking notes?'

'No,' he said, 'and that's a promise.'

She drew her knees up to her chin. She looked like a small Ice Monkey, almost, in her white veil. With Yackle in her white, too, they might be Granny Ice Monkey with Granddaughter. Two weird characters in their matching shrouds.

'Are you Mr Boss's daughter, or are you married to him?' asked Brrr. 'I can't see why anyone would commit herself to a clockwork oracle, unless it was the family business.'

'I am not married, and will not be so,' said Ilianora. 'I'm no longer fit for bearing children.'

'You have white hair, but you aren't that old . . .'

'I had myself closed,' she said, 'after having heard enough of human iniquity to despair of the species. Closed. So I tread the world lightly, lightly as possible, and I bring no infants forward to suffer as I have done. I worked with the underground vigilantes who struggle against the tyrant on the throne of the Emerald City – our Emperor Apostle – until I learned that in the service of their honorable goal they are capable of actions as dishonorable as the Emperor's – then I gave myself up for lost. I wandered without aim or ambition, a sad folly of a way to spend one's life.'

'I wouldn't know, being drenched in accomplishment each time I open a new door—'

She laughed at him; a bell-like sound so devoid of malice that it made his ears ring. Brrr pressed her to continue, not just for the story but because he was blushing. 'And the Clock found you and took you hostage?'

'You could say that,' she said, 'if you believe in oracles. Since I don't believe in fate, it can't hurt me. Its capacity to predict my days is nil. I have apprenticed myself to the Clock's company, and I serve as a kind of watchdog of its prophecies. The dwarf is unscrupulous, just doing his job; he doesn't care what mayhem is rucked up by the Clock. The boys who cycle through the company for months or even years at a time join because they are young and scared of the possibilities of life. A belief in preordained history is consoling to those with few prospects, and the boys generally come from the families of blue-coal miners or serfs. They see a little of Oz, watch the Clock tell its predictions and stir up trouble, and do the dwarf's bidding. I suppose they think it is a way to secure a brighter future.'

'Perhaps the boys know more than you do,' said Brrr. 'Maybe believing in the Clock is its own reward. You've never seen it tell your future for you?'

'I have no future. It wouldn't dare.'

'You sound very cynical.'

'You've seen enough of life to suggest I should be otherwise?' she asked.

'As I said, a bed of roses and a walk in the park, that's my life story. But look, here comes Yackle blinking back to life. She is an oracle without a bevy of spies or a clockwork instrument. She's the real goods. What might she say to you, if you asked her?'

'I wouldn't listen to it, and anyway I wouldn't ask her,' said Ilianora. 'Regularly I ask blank paper, and in all my life I've never known magic writing to appear on its blank surface.'

6

Yackle groaned and made to sit up; Ilianora on one side and Brrr on the other helped her. She murmured unintelligibly. Then she spit on the floor, something thin and bubbly – liquid lace.

'I thought you were dead,' said the Lion.

'More's the pity,' she replied, 'not yet, but I may have seen my way out at last. I've had a Sighting, and maybe the truest one I ever had. But you have to help me. Get us out of this hell-nook.'

Brrr glanced at Ilianora and raised an eyebrow. 'Lucky you,' he said to Yackle. 'I've already cleared the doorway.'

'It's very quiet here,' observed Yackle. She turned to Ilianora. 'Where are your friends? They haven't left without you, have they?' She became alarmed and turned back to Brrr. 'It depends on them – on the Clock – I have seen it.'

'Don't worry; they won't have left without me,' Ilianora replied. 'Give me your arm, old auntie.'

Yackle was irritable with fretfulness. 'Are the sisters still in Council, or have they fled in advance of the approaching army? Help me on these steps, will you? I seem to have caught a tremble in my knees.'

'We're here, on either side,' said Brrr. Yackle reached out her dry twiglike hand and squeezed the muscle of his right forward limb.

'Well, go ahead, you, and stop them if they are trying to flee without me,' said Yackle. 'I'm not going to miss this omnibus!'

Brrr and Ilianora glanced at each other. Brrr nodded, and shifted his arms so he could support Yackle, supplying both a handhold and a backrest. Ilianora hurried down the steps ahead of them.

Shadowpuppet stuck close to Brrr's side.

'I must rest a moment – a stitch in my side,' said Yackle. She leaned her forehead upon the stone wall and closed her sightless eyes.

'Was it upsetting? Your Sighting?'

Yackle said, 'You gave it me.'

'I beg your pardon.'

'You told me. You cued me to that line – "You have to leave the way you came in." You told me that was for me. And I saw that it was true – it is true for me, and it is true for you as well.'

'None of this will hold up in a court of law.' But he knew that she would hear the sweet mockery in his voice as encouragement.

'I'll tell you what I saw as it pertains to you. If you want.'

'For a lark, for a joke, to pass the time while armies are converging upon us . . . sure, what the hell.'

She reached her hand out, searching for his paw. He took it.

'The hunt for a Lion cub in the Great Gillikin Forest,' she told him. 'Several decades ago, I'm guessing; I was never good at counting years. Male humans wanted a cub for experimental use in a lab of some sort. I saw a day of floating leaves. You know, the forest in the fall, all red and gold. I saw a circle of men closing in upon a pride of Lions. Most of them scatter, but there is a nursing mother, too tired to run, and her mate stays by her side. A family group. Around them come the men. Beating the bushes, using nets and snares, carrying for defense those hot charred stakes pulled from a portable furnace. Closing in, closing in. That Lion king, that paterfamilias, he is alert, leaping back and forth. The noose is tightening. The Lion family breaks up, hoping to cause confusion, diversion, hoping some might survive. The father and the cub escape before the explosion.'

Brrr is calmer than he's ever been in his life. 'And the mother?'

'The gelignite is lit. The rocks split and tumble skyward. The mother is crushed when they rain back to earth. She protects the other cub with the arch of her rib cage, though her spine is broken. The men take him away from her breast.'

Brrr says, 'Umm – the other cub?'

'Yes,' says Yackle. 'There are two in the litter. The

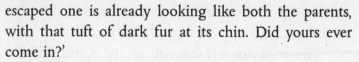

escaped one is already looking like both the parents, with that tuft of dark fur at its chin. Did yours ever come in?'

'No.'

'I suspect it was scared out of you.'

'I suspect so.' His voice was exceedingly calm, almost as if he were still practicing to learn how to talk, with very very concentration.

'You have to leave the way you came in,' she finished. 'That's not just for me, Brrr. It's for you, too. You arrived in a family, unlike me who arrived on a wing and a prayer. You are not supposed to be so alone.'

'I have no family.' No Cubbins, no Muhlama, no Piarsody Scallop, no Jemmsy, no allegiance to the yoke of his probation officer. Certainly no family feeling with a pride of tuft-chinned Lions who, it seemed, removed themselves to the Madeleines and saw fit to deny any relationship.

'You have time,' she told him. 'It's yours to do with what you choose.'

'They turned me out,' he said. 'Again and again. They all did.'

'I have to wait for magic,' she said. 'You don't have to. Don't wait for anyone else. Do it yourself.'

The light had moved on over the mauntery. Daylight, with its shifting dusty tremulous clarity, fell lengthwise down the shaft of the broad, foursquare stairwell. Yackle and the Lion and the glass cat.

Elsewhere in the mauntery, a cold silence, patiently waiting for – for what was to come. Whatever it was.

'Come on,' she told him.

The stairs finished at a broad terrace that itself debouched through arches into a cloistered courtyard open to the sky. Favoring his shoulder, Brrr's body leaned left, and his eyes trailed heavenward, noting the battalions of clouds that surged east. They were thick and grey enough to make the few blue patches look like water features – lakes, inlets, impossible seas – picked out in landmasses painted the grey of wet papier-mâché.

'It is a map of Oz,' he said, for a moment forgetting about the blindness of Yackle. But then he turned his attention to the structure in the center of the courtyard. 'Sweet Ozma,' he growled, 'that's a stick of furniture and a half, en't it?'

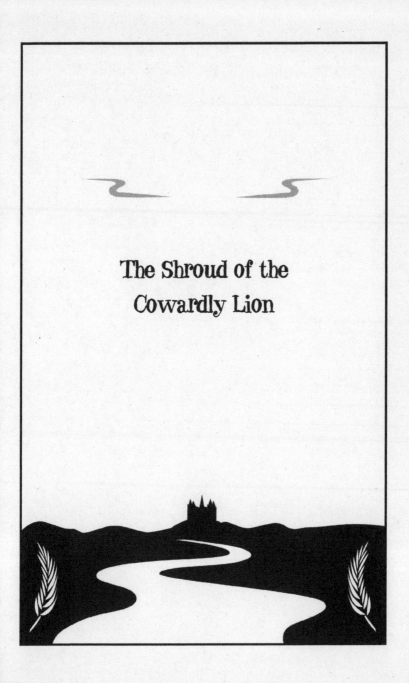

The Shroud of the
Cowardly Lion

1

Brrr delivered Yackle safely onto the cobblestones of the courtyard. He could feel the quickening of her pulse; it matched his own. He was aware of Ilianora standing to one side, neither demure nor deferential, just a handmaiden to her own life. The sun struck the silvery stitching in her veil. If she was a eunuchess, she was a striking one, coming forward to offer Yackle her arm.

'Well, there you are,' said the dwarf, poking his head out of a window halfway up. 'Never known the gears to stick, ever. But I think I just fixed it. Maybe it was balking until you arrived. What took you?'

'A vision took me,' said Yackle in a theatrical voice.

'Visions, schmisions,' said the dwarf. 'We got the corner on that market, darlin'.'

'This is quite an operation you got here,' said Brrr.

'The Clock of the Time Dragon, at your service. Well, not at your service,' said the dwarf. He pulled himself out of the window and scrambled down the side. 'All this time we've been pulling history out of a hat, and we never crossed your path before?'

The thing was massive – mounted on a flatbed cart, three times as high as Brrr standing upright. From a

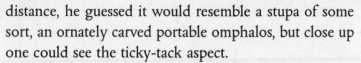

distance, he guessed it would resemble a stupa of some sort, an ornately carved portable omphalos, but close up one could see the ticky-tack aspect.

'It's due for a once-over-lightly,' admitted the dwarf, as if he could guess the Lion's opinions. 'Every little while we replace the fabric, do some touch-up work. But we've been on the road lately.'

'Can't tell by me,' said Yackle, urging Ilianora forward with little twitchings on her sleeve. The elderly maunt reached out and stroked the folded leather wing of the dragon, whose head and forearms finished the steeple-top scare of it all.

'Don't fondle the merchandise,' growled the dwarf.

'You are going to start it up,' said Yackle.

'I don't take orders,' he replied.

'Do what the lady says,' growled Brrr.

'I'm not giving you an order, Mr Boss,' Yackle told the dwarf. 'It's a prophecy. You're going to start it up for me before you leave here. If you're anxious to be on your way, and who isn't, I might add, you'll get it up to speed pretty damn zippy.'

'You may as well,' said Ilianora to the dwarf. 'She might be right.'

'You're the one don't believe in prophecies. What's got a hold of you, Missy Malarkey?' said the dwarf, but affectionately enough. He petted Ilianora's hand a little.

'Come on, Mr Boss,' said one of the boys, 'armies

THE SHROUD OF THE COWARDLY LION

on the way and all that. We're getting wanderlust.'

'Oh, is that what you call it, boy genius? Well, the gear's unstuck, so we'll push off then.'

'Wind it up,' says Yackle. 'I know more than you do, today at least, and it knows more than I do.'

The dwarf made a rude gesture he knew blind Yackle couldn't see.

Brrr swelled his chest. 'Mr Boss, I didn't throw out my shoulder and crash down the door so we could linger here exchanging pleasantries. I want to get out before the armies arrive, too. Now, I notice there is a well in the corner of the courtyard that is far too large for me to hide in but would accommodate you nicely, if you're scared of soldiers.' Then he did something he'd never done before and, sweet Ozma, hoped he'd never have to do again. He opened his mouth and picked up the dwarf by the largest, densest part of his body – his considerably broad shoulders – and he began to carry him, as a mama cat would her kitten, across the courtyard.

'Oh, all right,' growled the dwarf. 'Everyone's going nasty on me.'

'We're on edge,' said Ilianora. As if to authenticate the worry, the boom of cannon was heard in the distance.

A moment later the cannon sounded again, four, five times in sequence, and a hail of roof tiles rained into the courtyard. 'Sister Hammer is going to be none too happy,' said Yackle, ducking her head. 'But have the maunts all fled?'

'Fled, and left us locked up like that? The nerve,' said the Lion.

The dwarf climbed a small rack of stairs to the base of the Clock and disappeared inside a low painted door. Above the bartizans of the mauntery, above the Clock, new clouds of gunpowder smoke smudged a darker aspect across the celestial map of Oz. Brrr could smell the stink of saltpeter.

'Oh, for the eyes I once had,' said Yackle. 'You'll have to tell me what's happening, Sir Brrr.'

'I don't read omens,' he said, 'en't that your job?'

They fell silent. The dwarf could be heard moving about, setting pendulums free from their catches, winding trip-gears, muttering to himself. Stumbling. 'Ow. Damn it.' Then he reappeared, breathing a little heavily and brushing some sawdust off his elbows. 'Well, that's that; she's cooking. Let's see what the old gal comes up with this time. I hope it en't a nice little tragic-comedy about the beheading of several boys and the skewering of a Lion by any advancing army or such.'

'You don't know?' said Brrr. 'You didn't set it up?'

'Of course I don't know,' he snapped. 'I'm the servant here. When did you ever know a dwarf to be in charge?'

They watched. Slowly the interior clockwork built

up its reserves of power. Sounds of ticking and switching emanated from the depths of the cabinetry. There was a moaning, almost as of an orchestra tuning up, adjusting the parameters of its harmonies so as to accord.

Then the dragon began to lift its head. Notch by notch: in the costive silence you could hear the mechanism at work. Underneath the sequined scales a cleverness of hinges and loops was corralling the spine tighter, so the head of the dragon lifted, and the eyes began to burn red; the nostrils of the dragon dilated with a pornographic labial movement, issuing some hiccups of pale purple smoke.

'The dragon is smoking, too,' said Brrr to Yackle.

'I can smell that much,' she replied.

2

Brrr thought the dragon seemed uncertain what revelation to publish, if any. In a balcony to one side, made from half a porcelain teacup, a small puppet with a red mane emerged and mewed.

'Is that supposed to be me?' said the Lion. As if

disappointed in its reception, the puppet disappeared.

'You don't criticize the Clock,' said the dwarf. 'What, you think it responds to notices in the evening papers? To notes from some splenetic director? Let it be.' But he sounded confused himself.

'What's it doing?' asked Yackle.

'A marionette in an alcove now,' said Brrr. He peered, squinted, to make sure he was getting it right. 'With diamonds painted on his face.'

'Steady,' said Yackle, though whom she was addressing was unclear: maybe the marionette.

'Gone,' said Brrr. 'This is awfully patchy.'

'You're asking a lot of the Clock,' said the dwarf. 'To make sense to both of you at once – not sure if it can handle the task—'

'Over here,' said Brrr, 'get this. Another arcade.'

A red velvet curtain lifted, and a stage like a rounded dock slid forward on invisible rollers. The marionette with the blue diamonds on his face reappeared. The light strengthened enough so that one could see his fine rural tunic half slipped off his shoulder. His chest, though only a piece of polished poplar, managed to look sexy, the blue diamond tattoos circling around one nipple and then dropping in single file toward his abdomen. 'It's a man from the West, a Winkie I believe, in a costume suggesting money . . .'

But even Brrr's voice caught in his throat, to see the door of a cupboard open and a figure painted green, dressed in the black skirts of a novice maunt, step through.

'It's Elphaba, with the Winkie prince,' said Brrr. 'Couldn't be anyone else.'

'No,' said Ilianora. 'The Clock wouldn't dare. I don't buy it.'

Yackle kept her chin trained straight at the little stage as if she could tell exactly where it was, and what it must be showing. She gripped Ilianora's hand hard. 'Steady, steady, steady,' said the older woman to the younger.

'He's her lover,' said Brrr. 'The Witch's lover. Did she have a lover? Or is this propaganda?'

The dwarf didn't answer. He seemed just as captivated as they.

The embrace was brief and, if you could credit such a thing between figures of painted wood and cloth, passionate. Then Elphaba whipped away off-stage, and the lights went half down. They were beginning to come up elsewhere, on a lower section, a grid of iron behind which something was beginning to happen: a huge golden fish, a carp or something, float-ing ... But Brrr's eye was caught by a flash of movement on the darkened deck, and he whistled. 'Something else up there – look!'

The puppet of the Winkie prince had gone into a slump, perhaps a kind of postcoital doze, when a figure up on top of the wardrobe appeared. It was a funny little white pincushion sewn over with small mirrors that caught the limited light.

Brrr said, 'A little star up there? A small overweight star spying from the wardrobe?' But the bright lumpy thing leaped down with an undeniably feline agility, and stalked on stiff little furry legs to the sleeping lover. The creature sniffed the man up and down, from his soft breathing nostrils to his groin.

Brrr found himself holding his breath.

As if to protect Shadowpuppet, he reached down and snatched up the glass cat, turning its head from the entertainment. But no cat, glass or otherwise, yields to this sort of command, and it squirmed its neck about so its glassy eyes could follow the movements on the stage.

'Powerful entertainment. My little critter's rapt,' he said, as much to himself as to the others.

The white cat in the tableau ran to a doorway at the rear of the stage, and mewed – three harsh mews, cut off, more like words. Not so much 'meow' as 'now – now – now!'

Several bits of shadow, with masks and cudgels, shaped themselves into more or less human form, and they surged forward, four, five of them – the sleeping man woke, and cried out twice – and then the cudgels were upon him. The toy blood realistically sprayed the stage. The puppet cat watched, and then licked the blood off its mirrors.

The glass cat in Brrr's arms began to squirm. Brrr

held it more tightly. It protested with meows like insults.

'Now, settle down, you,' said Brrr. 'Don't want you running away and hiding just when we're getting ready to fold up shop here and skedaddle. Can't imagine either army would treat you as well as I do.'

'You oaf,' cried Shadowpuppet. 'I can't breathe.'

'What in tarnation's corner!' Brrr thrust Shadow-puppet away, as if it were possessed, but caught himself from dashing it to the ground. He barked at the dwarf, 'My only comfort, my pet, and you paint it a small villain? Is this how you catch your audiences, sowing discord and suspicion among them?'

'Don't look at me,' said the sergeant-at-hand. 'I'm staff, not management.'

'And you—' Brrr winced at the wriggling thing. 'You suddenly borrow enough language to lodge a complaint mightier than a meow? Have you been enchanted by this, this puppet play – or are you smoked out by it?'

'You!' said Ilianora. 'You were an informer on Elphaba and – and—' She nearly couldn't say his name. 'And Fiyero? *You?*' She grabbed Shadowpuppet from Brrr and squeezed it so hard its tail broke off, and splintered upon the cobbles.

The glass cat – *was* it a *Cat?* – reared and shot its claws. Ilianora, weeping, flinched away and flung the Cat on the ground. It didn't shatter, but a front leg bent laterally in an unnatural way, as if the Cat had taught its forearm how to cast a shuttle across a loom. It sat there and just managed to crane around enough to lick the blood from the stump of the severed tail. The blood was thin and brown, like shit water.

'Shadowpuppet! Were you spying on the Witch? Were you in the Wizard's employ? How could you – how you could – a traitor – a turncoat—'

'The word you want,' said the dwarf, 'is fink. Or, if you're being fancy, collaborationist.'

Brrr felt he suddenly understood what it might mean if he said *I am beside myself!* The world contorting again, long after he had thought it possible to learn anything new. It was like being back in the Great Gillikin Forest, suddenly recognizing that the musical repertoire of humans that he was overhearing was in fact language, implying meaning, implying a secret world he might uncover. The bone-icing creepiness of realizing that an Animal can masquerade as an animal! He hadn't known it possible.

'Oh, we all have our disguises,' said Shadowpuppet irritably. 'You think only a big Cat can practice sedition?'

The Cat hissed at them all. The dwarf continued, 'No need to get so worked up over it, Mister Lion. The episode depicted by the Clock didn't involve you, far as I could see.'

'No, it didn't,' said Brrr. 'But I took on

Shadowpuppet as my pet—'

'Hah,' said the Cat. 'No, sir, I took on *you* as an assignment. To end my long career in a last bout of usefulness, and look – I've all but been thrown out on my ass.'

'Assignment for whom?' asked Brrr.

'The regimes change, the posts are filled and vacated and refilled. I can hardly remember the current personnel. Think you'll take *my* deposition? Think again. Anyway, as if I owe *you* an explanation?'

'You do,' said Ilianora. 'If you informed against the Witch, you were an agent in the death of Fiyero Tigelaar. And he was my father.'

'Was he now,' said the Cat. 'Pity, that.'

'Nor?' said Yackle, turning her head toward Ilianora. 'Nor Tigelaar? Fiyero's daughter?'

'Nor was a girl, and that girl is dead,' said Ilianora. 'That girl died in Southstairs Prison . . . I go by the name of Ilianora now.' She dropped her veil back from her forehead. 'If a Cat can skulk around disguised as a cat, a girl can certainly disguise herself as a woman.' Her tone was cool and not particularly flummoxed.

Brrr had never known Fiyero, but long ago he had traveled to the Emerald City with the boy sometimes thought to be Fiyero's illegitimate son. 'Ilianora, listen: The Witch's boy – Elphaba's charge – was looking for you some years back. Did he ever find you?'

'Liir?' said Ilianora. 'Liir, you mean? Is he still alive?'

'Twenty years ago he was,' said Brrr.

'*Ten* years ago he was still alive,' said Yackle. 'He'd be, oh, twenty-nine or thirty by now. Excuse me for hurrying this along, but why don't you ask the Clock?'

'It does no good to ask the Clock,' said the dwarf curtly. 'The Clock only reveals what it will.'

They all turned to look at it again.

'You'd be thirty-five then,' said Brrr. 'Or so. You were older than Liir, right?'

She didn't answer. Her face was in her hands. The news that someone had once hunted for her seemed to be seeping in.

'You have someone who cares for you,' said Brrr. 'Somewhere. You don't need to languish in thrall to a dwarf. You don't owe him anything.'

'Don't mind me,' said the sergeant-at-hand. 'I didn't snitch on any Winkie prince. I don't take sides. I mind my own business. Little me and my own ten toes, each more blameless than the one next door.'

3

Yackle waved her hands loosely in the air, as if casting spells or shooing chickens. She began to get excited. 'Open your trove, Mister Boss, and let me at it.'

'You're off your rocker,' began the dwarf.

'Don't deny me my last moment.' Yackle rubbed her eyes with her fists, impatiently. Brrr thought: She'd force her eyes to focus one last time, if she could.

'Show's over,' growled the dwarf. 'You've agitated my virgin missus. En't that enough trouble for one day?' He began to slap up the hinged stages and secure the shutters. 'We gave it a chance, and it's paid us with a scrap of useless history. Who cares if that friable Cat once worked for ye olde Wizard of Oz? He's long gone, and it's Emperor Shell on the throne now. All that bunk of espionage and assault is ancient history and does no one any good, least of all the Cat, with its fragmented tail.'

The Clock disobeyed the dwarf and clattered its central stage open again.

'Huffy, are we?' said the dwarf. 'Feeling our oats, eh? This is a strange turn of affairs.' But he backed off a little, nonplussed.

'Look,' said Brrr.

'Easy for you to say,' replied Yackle, tapping one dead eyelid with her fingernail.

The Clock's machinery chirred with a sound like the tumbling of oaken dice. The hands of the dwarf fell at his side, but remained fisted, as if Mr Boss would strike the equipment if it dared an impertinent display. Brrr shifted to get a better view. Ilianora and the boys watched, too.

Through a mist that suffused the stage from vents in the flooring, a tall figure emerged. It stood about ten inches high. It sported a long white beard and a tall velvet hat – like a witch's hat but without the brim. The face was indistinct but furrowed with character; it looked like the business end of a pair of socks folded into each other. The face seemed pinched between the downward cone of the white beard and the upward cone of the black velvet cap. Stars and moons were picked out on the old gentleman's robe.

'What's *happening*?' asked Yackle. 'This is no time to fall silent, you lot.'

'Sorry,' said Brrr, and he began to describe what he saw.

In his arms the figure hugged an oversize volume, a folio of russet leather clasping vellum pages of irregular cut. Oversize, proportionally speaking, of course: in actuality, the prop was about the heft of a roast-wren sandwich.

The figure set the book down on the ground. He looked to the left and to the right, as if checking to make sure he was alone. Then, alarmingly, he looked at the small audience and winked at *them*. It was almost salacious. Brrr felt in the presence of rough magic.

'It's a book,' said Brrr. 'A magic book, I bet.'

'The Grimmerie,' added Ilianora. 'I knew it in my youth, back at Kiamo Ko.'

'The Grimmerie,' replied Yackle. 'As I suspected. What about it?'

Brrr and Ilianora took turns describing the scene. The figure opened the cover of the book. It was only a simulacrum of a book, not a real book: its pages were not more than five inches square, if that. When the book was opened flat, at a central section of pages so the versos and rectos spread evenly in each direction, the bearded puppet made some arcane gestures above the gutter of the volume. He let his beard trail along the stitchery, which seemed a nearly obscene gesture, certainly an odd one. Then he curled his fingers up and lifted his gnarled hands – Brrr could tell his hands were gnarled even though they were papier-mâché puppet hands. He knitted a spell with his fingers. It was as if, Brrr thought, he were writing in the air above the book. 'He's . . . he's conjuring something out of the book.'

'Of course he is. It's the *Grimmerie*. Aren't you getting any of this?'

'Don't be so snarky,' said Brrr, but mildly; he couldn't really fault Yackle. The air seemed to crackle and dry; his mane was going mad with static.

Yackle gripped each of her elbows and hugged herself. 'What's he calling up?'

Something began to lift off the page. It looked like origami being done by invisible fingers: a complicated fold of ivory paper twisted itself, unbent a limb, twisted again, uncorked a shoulder. Slowly the creature balanced on four limbs, then stood erect on two – the rear two limbs. A third pair of limbs scraped the air behind the creature, unfolding and unfolding until they were twice the height of the biped.

'Wings,' said Ilianora, in a gasp.

'A winged human,' said Brrr, 'made out of paper, I mean.'

The creature stood to full height only once, and some trick in the folds of the face made a little gleam of light come out – as if a torch had picked up a glint of reflection made by a drop or two of dried glue. The figure was naked and magnificent, a hobbledy old winged woman with a mane of paper hair wild enough to make Brrr jealous.

Then the creature's wings folded back, to pack into the woman's shoulders like a broad deformity, a pair of humps. The weight of them curved her spine a little; she stooped, looking older. This caused her hair to drop over her forehead, giving her a shifty look beneath its unkempt locks. The light dimmed some-how; only now could Brrr see that the paper had been crumpled before being folded, so the dozens of wrinkles approximated the veined sheen of old flesh.

'It is an old woman,' said Brrr. His voice went quiet. 'An old woman has just lifted out from the pages of the Grimmerie, and been deprived of the wings that helped her stand erect. The wings have folded heavily on her back, buckling her spine with the weight. And she is on her knees, now, and lying down, naked and old.'

'I know,' said Yackle tiredly. 'Naked and old and newborn. And never knew a mother's kiss. Tragic. But you've learned of your origins, Brrr, and I've learned of mine, too. Happy birthday.' Her voice sounded as proud as it did tired. 'Now what?'

The crumpled woman who had sprung from the open folds of a magic book slid offstage, never waking, never stirring. The bearded puppet was left alone. He picked up the book. He looked here and there – hunting for something. A puppet can do anything. He turned at last, and a scroll of paper at the back of the stage wound a new backdrop behind him. An approach to a towering house, almost a castle—

'Kiamo Ko!' said Brrr.

Ilianora gripped his paw. 'Wasn't Kiamo Ko bigger than that?'

'Everything seems bigger when you're young,'

explained Brrr. 'Anyway, this is a stage set, so how big can it be?'

'Give me my eyes,' said Yackle. She sounded like a crazy old lady, nothing more, but Brrr knew what she meant, and answered her. Brrr described what he saw.

The castle was painted gloomy and quaint, bats in the window and crossbones on the door: a bit over the top, if Brrr could rely on his own memory. But up came the magician, if that's who he was, in his tall hat and his unrespectable beard; he delivered air-knocks on the castle wall, and then he laid the book down on the floor before the doors, which anyway were painted shut. Once he'd accomplished this, the magician puppet was yanked into the fly space by the Clock's impatient gearwork.

'That's how the Grimmerie came to be at Kiamo Ko,' said Ilianora, almost in a whisper. 'I remember my mother telling us about it once. An old peddler or a mystic of some sort left it there, and years later Elphaba found it in the attic.'

The book sat on the floorboards. The rest of the stage set was bare. Nothing happened.

Shadowpuppet chose this moment to comment. 'A tiktok entertainment leaves something to be desired in the way of dramaturgy. The plot has gone slow here. Are we to wait here and watch the cobwebs grow, while armies are approaching? If you call this a reliable witness, Sir Brrr, why don't you just haul the Clock of the Time Dragon back to the Emerald City magistrates? Get it to deliver your deposition for you? If you trust it so much?'

'I'm not sure I'd take advice from you, Shadowpuppet,' snarled Brrr. 'Your transparency is just another one of your disguises, isn't it?'

'As long as we're chatting,' said the Cat, 'the name is Grimalkin. Malky for short. Shadowpuppet is just so . . . so *you*.'

Yackle threw her fists in the air and uncurled her palsied fingers as far as she could. 'Enough! Will nobody do as I ask? Dragon, dwarf, lady, Lion, someone: Ask the Clock for the book!'

Brrr was stunned. 'Ask where it is now?' he said.

'Don't you understand? I have seen how my story ends. It's here. It's here. In the clock. Bring it out.'

'It was a play-action, it was a fake book,' Brrr reminded Yackle. Was she losing it at last?

'Shhh, old mother,' said Ilianora, stroking the skin pleating on Yackle's trembling forearms.

Even the dwarf showed some remorse at getting Yackle all wound up for nothing. 'I'm afraid they're right, Mrs Mysteriousness. We're out of tricks. Show's over. Nothing to see here. Move along. Keep to the left. Tell your friends. Blessing of Lurlina on you, and all that rot.'

But the Time Dragon had other ideas. It flexed a forearm and draped an accordion-pleated leather wing across the central display chamber. It lowered its head with a clanking sinuousness both sinister and noble. Its ruby-glass eyes bulged in their leathern sockets. Its gooseneck armature struck forward, pinning Mr Boss to his ground. From its nostrils issued a smell of scorch that wrinkled their noses. Calamitously thick smoke spilled from the dragon sinuses, clouding the courtyard, watering every eye.

Brrr wanted to rub his eyes, but in his arms Shadowpuppet . . . Malky . . . was squirming to escape in the sudden fog. 'Stop, or I'll snap every limb off of you, one at a time,' Brrr rasped, coughing. He had to do with trying to rub his face into his forearm. When his eyes stopped streaming, the smoke was lifting. Everyone was suffering from the stinging soot. Ilianora was wiping her face with her silvery veil, the dwarf with his beard. The boys were clutching one another and whimpering: They had all of a sudden seen one revelation too many, and they wanted to go home. Yackle rubbed her eyes, too.

'Look,' she said, pointing. The dragon wing was lifting at an angle. Brrr stared: The Clock was taking orders from no dwarf. It had its own agenda. The second dragon wing had started to lift in the opposite direction, an effect like curtains parting at a window, before it dawned on Brrr that it had been Yackle who had told them to look. But he couldn't even turn to see what her face was like now that – could it be possible?

– her eyesight had been restored by the dragon smoke. He just obeyed her instruction, and looked.

4

A sliding panel of stage flooring moved out, a wooden tongue on oiled bearings. In a drawer, on a carpet of green and gold silk, the Grimmerie waited for them.

Brrr didn't need to describe it for Yackle anymore. He didn't need Ilianora to identify it. It wasn't a tiny stage prop. It was the real Grimmerie.

The volume sat half unwrapped in a traditional Vinkus hunting shawl, a fringed cloth with roses on a black background. There was something almost lascivious about the arrangement to Brrr, who had never admired books particularly. He didn't remember that a mere book might reek of sex, possibility, fecundity. Yet a book has a ripe furrow and a yielding spine, he thought, and the nuances to be teased from its pages are nearly infinite in their variety and coquettish appeal. And what new life can emerge from a book. Any book, maybe.

'Nobody has the clearance to touch the Grimmerie,' said Mr Boss, but his voice had gone faint; he was immaterial now, incidental, and they all knew it.

Yackle took hold of Brrr's paw. She regarded him up and down with real eyes, which were, Brrr saw, adamantine blue and cloudless. 'You're not quite as I'd pictured,' she admitted. 'A little baggy here and there. Still. Are you ready?'

Brrr was fairly certain Yackle wasn't the angel of death come to take him to the breast of Lurlina. Still, he raised an eyebrow enquiringly, his underarms dampening. 'I don't think I'm quite *that* ready,' he replied. 'I've made my fair share of mistakes and all, but hey. There's always next time.'

Yackle laughed. 'You idiot. Pay attention. Are you ready to choose, I mean. You came hoping to find information about the Grimmerie, and instead you stumbled upon the actual article. If you take this dangerous volume into custody, you might have redeemed yourself. There's rehabilitation in this for you – or so you'll be tempted to hope.

'On the other hand,' she continued, 'a different choice. A lot less fruitful for you, perhaps. Nothing certain about the outcome.'

But that was the whole point. There is never anything certain about the outcome of a child's life. She was reminding him about the child of Liir and Candle. Elphaba's granddaughter, just possibly.

'You think you came up from the crypt to tell me about—' But in the presence of either the dwarf or the tiktok oracle, Brrr kept himself from saying *the child*. Yackle saw that he wasn't going to give their secret away, at least not yet, and she grinned at him like a saucy schoolgirl. 'But,' he continued, 'you didn't come to tell me anything. You were sensing the approach of the Grimmerie, that's all. That's what you were doing.'

'Never mind about why I jumped out of my sarcophagus. That's ancient history now!' she said gaily. 'Anyway, whoever insisted that two things can't be true at once?' She put her old pale hand on the kinky hair of his chest where a medal for courage might have hung, did he still own one. 'Make the right choice, Sir Brrr, when your time to choose arrives,' she said. 'Oh, liberty at last!' Hiking her white sheets to her shoulder, she tottered forward with the tentative steps of the truly elderly. It was as if the return of her eyesight had reminded her how very infirm she must be. Ilianora moved beside her, ready to catch her by the elbow should she fall, but Yackle managed to keep her balance for the five steps left to her, from the crowd of Ozians to the threshold of the Grimmerie.

'Don't you dare touch that book,' said Mr Boss, the buzz of a fly, no more.

Brrr watched as Yackle reached out for the cover. It was made of a material he couldn't identify, something that had properties of leather and cloth both – the slick coolness of leather, the cross-grain of cloth. The color of the binding suggested light on water, as if the warm color was emanating from a depth inside the book.

The spine was set with jewels arranged in an arabesque – every color but emerald – and an iron lock to clasp the secrets tight. But the pin was freed from the staple, and the hasp lay back upon its hinges.

Yackle lifted the cover and turned it over. The book didn't allow any page to slide open; it turned itself to one page, a third of the way from the front, as if, for right now, the book consisted only of that page, and the other pages were glued shut.

'Do you know what you're looking for?' asked Brrr.

'No one knows quite the shape of their death,' said Yackle, 'but I daresay I will recognize it when I see it.'

The paper had a purple aspect at first, and the writing thereupon was silver. As they looked – they were all looking by now, even Shadowpuppet leaning forward, even Mr Boss, craning from where he lay pinned on the ground – the color subsided to a taciturn peach, not unlike the tanned hide of a pig. The ink seemed less silver and more black. Almost as if the book were trying to resemble other books, as much as it could.

'Ah,' said Brrr. 'Look, can you see that? A watermark.'

'What is a watermark?' asked Ilianora.

'Something I learned about in my years as a trader of etchings and drawings. A watermark is a kind of a ghost coin imprinted when the page is made by the artisan. A trademark. The emblem is an embossing done when the paper hasn't fully set; it presses the fiber tighter there, so when the page is held up to light, the image emerges. I never knew a watermark you could see without a light behind it, though.'

'This book has its own light,' said Yackle.

Brrr rested his chin on her old shoulder; she was strong enough to take it. Absentmindedly with one hand, while trying to read, she reached up and scratched just below his lips, exactly where he would have liked it best had anyone ever done this before.

Most of the text on the page shrank and moved off to one side, like dancers in the wings awaiting their next entrance. The watermark grew a little larger, as if to be seen all the better. Brrr could make out a form, though not the foreign alphabet that spelled a single foreign word beneath the watermark.

'Is that a symbol we're likely to recognize?' asked Ilianora.

'Is it lightning?' suggested one of the boys looking on.

'A crow with the legs of a stork,' offered Brrr.

'That's a pretty good description of Elphaba,' said Yackle.

'Is this her story?' asked Brrr. 'Or is it her book?'

'It was her book for a time,' said Mr Boss. The dragon claw had let him sit up, at least. 'Or in her keep, I should say; the Grimmerie was no more hers than it is mine. The book belongs to a magician from some distant land, the one who brought it to Oz for safekeeping.'

'Who do you mean?' asked Brrr. 'Do you mean the Wizard of Oz?'

'Please,' replied Mr Boss. 'Don't insult my intelligence.'

'The Wizard of Oz had no *power*,' snapped Shadowpuppet. 'That's common knowledge by now. No, Our Glorious Wizard *came* to Oz looking for this book, don't you know? And ever since Elphaba died and the book disappeared, everyone else has been looking for it.'

'You, too,' said Brrr, surmising. 'Your directive was to keep an eye on me in case I actually found out something and decided not to report it.'

'Oh, you'd never do *that*,' said Shadowpuppet mockingly. 'Not Sir Brrr, the most reliable agent we have in the field. Sir Brrr of such famously lofty *principles*. Heaven forfend. Besides, I'd never betray you. You've been such entertainment. Such a lark.'

Yackle laid her hands on the paper, palms down, as if reading the heat on the page.

'How long have you been here, guarding the book?' asked Brrr.

'You still taking notes?' replied Mr Boss. 'Oh, on and off, oh, eighty years maybe? You lose track when it's such a gas.'

'Even before the Wizard of Oz first arrived in the Emerald City? But why?'

The dwarf replied, 'That's a tale for another time, my comings and goings. I thought you were curious about the history of Our Miss Yackle. Which is all in the Grimmerie. Haven't you seen it now?'

'Put it together for me.'

'The Clock told it to you. You saw the story of the birth of Yackle – from the pages of this magic book. She was drawn out of here to do a job: to be vigilant over Elphaba's life. Not to interfere, not to intervene: to be a witness. That was enough.'

'That's all I did,' said Yackle, talking as much to herself as to them. They had to strain to make it out. 'All I ever did. I was a handmaiden. Rather long in the tooth to be a maiden, but it takes all kinds to make a world. I did give Elphaba the broom; I'll accept that much credit. But I didn't know what she could do with it. Nor did I know why she was the watermark in my life: the deep hidden thing around which my weird existence revolved. I only knew what I was compelled to do. And I know what I'm compelled to do now.'

'You take a lot upon yourself to guard this book,' said Brrr to the sergeant-at-hand. 'If the Emerald City gets hold of you, you're history.'

The dwarf shrugged. 'I have a job and I do it: I protect the book. The Clock of the Time Dragon was magicked up as a kind of reliquary for the Grimmerie when it's needed. I don't ask questions. Elphaba seemed to be the one most capable of reading it correctly. Given her bloodlines, maybe, her natural talents. And she found the book where the magician left it, and used it, and showed the Wizard of Oz a page of it. He hunted for it ever after, but when Elphaba disappeared and the Wizard abdicated, the book ended up with her erstwhile friend Galinda. Sorry: Glinda, onetime Throne Minister of Oz. Our Miss Glinda returned the Grimmerie to me when I was passing by her country estate, Mockbeggar Hall, some years ago. It's been safe here ever since, until today, when the Clock determined it was time to reveal its treasure to you bozos.'

'Yackle,' said Ilianora. 'Yackle, what are you doing?' and Brrr realized he had been watching the dwarf, and clutching the Cat, keeping the troublesome elements under control, his back turned from Yackle and the Grimmerie.

She had slipped her winding robe off her shoulders like a shawl.

While she had been speaking, the watermark had returned to fill both pages of the open volume, and the page had gone from ivory to pale spring green. It looked more like Elphaba than ever, with her sharp nose and slightly crooked hat, and her zigzaggy bony form at the ready for flight, for battle against some treachery they couldn't see just off the margins of the page.

The lines of the watermark glowed a yellower, fiery green, and the shape of the Witch contorted, as if working out a kink in her lower back.

Then the watermark rose off the page. It did not flesh out, like a suddenly luminous puppet or like a radioactive green parrot, but retained its drawn outline, its crude symbolic origin. It reared, it rose in a sweep of cape, it lifted like a green flower from a bed of words and red roses on a black fringed background. It was not Elphaba; she was not here; her time was over and done. It was the mark of Elphaba, though, vivid as ever. Their eyes stung, to see her again, or for the first time.

'Of course,' said Yackle, turning for a moment and glowing at Ilianora. 'You have a brother. Of course you must go on! Because history can't be vexed by small players; don't you know?' She looked at Ilianora, at the dwarf, at Brrr, with an expression too complex, too pungent to understand. 'Don't you understand? She's coming back—'

Brrr thought, for an instant – but what does she mean? In her weird seeingness, can Yackle picture Muhlama H'aekeem? Or does she mean the lost Ozma, or Elphaba, who melted away, or the fairy goddess

Lurline, or the Kumbric Witch, or even Dorothy the interloper?

In any case, Yackle let her shroud slip to the floor, and from her naked, poxy back unfurled two capacious sails of feather and strut and papery light. Unused these dozens of years, they had lost none of their power to elevate. Yackle rose in the air in the courtyard of the House of Saint Glinda, her calloused heels showing the dirt and detritus of the cobbles, the skin around her shanks and buttocks sagging, bruised, vivid with ancient life. She said nothing more, but as the watermark of Elphaba began to sink back again to flatness on its page, Yackle followed it. She disappeared into the Grimmerie like a diver entering the deepest parts of a magic pool: slow-motion, full of grace, the toes in the gleam; casting off wretchedness, casting off the shroud. She folded magically into the Grimmerie, her third and fourth dimensions laddering accordion-like into the secret unnamed dimensions of a page. They all leaned over the great book to watch.

But she wasn't fully done. Just before her arms and wing tips and head lost their material shapeliness, her hands twisted in the air. Brrr, who had met Yackle only twenty-four hours earlier, knew her well enough to guess what she intended. He reached over the book as one will lean over a precipice. Shadowpuppet-Malky began to squirm and yowl, but Ilianora grabbed its rear paws. Together she and Brrr delivered the glass Cat to

Yackle's hands. Only a vowel-less snarl was left behind as Yackle's wing tips and wrists and tendrils of hair and the glimmer of hostage Cat disappeared into the pages of the Grimmerie.

'I've sworn off taking sides,' said Ilianora fiercely, 'but good riddance to bad rubbish. I hope it finds itself in some sort of a pit of hounds in there.'

'That hissy little piece of work won't do any more damage while penned in that book,' said Brrr. 'Just hope it doesn't try to claw its way out from the inside.'

They peered to see if Shadowpuppet was pictured on the page, or even if Yackle was, but the letters had come crowding back. They'd enlarged, and begun to superimpose themselves yeastily, one upon the other, so that only the spaces between the loops of printed letters showed like dwindling dots of light. Then the words darkened entirely and screened the paper with darkness. In the sea of black remained the watermark, faintly, vernally. No other image, no Yackle, no Shadowpuppet. No prophecies about Liir and Candle and their daughter.

The Grimmerie shut itself; the Clock withdrew the book into a hidden chamber, the dragon up top sighed and clanked rather noisily to a finish – Show's over, folks – and they were out of the realm of mystery, and back in the realm of war.

5

Though they all stood for a minute, in between moments, as a light wind pushed into the courtyard, and a smell of smoke and greenery strengthened. It whisked their spirits in silence; they felt upbraided by possibility; they felt taunted by the aesthetic appeal of justice. They felt hungry, and several of them felt horny, and the light flickered as a flock of birds coursed against the sun – too high to be identified, too high to be heard, but not too high to be influential.

6

Although Brrr was halted among this latest grab bag of companions, he was alone in the anointment of a quickly stinging grief. A hollow feeling, before forgetfulness rushed in to blanket and anaesthetize. Yackle had not been his antagonist after all. He'd learned this just well enough to feel the ache of her departure. Even the thorn in the paw makes sense while it stabs, and she was both thorn and balm.

His reverie was broken by the sound of footsteps. The Lion looked up to see Sister Apothecaire stumping along a rampart. She brandished a ring of keys and was blathering nearly incoherently.

'Slow down,' called Brrr. 'Take a breath. You'll pop a button or burst a spleen.'

'They're advancing, oh sweet Lurline,' said Sister Apothecaire, in her panic reverting to pagan sensibilities, for Lurline had come from history and gone into myth long before faith in the Unnamed God had called maunts to live in community and service. So long ago that no one could ascertain the chronology of it.

'While we were in Council, and we left you locked up – oh – you're out' – she noticed – 'the Munchkin-landers have come up with a startling crew of backup patriots! Lord bless 'em! But they're converging from the east, and it looks as if a battle will indeed be joined right here, on the very skirts of our precincts. And the good sisters at last have fled, that toady Sister Doctor leading the gallop! I said I would hurry back to release you, once we had remembered about you, and no one protested. Who wants a blot like that in our copybooks? So here I am. Consider yourself released. Shoo.' She waved her hands. 'Where's Mother Yackle?'

'Safe,' said Brrr.

'You're a brave woman, good Sister,' said Ilianora, starting to help the dwarf strap up doors, slotting the stages like drawers back into the bureau of clockwork.

'Brave or good, coward or bad, I don't know and I don't care,' she said. 'Get out while you can. I have the keys and there is no governing Council or Superior Maunt to stop me. I'm going to open the doors to the Munchkinlanders and give them a fighting chance. Unless you want to be caught in here with them, take to your heels, at once!'

'Which way should we go?' asked the dwarf. 'We have precious cargo.'

Do we? wondered Brrr. He supposed that Mr Boss was referring to the Clock of the Time Dragon and the Grimmerie. All the rest of them – Ilianora among them, even the dwarf himself – were more or less dispensable.

Sister Apothecaire replied, 'I don't know which army would trouble you least. It's your choice. Munchkinlanders are sweeping up in a shallow curve from the eastern edges of the oakhair forest. It's a counter-attack in advance of the arrival of the Emperor's armies. We maunts evacuated to the northwest – deeper into Gillikin, whether I like it or not. The pincers are closing exactly upon this troubled house: It stands precisely where the East and the West will meet and have their bloodshed, and in a matter of quarter hours, not days. I have sung my alarum to you, now fly if you will; be it on your own heads if you won't. I must be at the ready. I will offer flame and pitch from the ramparts to any EC soldiers, or sanctuary should the Munchkinlanders get here first.'

'You can't rely on virtue and vice being so evenly distributed,' said Ilianora.

'I am not talking about vice. I'm talking about clan.'

A pride of maunts, thought Brrr, is rather a self-made thing, isn't it? And temporary, if it could dissolve under pressure of war into the clans from which its members originated. Still, there is no law that says all decent things must be permanent. Perhaps family itself, like beauty, is temporary, and no discredit need attach to impermanence.

Having delivered her ultimatum, Sister Apothecaire turned, but she was moving so fast that she couldn't stop herself. Her foot twisted on a crack between the stones of the staircase, and she tumbled nine or ten feet to the ground, and there she lay still.

'She won't be dead,' said Ilianora, but Brrr thought her statement more hope than prognosis.

The dwarf wouldn't wait for a report. 'Leave the little old fussbody for her countrymen to tend. We'll be off and away with the fairies, as advised.' He barked orders to the acolytes to withdraw the bars from the main gate, and then to position themselves for flight.

Four boys put themselves between the shafts of the

cart, and the others went behind to push. But Ilianora said, 'Mr Boss, we can't be sure the Munchkinlanders will arrive first. If the Emerald City Messiars beat them to it, this maunt may be in danger. Lay her on the coachman's seat, and we'll study her situation when we can pause for a moment to breathe. Brrr, help me.'

'Oh, my Lady Lovely, are you planning to leave us? Are you nominating a successor? Or are we abducting a goodwife for me in my ripe old age? Such a cranky one! And won't she be surprised when she wakes up. Sure, take her along.'

Brrr and Ilianora lifted Sister Apothecaire, who was heavy for one so small, and they settled her in a supine position. Her eyes were closed but, as far as Brrr could tell, she appeared to be breathing.

'Well?' said the dwarf, scrambling onto the buckboard, 'you're coming with us, Cowardly Lion?'

'Is that an invitation or a prophecy?'

'I came to get you, didn't I? That's what the Clock told me to do.'

'You came and found me, true, but maybe my use to you was only as bait. To draw the Grimmerie to Yackle so she could take her leave. And where are you going anyway? Are you converted to Elphaba's old cause, to see her rise like that before us?'

'Elphaba's dead and gone,' said the dwarf equably enough. 'We stay neutral, we keep our nosey noses clean, we take no sides, and we watch our backs. So linger here and stew about it as long as you like. Send us a postcard from whichever military prison you end up in. Whee-up, gee-up, knees-up, boys.'

Brrr was stuck with the conundrum. His job was done. He had been ordered to find out what had happened to the Grimmerie, and he had done far more than that: He had located the very book itself. Why let it escape? He might as well go with them, keep them in range. When the time was right he could choose to turn them over to the Emperor's army. Once he felt ready to make that decision. The proper number of the dwarf's slurs and indignities having mounted up to legitimize it.

Think of the glories that might accrue to Sir Brrr if he arrived back at the Emerald City with the Clock of the Time Dragon, and the Grimmerie safely interred within.

Think of the possibilities if he did not. He could fall in with the company of the Clock now, and perhaps – if they escaped to the West, along the banks of foul Kellswater – he could trip the brakes on the dreadful apparatus and drown the tiktok dragon and its bullying prophecies in the deadening water. Then no one could ever again use the Grimmerie to learn how to attack another soul.

'Make up your mind, and on your own head,' said the dwarf as the Clock of the Time Dragon began its slow creaky exodus into its future.

Ilianora turned to him and held out her hand. 'Don't be bashful. You would make a good companion for the company of the Clock. You know as much as anyone does, now, about where it came from and why we tend it.'

'I don't know why you tend it,' said Brrr, but he flipped his notepad closed and pocketed it. 'That's beyond my brief to care about, Ilianora, so don't spend your breath. Let's get out of here.'

They passed under the portcullis. The broad stretch of the Shale Shallows lay to the west and south, wheat fields to the northwest. On the horizon they could see emerald green pennants of the advancing army, though from this distance the wind masked the sound of their snapping. Had the EC battalions paused to reconnoiter? Load their cannons? Was some general busily braying a rallying oration?

'Why did that otherworldly magician bring forth Yackle to oversee Elphaba?' Brrr asked Ilianora. 'If his goal was merely to hide the Grimmerie, he didn't need to use it to meddle in the affairs of this world. Look at the harm it's done.'

'All my thoughts about history are sifted through my own warped fate. I have no conclusions,' she replied. 'I can't imagine why Elphaba deserved an angel to hover on her sidelines, even a paper angel, when the rest of us have to deal on our own with what prison and torture befalls us.'

'Prison and torture?'

'I'll tell you one day. But not while you're on the payroll of the Emerald City, no thank you. Not when the EC has supervised the extermination of my kin.'

'They're not all dead,' said the Lion. 'Liir may not be dead. And he went looking for you, all the way into Southstairs, I'm told.'

'There is that,' she said.

'We could leave the dwarf to his misadventures,' said the Lion. 'We could try to find Liir.' So was he signing on to Yackle's hopes? Was he being seduced by her wily trust in him? Or perhaps he was remembering Dorothy's long-ago request of him, that he remain a companion to Liir. 'I'm not looking for much,' he continued, shrugging. 'Not for romance, believe me. You and I are well matched in our hesitations. But romance isn't the only thing that draws two individuals together.'

They walked more quickly, almost trotting, to catch up to the Clock of the Time Dragon, but still they hung back far enough to speak privately for another moment or two. The steep walls of the Cloister of Saint Glinda fell behind them, a stone cloak they were escaping. As the armies drew within earshot of each other, the doors of this holy keep would be opened to all.

'I don't want your company while you are in the employ of the Emerald City,' she said at last. 'Not when they were behind the stationing of your Cat as a spy. Not when they were behind the deaths of my father and my mother and all my siblings. Everyone.'

'Everyone but Liir,' he said again, trying to convince her of something. 'Liir waits for you somewhere. We can find him.'

'Have you other work you must finish?'

There were so many campaigns he had left midway, out of shame and confusion. One couldn't fix much in one's messy past, of course. Perhaps none of it at all. He couldn't stitch up history so that Muhlama returned to him. He couldn't go back and pull the trap off Jemmsy's leg. He couldn't apologize to Dorothy for his failing to warn her against the wickedness of the Wizard of Oz.

'It's hard to know what to do,' he admitted. 'I look at that great book of magic, and all the mechanisms set up to guard it from eyes that would steal its secrets. So much fate seems wound up around it, including whole lives – yours, Yackle's, maybe Elphaba's, maybe mine. With so much written in magic, how can we hope to become agents culpable for our own lives?'

Ilianora laughed. It was the first time she had laughed in years, guessed Brrr, for even she looked surprised to hear the sound coming out of her mouth.

'You and I think alike,' she said. 'How improbable. But I don't put much faith in a magic book. For everything that is revealed, more is concealed. What good is that Grimmerie going to do us? A magic book can ingest a troublesome old crone: so what? An army can't disappear into a book of magic.'

'Fair enough,' he admitted. 'Can it bring a single dead soldier back to life?'

Ilianora was busy unlatching a satchel slung over her shoulder. She reached inside and withdrew a small notebook. 'Look,' she said, opening it up, fanning its blank pages in his direction. 'This is a book, too, and precious little is written in it. It's just as accurate as the Grimmerie, and maybe more so. Don't be chagrined by its blankness. Be liberated instead. Go on, it's yours. I have never written a word in it worth saving, so what I give you isn't magic or the benefit of my thinking, but my belief in the blankness of our futures. Charms only go so far. Here, take it. Whether you write your own story in it or not, that's your affair.'

He took it from her, mostly because she seemed eager to release it to him.

'A blank book for a court reporter to take depositions in?' Was he teasing her, just a little? He was.

'Take your own deposition,' she said.

He looked sideways at her. Her veil came down farther over her forehead, hiding even the tendrils of hair that had been blowing across her forehead, but her chin was up. Her eyes were dry and true.

'You go on ahead, then,' said the Lion. 'We'll find

a future uncharted by any tiktok charm. We'll make our luck as we go along. When I get back.'

'Why?' asked Ilianora. 'What are you doing now? Where are you going?'

He wasn't sure even what his answer would be; he waited to hear the words from his own mouth.

'The cottage there.' They were passing a small stone hut with a roof of oakhair thatch. A kitchen fire was still burning in the chimney, and beyond, in the light, a field of wheat rustled like gold on water. 'One of the maunts mentioned that an elderly couple lives there, and their sons have gone off to war. The rain will come soon, and the wind, and an army will trample this field by tomorrow. I have learned enough about prophecy to say that for sure: Its future is drenched in blood. Let me harvest wheat before the catastrophe. I've done some agricultural work in my time. I can bring in that crop for them. Better they should have something to sell to the mill when the battle is history and their sons are dead. Better that wheat should go for bread. No? No?'

'Go, then,' said Ilianora. 'If you must. Someone might as well chase the schoolchildren away from the lightning-wreathed hill.' She didn't look at him, but drew her veil tighter, and covered her mouth with it. Was she covering a smile – did she believe he was lying, out to betray the company of the Clock? – or did she think him a hero, for having so far-fetched a notion of charity?

Brrr bounded forward and pulled from the back of the Clock of the Time Dragon the shroud that Yackle had left behind. She wouldn't need it now. He dressed himself in it. Not a white flag of surrender but an advertisement of his neutrality. A plea to let him pass.

'Go,' she repeated. 'Bread for the aged and the desolate. It's as good a job as tending the book. Maybe a better one.'

'We'll look for Liir,' he said. 'When I come back.'

'We'll look for Liir.' She was trying the idea on for size: the idea that someone might be left to her, after all her losses. Her color was high, making her own veils look like the glazed white paper in which Shiz merchants wrapped freshly cut flowers. Which made her a kind of bouquet. 'You and I together? You'll catch up to me?'

'I'll catch up to you.'

'Is that a promise?' But she wouldn't have heard an answer even if he had given one. The dwarf was braying out that the boys should push, push, put their backs into it. The dragon's sallowwood limbs were creaking and its leather wings fell to flapping in the commotion, like a bellows swung about in a circle. A mile or two off, the music of war went tintinnabulary. Clarion horns of the hunt sounding, thunder of horse hoofs on stony ground, shatter of artillery, the clamorous ringing of swords.

Louder than any of that: men roaring like beasts.

The Lion turned into the wind, on the run once more. Neither an envoy of the EC, just now, nor a foot soldier of the underground opposition. Not even a neutral protector of oracular justice and magic hopes. He was a free agent, a rogue Lion, just as he'd started out in the Forest. A rogue Lion with the beginning of an education.

He headed for the sag-roofed, slipshod cottage. He had so little time. He would frighten the old couple there with an offer of help. It was neither the least nor the best he could ever do. It was simply an action that didn't follow obviously from all his earlier campaigns. It was an exercise in refusing to barter. It was an exercise in refusing to play dead. And that was the only way he could imagine how to vex history.

A plodder, he watched his feet on the ground. Had he turned to look up, to review the map of Oz in the clouds, he'd have seen the first stain of battle smoke rising against the white. Lightning was waiting in the heavens, of course. Sooner or later, the lightning comes to us all. In the meantime, for a moment, the clouds had rearranged themselves, and he might have said that they looked like a flying creature, a shadow angel, all light and impermanence. But the clouds suggested this only to themselves, while he kept his head down, bent to his task.

Who would have thought my shrivel'd heart
Could have recovered greenness?
  – George Herbert, 'The Collar'

Acknowledgments

I'd like to thank a coterie of early readers for giving such useful comments. Mistakes that remain are mine. The readers include David Groff, Betty Levin, Andy Newman, and William Reiss of John Hawkins and Associates; and at William Morrow, an imprint of HarperCollins, Cassie Jones and Johnathan Wilber.

Four years ago, to prepare for writing *Son of a Witch*, I reread *Wicked* for the first time in quite a while. I was startled to see something I'd never noticed before: a little plot device I had worked up to explain the mysterious presence in Elphaba's life of the dwarf (in *A Lion Among Men* called Mr Boss). I saw that his character, his origins and situation, and his employment and employer bore an uncomfortable similarity to aspects of Susan Cooper's novel for children called *The Dark Is Rising*, which I'd read some fifteen years before writing *Wicked*. While I have had fun in the Wicked Years slipping sidelong references to books by L. Frank Baum and other inspiring fantasists, and to the famous MGM film of 1939, I didn't intend my homages to descend into appropriation or plagiarism.

At once I wrote to Susan Cooper – a long-standing

friend and colleague – and I apologized for the accidental theft. She answered with her usual clarity and courtesy, citing a remark by J. R. R. Tolkien (who had once been her teacher at Oxford) that reminds us of the differences, in ancient storytelling, between invention, diffusion, and inheritance: 'Speaking of the history of stories and especially of fairy-stories we may say that the Pot of Soup, the Cauldron of Story, has always been boiling and to it have continually been added new bits, dainty and undainty.' Had she been possessed by a litigious mood, she might have gone on to quote: 'There are many things in the Cauldron, but the Cooks do not dip in the ladle quite blindly. Their selection is important.'